This is a work of pure fae propaganda.
Read at your own risk.

MINNESOTA 2049
Spring Break River Run
Duluth
Stinkwood
St Cloud
Edgelands
Strangelingtown
Twin Cities - occupied
1. Pack van
2. Rescue Dusty
Get first runner
3. Rendezvous w other runners
Get second canoe
!!! AVOID DIV 51 !!!
4. Deliver Runners to Strangelingtown
5. Lumber Punks gig

Strangeling

Children of the Broken Dawn
Book 1

Kira Hagen

Whispering Candle

CONTENTS

In Thanks

In thanks to my husband and son for putting up with me while I was off in other worlds, my birds for being just badly behaved enough to pull me back but not actually murder each other, and to my mom and dad for all your support over the years. Mom, you backed me on every daft art project I ever got into, and it made all the difference. Dad, sorry I never actually learned how to handle a chainsaw, but all the solarpunk and gardening stuff in this book is entirely the result of your influence.

This book is of course not my creation alone. With thanks to Celeste Jackson for proofreading, Segomâros Widugeni for insight into Gaulish swearing, Morgan Daimler and John Beckett for reference material. David Christian helped brainstorm what would make some of the weird science aspects of this work; "Anita Mann" comes courtesy of my old friend Micheal Sichmeller; and the name for Aisling's band was inspired by Leif Rafngard's comment that grunge music is just lumber punk.

And huge gratitude to my beta readers; thanks go especially to Tara Stone, Angela Chervenak, Lisa Hario, and Mark Fitzpatrick - your encouragement kept me going, and your feedback made this a far better book than it started out!

ALIASES & PRONUNCIATION

Aisling Lingren *pr. Ash-ling Ling-ren,* aka The Green Lady; nicknames: Dusty (friends), Slayer (Twin Ports Free Strangelings), Rue Libertie (Underhill Railroad), Alfhilde of the Mead Horn/ Hildie (SCA)

Arthur Hart, formerly Arthur Holt

Bethanna *pr. Beth-ann-a*

Brennos *pr. Bren-noes*

Connor McMann, formerly Commairge Sciatho an Briargard, aka Anita Mann (stage name)

Coral aka Siren (Underhill Railroad)

Daire *pr. like the English word "dare", not the Irish pronunciation*

Derdriu *pr. Dair-drew* aka Deirdre (*Deer-druh*)Lingren

Maddoc *pr. Ma-doc*

Manannan *pr. Muh-nan-an*

Rellen pr Rell-in

sidhe *pr. like English "she"*

Siobhan *pr. Shuh-vaun*

PART ONE

THE DAYS BEFORE

1

EDGELANDS
PATROL

ARTHUR

The sky stretched brilliant blue above my Jeep, its flawless dome cracked by a solitary launch contrail. The craft creating it gleamed through my binoculars, its odd organic lines as elegant as they were alien. It rose, arcing up to Beyond. The ship seemed almost to dance as it soared away from the stolen Twin Cities.

Spacecraft... damn. The Elsecomers got the dream.

One of my men started explaining to the new kid about how we record intel on the invaders, as well as the cryptids we were currently patrolling for.

...and left us the nightmare.

The sight of a ship was nothing new; we saw odd lights and trails in the sky all the time, and this launch was on a predictable schedule. Earth's invaders didn't deign to communicate with us locals, so it was hard to guess what they were up to, but we tracked their activities. They seemed to have spacecraft, anyway, and some kind of weird, mutagenic sorcery. Or perhaps it was technology indistinguishable from such; easiest to just call it magic. Regardless, it had broken the world, wrecking our best tech and Changing people into beings out of myth and folklore.

The air began to somehow thrum, something no one else in the troop ever admitted to feeling. There was a sudden flash of light at the tip of the contrail, and the ship disappeared, as if it had pierced the surface tension of reality and... well, I had no idea, really.

Off they go. Wonder where?

Some bird I didn't recognize started singing across the river, its haunting trill somehow as alien as the starship.

Must be nice to come and go at will, I thought, getting back into the Jeep's shotgun seat and putting away the binoculars. I straightened the sleeves on my army uniform, trying to ignore their prison-orange trim. There was no more coming and going for me. Strangeling Brigade was a forced-labor division, kept away from humanity for everyone's safety. My pointed ears and the antlers growing from my forehead made it instantly obvious why I'd been enlisted.

Still army life, though.

I heard Lieutenant Birch, team lead for the human side of Division 51, confirming the launch in his voice recorder. We didn't patrol alone. The human soldiers were all under strict orders to shoot the second it looked like any of us strangelings were going bad. I reinforced the importance of those orders at least once a month.

I need that failsafe.

Deep in the darkness inside me, something shifted and growled at that thought.

Not that I'm certain they'd actually follow the order...

Birch finished his notes and waved that he was done.

In the sky above us, the wind began dispersing the starship's trail.

We collect intel, but never get answers.

Every bit of info might someday help us regain control of Earth, though.

Someday.

They have starships.

We have the junked out remnants of the world Before.

But... someday.

The spring breeze blew through my hair then, seeming almost to laugh at such hubris. Pale sunshine kissed my face. I grinned ruefully to myself.

Brooding is pointless.

And until "someday", the weather's lovely and the land's waking up from winter. Can't complain.

Along the Mississippi, fifty miles upriver from lost Minneapolis, the cottonwoods were blushing with the first faint greens of spring. Pussy willows bloomed in the low areas and the final bits of snow from last week's blizzard were dripping away into the thawing soil. The river was running fast and high, chunks of ice from up North swirling on its surface. Breathing in the gusty spring air felt like inhaling raw *life*.

"You're in a good mood, Captain," Sgt. Jones said, putting the Jeep into drive and pulling back onto the dirt track we were patrolling. He was a big black guy who'd already been in the army for a while himself before getting exposed to some of that mutagenic magic. Fine mahogany brown fur covered most of his body now, and he had bat ears and weird folds over the bridge of his nose. Minor Changes, as such things went. He was good at what he did and didn't want to do a damn thing extra, so he delegated well and didn't cause problems. It was just about everything you want in a subordinate officer, though he *could* have been a little more enthusiastic about our work.

"It's finally spring, and we get to hunt a new type of monster tomorrow!" I replied, grinning widely as he twisted the steering wheel to avoid a sapling growing out of the disintegrating asphalt. Getting away from our usual patrol along the edge of the Elsecomers' no-go zone was always a treat, not least because we got to drive on roads people actually maintained. "Have you ever gone after a man-eating stone giant?"

"Nope, and yet I still feel my life is complete," he replied, swerving around a pothole larger than the Jeep. "And *sure,* it's the *giant* you're looking forward to chasing."

Soon, that voice down in my darkness whispered, more in impressions than actual words. I felt claws stretch inside me. *I'll catch her soon. She'll be after the giant, too. Then we'll...*

"That girl's a public safety hazard," I said, ignoring it. Better not to give the faery whispers any attention. They had too much power over me already. "Somebody's gotta bring her in."

"Still think you're just trying to find a girl prettier than you," Jones said, shaking his head. "Bet you don't even know what you'd do if you caught her."

I gritted my teeth. *Pretty* was not a word I'd ever imagined describing me, and my strangeling Change had left me looking like I'd just stepped out of a classic fantasy film... except that unlike Middle Earth's elves, I got to grow flipping *antlers* out of my forehead. Now I can't wear a helmet or most hats or ever forget that Elsecomer magic has deformed me.

Jones was right, though. I had no idea what I'd do if I caught her. I mean, arrest her, of course. But after that?

She irradianced me. She broke my life and turned me into a monster. She's working for the invaders.

Well, maybe. I've never seen signs of her doing intentional harm.

But she's a monster, like me, and monsters need to be killed or caged!

"Who are you talking about?" the new kid asked from the back seat. Recent inductees did a couple ride-alongs with the team leaders when they first started patrolling. Omar Hassan was of Somali descent, from a family that escaped Minneapolis just before the Elsecomers took the city. He'd Changed on his seventeenth birthday and gotten incarcerated with us last month. His hair had gone whitish blue and marks like lightning appeared all over his skin, and moth-like antennae twitched on his forehead. We'd been having electrical trouble with every system he was around, so he'd probably end up developing some magic along those lines. At least he'd finally stabilized enough to get into a car without shorting out its systems.

"Captain's hot blond nemesis," Jones replied. "The 'Green Lady of the North'. He goes frothing at the lips crazy every time she's nearby."

"Oh, I've heard of her! With those free strangeling guys up by Duluth, right? They fixed some medical gear that saved my aunt. Have you actually seen her?"

"Yes, and being a connoisseur of the feminine..." Jones made a chef's kiss to the air. "I mean, give *me* some curve on a woman, but scrawny blondes apparently do it for Captain. She's a similar strangeling to him, but seems to actually enjoy it."

You fucking idiot, I thought. *She's dangerous.*

"She's not a strangeling. She's an Elsecomer elf," I snapped. "One of the Beautiful Monsters. And when you saw her, she was cuffing a *bomb* to your hand."

"Captain blames her for his Change," Jones said sympathetically. "It's hard on him, having someone out there who's both prettier than him and better at hunting monsters."

I bit my tongue and made myself count to ten. Jones looked sideways at me, trying to contain his grin.

"A *bomb?*" Hassan asked, aghast.

"We thought so at the time," I grumbled.

"Her team was smuggling something into the Edgelands back in January," Jones said, chuckling. "They do that a couple times a year. We knew they were out there; found ski and sled tracks. Captain senses her somehow, goes nuts every time she's nearby. So we had multiple patrols out, and she blasted into mine like some comic book speedster, grinned, and cuffed what looked like a briefcase bomb to my wrist. Then she flashed away."

"Shiiit..." Hassan said.

"It had a walkie talkie attached. We could tell there were electronics inside, and something that smelled like ammonium fertilizer. Guy on the walkie told us to hold our positions, or it'd blow. While everyone was freaking out about that, they got past us," Jones explained. "Captain eventually got me on one side of a fairly blast-proof door and had Gregor, he's the big guy with rock skin, break the cuff. Guy on the radio said we'd had it, he was triggering his bomb. Gregor threw it as far as he could, and 'Never Gonna Give You Up' started singing from the suitcase in mid-air."

"It wasn't funny!" I said, as Jones guffawed.

He and the rest of my troops had thought it was *hilarious*. And the monster hiding inside me had gone positively rabid with rage.

"It was the best Rick-Roll *ever,*" Jones said. "I laughed for two days."

And I spent three days in the snow trying to track those bastards down before coming home with frostbite. Not sure how I even kept all my toes.

We turned a corner onto an even worse road. A flock of brightly colored draclets burst out of a tall cottonwood in a rainbow of brilliant colors, squawking like parrots. We watched the little cryptids wheel and fly out over the river for a minute.

"What are *those?*" Hassan asked, fascinated.

"Pocket dragons. Draclets. They're an invasive exotic out of the stolen Cities. Annoying, but mostly harmless. They act like escaped pets."

"*Coooool.* Do they breathe fire?"

"Nah. Their saliva is corrosive though, and they like chewing on rubber and plastic, sometimes metal," Jones said. "Gotta keep 'em off the cars. Little fuckers eat windshield wipers like licorice sticks."

"You'll probably stay with the gear when we go hunting off-road, to keep them off the vehicles," I said, and his eyes widened. "No, not alone. We do everything with at least a partner. But they'll go after the tires, window lining, wipers, and radio antennas."

"Speaking of radios..." Jones said, glancing at me.

"The Green Lady's team has a guy with power over technology," I sighed, tapping my fingers on the Jeep's door. "The military wants him, *bad.* He's blocked our radios, stolen our patrol schedules, and broken the code Lt. Birch came up with for covert communication. And whenever they're smuggling through the Edgelands, we have to assume they hear every word we say on the radio. So keep that in mind if you need to use your walkie when they're around."

"Birch's code was the *Klingon language,* Captain," Jones groaned. "He shouldn't have been at all surprised to have another obvious geek figure that out. Or tell him he had a flat forehead and his father smelled of elderberries."

Which he considers the highlight of his Div 51 career. Half the reason we haven't caught the smugglers is that none of my people want to, I thought, grinding my teeth internally. *Especially since that guy said they were trying to figure out how to free us all.*

As if strangelings can manage freedom.

"Captain's hoping to catch the Green Lady when we're hunting up North, but she might show up down here any day now," Jones said. "Her runs are almost always on university breaks. We think she's a student."

Hassan blinked.

Yeah. I have trouble believing one of the invaders could be a college kid, too. But the timing lines up.

"Can I ask about how things work here?" Hassan asked. "Because we've got a captain and a couple of other officers, and Lt. Birch is supposedly in charge but Captain Hart seems to give all the actual orders?"

"Birch is in charge," I said, though it still stuck in my craw a bit to say those words.

It's safer this way.

"Captain's in charge, and the lieutenant is alive despite all expectations purely because they work together," Jones contradicted me. "But for the human authorities, Birch is in charge. Captain's the one we follow into and out of battle. Birch is like his trainee."

"*Aide.* I'm only a captain informally now," I said. "The military doesn't like acknowledging how many people get irradianced in the line of duty, so they strip us of rank, change our names, and have moving public memorials for us. Then they toss us 'walking ghosts' into the strangeling prison brigades. Apparently, I've got a very nice headstone down in Rochester."

"We had cryptids killing our officers like flies before Hart got incarcerated," Jones explained. *"Consistently* their first target. And hardly any privates lasted more than a year or two, on either side of the troop. The army wasn't even sending trained officers anymore, just told the human part of the troop to elect leaders from the ranks. Then they bitched about how our incident reports were shit, so since officers didn't last, the troop elected a nerdy kid fresh out of basic to make them happy."

"You mean Lt. Birch?" he asked, glancing at the human soldiers' junked out troop carrier lurching along behind us. We had stenciled *Strangeling Brigade Goes In First* across the hood; they're our words now. The Changed troops used to get driven in at gunpoint on monster fights; now we go first because we're *better.*

Or because it takes monsters to fight monsters, I thought grimly.

Our freckled, towheaded "leader" waved cheerily back at us. He's twenty-three, three years younger than me, and we all hoped very hard that someday he might look like an actual adult.

No one's holding their breath on that, though.

"He got stuck with us because he wrote some sarcastic furry fanfic featuring his old officers," Jones chuckled. "Got sent over to Div 51 for insubordination. His heart's in the right place, but his head's somewhere off in the Delta Quadrant."

"Birch was doing his best," I said, sighing internally. "For a certain value of the word. He just needed real training and some structure. We're as effective as we are *because* he's good at writing fiction."

"He's basically our liaison with the real army and human world now," Jones explained. "It takes about five seconds here for the new human soldiers to realize they're in much better hands with Hart leading the troop. He was already military and had full officer training, after all. Bit of a hero, in fact. It's their lives on the line if they report the actual situation."

"You mean there's *no one* in this unit that volunteered for it?"

"Well, Birch enjoys himself," Jones said, and I gave him a *look.*

"Dude pretends he's on Away Missions while patrolling! He's got a handheld voice recorder and keeps 'officer logs' of every outing! Then he writes fanfics based on them."

Of course he does.

I NEVER want to learn what goes on in his stories.

"Human soldiers don't get sent to Div 51 because they're standard army issue," I said, sighing internally. "We get the... ah... interesting ones."

"He means the weirdos and misfits," Jones said, shrugging as he swerved around another sapling growing in the middle of the road. "Works for us."

It wasn't inaccurate. I stared out at the passing trees, the weight of everything I'd lost with my Change hitting me again. I'd been "promising" once, fast-tracked into an officer career, with a solid family behind me and a fiancée ready to start a new one. The people I'd worked with had volunteered for service and been good enough to be placed in elite units. I had *loved* it.

I'd had a future. I'd had a life...

Something large moved between the trees.

"Cryptid!" I yelled, and the patrol skidded to a halt. Weapons fell into ready hands, both human and strangeling.

The creature slunk between the trees towards us, bulky, huge. It moved like nothing earthly.

A sudden shiver ran through me, electric, making my ears twitch and antlers tingle. Darkness stirred inside me, waking up.

What stepped onto the broken road looked like the toothy cousin of a water buffalo, seven feet tall at the shoulder, all claws and fangs and heavy slabs of muscle.

That thing is not *an herbivore.*

It looked at my troops and licked fanged chops. Drool oozed out of its mouth, falling in thick cords past its teeth. It eased back, muscles tensing, preparing to charge us.

Something inside me purred, and a smilodon grin answered that challenge.

But it is prey. My prey.

In my core, darkness stretched its claws. Teeth glinted through shifting green shadows. I felt my hands put down my gun and reach for the combat knife at my hip, and there wasn't a thing I could do to stop them.

"Shit, it's happening agai..." I managed to choke out before the faery monster inside me surged out of its hiding place and took over.

Everything went black.

"Captain. Captain! It's down. It's dead. You're okay. Everyone's okay. Put the knife down. Oh gods, don't lick it, that's disgusting."

Birch's voice came to me as if echoing from miles away. I was... where was I? Down in darkness, bound, where writhing silver vines held me in place, holding me, gagging even my mouth. But also, *not*. Something delicious was on my lips, but iron burned my tongue. I stood up and my body moved with clean, inhuman fluidity, lithe and elegant, explosively powerful.

"You want *him* back?" my voice asked. I caught a glimpse of Birch, terrified, looking like he was staring down a demon. He nodded, the whites of his eyes showing all the way around, holding his ground.

Magic flickered out from me, reaching for his mind, and slid off strong mental shielding.

It wasn't just his writing skills I valued Birch for.

"Please give us back our captain," he repeated, extremely carefully, holding empty hands up. "The beast is dead. You've had your blood."

My shoulders shrugged carelessly, but I felt the stab of pain run through me, like pure distilled loneliness.

"Oh, fine, he's good enough at cleaning up messes," my monster said, and suddenly I was falling upwards into my body. There was a disorienting sensation of everything spinning, of vines flexing and coiling around and through my mind and soul. The world tipped. I went straight to my knees. A bloody knife dropped from my hand, skittering off the very efficiently dead beast in front of me. Jones and a half dozen of my closest troops looked up around me, moving like a hunting pack, eyes glowing with feral magic.

They went completely still. Jones blinked and shook his head, and the others followed him.

"Ah, not this crap again," he said, as I pulled myself to the edge of the road and started heaving.

2

ILL WIND

AISLING

I was as restless as the rough March wind. The raw breeze made spinning my aunt's mixed cattail and nettle fibers an exercise in frustration, much like visiting home. Sitting by the front door of my dad's fortified apartment building, I watched my extended family clean the killing field gardens. I dropped and wound my spindle over and over and over. Bits of cattail fluff blew away with every fall. The damn stuff's good insulation, but too short to spin on its own. My aunt had carded nettle fibers in with the fluff for support, but some of those fibers hadn't been well-retted and were over-stiff for hand-spinning. The mix was both too fine and too coarse, and barely held together.

No one wanted me in the garden. Green thumbs ran in the Lingren side of my family, but I was just good at killing things. When Aunt Dahlia saw me pulling up her naturally reseeded amaranth seedlings, she banished me to the front steps. The spinning basket held nothing I could murder, she said, and if I couldn't tell weeds from reseeds, then I could be useful *away* from her "babies".

It was probably another subtle dig about me becoming a spinster. I was a twenty-four-year-old grad student in a field no one wanted to hear about, and "too opinionated" to have serious dating prospects. I mean, *whatever*. But she brought up our Duty to Maintain Humanity every chance she got, and I was utterly sick of it.

Not exactly something I could help with, anyway.

I glanced at my dad, sixty-something and enthusiastically shoveling last fall's organic detritus into a rusty wheelbarrow. Dead beanstalks, old potatoes missed at harvest, and all winter's untidy muddle had been cleared into a fresh compost pile. Cover crops had been turned under and chickens set loose to scratch and manure the whole place, excepting, of course, any now-carefully protected reseed patches. Just *lovely* to learn my family trusted the poultry more than me in the garden. Aunt Dahlia had passed out hundreds of little pots to go into every South-facing window on the building, full of tiny seedlings ready to grow as big as the spring sun could make them. We couldn't count on frost-free nights until June, but when summer comes, Minnesotan gardeners hit the ground running. Supplies don't always get through anymore, and sometimes there are *things* outside the security fence. The garden needed to produce, and it did, enough to hold the family through at least a two-week siege.

I know, because one happened when I was fourteen.

Spin and drop, spin and drop, wind strong thread for weaving warps... do something useful, Aisling, don't glower at your family... spin and drop, spin and drop... spin and drop dead of boredom...

The siege happened just a few weeks before Mom died. We'd been visiting my cousins and got stuck in the compound while cryptids howled and gibbered beyond the fence. When the food was almost gone and Mom's medicine supply long exhausted, we finally got a night as black as pitch. I slipped out into the dark, taking just a kitchen knife. By dawn, gore dripped from every inch of my skin and hair, and I knew who the worst monster in the night *really* was.

And I'd rather be out in the dark again, surrounded by rabid rat goblins, than dealing with another heaping helping of familial disapproval!

I dropped and wound my spindle, hating how stuck my life was. Desperately, pathetically, I wished something, *anything*, would happen.

Then a sheriff's squad car pulled up outside the front gate, and I cursed my stupid wishing roundly.

"It's an ill wind," I heard my aunt Thelma say, looking at the sky and then at the car. "Blowing in ill news."

Sudden sunlight slipped through the blustering clouds. It gilded the car's bolted-on armor and re-bar window guards, and seemed to give the sheriff and his deputy brief halos. They had welded an old snowplow to the car's front as a battering ram, and a tuft of bloody, unnaturally orange fur stuck to the bottom, neglected whenever it last got hosed down. The skull of some toothy, four-horned cryptid grinned from where a hood ornament should have sat.

Did I screw up? I wondered as my pulse started pounding. It did that every time law enforcement came around. The choker binding my illusions seemed to tighten around my throat.

We scrubbed the jackhammer after dismembering that corpse. With bleach!

I set my spinning carefully into its fiber basket, spindle on top to hold the roving down, and readied myself to fight or flee... or, more likely, just keep hiding.

I hate hiding.

A sleek, expensive little hybrid electric car slid into the space behind the sheriff's car, and my cousin Trey slipped out of the driver's seat. He was a few months younger than me, lean and blond and handsome in a spare way, and his only redeeming qualities involved using guns well. He pulled one out of the back seat, some sort of assault rifle, and grabbed ammo with his other hand. Then he sauntered casually over to the sheriff's window, juggling bullets between his fingers.

Sheriff Rudy hit his siren for a second, turned it off, and then hit it again. That code meant, "Threat, but not imminent, come out for info."

No, I decided. *If they thought they were arresting a sketchy local superhero, it wouldn't be local law and my worst cousin stopping by. It'd be a full surprise military raid, with everyone the remnant army could pull in.*

The sheriff said something to Trey that made him smile, but it didn't reach his eyes. My cousin made a joke and slid ammo into the big gun. I glanced around at my family. No one looked too worried. They didn't know about my stuff, though. If my issues ever came to light, the resultant catastrophe would sweep up all of us, and they had no clue. It needed to stay that way. They drove me crazy, but they kept me human too... as much as anything could.

I can't let them get hurt.

Someone sat up in the back seat of the sheriff's car, and I could feel the Radiance swirling around her before seeing who it was.

Well, that explains Trey's presence.

I wondered how many executions had paid for that shiny car of his. Our broken world necessitated messes, but the sheriff still held an elected position. Slaying a monster actively tearing up humans was one thing; pulling the trigger on some teenager just starting to Change, sobbing and begging for mercy, was another. I mean, some more stable strangelings lived out brief lives as prison labor, but over half got shot as their Cascade started.

The neighbor kid put her face to the window, more vulnerable than I'd seen her since her dad walked out, years and years ago. Vicki's expression that of someone stepping in front of a firing squad.

No. Not her.

I used to babysit Vicki Marweg before I left for college. She was due to graduate high school in June, with a full military scholarship already lined up. Radiance twisted and turned in the air surrounding her now, invisible to everyone here but me. It'd take a miracle to keep her human long enough to get her diploma now. Vicki's little sister fled into the building, yelling for their mother. My stomach sank into the dirt under my bare feet. There were too many witnesses. Helping her could out me. Outing what I really was could get my whole family executed. Treason Against Humanity was an automatic death sentence, after all, even if I was technically just the *result* of it. I didn't think even my dad had realized what Mom was, though; he could be amazingly oblivious.

Almost the whole family was guilty of Contact with an Elsecomer because of her, also an automatic death sentence. None of them knew, and I had to keep it that way.

Let some Way open, I prayed to the god of my mother's people. Silver branches shook within me, futures and potentials knotting together and fraying apart. I stood up and followed the path they presented.

My kin and neighbors had put down their shovels and rakes and gathered around the front gate. It was late afternoon, and their work was almost finished, anyway. I glanced up at the building's roof. A twelve-year-old second cousin was up in the sniper nest, .22 rifle in hand, peering down to see what was up. The gardens double as a killing field, enclosed space in which we can shoot anything before it gets too close to the building. The fortifications aren't high end, just eight-foot chain link fences with lines of barbed wire strung along their tops. Another length of chain link lies flat on the ground outside to prevent digging. The fences mostly keep out the whitetail deer that'd eat the gardens, but they slow down cryptids nicely too. Probably the steel they're made of does more than the actual barrier they present, but it works well enough.

Most of the residents were already outside for the work party, and the rest filtered out as I watched. My dad and a couple of my adult cousins, some of their horde of kids, and the few sets of neighbors that weren't close kin gathered by the gate. I mean, Stinkwood's tiny; they were probably relatives. I just didn't know how close.

Which is why I don't date in town anymore.

Vicki's sister and mother came running out the door and straight to the front of the crowd.

I kept myself to the back.

Sheriff Rudy opened his door and climbed out. He was a bit of a good 'ol boy: paunchy, past his prime, and fast with a gun... but nothing else.

"Well, folks, gotta bitta bad news," Rudy said, ambling over. Trey and Deputy Jenkins stayed over at his car. "Seems some contaminated food got passed out at a track and field meet over in

Carlton. Already had one Change, and a half dozen other kids need to be kept under observation for a bit. Miss Marweg here's one of 'em. So this all's just a precaution, but her family needs to get her an overnight kit. Anyone wants to say goodbye, just in case, you all actually have a chance for once."

There was a moment of horrified silence. Vicki's mother collapsed to her knees.

"Who Cascaded?" one of my kid cousins asked. Julian was about to graduate high school himself. He probably knew whoever it was.

"Sara Little," the Sheriff answered. I heard a couple of gasps from the crowd. She was Vicki's best friend, and they were together most of the time; everyone here knew her. "She got away into the woods, headed into old Jay Cooke Park. Sounds like she's turning into something big, dunno what, so we'll assume she's gone troll and is in the Hunger. Got a buddy with dogs coming over from Hermantown; we'll find her. Lock the gate after we leave, though, and keep someone on watch till you hear she's down. Standard precautions."

Not Sara too, I despaired.

"Ma'am, can you please get up?" the sheriff asked Mrs. Marweg. "Your daughter's fine so far, and she needs you to pack an overnight kit for the quarantine cell. Everyone else, go say whatever you need to."

The crowd shuffled over to the sheriff's car, and Rudy's deputy rolled a window down for people to talk to Vicki. Then he got out. He caught my eye and nodded for me to join him.

That way, whispered hidden silver leaves.

Deputy Luke Jenkins had been in school with me and my crew; well, a senior when we were mostly in eighth grade, and we got him in some hella trouble at one point. He was a decent guy, though, one of those too-rare cops who actually wanted to protect people. He'd just seen too much of what I really am. I had to play it cautious. I settled my basket over my arm and slipped out the gate.

Just another local human girl, I thought, trying to wrap normalcy around me. *Old flannels and farmgirl braids and calluses from chopping her own firewood. Just that, and nothing more.* Trey saw me checking my reflection in the car's window and rolled his eyes. Idiot. If he wanted to think I was sweet on Luke, let him. Guy's another cousin (third, twice removed, I think) and law enforcement was *definitely* not my type. Anyway, Luke was married and had a toddler. My illusions were holding; that was all I'd needed to see. I looked as harmless as anyone does, living after the end of the world like we do.

Not that the bondage warrior look ever took off here. Minnesota's weather would either freeze or burn your bits off if you tried it, somewhat seasonally dependent.

Waste of a good apocalypse.

Mostly, we all just looked really poor. That's what really happens when everything falls apart. I mean, kudos to the sheriff for what he'd done with his car. If I hadn't needed to be invisible, I'd have tricked out my pickup like a total road warrior. Seriously, I'd killed *much* cooler monsters than Rudy had.

Life in the fucking wardrobe...

"Afternoon, Dusty," Luke said, using my highschool nickname, and nodded towards the girl in the back of his car. "So..."

"Can I get something for her?" I asked. "Or for you?"

He gave me cop eyes. I tried to seem like I had no idea what he was implying, but it's hard to look innocent to an officer who's previously cuffed and booked you. I mean, in my defense, I did not *start* any of that shit on prom night.

Sure ended it, though.

"She gonna go?" he asked, too quietly for anyone by Vicki to hear. Trey glanced up sharply. I glared at my cousin and he shrugged and looked away.

"Think that's in fate's hands now," I said.

"I'm not asking fate," Luke answered. "I'm asking *you.*"

Dammit. He does *know something.*

"Been only five years since the invasion that no Stinkwood kids Changed," he said quietly. "And we both know what years those were."

The ones I was in school here. And it was completely inaccurate to say no one Changed then; more like, no one visibly Changed.

I had hoped no one noted that. Dammit. I stared at my feet.

"Heard about what you're studying now," he said. "Monster biology, dissections. I'm heading over to join the Duluth police force next month. They said they've got a grad student who comes in and consults with them on cryptid forensics. Wasn't surprised when I heard it was you. So..."

He nodded to Vicki.

Dammit.

"Yeah," I mumbled. "She's gonna go."

"Anything you can do 'bout that?"

"Asking the monster biologist?"

"Asking the local witch."

All things considered, Luke thinking I'm just a witch is probably a good thing.

I kicked the ground and nodded, pulling my drop spindle out of the basket.

We can make this look like human witchcraft. That's doable. Everyone here knows I'm more or less a pagan, anyway. It's one of the few things I'm not closeted about.

"Hey April!" I called over to Vicki's little sister. "Come over here."

"What's going on?" she whispered. She was a scrawny little kid, with enormous eyes and over-thin cheeks. "Can you do something?"

"Maybe. Get me some hair from Vicki's head and ask her exactly how tall she is."

She blinked at me, then bounced up with sudden hope and ran to the car. Guess it wasn't just the deputy who thought of me as the local witch.

"Luke," I said quietly. "If this works, I don't know if it'll be permanent. I've never been able to totally *stop* a Radiant infection, just slow 'em down."

And sometimes shape them. But we're not going to say anything about that.

"I'll monitor her," he said. "She's the only one of the quarantine group I felt was gonna go."

"Got your own sense for that?" I asked. Trey's ears sort of twitched. Luke shrugged noncommittally. Okay. If he was protecting his own issues, he'd be quiet about mine. And he had a kid. These things intensified with every generation. He'd guard his family.

April came running back, some long, dark blond hairs clenched in her little fist.

"She's five foot eight," she breathed, handing me three hairs.

"Good," I said, laying them across my left wrist. I took the first one and aligned it with my spinning fiber. Eyes closed, I cautiously opened my connection to the Tree that Grows Between Worlds, the source of fae magic, and reached into the Radiance sparkling around Vicki. With the heavy steel all over the car, it wasn't easy, but it felt... doable. I spun the spindle and dropped it, Vicki's hair twisting in with the long nettle fibers and short cattail fluff as it fell. Three times I dropped and wound the spindle, adding a blond hair with each fall, spinning the Radiance writhing into Vicki through the thread. Then I pulled off the last six feet off the bobbin end, running the thread through my mouth to wet the yarn and set the twist.

"Cut this two inches shorter than my feet," I said to April, holding an end of the thread up to the crown of my head. "I'm a little taller than Vicki."

She pulled out a little pocket knife and sliced the end of the thread. I wound it up around my hand, set the spindle back in its basket, and knotted a little loop into one end of the yarn. Then I went over to the car and waited for a chance to talk to Vicki.

"Hey kiddo," I said when I finally got up to the window, like I used to back when I babysat her years ago. "Heard you're going running in some dangerous woods. Mind if I give you a little luck-wishing to help get you through?"

"You're the one who likes running in the woods, Dusty," she said, her eyes bleak. "But you always got us back out. Sure."

"Put your hand out the window."

She put it cautiously between the bars. The steel didn't seem to bother her yet, a good sign. I set the thread I'd spun against her wrist, and finger-crocheted a little bracelet with the yarn, binding the flow of Radiance pouring into into her through the string. Her incipient Change slowed with every twist and knot.

"How long are they keeping you for?" I asked casually.

"Three days," she said. "I... I kind of feel something. Like that tingly electric feel is fading."

"That's probably good," I said, like I was operating on hope and guesswork. "So what happened?"

"Sara's family got a package of charity food," Vicki answered. Her hand went to the little unicorn pendant Sara gave her for her tenth birthday. They'd worn matching ones ever since. "There were some pemmican bars in it, a venison and cranberry mix. Nobody in her family likes cranberries, so she brought them to the meet. Most of the team tried them, but she and I were the only ones who actually liked them. Then suddenly she doubled over and started screaming, and when she looked up at me, she was growing tusks and sprouting black fur all over her body. When she realized what was happening, she ran into the woods. On all fours."

A fast Change, and a bad one, then.

"Well, she didn't hurt anyone, that's something," I said.

"Dusty, can you find her?" she whispered. "Can you help her? I remember your... friends... in the forest."

"Vicki, I..." I said. "I don't know. I can go for a run tonight. But I'm heading out of town for a couple days tomorrow, and..."

She stared at me with those needy puppy eyes that got me to do things for her when she was little.

"I'll do what I can," I finally said, tying the bracelet closed around her wrist, too tight for it to come off easily. "Good luck in quarantine."

I stepped away and back over towards Luke, stuffing my magic back under wraps, making myself as human as I could. It felt like I was cutting off my fingers.

"You shine when you're doing magic," Luke said quietly, and tapped his forehead. "In here, I see it. What *are* you?"

"The village witch," I said, a wave of despair washing over me. "Oh gods, I can't take losing people like this."

He nodded bleakly, understanding. We just stood there for a moment, our shoulders drooping. No matter what we did, it wasn't enough. Then he nodded and strode off to have a word with Trey.

I need to get out of here.

My pickup was parked down the block. I tossed the spinning basket in the front and grabbed something from under the passenger seat. Then I turned away from the safety of fences and walls and crowds and just ran.

I heard my cousin say something disparaging behind me, and then I was out of range.

Well, fuck him. Trey's just an asshole.

Now, to really take care of things.

My magic stetched out from me, igniting the bondnet links in my mind.

Guys, I think we'll have another Runner for the Underhill Railroad to transport tomorrow, I projected into the mental network I share with my strangeling friends, the ones people don't realize Changed back in high school. Like me, they hid their fae sides. All of us lived closeted lives, deep "in the wardrobe", pretending to be human.

Who? Rigs sent back. **I can see about finding a second canoe.**

We've probably got too many for just one now, anyway, Coral added. **We'll be slow in the water, and there's still ice on the river. It's a bad combo when we also have to get past Division 51.**

Sara Little, I answered. *Sportsball's friend, the one I had you track down the Black Panther film for five years ago. I'm off to talk to some owlies about finding her.*

You'll need something to trade, Rigs reminded me.

Already got it.

Losing it was going to suck.

3

THE FISH BALL

CONNOR

"This is the worst fucking planet in the galaxy," Enzo said, hefting his shield next to me.

The sunset glowed pink and gold on the Mississippi, and the lights of the city formerly known as Minneapolis were shimmering to life through a lavender twilight. Architecture native to a dozen worlds rose from the old human foundations of the city, arching and tangling in an opulent fantasy of galactic engineering. Overhead, a pair of sleek cruisers swooped through the dusk towards the starport. The faint strains of a string orchestra drifted out of downtown. On Bohemian Flats, floodlights flicked on and glared over a grassy field half flooded with spring meltwater.

The riverfront meadow would soon be a slimy mess of a battlefield, *again*. Just like it'd been once a month for the past seven years. Crowds gathered on balconies and bridges to watch the idiotic spectacle. Vendors walked through the crowd selling popcorn and cotton candy. A flock of squawking draclets flew in and took perches on the trees and floodlights, settling in as if to watch a circus performance.

If this is a circus, does that make us the dancing monkeys?

Dark ripples spread in ominous circles near the shore.

My partner in the city guard, Rellen, readied his blade. He nodded agreement and gagged at the stench wafting in from the water.

I groaned and raised my shield too. The Freeport Guards' white and silver armored uniforms shone through the gloaming, graceful lines and high-tech fabrics well-befitting our culture's elegant aesthetics. Our slim, curving armaments complemented them, luminous in the twilight.

The getup makes my butt look fantastic, but my hair's too curly to come out of the helmet looking anything but *flattened*. The damn thing rubs my pointed ear tips, too, and coming out of battle with chafed ears is just the *worst*. Also, while the expensive fabric sheds visible dirt well enough, the stink from these Fish Balls does not come out *nearly* so easily. I washed my uniform *six times* after last month's fight and still had to take it to a professional cleaner.

"Gods Between Worlds, I wish we could just fry the fucking fish men," Rellen said, making a face at the water. He's got straight dark hair that he ties back, and it looks fine when he takes off *his* helmet. "We could be done in ten seconds and never, ever have to smell them again. Or clean their crud out of our boots. And hair. And everywhere."

It's the "everywhere" that really gets you.

Something large breached the waves, then disappeared again below them.

"Why did they have to attack *tonight?*" I wailed. "Usually it's the day *after* the full moon! I should be on the runway for Danielle right now. She's going to be *devastated*."

"At the starport?" Enzo asked, confused, changing his grip on the stupid spear he'd been issued. It was ceramosynth, which holds a better edge than steel but wasn't half as good the bound nanotech weapons some of us had.

"At the *drag bar*," Rellen corrected. "Danielle's the up-and-coming designer he's been modeling for."

"You sure picked up some weird hobbies here on Earth, Connor," Enzo said. Rellen nodded agreement. I rolled my eyes at the uncultured barbarians next to me.

"I found a local community that *loves* drinking and being fabulously beautiful," I said. "It was a natural fit. You guys are *jealous* of how well I'm integrating."

They both just stared at me for a moment.

"I'm surprised you're only going for guys now," Enzo eventually said. "Don't remember you being that picky before."

"Ha," I said. "You haven't seen the women who come into those bars with their gay friends."

"Oh?" Rellen asked, perpetually rather desperate.

"Smart women with good taste," I said. "I mean, *obviously.*"

"So you aren't any pickier than you used to be," Enzo said.

"Meh," I said.

Okay, so I used to sleep around... a lot... back when our world was ending. I actually didn't anymore, well, *much*, but why let anyone know? Far too many people already thought I was irreparably broken.

Dark shiny blobs glooped their way out of the Mississippi. Moonlight glinted on their fins and the primitive spears held in their armlike fins and tentacle whiskers. The smaller ones were the size of dolphins, the largest almost van-sized. I hefted my sword. We were armed with ridiculously basic weaponry ourselves, stuff that's normally backup weapons *only*, swords and shields and spears. Diplo thought we should meet the idiot monsters with more or less the same level of tech they used, and thus prove our superiority the old-fashioned way. Hopefully, this would lead to... something? It'd been justified like, "...blah blah respect blah blah diplomatic relations blah blah..."

Okay, I actually drank my way through the whole talk about the mutant catfish. Like many things on Earth, it was simply too loony to deal with sober. No one believed the reasoning, anyway; the fish-men were too insanely dumb to negotiate anything. Establishing diplomatic relations with them was a grim joke. Unfortunately, many people thought we'd done enough genocide lately, so even when monsters came out of the river roaring about conquest... I mean, seriously, they *do*... apparently now we have to dance around and act as dumb as they are.

"Are my hobbies any weirder than fighting semi-sentient fish every fucking month?" I asked. "Nothing on this planet makes sense. I'm just giving that its due. And walking in those heels is *fantastic* for my balance."

The good money was on one of the older, more whimsical weapons trainers instigating the primitive weapons policy. Mostly likely it was my primary mentor, Maddoc. Further orders said we shouldn't kill any more fish-men than absolutely necessary, which gave that some credence.

Semi-sentient fish are going to invade every full moon? I could easily imagine him saying. *Great! Let's make a training exercise out of it! Everyone use non-lethal force so we can do this again next month! These fish-men shall be the frosting on the shit-cake of our Return experience!*

Except, of course, that the old man doesn't explain himself.

"You should wear stripper heels at next month's Fish Ball!" Rellen said. "Fifty creds say you can't keep your balance."

I mean, the policy makes some sense. There's practically nothing else for the Guard to do around here. Whatever distracts from drinking, making stupid bets, and missing our annihilated homeworld, right? If the mutated catfish had been just *slightly* more worthy, better smelling opponents, I wouldn't even have minded. But they were stupid, awful, and their stench got into your hair and *lingered.*

"I'll double that," Enzo said, grinning. "Hundred creds if you show up in heels. The big platform kind, at least a hand's-breadth tall."

After last September's Fish Ball, we spent an evening watching old local monster movies from before the Return. We collectively decided the fish-men were Godzilla's wet farts, risen from the deep to torment us for destroying the King of Monsters' fan base. The sheer stench really has to be experienced to be believed.

"You guys just want me to end up with that *horrendous* trophy on my locker," I answered, as more fish-men heaved themselves up onto the bank. There were more of them than usual. A lot more, though most were on the smaller side. A little frisson ran through me, a feeling that tonight's battle could be more than we'd expected. "But seeing what Danielle could come up with as a fetish version of a Guard uniform might be worth it."

"I can think of a few other people who might order some of those," Rellen replied, glancing down the line of Guards.

"How often did we have to listen to the elders reminisce about the epic battles of their youth on Earth?" Enzo asked in disgust. "It's almost too bad they killed off all the Fomorians. All we're left with are these loser fish we could off while dressed as dancing girls."

"We should do that. All dress up together," Rellen said with an annoyed glance at his sword and shield. He much prefers firearms to melee weapons, sensibly enough. "It'd hardly be more ridiculous than *this* nonsense."

"RELLEN! ENZO!" Captain Bhairton bellowed. "Do I hear you instigating McMann into something even dafter than that affair with the eel?"

"Sir no sir!" they answered in unison, winking at me.

"And Connor, what is department policy on embarrassing our entire civilization and culture?"

"Not more than once a year, sir!"

"Never! Try 'never'!"

"Yes sir, I'm trying, sir!"

"Try harder!"

I couldn't help it. A giggle escaped me. The captain rolled his eyes at me and looked at the line of fish-men flopping their way towards us. He could say whatever he wanted; I knew he had his own bets in the pool for what the next big Connor Incident would be. Being under a century old and one of the youngest of our people came with *some* benefits, at least in terms of what I could get away with.

"Ready weapons!" he yelled at us. "Tech crew, we good?"

Sveta threw us a thumbs up from her floating control center. Lady Morganna, our *Rí*, had taken the pale, lavender-haired strangeling girl as her ward after she caught the kid robbing a Raven armory in Moscow eight years ago. Sveta is twenty-something now, looks elfin but punk, and is way too technologically proficient. She's like a little Russian manic pixie nightmare fiend. I'd been instructed to treat her like a kid sister, and she'd *more* than made herself at home in that role. We couldn't see them, but she had a swarm of tiny invisible cameras called Eyes flying through the surrounding air, ready to record the entire fight from a dozen perspectives. The biggest "fail" of the night would be made into a horrifically entertaining video clip and posted on Stellnet for the galaxy to laugh at. The guard responsible would get the world's most awful trophy stuck to his locker all month.

So far, I'd avoided that.

My luck was about to run out.

4

The Old Tank in the Woods

Aisling

Deep in the woods, where roads don't go anymore, strange purple vines twist and wind around an old rotting army tank. They bloom regardless of the season, huge blossoms in a toxic shade of violet. Back during the invasion, a year before I was born, the local Guards base tried to save some of their stuff from disintegration. They hid gear at the end of an overgrown logging road a few miles outside town. It didn't help. The Elsecomers found it anyway, and hit it with a Radiant weapon. Now the tank sits contaminated and abandoned, rusting away, mutating whatever comes too close.

Except things that are already Radiant. Except things contaminated since birth.

Which makes it a good place to meet such people.

I glanced down the road behind me, but no one was following, so I leaped over the edge of the road and into the forest. My bare feet hit the ground on the far side of the drainage ditch and I pushed through tangled underbrush and into more open space under the pines. There was a deer trail back there, but with the woods a mess of late spring muck and snowmelt, it wasn't as obvious as usual. The ground made slurping noises as I ran, slow-thawing mud squelching between my toes.

Trees flashed by me and a mile disappeared beneath my feet. I pulled rocks off a pile of fieldstones outside a long-abandoned farm, then ditched my threadbare jeans and flannels in a watertight tote I'd hidden there years earlier.

Time to lose the farm-girl look. Can't let the worldless tribes know my daily-wear face.

I stood naked in the snow for a second, the chill bringing my skin alive. My fingers fumbled at the choker my human self always wears. It's nothing visibly very special, merely some dark hemp twine and a polished chip of blue-gray moonstone. I could hold illusions without a focus easily enough by then, but... my mom wove it for me, knotting magic and illusions through its strings. Sometimes I feel like I can't breathe with it on; more often I feel like I can't breathe without it. Even after what Mom did, near the end, I still miss her. There was a comfort in wearing something she made to protect me.

But sometimes you can't play it safe.

I found the clasp and pushed the knot through it. My human seeming melted away. It's tall, plain, and very Northern. The local side of the family is mainly Swedish-American, so I look lanky and blonde and wear horse-girl braids that reach the small of my back. A casual observer might think my ancestors probably milked a lot of cows whenever they weren't fishing, which is both fair and completely accurate. The Lingrens were all pretty typical Minnesotans; some were even *enthusiastic* about ice fishing.

Real me stayed under wraps, and only got out when I need to talk to aliens or really cut loose. Living as my illusion and tying my magic up in knots kept my mental self-image human. When I ran into someone with a bit of Sight, like Luke, they usually just thought I was a weirdo, not some invader's half-breed spawn.

To be fair, I'll probably be weird by the other side of the family's standards too, if I ever meet them.

My hidden self emerged, moon-pale and misleadingly delicate, with pointed ears and some apparently odd beauty no one's ever described well. My team teases me about it, anyway, saying I don't look old enough to buy beer. If that's not a good reason to live with an illusion on, I don't know what could be. I'm twenty-four and live after the apocalypse in bumfuck nowhere. "Dry" is not an option. I have to think of myself as mostly normal and local, though, so I don't look in mirrors when that face is out.

But ditching the illusions felt *good*. My magic stretched out, unfurling, making the land *sing* to me. I gloried, for a second, in being briefly, nakedly, unashamedly *myself*.

My mother's otherworldly green armor came at my call, fifth dimensional nanites swirling around me. It defaults to something really sci-fi looking, but I prefer making it look like old leathers from Middle Earth. No one would mistake me for a human with it on, but I don't really look like an Elsecomer either. I shrugged, settling it into place, then stepped off the trail and ran cross-country the last two miles.

Gods between Worlds, I thought, flashing across a stretch of open snow, *I wish it was possible to put on enough speed to hit escape velocity on my life.*

The light... changed... when I got close to the abandoned tank's clearing. The sun was close to setting, but the air turned silvery and numinous. There didn't seem to be anyone or anything else around, but I took my time and went in slow and cautious. Making a mistake out here could get me killed.

Shadows hid me in the forest's edge. The faint traces of fog that always haunt the clearing drifted over the tank, and for a second I saw not a tank but a sleeping beast, something with steely ropes of muscle and the same vines draped over it. In the swamp beyond the woods, a stiff breeze gusted and teased, filled with the scents of melting snow and thawing mud. Here, though, was slightly *Elsewhere,* and the air hung still and expectant. Pod-like cocoons hung from the purple vines, something new, and embryonic creatures twitched inside them. The late afternoon sun slunk through wafting vapors, a pale silver disk in a pale silver sky. Its wan light shimmered as if it fell through water, and something like an *awareness* pulsed through the eerie gloom.

It's not a ghostland, I felt. *Not yet. And it won't be, if I can help it.*

I waited, wary, *listening,* in case I'd somehow missed a sign of something dangerous. Horrors haunt these woods, sometimes. I'd rather I see them before they see me.

Nothing. I tipped back my head and sang out the Call to Trade.

Silent wings flew over my head a minute later. A cream and brown owlie landed on a pine branch fifteen feet from me. The little alien was about a foot and a half tall and looked like a cross between a barn owl and a squirrel. It's an awfully cute look for what are basically an entire species of street vendors, scammers, and gossips. He stopped to preen his face with little squirrel paws before acknowledging me.

"The Call is Answered. Aulen u'Michii of the Pinesong Mihooli greets you," he said in formal Market-Tradish.

Great, Michii's son. What did I do to deserve this?

I adjusted my expectations about how well this might go downwards. He looked at me, equally unimpressed, fluffed his feathers, and switched to the simpler variant I speak, Barter. "Whaddaya want, o *lost* child of the starborn?"

I grimaced at the description, however accurate it might be. Aulen was reminding me I didn't have the muscle of my mother's people to flex behind me.

"Hellos give I, from the Underhill Railroad to Aulen. Aid seeking-come-I. Girl lost-is, was human," I answered in Barter-Tradish, a bit shortly, knowing my limited knowledge of the language sounded awful. Mom taught me the basics of her people's language, but not the one that'd be actually useful. She didn't want me talking to aliens. Or anyone, really. "Strangeling now. She very tall is, half again bigger than human, dark in color, maybe hairy all over. I message to her want-give. You seen?"

The owlie huffed and stared at me.

"Do we *have* to do this?" I said in English. "I just killed a huge cannibal stone giant that was attacking people near the Temperance River, and kept a major military action from going through your nesting zone there! The soldiers would have wiped out all the Mihooli in the region!"

"*That* was Stonenest tribe. *This* is Pinesong."

I made a face and proceeded with the formalities.

"Fine goods to trade have I," I said, rolling my eyes internally at the hassle of this. "A folding solar charger and these two AA batteries. They used-are, but hold an eighty-three percent charge."

The owlie fluffed his feathers and cocked his head sideways, then flew down closer to inspect it.

"This charger has space for *four* batteries."

I cursed internally and pulled out the other pair, placing them with the others. If you didn't do something like this, owlies won't respect you. He nodded, tasted one, and signed *acceptable* with his tiny hands. He fluffed and hopped back to his original perch.

"Wait here. We will go searching," he said. "What message to give? English speak, I will remember the sounds."

"She's directly that way," I said, feeling her through my landbond and pointing Southwest. "About ten miles. Sara, called she."

He puffed and made an impatient head-bob.

"Tell her, 'An agent will meet you tonight, 8 pm, under the Interstate 35 overpass by the old casino, Westbound side. Climb into the back of the pickup that pulls up and hide under the tarp, then follow instructions as they're given to you. The Underhill Railroad will get you to safety.' Do you need that written down?"

"We will manage," he said, as short with me as I'd been with him, and bent his legs and leaped into the air. A couple wing strokes, and he was away. Owlie hoots echoed off into the distance.

I waited on a glacial erratic from the last Ice Age. That's a boulder, if you weren't raised by a science nerd who thought kids books were boring and had you memorize nature guides instead of moo-cows and baa-lambs like a normal parent. Back in high school, I used to come out and sit by the old tank a lot. I'd plop down on this rock, drink bad moonshine, and poke at a hole Mom's magic had left in my memories. She did something to me to "ensure I survived her death", and it left aching blank spots all over the year prior to it. The wipe had fucked me up, my emotions and empathic gifts in particular, and it took me years of intentionally working at it to feel anything vaguely like normal. I still didn't really date. I was hardly celibate, I just didn't try for anything involving *commitments.* Too risky, too painful. Too easy for things to go *very* wrong.

Silence stalked the forest. This clearing was really close to going ghostland, with Presence like that making itself felt. Melting ice-water dripped. Pods twitched on the vine, shapes convulsing inside them. Birds sang in the distance, but not nearby.

My belly grumbled. I wondered how long this would take. My aunts had brought wild rice hotdish over to Dad's place and I was ready for a big plateful. It had been four-ish when the sheriff showed up, so I probably had an hour before they served dinner.

I wished I had some 'shine to drink, but the guy I used to get it from died in a shootout with mutant raccoons two years previous. The Rax had taken over his operation, but I was banned from buying from them for *reasons.*

They were something Mom had blamed on me. I thought Rocket Raccoon was the best Avenger when I was little. Mom let me watch the DVDs with him because anything with a cute animal on the cover was a kids' movie, right? Then she wondered where I learned to talk like *that.* But the first sentient racoons showed up when I was obsessed with him, and she had thought my weird hybrid magic was contagious. Maybe she'd been right. The moonshiner's death wasn't the only one I was responsible for, if so.

There was this cute soldier, braver than most... I don't even know what happened. He helped me kill some wyverns up the North shore, and then I saw his funeral on the news a few days later. They said I irradianced him, but I don't know how. That was it for me trying to work with local authorities, though.

I really wanted some 'shine. Staring at a rotting hulk and drinking terrible booze wasn't a healthy coping mechanism, but the rusting tank and strange flowers kept things in perspective for me. The human half of my heritage had irredeemably fucked up the world; the other side outright broke it, and maybe saved it too... but in the *weirdest* possible way.

And there's nothing I can do about any of it, except try to contain the worst of this cascading clusterfuck.

Over on the tank, a pod started jerking around and split down one side. Pale green hands reached out, tiny as a mouse's, and pulled at the hole. A creature vaguely like a pixie emerged, wet wings clinging to its back. It started crawling towards the tank, somewhere solid to sit while they dried, then winced away from the rust. I walked over and cradled my hands together, holding them in front of it. It crawled blindly into them, its eyes still milky, and I moved it over to the other side of the boulder I'd been sitting on. I shifted the others over as they hatched.

Some of the mist cleared, and we sat together in silence as they bathed in the late afternoon light, stretching out damp, translucent wings. They could almost have stepped out of the pages of a Victorian book of fairy paintings, though soft green fur covered their bodies and they somehow made me think of little chipmunks. Their wings looked like those of luna moths.

I shifted on the boulder, getting stiff, and they all turned, bug-like, to look at me. Their eyes shimmered like polished jewels, amethyst and citrine and emerald. Serrated teeth glinted in their tiny mouths. I sighed, shaped a golden armor claw over a fingernail, and sliced open a minor cut on my left palm. I held my hand out to them. The first one to hatch cocked its head sideways and leaped over, and sat on my fingers and examined my face for a minute. Then it lowered its head to the blood, lapped delicately at it, and shivered so hard it blurred for a second. Golden lines spread through its wings, and its face gained sharp fae definition.

"Welcome to the world, little one," I said to her. "Good luck to you out there."

She jumped to my shoulder, and her hatch-mates descended. They drank my blood with delicate politeness. With the connection thus formed between us, I grabbed the excess Radiance in the clearing and poured it into them, shaping their magic into something that could *fit* in this world. Three minutes later, they rose from me in a shimmering flurry of jeweled wings and flew away into the forest. An owlie hooted in surprise a couple hundred feet away.

I sighed and stood up.

"The message is delivered," Aulen called down to me, swooping back into the clearing. "And the meeting arranged."

"Good-is-it to conduct deals with the skilled and resourceful," I answered formally, pulling the little charging kit out and placing it on the boulder. "Fair winds and solid branches to Aulen u'Michii. Our deal is complete."

He chuffed, pleased, and hooted. A couple more owlies flew into the clearing, carrying bags held between their feet. I left them to their loot, wondering how the hell I'd replace it. I was already totally broke after replacing my dad's chainsaw. Going without batteries until I got my next miniscule paycheck would suck.

On a side note, don't try dismembering stone giants with chainsaws, you'll just wreck the saw. Then you'll have to break into a rental place at 4 a.m. and steal a jackhammer. After that, you'll need to give your dad a new "gift" chainsaw and let him think you'd done something so stupid you couldn't even talk about it. Also? Chainsaws aren't cheap. It was a total buzzkill on what had otherwise been an awesome adrenaline high.

And Dad keeps shaking his head in some combination of disbelief and disappointment every time he looks at me. If I hear, "Any daughter of mine should know how to use a chainsaw properly," one more time, I'm going to scream. The giant didn't totally harden right away and then the blade got stuck - how is that my fault? Not that I can explain...

"You go soon to the Edgelands?" the owlie asked, surprising me, and I nodded. "Move swiftly there. The traitor recovers his magic, they say, and knows when others walk his lands. He will pursue you again."

Well, fuck.

As if sneaking around that close to the stolen Twin Cities wasn't dangerous enough, it was my cruddy luck to have someone with magic like mine get stuck in the St. Cloud prison labor brigade. Division 51 hunts me every time I'm down there, and the guy also has landbound magic. Strangelings *can't* turn into something like me, though; my mother had been insistent that the magic behind the Broken Dawn might reshape random humans, but our people's relationship to it was... different. Her reason for telling me that was lost in the fog of missing memories. The owlies thought he was probably an Elsecomer exile, but that seemed unlikely to me.

The asshat must be part of the organization Mom was hiding from, I reflected. *Fucking Squids. He'll doubtless be after me again.*

"Are you *positive* he's an Elsecomer?" I asked Aulen, though. "Division 51 always uses mostly human tactics."

"We got a message to kin in the Freeport, and through them to the Guard there," Aulen said. "My uncles are convinced it's a case of *clandestine* exile."

"Clandestine?" I repeated, not sure I understood the word he'd used and, well, dubious. Owlies are both terrible gossips and the worst sort of conspiracy theorists, and they will at least play at believing *anything* they find entertaining.

"The Guard denied anyone has been exiled, so *that* likely means it's all highly classified state secrets. Probably the outlaw is related to someone important, and that's why they dumped him out in the human lands instead of just killing him. But only a renegade would break the Compacts as he does."

Well, that made things clear as mud.

For a minute, I just stared at the owlie.

I don't think the guy is a renegade. A real Elsecomer wouldn't fall for the ridiculous shit my team pulls getting past Div 51.

"We can take a message to the Freeport, let them know you're out here and need rescue," Aulen said, both helpful and dubious himself. No doubt potential reward money was involved.

"Fuck no," I said in English. "I'm not one of *them*. And if you want me to keep clearing monsters out of your nesting sites, you won't say a damn word about me to anyone there."

The owlie cocked his head sideways at me.

"Deal not-desired is," I replied in Tradish. "Information appreciated."

"When you get taken captive," he said, fluffing up again. "We'll take word then."

Arguing was pointless. Hopefully, whoever they talked to would simply ignore them again. I kicked some remnant snow, nodded in acknowledgment, and tossed up a look-away glamour. Then I took a second to reach out telepathically and update my team with the rescue plans. Everyone sent back general feelings of assent, but they were busy with other things.

I jogged back to the old farm and put my choker and clothes and human seeming back on. Then I scrunched up my eyes and pulled in my magic, burying elven-me under layers of bindings and glamours. The world went dull and gray around me, and cold bit my skin.

So we head for the Edgelands tomorrow. Just gotta keep one step ahead of that guy, and out of Div 51's reach.

I shrugged on a *don't see me* glamour and turned towards Dad's place. I spent the final walk back wondering again how the hell someone with magic like mine had ended up in a prison labor brigade. No one was sticking me in a box - why did he *stay* there?

5

PYRES

ARTHUR

O ther people did what forensics we bother with on the cryptid, mainly some photos and measurements, then dragged the body down to the river sand and built a bonfire over it. Better not to have every scavenger in the area get irradianced by the cryptid's remains. Field rations got passed around, and Jones dropped a blanket over my shoulders.

I stared at the fire, trying not to think.

"Captain, whatever happens... you don't go *evil*," Birch said, walking over next to me. "When... the other guy... comes out, it's no worse than a big cat or a wolf or something wild. Never hurts anything but the monsters. Seems to just like hunting."

"That *thing* tried taking over your mind," I reminded him.

"Lucky I've got friends who taught me how to block fae mind control, huh?" he said, taking a seat on a log opposite mine.

"Think you could convince them to come teach a class to the other troops?" I asked.

He blinked, and his eyes went wide. Then he forcibly bit his own lips together to hold in his laughter.

"Um... I don't think you would get along with the teacher," he said, trying to keep a straight face. "The girl who taught that lesson runs utterly wild. She's one of the Viking re-enactors at the camp I go to every June. You'd probably kill either yourself or her after five minutes in a room with Naked Fuckin' Hildie."

Wait, Birch has a friend with a nickname like that? Our Birch?

"This I gotta hear," Jones said, joining us. "M'dude has actually seen a woman in the buff? In real life?"

"Look, Hart sent me looking for the Green Lady at an event where she'd been seen previously. The best candidate I ever found was a Range chick who drives a crappy pickup, knows the lyrics to like every Weird Al song ever, and shows up drunk and naked to public exhibition battles. Not exactly a deadly, sophisticated alien."

I blinked. This was not how I'd envisioned Birch's social circle.

"*That's* who you learn magic from?"

"Well, some of it. Hildie teaches the resistance part. Brought a friend along for the training. Redhead, *hot,* body like a movie star and the voice of a flipping angel. She showed up for an evening to drink with Hildie, who I guess is a roadie for her band or something. After the stick jocks had passed out, Erika the Red pulled out a batch of Strawberry Surprise, and she said we were going to drink it until we learned to resist glamours."

"Strawberry Surprise?" Jones said. "Doesn't sound too rough."

"The surprise is that there are *no* strawberries. It's moonshine and habanero sauce, among other horrible things. Slamming a shot can make a strong man wish he'd never been born."

"And you?"

"Spent half the night curled up sobbing," Birch cheerfully admitted. "Erika passed out glasses. Then the redhead started telling us how much we wanted a drink, and a few shots and some screaming and vomiting later, most of us figured out how to fend her off. What you do? Doesn't hold a candle to the glamour she could pull."

"What was she?" Jones asked, frowning.

"A musician. Looked perfectly human. Well. Almost *too* beautiful, but then she is a performer. Her magic felt fae, though. I halfway thought she was passing."

"Maybe she was an Elsecomer? One of the Beautiful Monsters?"

"No fucking way. She and Hildie spent half the night filking 'Lumberthumpin'' to make verses about dating in the SCA, and the rest trying to decide which dive bar in Superior was the most godawful."

"*Lumberthumpin'?*" I asked, dubious.

"Oh, it's this terrible song some little band up North wrote about trying to date in their hometown. The redhead might have been the singer, actually. It was popular on local radio a few years ago. It has verses about finding out your date is your cousin, romantic evenings ice fishing, and lucky blaze orange camo lingerie."

Jones laughed.

"This fucking state..." he said.

"Why would someone possibly fae but passing help a bunch of humans like that?" I wondered aloud. "Staying completely hidden would be more sensible."

"She was in the slave trailer with Erika when the redcaps raided the festival five years ago," Birch said. "Luckily, the Green Lady showed up and slowed the raid down long enough for a rescue to reach them. But Northshield's all prepping; they think an actual war with the 'caps is yet to come, and someday she'll show up and call them all to battle. They want to be ready when she does."

"Wait," Jones said. "Your human friends are willing to fight for someone that *Else?*"

"Oh yes," he said. "Call them on it, and they'll say '*She's ours, and the old gods favor her. Beowulf was part monster, too. Someone like that calls you to battle, you* GO.' They're all daft, but they mean it."

I shook my head. When she'd irradianced me, almost five years previously, she'd been a lunatic kid with *no idea* what she was doing.

But when she'd called, I'd followed her straight into battle, too.

It had felt *right* in a way nothing ever had, before or since.

And then exposure to her wild magic mutated me into a monster.

Maybe in a couple of days I could talk to her, after I got back from my trip. Vicki might be out of quarantine by then, too.

Dinner was at Aunt Thelma's apartment, a floor below my dad's place. Gram and Aunt Dahlia had brought hotdish over in some crock pots that they just plugged in and let simmer. The world had lost a lot of its tech in the Elsecomer invasion, but here in Northern Minnesota we run mainly on hydropower, and the invaders left clean energy alone. As long as the rivers are high enough, we still have municipal electricity, most of the time, and a wide array of kludged-together wind turbines, solar panels, and micro-hydro generators for backup power. Out here, it was just the most fragile and modern electronics that were done in, and the higher above ground the worse they got hit. In a state full of chronic hoarders with basements built as tornado shelters, it meant we weren't knocked back to the Stone Age so much as to the mid-1990s.

Apocalypse enough, really.

"Food will be on as soon as the kids get here," Aunt Dahlia called from the kitchen as I walked in. She glanced at my bare feet and shook her head. Didn't bother saying anything, though. Dad looked at me and raised his eyebrows. I just stuck out my jaw and kept quiet.

Don't say anything suspicious. They'll all just think I ran out because of what happened to Mom and baby Jamie, not to take care of this.

I pulled out a chair and reminded myself to be on good behavior. It's flipping hard whenever Trey is at the table, though. I braced myself for whatever was to come.

"Has anyone heard what triggered that poor girl?" Aunt Dahlia asked. Every time someone Changed, people tried figuring out what caused it. Sometimes there was an obvious, Radiant reason, like eating contaminated vines off a blasted tank. Sometimes there was nothing.

"Bad blood," Aunt Thelma sniffed. "And bad habits."

My knuckles went white under the table.

"Thelma Louise Lingren," Gram snapped from the corner, not looking up from the latest baby sweater she was knitting. I wondered which cousin was expecting now, and decided it was better not to know. "I did *not* raise you to be a judgmental bitch!"

My aunt gasped and her mouth went white. Now and then I wondered how Thelma had avoided a redcap transformation; her husband hadn't, after all. My best guess was that she was just a gossipy old busybody, not a hate-wallowing fascist. Sometimes it seemed like a thin line. And when push came to shove, she showed up. With hotdish and cookies. I guessed that was something.

Aunt Dahlia sighed loudly.

"Sara was *Black*, not contaminated, and Vicki said it was some charity food," I said. If anyone around here had bad blood, it was *me*. "Blame whoever provided *that*. Sara was a good student who actually followed the athletic code of conduct, unlike most jocks. I never even saw her drinking beer, and I babysat her and Vicki for five years and saw both of them regularly after I left for college. Exactly what habits are you talking about?"

"Well, I *heard...*"

Thankfully, the doorbell rang then. The hooligans, Jackie and Evan, came in with Lucy, who was just old enough to have her own car.

"Hey kids!" I called as they hung their jackets on the coat rack. "Guess you're with me this evening."

Lucy stifled a laugh, and Jackie looked dismayed. She was fifteen and a "rebel", and convinced my study track was evidence I'd sold out. Evan bounced obliviously into a chair and started grabbing dinner buns. He was a small, scrawny ten-year-old and could probably eat an entire cow without putting on a pound.

"Watch out, kids," Trey said. "Aisling had a hot date with Bigfoot and she's all cranky because you're box-blocking her tonight."

"Trey, shut up," I said, glaring at him. "I have some errands to run and didn't expect to have kids in tow."

"Yeah, Bigfoot would be out of your league anyway," he answered. "And probably isn't a musician."

"The only bigfoot I've ever met is already married, with a very happy wife. She says the shoe size thing is dead on. Think she had her fifth on the way last time I saw her."

Trey looked at me like he was trying to figure out if I was finally outright lying, and I gave him a perky grin.

"Dude, Aisling, learn how to use makeup and even you could land the guy or girl or weirdo cryptid of your dreams," Lucy said, pulling off her fake zebra fur jacket. *Her* cosmetics might have been applied with a spatula. "Your skin's more pasty than the belly of a dead fish. Bronzer, try it! You might finally get a relationship that lasts beyond when the band van pulls away."

"Lucy dear," Gram said sweetly, needles still clicking away. "Aisling is apparently your only cousin who has learned how to use contraceptives. You could learn a thing or two from her, before I have to start knitting mini-sweaters for some *great* grandchildren. Don't give me that look, Trey Lingren, if you can ever convince a girl you're not a serial killer, *then* we'll see how you do. Aisling's responsible and should enjoy herself. Lotta fish in the sea!"

Kill me now. We are not discussing any of this at the dinner table! I thought. *And relationships are too dangerous for someone like me.*

"Too busy with finishing my Master's to deal with dating," I said, dishing myself some mashed potatoes. "The lab's doing fascinating stuff right now. Last week I got to dissect a real chupacabra! It was a mess inside, though; some logging truck hit it at full speed. Looked kind of like a kangaroo on the outside, but the internals were fascinating. What wasn't oozing hemorrhaged goo, anyway. Most of it looked like this gravy, but redder."

I heaped a big ladle-full onto my potatoes.

"Chunkier, too," I added, just because.

"Aisling Sorcha Lingren!" Aunt Dahlia snapped. "We do not discuss dissections at the dinner table!"

"I think it's interesting!" Evan piped up. He was ten and supposedly had cheered on his sister burning down Aunt Thelma's kitchen. "What's a chupacabra?"

"It's like Mexican for *goat-sucker*," I said, going all in on my mad scientist impression. "And it might have hitched a ride North somehow. They're like mangy kangaroo vampires that attack livestock. Their tongues are this weird funnel shape, and they stick it in the holes their teeth make and slurp out the good stuff."

"Aaaashling!" Dahlia repeated, drawing out the ash sound at the beginning of my name. My mom gave me a name that means some kind of hippie BS in Irish, her "dream of the light of the blooming tree", she said, but in English it sounds like I'm a child of the ashes. Which may be accurate, but I don't have to like it! Only my family calls me that name now, and some of the worldless aliens who insisted on a true name before they'd deal with me. I have different nicknames and I.D.s for just about everything else I do.

Get raised by someone in hiding, grow up paranoid. Way of the world.

"World's gone bleeping nuts," my dad said, shaking his head. "Lab work didn't involve monsters in my day. Pass the gravy?"

"Your lab work once had you thinking you were a six foot tall goose who could see through space-time!" Aunt Dahlia exclaimed. "And Evan, that is a *fork*, not a shovel. Slow down and chew!"

"Oh, well, it *was* a mycology lab," Dad said, smiling at the memory. "One of the grad students put the wrong mushrooms into the omelet while we were cramming for midterms. Ahh, sometimes I miss the taste of eggs fried over a Bunsen burner."

"How'd you do on that test?" I asked.

"Fantastic. The professor had them too and thought we all made A+ goslings."

I wish some of my profs would get stoned and go easy on me.

"Everyone has their food?" Aunt Thelma asked. "Let's say grace. I want us all to pray for the soul of that poor girl we just lost to the Elsecomers' demonic powers."

Gram sighed loudly.

Trey bowed his head and crossed himself piously, as if he'd ever been the slightest bit religious, the unrepentant faker. His eyes glittered at me, daring me to say something. I gritted my teeth and kept my mouth closed.

It was a waste of effort.

I bit my tongue until it was practically bleeding, and dinner was a disaster anyway. Jackie got into a screaming fight with Thelma about five minutes after sitting down. My aunt implied maybe Sara had Changed because she'd been caught making out with another girl on the basketball team. Lesbian activity was *definitely* a stop on the road to Hell, after all. Jackie said in that case, she planned to take over the place. Gram gave her a thumbs up. Lucy added that her friend had waitressed at The Rendezvous when The Sparkling Cowboys last played, and it sounded like Jackie would have to fight me for the throne. Trey piped in that I just slept with losers, regardless of gender, and things went downhill from there.

7
FRUSTRATED

ARTHUR

M y fists pounded into the punching bag, far faster than I'd ever been able to hit when I was human. I bounced a step away, my bare feet sure on the mats of the Box's improvised gym. I'd wrapped my knuckles, but blood was already seeping through.

She stole my kill. Again!

My leg snapped up, and I kicked the bag as hard as I could. Old chalk dust puffed off it.

"What's going on? What happened to heading North?" I heard Sergeant Black quietly ask Jones, opening the gym door and peaking in. Serena handled intelligence for our unit. She was a former analyst whose Change left her looking like that cat-headed Egyptian goddess. They were across the room, but every word they whispered was perfectly clear to my Changed body's pointed ears.

"Take a wild guess," Jones' bass voice rumbled from where he was lounging against the wall, keeping an eye on me. "What usually puts Captain in a mood to murder the gym gear?"

I slammed an uppercut into the bag. Discipline and iron self-control keep the monsters in us from taking over, but mine were frayed to bits. Strangelings can't manage freedom. I longed for it, oh god I longed for it... but I knew the darkness in myself, and in too many of my people. It waited, famished, *starving*, a spree killer lusting to run down prey and feast as its blood pumped out into the eager land...

"Greenie already offed the giant?" she hazarded. It wasn't hard to guess. Story of practically every mission Div 51 got sent on up around the Duluth area. That green-armored elf-witch had even thrown a stinking, muddy monster head into our camp once. She was gone before I could get halfway up the cliff she'd tossed it from. The head looked like it'd been in the ground for a week already. Birch had just looked at it, said, *Oh, guess that's why we're not finding any tracks.* An hour later we'd been on our way back to our prison in St. Cloud, as if the woman who'd offed it wasn't a significantly bigger threat than any of the monsters she killed!

"Yup," Jones drawled, and I spun and hit the bag with my other foot, directly where one might imagine a renegade Elsecomer's throat might be. "So what's your money on, Serena, murder or marry?"

"I'm not touching your stupid bet with a ten-foot pole," she said. "Gonna get some grub if we're not traveling tonight. Join me in the mess hall?"

The punching bag's support made a groaning noise like it was on the verge of breaking. Both officers jumped and stared at me.

"Will do," Jones sighed, leaning back again. "Eventually."

"Yeah, I see what you mean," Black said, shaking her head at the bloodstains on the punching bag. "Well, can't say I'll miss five hours of potholes in trucks with no suspension, then a bug hunt down an icy canyon. Hadn't eaten because that ride makes me so carsick. Anyway. William got the DVD player working again, and he's setting up a movie in the rec room. Come join us when Captain's done destroying the gym?"

"Yup," Jones said, settling in further.

When the door had closed again, I slowed down and leaned my head against the bag for a second. The antlers growing out of my forehead poked into the canvas. They still felt odd, alien, not really part of me.

"I don't need a babysitter, Jones," I told him.

"Sure you don't," he answered, making no sign of moving away.

"I'm fine," I said, the lie grating as it slipped through my teeth.

I wasn't. He knew it, Black knew it, the whole bloody troop knew it. Every time the Green Lady danced past me, I ended up like this. The fae magic roiling inside me went into rabid fits every time she was nearby, and had been doing so since the first time she stole a kill from me, four years ago.

"What *you* need is to get laid."

"Uh huh," I said. Fat chance of that. I pointed at the antlers. "You know any willing civvie girls that'd be into this?"

I mean, holy fuck, was he ever right. It'd been four and a half years; I hadn't touched a woman - or anyone else - since the morning I woke up with aching bumps on my forehead. And god, had I been turned on then, feeling like something wrong with me was finally becoming right... when the exact opposite was true. If Laurie hadn't seen the budding antlers, and started screaming... I don't know what might have happened. If I'd gone into the Hunger then, I could have killed her on the spot.

"M'dude, I know an entire studio of movie starlets that'd love to do you," he said, stretching and putting his arms behind his head.

"*Sure* you do."

He laughed. Jones had been joking that he had a secret identity as a superhero of porn for the last three years. He and a team of our most stable members went out to work road repair projects on weekends, but they always said that they were "off to the studio". It started with jokes about filling potholes and got more and more elaborate over time. They came up with stories about what they'd *rather* be doing while working, I assumed, and those were everything you might expect of prisoner fantasies. The guys who went out sometimes came back smelling of beer or pot, but I turned a blind eye; they didn't get any other pay for their labor, and we were all just incarcerated for Changing, not actual crimes.

Maybe I should go out with them. I would kill to have a real beer again.

My hands smashed into the bag again, *left right left spin kick sucker-punch.*

If I couldn't control this ridiculous rage, I could at least direct it somewhere harmless.

I hadn't gone fully into the Hunger, not like some do. I just lived with this never-ending gnawing rawness that I knew was somehow the Green Lady's fault. It wasn't logical. It made no sense, and knowing I was going crazy didn't do a damn thing to stop me from tipping over the edge every time she was nearby.

"Maybe go for a run?" Jones suggested. "Stretch your legs a bit?"

"Like we have enough space for that... oh. The courtyard. Yeah, that's a good idea."

"Drink some water before you go," he said, and I grabbed an old plastic water bottle and chugged a bit from the locker room sink. The face of my demon stared back from the mirror, inhumanly handsome, the lines of the face I'd been born with barely recognizable in it. Almost human, but for the antlers, a stark reminder of my awful Change. Ears as pointed as a deer's swept back with them, highlighting cheekbones pre-invasion Hollywood would have killed for. My skin had smoothed from showing the faint brown of a drop of unspecified ethnic heritage to a golden tan that never faded, and my eyes turned the golden green of sunlit leaves, with pupils slit like a cat's. Auburn streaked silky hair that had once been simple brown.

My Change had left me as beautiful as I was monstrous.

The Elsecomer elves looked a lot like this. I'd never heard of any with antlers, though, and the pair I'd seen up close had round pupils, so that was... something.

The Devil's own looks, and they keep me single.

I wish I at least had a dog.

It wouldn't be that hard to smuggle a puppy in, actually.

Yeah, and someone with less self-control would eat it within the first week, I thought cynically, shaking some feeling back into my hands. *I can't risk that.*

Not least because someone eating my dog would probably make me snap.

I had a very bad feeling about what might happen if I ever snapped.

My monster had taken over on hunts a half dozen times now. I came back to myself with a bloody knife in my hand, my gun holstered or discarded, and an efficiently dead cryptid at my feet. The last three times, I had somehow even pulled my closest troops into that state with me. Their eyes had glowed around me like a hunting pack's when I came out of it, before they blinked and my magic's influence faded away.

Part of me had exulted in seeing that.

I didn't know how much longer I'd be able to trust myself.

Or if I could even trust myself now.

Jones opened the door, and I padded silently out into the hallway. No locked doors in here anymore, nor jailers wandering the halls. It was partially actual confidence that Strangeling Brigade was doing better. Apparently, we self-regulated better under my command than had ever happened before I was forcibly enlisted. Walking through the prison doors was a low level Radiance Event in its own right, though, and no one wanted to risk that. We had a couple of former prison employees in here as inmates now, in fact. No sane human wanted to work inside the Box. Everyone assumed we had too many strangelings together in one place, somehow turning exposure to us into a Radiance Event.

And it was partially that I could nudge the minds of people wanting to come in towards a... *better*... decision.

I *had* to protect what was growing in the old exercise courtyard. It was as fundamental as gravity, and as inescapable.

The fae weirdness that had taken over out there made us forget it when we were out of range. A vast tree grew impossibly far away, in the center of the space, but one could walk to its base in twenty strides from the courtyard door. I told myself over and over that I needed to report this... then forgot about it before I could. I penned myself notes, and shredded them. Once I wrote directly on my wrist, and came to all bloody, with no idea why my skin was scratched raw. The faery monster inside me, whatever else I might say about him, was absolutely committed to defense of this weirdness, and if I couldn't control him on this one thing, at least it was harming no one.

So far.

Regardless, right now I needed space, and to run, and at least with the faery tree growing out there, I could have that. Jones opened the door, clapped me on my back, and headed off towards the rec room.

I stepped into the meadow. Eerie moonlight flooded me. Night-blooming flowers swayed in a fragrant breeze, and some unearthly bird sang in the distance. I closed my eyes, quit trying to hold on to both my rage and my humanity, just for a bit, and let the night take me.

8

LITTLE COUSINS

AISLING

"I don't think you can actually *choose* to Change into a Japanese sex-tentacle monster," I told Jackie as we were walking out to my pickup after dinner. "Even if it would make your girlfriend super happy."

"Why do you stay in the closet?" she asked accusingly. "Everyone *knows* you're not straight. Thelma's asked us all to pray for you often enough."

My shoulders tightened up.

"Don't need the drama," I said shortly. "And I'm bi, I *might* bring a guy home someday."

She frowned at me and kicked the snow.

She's not going to understand.

And I can't explain that I want the family to love me until they inevitably learn I'm a monster.

I climbed into the *Millennium Partridge's* pickup bed and started loading firewood into the gasifier barrel. Wasn't a lot of gasoline to be had anymore, so when I was flush with battle loot a few years back, I bought an ancient junker pickup. My friend Bob converted it to running on wood gas, *et voila*, I had my own post-apocalyptic ride. Something new fell off it every month, but I could chop the fuel for it myself. Had to be careful of the axe to avoid iron burns, but the pickup got me around. Usually. Mostly. The *Partridge* has all the *Falcon's* mechanical problems, but absolutely *nothing* in common with a swift bird of prey. It made weird pounding sounds similar to a ruffed grouse in mating season, and frequently froze up just like an idiot forest chicken.

Driving the junker did wonders for preserving my secret identity, or so I kept telling myself.

Aaand it won't start.

Trey came out after us, waved a jaunty goodbye, and jumped into that sleek, sporty little hybrid-electric. It was a far, far nicer ride than mine. Surely that strut in his stride had *nothing* to do with seeing me under the hood... again.

"It'd sure show Thelma if I *did* Change into something like that," Jackie said. "Can you help me dye my hair blue after we run your errands?"

"Sure," I shrugged, thinking no one had any right to assume I ought to be a *good* babysitter. I slammed a thingy with a wrench, just like Bob showed me to do. The engine made a chugging sound when Jackie turned the key. "It'll make you really noticeable, though."

"That's kinda the point," she said, like I was stupid or something. "Out and proud! I'm not living *my* life in the closet!"

"Sometimes it's better if no one sees you and you just do what needs to be done," I answered, rolling my eyes internally. "And that said, I'm about to go do a bit that needs to be done. It'll take me about an hour. Where do you want me to drop you off while I run my errands?"

"I can help you!" Evan piped up.

"Look, you guys are too old to need babysitting. This is ridiculous. I'll just drop you somewhere and then come back for you, okay? Maybe Mooseburgers? Or a playground?"

"Yeah, Mom didn't leave us any money, *you* don't have any, and it's cold and we're too old for playgrounds," Jackie said dryly. "What are you doing?"

"Absolutely flipping nothing anyone not involved needs to know about," I said, putting the key in the pickup's storage box and getting some gear out. "Which is what you will tell anyone if asked. That I bored you almost to death, okay? You guys want to stay with me, you'll have to swear by the breath in your lungs to speak no word of what you see, except to those I okay."

"That's... weirdly specific," Jackie said, hesitating. Good. She had *some* sense.

"Seeing this could get people killed if you talk," I said. "I don't actually object to getting you involved, but my errand isn't safe. Or exactly legal."

Jackie bit her lip and thought about it.

"I swear to keep quiet! By the breath in my lungs!" Evan said, bouncing up and down on his toes like a hyper squirrel.

"Fuck," Jackie said. "Okay, me too."

"Then so be bound," I said, tying the oath with magic and a twisting gesture of my right hand. Evan gasped, and the breath whooshed out of Jackie's mouth like she'd been kicked in the stomach. Huh. The two of them were more sensitive than I'd have guessed.

"Aisling, do you know magic?" Evan asked, delighted. "Can I learn?"

I grinned at him, put a single finger to my lips, and pulled a few more things out of the lockbox.

"Is that a crossbow?" Jackie asked as I handed it down to her. "Wicked!"

"Why would your most boring cousin have anything like a crossbow?" I asked, making my eyes big and innocent. "Put it on the front seat for now, and the bolts next to it. Then grab the box behind the driver's seat. Don't open it; it's shielded, but the contents are Radiant."

Evan's eyes went huge.

"Aisling, that's, like, radioactive," he said.

"Not exactly," I answered. "It's a form of magical energy that opens up... possibilities. I've had my hands in enough Radiant guts that I know I'm not gonna Change. The jerky inside came from a cryptid out of the ghostlands. It'll help someone who's started Cascading, and hopefully get them through the Hunger while keeping them sane."

"Are we rescuing Sara?" Jackie whispered, her knuckles going white on the edge of the pickup bed.

" *We* are simply pulling over on the side of the road at a particular place. Then we'll drive to another particular place and hand an envelope out the window. We will see nothing and no one and speak of exactly that later on. Got it?"

"Who gave you the envelope?" Evan asked.

"No names," I said, checking the fire in the gasification chamber. We were good to go. I hopped out of the pickup's bed and opened the driver's door, and grinned. "But she's known for wearing green armor."

The kids slid in the other door and we pulled out and headed towards old Interstate 35, my pickup chugging like an asthmatic smoker. Of course, the highway doesn't go to any other states anymore, what with the Taken Cities and their fifty mile buffer zone in the way, but it was still the biggest road in the area.

"You know *her*?" Jackie asked, fiddling with the radio.

We passed the old sign marking the entrance to town. It had been set on fire in the redcap raid that got Rigs' parents and Trey's mom, and most of the town's old name had been burned off. Some enterprising teens had spray-painted its post-Dawn nickname over the char in blaze orange. Now it said Welcome to Stinkwood: Gateway to the Iron Range!

"*Know* is a strong word," I said. "But now and then, she helps an organization I work with."

"What's that?" she asked.

"Go back to the news," I said, catching a sound bite.

"*...planned joint military exercises to take down the Temperance River Giant have been called off after foragers discovered its corpse late this afternoon. It apparently turned to stone at death, and someone dismembered it with a jackhammer to keep it from regenerating. Score marks all over the corpse show it was attacked with an extremely sharp blade and eventually bled out. Astonishingly, no one heard anything, neither the fight nor the jackhammer. A local construction rental business said they* *found one of their jackhammers propped against their front door this morning. With it was an apology note, two hours' rental payment, and a $20 tip attached, supposedly from the 'Twin Ports Free Strangelings'. They are an anonymous group known to be associated with the so-called Green Lady..."*

It was hard to contain the grin wanting to spread across my face.

"Wow, I guess she is in the area now," Jackie said. "Is she really a renegade Elsecomer?"

I shrugged.

"Why do we call the invaders Elsecomers, anyway?" Evan asked.

"Nobody knows where they came from, or if they're mythological elves or aliens," Jackie said. "Some people think they're from Fairyland, because of their magic and the Changes they cause. Other people think they came from another planet. The leaders look like elves, but they have ships and weapons that are pure sci-fi. The day they invaded, cracks opened in the sky, full of stars and nebulas, and by the time those closed, humanity had lost most of its tech and all our big cities were under occupation. All we know is that the invaders came from somewhere *Else*."

"Why would one of *them* be out here, though?"

"I don't think the Green Lady is really one of *them*," I said. "Her accent's local."

"Ya, sure, you betcha, da Nortwood's own alien elf sounds like dis?" Evan said, throwing on the outstate accent extra heavy.

"Ope, uff da, doncha know, dat's it, dead on," I answered, laughing.

"What do you think the invaders are really like?" Jackie asked.

Dangerous question.

I shrugged. To be honest, I really didn't know. My mom was the only one I'd ever met, and she'd been a mess of paranoia and despair, especially at the end.

"I bet the taken cities are total hellholes now," Evan said. "I bet it's awful in them."

"Nobody human knows," I said, and pulled into the parking lot of an abandoned gas station by the Carlton exit.

But the owlies say they're awesome and half of them regret leaving.

I reached behind the seat, twisting around, and loaded the crossbow, keeping it pointed towards the pickup floor. I chewed on my lip for a second. "Either of you ever used one of these?"

"I have," Jackie said.

I raised my eyebrows.

"Sorry, you're not the first person to swear me to secrecy while doing illegal shit," she answered.

"Fair enough," I said. "So, trigger's here, and it's moderately sensitive. That crossbow's just a backup plan. If our passenger is in the Hunger or goes into it, try to take a shot and slow her down. But if she's coherent enough to make the rendezvous, chances are she's managing. Evan, reach under Jackie's seat and pull out the bear spray so you have something too."

"But what if..." Evan said, the seriousness of what we were doing finally hitting him.

"Then I'll kill her," I said simply. "I don't want to, but I won't let you kids get hurt. Hold that pointed down, Jackie, and keep your cool. She's waiting over there under the overpass."

9

DEVOURED

CONNOR

Evil stinking monster blobs glooped their way across the Flats, roaring about conquest. Well. Their charge was more like a galumphing waddle, but... they did their thing. And we might have been stuck in ridiculous circumstances with stupidly primitive weapons and absurd policies and all that, but we got to *hit* things. Let no one tell you it isn't incredibly therapeutic to hit things when you're frustrated as hell.

We try to make a good show of at least the first few minutes - elegant, coordinated, synchronized. But after the fish-men have been on the field a bit, it turns into a giant, slimy sliding rink.

The fish-men hit our line in a gooey, squelching wall of stench, an eye-watering reek redolent of rotted algae and decomposing fish. And finally, *finally*, we could cut loose. I whirled and opened the side of the closest one with my sword, slamming my shield into the eye of the one next to it. It thrust a spear wildly at me and I ducked under its tentacles and sliced them all off, then took off the fin behind them. We were supposed to avoid killing the monster fish; making them less able to damage us next time, however, was just fine.

Things descended into general glorious bloody mayhem for a few minutes, and I briefly forgot about irrelevancies like stink stains and missed modeling gigs and everything but the sheer physical joy of cutting loose. And *maybe* I got a little carried away. I certainly got carried away from the line I was supposed to be in, not that it was really tight anyway, and further towards the river than I should have let myself go. But my ceramosynth blade was light and agile in my hand, my shield felt like a part of my arm, and my body flowed between monsters like I was dancing.

This is what we're made for, we sidhe.

I lost myself in the moment.

Little thing, though: most of my magic had broken with our world's fall. My power had been too landbound; when the Eaters of Worlds took Briargard, I lost everything combat-oriented. I had to fight purely the old-fashioned way.

The guys around me? Not so much.

Lieutenant Sharrah blasted a large fish-man sideways with her magic, and she didn't anticipate it knocking a smaller one off at an angle when it flexed its tail on impact. The field was a slippery mess by then, and I barely even glimpsed the creature before it slammed directly into my back. The hit knocked the wind out of me and sent me sliding at speed across grass now ridiculously slick with slime, guts, and fish blood... downhill. Towards the river.

I rolled and tried to get back to my feet, but another big one slammed its tail sideways into me and I shot off even further from the lines. My sword was knocked from my hand. I heard yelling behind me and saw a gaping maw in front of me, the mouth of the biggest fish-man I'd ever seen. Nothing could stop my momentum; fish goo slicked everything around me. Darkness yawned, engulfing me in a stench so thick I could almost grab it with my hands.

No such luck. Nothing to grip. Slime everywhere.

I slid directly between the fish monster's jaws, and it gulped me down into stinking oblivion.

It's over, I thought, curling up as I fought against the fish's gullet, trying to keep my shield between its convulsing throat and my face. The darkness inside the fish was more than a lack of light. It was primal, devouring, a blackness of the soul, a creeping blight of infectious despair. I'd felt it before, in a recurring childhood nightmare where a demon ate my mother. It was a child's way to interpret personality changes after she took head trauma in a riding accident, I was told, but that stench stuck with me through the nightmares. This darkness felt the same: ravenous, filthy, eating not just flesh but soul.

It's finally over. I can let go and die like I should have, with Briargard. I'll go to the afterlife and be with my world and people again.

There will be peace.

Silence.

Darkness.

Like I've wanted for so long.

Then incongruously, resentfully, a thought intruded on my despair.

Danielle's going to be so disappointed. She made her last set for my measurements.

Then:

I'll never get to see her spring collection.

I'll never dance again.

If they recover my corpse, it'll stink like evil fish.

No one's ever going to talk about my death without giggling about how it was the dumbest one ever.

No one will remember me without remembering these horrible creatures.

And finally, clarity.

Fuck this shit, I am NOT going into the dark.

No mutant fish is killing me!

Something wild and brilliant lit inside me, and for a second I thought my magic was coming back, *at last*, in my hour of need. No shields bloomed around me, though, no magic roared like a rocket to shoot me out of the fish. And yet, there was *something*. Something bright and fierce and focused as a sword's tip, something that did not suffer evil, something that blazed against the dark. My backup armor sheathed my body, fifth-dimensional nanotech coming at my silent call, and hilts formed in my palms, cutting into the flesh of the fish-man's belly even as I shaped the blades, one in each hand.

The next minute was just striking and tearing and madness. I ripped myself out of that fetid stomach, covered in mutant fish guts and blood, and there was nothing about rules and regulations or "diplomacy" left in my mind when I pulled myself from that stinking belly. I looked at the river flats, at the battlefield heaving with monsters, at my coworkers ineffectively trying to cut themselves to me. Rellen was the only one already by me, stabbing the huge fish through its eye; the rest of the guards were still trying to cross the field, still obeying the rules, still holding back.

Inside me, something snapped.

What happened after that is a vague red blur in my memories, but I saw the footage later. Damn clip went viral on Stellnet. Sveta even won some award for the editing. In it, I pulled myself to my feet next to the twitching corpse of what turned out to be the catfishmen's war leader, stabbed it in the heart, and twisted the blade as I pulled it out. I looked at the field, and sidhe light spilled out of me brighter than the floodlights.

One of my best friends, Faron, out with a space unit now, is prone to berserking in battle. I'd always wondered what it felt like.

That night, I found out.

Fuck Diplomatic, I vaguely remember thinking. *These things DIE.*

And then I moved in a way I wouldn't replicate again for years, flashing through my enemies almost as fast as my mentor can, and started killing every oozing black monster in my reach. And the other fighters my light touched, they got caught in it too, and dropped half-assed ceramosynth weapons to the grass and pulled out nanotech armaments, sharp as a satirist's wit, and laid into the monsters with all the will they'd formerly held back.

My father led sword-wielding armies in his day. That night, I pulled one to me. We drove our enemies back into the murk they had slithered out of, killing over two-thirds of the ones who'd crawled onto my land's shores. And I turned my bloody head to the stars and screamed in defiance and relief and gods know what. The video I saw ended there, and things in my memory are fuzzy.

I came back to myself flat on my back on the river bank, my old weapons master dumping a bucket of water over my head as I gasped and sputtered.

"Well done, m'boy," Maddoc said, the brogue of ancient Wales still heavy on his tongue. His narrow features had wry humor and some pride in them. "Always knew you had that in you. Now get up and find a shower. You stink like the sewer behind hell's fish market."

He reached out a hand and pulled me to my feet, and I stumbled with him back to our staging area.

I got treated for shock in the back of the Guard's medical transport and eventually got taken back to headquarters. I walked into the locker room shower with all my armor still on and stood in the steaming water until I couldn't see a single drop of stinking blood on it. Then I dismissed the nanotech and scrubbed half my skin off, trying to get rid of the stench. When I finally realized I couldn't get any more of it to go away, I wrapped my towel around myself and went to my locker to get my street clothes.

The world's most godawful trophy was already stuck to it, staring at me with flat plastic eyes, mind-numbing in its hideousness. I should have expected it; no one else had ever gotten actually swallowed at a Fish Ball. The base part of it was an old pre-Return animatronic singing fish, with a half dozen gilded truck balls attached to the base plate and bits of tacky human garbage randomly glued on around it. A motion sensor in it activated when I opened the locker's door, and I jumped almost an arm's length in the air when it twitched and started singing "I Will Survive".

But I thought, *You know what? I will.*

"Fuck the paperwork," I said when Rellen tried to get me to come in and fill out incident reports. "I have a runway to get to."

An hour later, my lips scarlet and rhinestone bands glued into my eyebrows, an aquamarine tiara that matched my eyes pinned into a beehive wig and my outfit shining like a mirror-ball, I had Danielle request that song. Gloria's voice pierced the air as I strutted out to shake my fabulous, ostrich-feathered ass at fate, and darkness, and the horrid *things* that crawl out of backwater planets' primordial goo.

"Ladies and gentlefolk of all sorts," the announcer's voice boomed through the club. "Please welcome *Anita Mann!*"

My people, the ones who'd adopted me here as one of their own, roared approval, and I threw my hands up to the blazing strobes and just soaked my soul in the light.

It was time to *live* again.

10

Taxi Services

Aisling

"Dogs," Evan said as I pulled out of the old gas station. "I hear hunting dogs."

I did too, belling loudly and coming in fast. I slapped my pickup's radio.

"Slayer to Tech Support," I said. "I need a local scan for surveillance cameras."

The radio crackled, and Rigs' magic flared out around us, seeking. Evan and Jackie's eyes went huge.

"Clear, you're in a dead zone, but there are some in the parking lot of the old casino four hundred yards away," he said. "People with walkies are approaching from the Northwest. Speed indicates horseback. Have you made contact?"

"About to," I answered. "Windows down, kids."

"Who is that?" Evan asked, fascinated.

"You're not alone?" Rigs asked.

"Got stuck babysitting," I said. "But the kids are oathed to secrecy and have no credibility, anyway."

Jackie made an offended face at me, and I shrugged. She crumpled a little, realizing what I'd said was accurate.

Knowing the trackers might see my tail lights, I didn't stop, just slowed to a crawl. I rolled down my window, thumped the outside of my door, and called softly into the darkness.

"Taxi!"

A large, shaggy shadow rose from the ditch and threw itself with inhuman ease into the back of the pickup, then dove directly under the tarp.

"Evan, hold the can out the window and spray the bear spray down on the asphalt. Get a bit on the car. Good. Now roll up the window."

There was a sneeze and whimper from the back.

"Sorry 'bout that," I called. "You'll find a pack of jerky back there if you're hungry. It's special stuff, will help get you through."

The flashing lights of a sheriff's car zoomed off the interstate off-ramp and directly towards us.

"Steady, now, everyone," I said, and slowed down and waved frantically at another deputy sheriff, throwing a touch of *don't recognize me* glamour over my car. Didn't know this guy; hopefully he didn't know me. Fear stained the night around my pickup like a heavy cloud, rising off the kids. I rolled down my window like someone in a panic.

"Officer!" I yelled, pointing back towards the abandoned gas station. "Back that way, some big cryptid! We had to use bear spray to protect ourselves!"

Light bent around my will and magic. On the edge of the woods, illusionary red eyes blinked at the deputy, and a hulking form dove away into the trees.

The deputy threw me a thumbs up. Sirens wailed, and he hit the gas. I pulled away. In my rear-view mirror, dogs and horsemen came out of the woods and pounded up to where we'd picked up Sara. The lead dog got a whiff of the bear spray and turned away, sneezing violently. The deputy waved the posse towards where he'd seen my illusion, and the hunting party wheeled off on a wild goose chase.

I rolled my window back up, slowly accelerating, and turned to the kids.

"These aren't the fae you're looking for," I said, making the little wave. A relieved snuffling laugh came from the pickup bed. Then we heard a large predator ripping into the jerky. Hoped we had enough for her. "And the bear spray will screw up the dogs' noses enough to confuse things even more."

"Ais..." Evan started.

"No names while we have a Runner with us," I said, even though Sara would, of course, recognize me and my junker pickup. "The Underhill Railroad runs on compartmentalization of information."

"The Underhill Railroad?" Jackie asked. "Can you tell us about it?"

"Explanation's a bit long. The story of the old United States, back when the states were united, had freedom and slavery as its central narrative. For the early part of its history, the country enslaved a lot of people, mostly stolen away from homes in Africa. Not all the states allowed that. In the big scheme of things, debt slavery is more profitable for the business classes than outright owning people, since then they don't have to provide housing, food, or health care. Anyway, escaped slaves would run North for freedom. A secret network of sympathizers, called the Underground Railroad, helped them along their way."

"We read about that in American History class," Jackie said. "Harriet Tubman, right?"

"And many others. Those classes gloss over a lot. They almost never talk about the great African kingdoms or histories of the places where the enslaved people got stolen from. So, I'm just another white girl. I knew jack shit about all that except, as you guys know, I'm a nerd and love old superhero movies. A kid I knew was having some problems with racist asshats at school. I thought she might like the Marvel film that took place in a fictional African country called Wakanda. *Black Panther* was full of high tech and superheroes, really awesome. She turned into a super fangirl."

There was an indrawn breath from the back.

"I do historic reenactment every summer. Dressing Norse makes me feel like I'm standing shoulder to shoulder with my shieldmaiden ancestors," I said, and smiled at the kids. "Thought we could make her a Halloween costume like the warrior women from that film. But I ended up having to do some research for the cosplay, and it turned out the librarian really *knew* that stuff. She was an old Black Lives Matter activist and a bit of a historian in African and African American studies. She helped us find some outstanding books through interlibrary loan. I made sure the girl knew how to use her 'prop' spear before she wore the costume, and in pretty short order, she quit having trouble."

I grinned and shook my head ruefully. I'd gotten in a bit of trouble over that myself. Totally worth it.

"A month later," I continued, "My friends were researching something else for someone with a different sort of problem. A strangeling sort of problem. And we took a bunch of books on mythology and paranormal studies up to check out, and that same librarian was working. She looked at us over her glasses, and said, 'Kids like you don't need books like *this* in your checkout history'. I mean, we hadn't even thought about it, naïve little things that we were. Then she pulled up some books on the history of the Underground Railroad and said *that* was what'd actually be useful to us."

"And?" Jackie prompted, when the silence stretched.

"And it was. When we came back, she told us about the Underhill Railroad and getting strangelings to safety. We were enthusiastic recruits by the end of the conversation," I said. I pulled the pickup over to the side of the road by the ruins of a school that'd been derelict since well before the invasion. "Underhill is another term for faeryland, because the sidhe of Irish myth ceded sunlit Earth to humanity, retreating through hollow hills to the Otherworld. And now we run Changed fae to somewhere safe, like our abolitionist forebears."

I knocked on the back window, slid it open and passed an envelope back.

"Instructions for the next stage of your journey are here," I said. "There's an old root cellar behind the ruin that's stocked with canned food. You can warm it up with a few candles. Good luck on your trip, and say hi to Mrs. Rowan when you arrive."

"Mrs. Rowan?" Jackie asked.

A gigantic clawed hand took the envelope delicately from my hand. Jackie and Evan froze. A large, dark shape eased out of the pickup bed. The shocks groaned, and the truck lifted up a couple inches.

"The librarian," I said. "She had to run for safety herself a few years ago. Grandkid of hers Changed, and she went with him down the Railroad."

"Where do free strangelings go?" Evan asked.

"Over the rainbow," I sighed. "There's a place. People have been going there for over twenty years. Details are secret for safety reasons."

I flipped the lights back on and we pulled away and headed back towards town, taking back roads to avoid the hunting party.

"Dusty? Slayer? Tech Support?" Evan asked.

"Compartmentalization of information, like I said," I told him. "Mostly only family calls me Aisling. I've got nicknames and codenames for every different group and hobby I'm in."

"Tech Support?" Evan repeated.

The radio crackled.

"It's an excellent superhero name," Rigs said. "No one would get a damn thing done without tech support!"

The kids looked dubious.

"Just you wait," I said. "You'll see exactly how right he is, sooner or later."

"Slayer sounds cooler," Jackie said. "Like the '80s metal band, right?"

"Like a vampire-slaying cheerleader," Rigs said. "And don't believe a word she says if she claims it's about something else!"

Neither kid recognized the reference. I sighed.

"Gonna need to have some movie nights and educate you guys," I said.

We drove through the darkness in silence, our road winding through empty bogs and forests. A gibbous moon faded in and out of the clouds. Dark swamp hemlocks swayed in the wind. Strange eyes glinted in the headlights of my truck and darted away. Low mist drifted across the road.

"Why'd you let us see this?" Evan finally asked. "You could have ditched us. Everyone else does."

I raised an eyebrow at him and Jackie.

"Figure it out," I said. "Now, plausible deniability about tonight. We're going to go do something that will make people's brains turn off if you tell them how you spent the evening. Ever painted miniatures? My friend Bob has been trying to fix his water heater all day, and is behind on getting ready for a Warhammer tournament in Duluth next week. He asked for help priming a new army he's making."

"No..."

A couple hours later, Jackie had blue hair, Evan had a budding Warhammer addiction, and the Railroad had recruited a couple additional sets of eyes.

I didn't think anyone would ask me to babysit again soon.

MOONLIT
CREATURES

ARTHUR

I don't know how long I ran, or exactly where, but the meadow was green and seemingly as endless as the starlit sky above it. The only thing it really had in common with the frigid local night was the moon, and even that wasn't actually in quite the same phase. Time moved oddly out there, but after a while I found myself at the base of the impossible tree, collapsing into a nook between its roots. Twenty people holding their arms out couldn't have reached around the trunk, and when you looked up from the base, you could see the Milky Way shining through its branches, stars blurring together with its shimmering leaves.

When things got bad, I would go to the tree and curl up in its hollows, like a little kid running back to his mother's embrace. I didn't know why it felt like that. My dad used to take a couple beers and sit at Grandpa Holt's grave when he was going through things, now and then, and going to the roots' embrace always felt like I was doing something similar.

I wished I could call home to my parents and try to figure out some of the mess I was going through. Strangelings don't get phone calls, though, as we're considered dead and kept away from the living. As we should be. As I knew all-too-well we should be. The monster in me made that *entirely* too clear every time he came out.

Everyone likely thought I was dead, anyway. They'd all been at my funeral. It was televised state-wide. Thanks to surviving a suicide mission early in my service and getting labeled a hero for it, I got to watch my own memorial on the prison's television. I didn't even know if my parents had been told I Changed, or if they thought that casket held my body. I missed my family horribly, both the one I was born to and the one I'd meant to make with Laurie. She'd moved on and started over with someone else, I'd heard, and had twins last fall. And why not? The promising young officer she'd planned to marry was gone. There was no Arthur Holt anymore, just 'Captain' Hart of Strangeling Brigade, who was neither human nor fit for human company.

I leaned my cheek into the bark and stared up to the impossible stars, wondering again what the hell I was that this faery weirdness could make me feel almost like I was with family again, when I'd lost the right to ever feel such a thing. I'd lost the rights to so many things.

But I did *nothing wrong,* the lost voice inside me protested as I tried unsuccessfully to hush it again.

Living in the Box is not a punishment! I told new troopers when they came in, trying to make myself believe it. *We are called, however reluctantly, to the defense of Earth and humanity. The Change equips us with tools beyond those given ordinary man. We have become exceedingly dangerous weapons; in the field, we will be the best of the best and we will train to use every new strength we have gained. However, every wise warrior knows to sheath the deadly tools of war when they are not in use. Our old lives are gone, and the Box is the holster in which we rest between patrols. We have lost our humanity, but we can still shield those who have not. This* is *our purpose now.*

Sometimes I wanted to just be a person, though, not a weapon. I wanted friends outside work, a bed that wasn't a frozen prison cot, some drinkable beer, a dog, and at least the possibility of a girlfriend.

The stars hung cold and distant above me. Wind sighed across the meadow. I could almost feel like the surrounding roots were a mother's arms. I let out my breath and leaned into them, not caring if I was deluding myself, and the breeze tussled my hair almost affectionately. Slowly, the tension ran out of my body, and the predatory rage with it.

Strange stars wheeled above me. I wondered whose skies I looked upon.

The wind blew across the meadow. The nightbird's song went silent. I leaned into the tree and dozed off.

The breeze woke me, eventually, tussling my hair again like a mother waking her child.

On the far side of the tree, someone started singing, and soft magic gathered in the air.

I got to my feet and went to investigate.

A marble-rimmed pool lies amongst the roots on one side of the tree. None of us built it; it was just there one day. Silver moonlight flooded its glen, and fireflies danced through the night as if it were late summer, not nearly the spring equinox.

My quartermaster was sitting alone by the pool, with a bucket and a bottle of something that glowed faintly green.

"Brewing hooch?" I asked, grinning as I walked over, a sudden bounce in my step.

"Needing some, or should I deny everything?" William asked back wryly. The moonlight glinted on his curling horns and hooves. He'd turned into a classical satyr after a career in hotel management; some Radiant grapes were apparently to blame. His field skills were minimal, but he was everything you look for in a camp manager, aside from certain depression issues common to everyone stuck in here.

"I could probably be convinced... whatever you're making smells exquisite."

"Try a sip, then I'll tell you what's in it."

He poured two shots and handed me one. The liquid glowed faintly and shimmered with a slight iridescence. It looked like pure fae magic, swirling enticingly in my glass. Probably a terrible idea to drink it.

I so rarely indulged my terrible ideas anymore. When I'd been a young teenager... oh, I'd had a few wild years. Wanted to try *everything,* and possibly everyone too. Then some girl I could barely even remember, Ashley or something like that, had broken my heart into tiny pieces when I was sixteen, and in the morass of loss and grief following that, I decided it was time to put childhood behind me and become Responsible. I'd gone into early enlistment and the army as fast as I could after that. Now here I was, with well over a hundred people under my direct command, shielding the entire middle of the state from monsters. I was drowning in responsibility.

My glass clinked with William's and I knocked back my shot. Oh hell, did that have a *kick.* I mean, it wasn't really terribly alcoholic, we just got nothing but kiddie 3.2 beer in here, and that on very rare celebratory occasions. Birch's salary afforded an occasional bottle of something nice, but he wasn't much of a drinker "unless mead was involved". And this... this was on another level. A really, really good one. Good enough that even the gnawing hunger that always chewed at me seemed to soak it in and actually relax.

I leaned back against a root of the tree, which was almost as tall as I was, and let out a deeper breath than I even knew I'd been holding.

"More," I said. "I feel muscles unwinding that haven't unknotted in years."

"Since you were imprisoned?" William asked, pouring a refill.

"Since I last got laid," I admitted. "Feels like an eternity. Jones was giving me grief earlier."

"You know there are plenty in here who'd be willing."

"Yep. And every one of them is under my command, except Jones' imaginary 'starlets' who are decidedly under *his*," I said, and we both laughed. "Fastest way to break down order and a potential disaster of the first degree if I ever indulged. So, what's in this?"

The liquid in my shot swirled and glowed.

William raised an eyebrow. I shrugged and drank another shot. Oh god, it was good: rich, faintly floral, with a slight sweetness like basswood honey and a kick like vodka.

"Well?" I asked.

"I am not always so good at suppressing my fae impulses..." William said, looking at his own drink.

"Aren't you the oldest of us?" I asked. "I'd say you've done pretty well."

"It's ten years since I Changed," he said. "And it is my shame, perhaps, that my memories of being human fade. But I have always paid attention to my body, to staying fit and eating well and caring for myself and those around me. When you're in touch with it, it will tell you what it needs, and sometimes you'll see what others need as well..."

"What do your fae impulses tell you to do, if you don't mind me asking?" I wondered aloud, curious. The subject was one we tried to avoid in here, but drinking together made it seem acceptable.

"Oh, everything satyrs are supposed to, I imagine," he said, still not looking up. "Eat, drink, make merry with any beautiful young things that wander in out of the moonlight..."

Wait, is he hitting on me?

I blinked at William. He looked back, his face carefully neutral.

Nah, couldn't possibly be. Not when I'm like... this.

"And you, Captain?" he asked, sighing.

"Right now, wanting to run down the so-called Green Lady and make sure she never steals another kill from me," I muttered.

William tried to hide a smile.

"There's a chance she'll be making one of those runs into the Edgelands soon," I said. "Maybe I'll finally catch her."

"Ah. Yes. You know there's a betting pool on what would happen if you ever actually did?"

"Of course. Birch has money down for 'murder' and Jones has just as much for 'marry', god knows where he got any cash, but it's just to annoy me. He tries pushing it every chance he gets, when he isn't just praising her for saving us from having to do our jobs. I think he's trying to make me just give up on catching her."

"Well, Jones, unlike some people, doesn't like actively seeking out trouble."

"Because I do enough of that for all of us?" I asked, rolling my empty shot glass in my hands, knowing he was right. Strangeling Brigade had never *needed* to become more than basically competent; I was the one who pushed for military excellence and actively hunting down the threats to our land, not just patrolling wherever we got sent and hoping we didn't run into anything. *Some* people in here would have greatly preferred the latter option.

"It would not be my place to comment. Or wonder if that, too, is a fae impulse," he said, pouring another glass for himself. Then he passed me the bottle.

Argh. It could be. No, I've always been like this. Haven't I?

"Can you imagine free strangelings?" I mused. "Being like this, but... out there?"

William drew in a sharp breath, and his shoulders drew up tight.

"I'm sorry," I said. "The so-called 'Twin Ports Free Strangelings' took credit for killing the giant, and the thought..."

"They probably eat people in secret," he said, a minute later, his voice cracking just a little. "Or if they haven't yet, it's likely inevitable."

I nodded and stared bleakly into the pool. I couldn't tell if the stars in its depths were reflections or lights deep, deep underwater.

"So, what *is* this stuff?" I asked again, pouring myself a third shot. That aching hunger in me was actually feeling halfway manageable.

"Sap tapped from our tree here," he said, taking a drink and sighing as if it soothed his soul like a balm. "And a bit of fermentation magic."

I froze, my drink poised on my lips, and set the glass down on the edge of the pool.

"Do you really think that's wise?"

"Wise? No," he answered. "But perhaps necessary."

Shit. Everything in me was saying he was right.

"We don't know what we've become," William continued, playing with the glass in his hands. "We don't know what we need."

I sighed. It was too true.

"God, I wish we could talk to someone who *actually* knows something," I said, looking at the liquid swirling temptingly in my glass. Wind sighed through the branches of the vast tree, sounding like voices hearing and acknowledging my words.

What the hell.

This wasn't something to waste. I picked up the glass and downed it.

"Maybe wait a few days before sharing this around more, and we'll see if it does anything to us," I said. "Go ahead and make more, though; this is the first time since I Changed that the monster in me is feeling halfway sated. Might help people too close to the Hunger."

He nodded, and I sighed again and made myself head back indoors.

12

AN EVENING IN

AISLING

It was after ten when I dropped the kids off at Uncle Ron's house. Maria's car was in the driveway and we could see her passed out on the couch from the front window.

"Well, you guys have your reading lists," I said. They also had little packets with some basics of how to help a new strangeling manage the first twenty-four hours, and some well-packaged, heavily warded Radiant jerky, just in case. Too many kids were Changing now; it was just about inevitable that sooner or later, some friend of theirs would go. "Gonna be okay?"

"Not the first time Mom's gotten like this," Evan said cynically.

"How many days of spring break do you have left?" Jackie asked. "Can we hang out again?"

"Three days, but my friend's got a gig in St. Cloud and her regular bassist flaked and took off with some new girlfriend, so I'll be heading off with her tomorrow," I said.

The kids stared at me.

"Aisling, I've heard you play kazoo," Jackie said. "You're terrible. Are you saying you're in a *band?*"

"Hey, I know some riffs!" I said. "Okay, I'm mostly the roadie now, but once Coral starts singing nobody notices her backup, so it doesn't matter that my playing is crap. She just needs someone behind her who can kick in the teeth of any pervs trying to get on stage."

"Oh, that makes more sense," Evan said, and I rolled my eyes.

"Hey, our high school band had a song actually play on the radio! It was even briefly number one on the Duluth stations."

"What song?" Jackie asked, disbelieving.

"Uh... okay, but don't tell family. We were the 'Lumber Punks' and the song was *Lumberthumpin'*. The verse about finding out your date is your cousin was about Steve Riksby and me, back in eighth grade."

"*For real?*" Jackie exclaimed.

"Yeah. I didn't even really realize he was interested in me, but he thought I was introducing him to my family and things might get 'serious'. Brought him over to show him Uncle Trevor's sci-fi collection and Dad was like, 'Riksby? Jon's boy? He was my second cousin! We were best friends in grade school! Great to see our kids playing together!'"

"Oh *damn*," Jackie said.

Evan tried to swallow his giggle and failed.

"Yeah, don't date in town, the gene pool here is *shallow*. Anyway, Bob said you guys are welcome to come paint miniatures at his place whenever you want to," I said. "And Jackie, I know you like playing with fire. He does blacksmithing and welding on the weekends, you might try it out. Said he's doing a bronze pour Sunday, making some Norse jewelry so our SCA characters look cooler at Viking camp this summer. And he's safe, his type is big burly guys from the gym, you don't have to worry about harassment. Take nothing to eat, drink, or smoke from his friend Benji, though. You might wind up convinced you're a trenchcoat full of drunk ferrets and forget how to human."

They blinked at me. I sighed.

"Anyway, if you ever have a... problem... and can't reach me, go to Bob. He's solid."

"Is he in the Underhill Railroad too?" Evan asked.

"Not a question you get to ask yet," I said, messing his hair with my hand. "Remember, your first test is if you can keep quiet, and I don't mean for a couple of days, I mean for months. After classes start again, I'm going to be crazy busy, so don't count on seeing me until after I finish my Masters."

"That *sucks*," Evan said. "When are you going to teach me magic?"

"You've got your reading list. Remember what I said about actually checking out folklore and paranormal books, but hit the library and *memorize* that section. There's a good bit in my room at Dad's place, too. You can borrow stuff from there. Just write what you're taking in the notebook on top of the bookshelf, and bring the book back when you're done."

"Okay, I guess that's a start," he mumbled, and I smiled at him.

"Good night!" Jackie said, opening her door. "And thanks for taking us with you! It was so much cooler than I expected."

"You kids be good," I said, and hugged them both goodbye. "Take care of each other."

I drove back to my dad's place and parked on the street. A light was still on in the window. Dad was reading at the kitchen table and startled briefly when he heard the door, then waved absentmindedly at me and went back to his book. If it isn't about mycology - that's mushroom science, in which he did a doctorate - or theoretical physics, his hobby since retiring - he's not very interested. He'd never showed any hint he had known what Mom was, or what I am. I don't think he'd actually have judged or cared, but it was safer this way.

"Leftovers are in the fridge if you're hungry," he said. "How long are you home for, again?"

"Dad! I left you a message on the machine that I was coming home for all spring break! But I'm actually taking off overnight with friends tomorrow, will be in St. Cloud for a day or two."

"Oh, you'll have to show me how to check that damn thing again. It's been blinking since... hmm. Actually, maybe it just always blinks."

Dad's ability to focus on deep, complex science was balanced by his complete inability to manage more than the most basic functions of everyday life. Our antique but functional answering machine never got checked; "voicemail" was just not a thing for his generation, even after all our wireless and digital connections got blocked and we didn't have any other options beyond old junk hoarded in basements and storage units. He claimed not to mind since he'd always preferred analogue; apparently he'd been quite the crunchy-granola hipster, back in the day.

Dad's personal hoard was of every science and natural history book he could save, and they spilled out of the shelves built into every wall and covered every open surface not already supporting his *specimens:* random rocks, dried mushrooms, or taxidermied critters. Some stacks of more solid books even served as end tables in places. To call the place cluttered would be an understatement.

"I mean you're always welcome, of course," he said. "I just need to know how much to cook."

"Are you short on food? I can go hunting," I said.

It was off season and no one was *supposed* to, but no one really enforced hunting seasons when so many people lived on the edge of starvation. Nature was doing just fine anyway, considerably better than humanity. My night vision meant I could go out in the dark with a bow and get something quietly, with none the wiser. It'd been a literal lifesaver for my family a few times.

"Nah, no worries. The Silbertsens were culling their rabbits and I have a couple in the freezer. Just gotta thaw one. Said they'd give me a couple of bunnies if I want to raise some myself."

"Oh, that sounds nice. You'd have enough clippings from the garden to feed them over the summer."

He nodded and jotted down a note, then glanced up at me.

"Going out again tonight?"

"Nah," I said. "Already checked around. Bob was tucking in early, Rigs is tweaked out on energy drinks and working on some consoles to sell, Benji's too stoned to talk, and Coral's singing in that dive in Carlton that banned me."

He looked at me over his bifocals.

"Remember that kid with a BB gun who shot the hay ride horses at senior prom?" I said. "He's the owner's son, runs the place now, and doesn't think the reason he's missing his front teeth should drink in his bar. It's a dump, anyway."

Dad sighed. I might work in a lab, but I don't think I was quite the daughter he'd imagined having.

"Ok, well anyway, I'm going to drop my pickup at Bob's garage tomorrow. Took the hooligans over to his place this evening. He's going to look at the starter issues while I'm off with Coral. So I'll be back in a day or two, but don't worry about cooking for me."

"Stay safe if you're out in the woods," he said, looking over his bifocals at me. "That friend of Vicki's evaded the trackers. Supposedly tried attacking a woman and a couple kids in a gasifier pickup. They hit her with bear spray, and the dogs all got it up their noses and were useless for the rest of the night."

"Oh no, how terrible," I said.

"If my sisters found out family grandkids were out helping hide monsters from the sheriff's posse, the person who was responsible would *never* be welcome at a family gathering again," he said.

"Well, that sounds like a fate worse than death," I said, getting myself a beer out of the fridge and pulling out some popcorn. "Those kids have way too much undirected energy. Need some hobbies."

"*Safe* hobbies," he said.

"We spent the evening at Bob's painting miniatures! And he might teach Jackie how to weld, put her fire obsession somewhere useful."

"Miniatures?" Dad asked, horrified. "Like Trevor used to paint and game with?"

"Exactly," I said, putting some popcorn on the stove.

"Those aren't a hobby, they're an obsessive, expensive way to waste years of your life!"

"Hmm, did anyone ask me if I wanted to babysit tonight? Or if maybe I had plans that didn't involve little kids? Nopers, I don't remember any of that. Jackie has blue hair now too."

"My sisters still think you're the good one, you know," he sighed, resigned. "Or did until today."

"That's *just* compared to Trey," I said, and he shrugged like I had a point. "He and I might be the only unmarried cousins from our generation, but that doesn't mean we've got bottomless free time to babysit everyone else's unholy crotch-fruit."

Dad sighed, giving up, and went back to his book. It was titled "Physics Beyond the 4 Dimensions." He scrawled something into a notebook next to it.

"What are you working on?" I asked. Some of that looked like things Mom had talked about in relation to the source of her people's magic, the Tree that Grows Between Worlds.

"Oh, was thinking about what I heard about Vicki's friend. She was what, a skinny five foot six? Seven? But the description of what she was turning into said she was over seven feet tall already and *bulky*. That Radiance stuff, it's got to work multi-dimensionally, there's no other accounting for it. Mass has to come from *somewhere*. But where? And why?"

"Huh, good questions," I said. "I'm avoiding thinking about anything with math or evenly vaguely related to my degree work until Sunday, though. Want to watch a movie with me?"

"Nah, gonna keep working on this," he said, and bent his head back to his book.

Oh well.

I hooked up a DVD player and started browsing my lost Uncle Trevor's collection of films. He left all his boxes of wonderful Before-Times geekery (and no small quantity of gay porn) in my grandmother's basement when he moved to Minneapolis, ten years before the city got taken and all the humans there presumably died.

Uncle Trevor's geeky collections got me through a lot of shit. I kept a little shrine to him, surrounded by Star Wars figures, many-sided dice, and Warhammer miniatures on top of my dresser. Most magnetic media - hard drives and video cassettes - had died in the Elsecomers' EMP waves when they took Earth, but DVDs and CDs were just fine, and plenty of people had old players stored in their basements, and some survived. Not much new entertainment got made anymore, but we at least had movies and TV from about 1995 to 2015 to keep us going. I liked fantasy and sci-fi a lot better than anything having to do with the actual world we'd lost, the early seasons of *Buffy the Vampire Slayer* excepted. Getting reminded of everything the generations born after the Dawn would never experience didn't make for *fun* entertainment.

Eventually I decided on the extended version of *Fellowship of the Ring*, sat down, and grabbed an almost-finished sweater I'd been working on for the last month. Stress-knitting kept me sane sometimes; I mean, you stab yarn with sticks a few thousand times and get clothes – how awesome is that? The pattern wasn't anything complicated, just a basic fisherman's rib in muted pine green that I was working in-the-round. It'd look good (and unobtrusive) on my Railroad persona, and I'd gotten the wool in trade for a leg of a deer I bow-hunted last fall. I spun the yarn over the winter holidays. Probably I'd leave the sweater in Strangelingtown after dropping off our Runners; they always needed warm clothes, so I was making it a bit oversized so it'd fit anyone. Dad eventually joined me for a bit, then yawned and went off to bed. I needed like half as much sleep as a human, so staying up wasn't a problem.

I wondered again, needles clicking away as I finished the sweater, if my mother's people were anything like the elves of Middle Earth. I'd tried asking Mom once, when I first saw the film, and she laughed until she choked and never actually answered because then she was crying too hard. Legolas was hot, anyway, even if my tastes had grown up a bit since then. He was still worth a sigh or two, especially during the final fight scene. I'd spent *hours* practicing his fight choreography. When I was little, Mom had put me in one gymnastics class after another to explain away my inhuman balance and reflexes, and I'd finally felt like the lessons were useful when I started using those skills to learn fight moves from movies.

After the film, I sat in my teenage bedroom and watched the moon through a grubby window. When I was younger and we still had the farm, before things went bad, Mom and I used to sneak out and race its shadows through the forest. Night's magics sang through us as she taught me the arts of her people: fighting, empty-handed and with blades, the minor magics she could still manage, and some of the lore of her lost world. We ran silent-footed through the woods and the waters, slipping through all the between places where one thing might shift into another, and perhaps become something it wasn't otherwise allowed to be... like, true to itself, and free.

Part Two

The River Run

13

A Day in the Edgelands

Arthur

We were back on our regular patrol the next day. Riding shotgun, Jones at the wheel and a competent troop around me, life was feeling pretty good. The tree-sap vodka hadn't given me any sort of hangover; possibly the opposite, if such a thing were possible. I'd barely felt more than a tiny ache of that terrible dysmorphic *wrongness* today, and for once my skin actually seemed to fit me. I kept getting flashes of this *other* sort of awareness, of everything alive around me, but it was just weird, not bad.

I also knew where each one of my troops was, the way you just know where your hands are. Maybe I'd lost my birth family, but I had these guys, and that was something. They were *my people,* even if only half of us got counted as people now.

"Feel anything near us, Captain?" Jones asked.

"She's not here yet," I answered, drumming a finger against the Jeep door. The steel bit me, but I ignored the burn.

"I said *anything,*" he replied, rolling his eyes, "Not your freaky personal obsession."

I closed my eyes, casting out with my magic into that strange sense for the land and the flows of power through it. This was a borderline thing for me, damn useful, but prone to pulling up some of the worst of my fae impulses. It made me want to throw away my shoes and steel and run howling into the woods, then chase whatever ran from me. Today the land was singing spring's joyous music, but the urge was still there.

I am *hunting,* I told the darkness inside me. It growled back, not quite satisfied.

"Two o'clock. Mile or so that way," I said, pointing. "Dunno what's over there, though. Four or five medium size cryptids, couldn't say what sort or what they're doing."

"So are we after monsters or the Green Lady today?" Hassan asked from the back seat.

" *We're* after threats exiting the Edgelands," Jones said. *"Captain's* looking for his girlfriend. She shows up on school holidays sometimes. Helluva way to waste spring break if she *is* making a run now."

"So what has the Green Lady done that's so bad, anyway?" Hassan asked.

"Blue-balled Captain repeatedly," Jones shrugged.

"The Green Lady is a legitimate threat," I said, glaring at him. "She irradianced me and god knows how many others since then. We need to know what the hell she's doing."

"Who cares?" he shrugged. "Whoever she is, she's saved us some major trouble over the years, and at least eight hours of miserable carsickness this week alone. When's the last time we had to hunt something near Duluth that we didn't find already dead? Two years ago? Three? And some of those things she's taken down were big muthas. I, for one, much prefer somebody *else* fighting them. My fan base would be devastated if something happened to the Bat-Bod."

Not this again, I thought.

"She's trafficking with the Elsecomers!" I snapped. "Why else would someone keep coming in and out of the Edgelands multiple times a year? And that bladed weapon she uses is Elsecomer tech; nothing human-made cuts that sharp."

"Maybe she's visiting Grandma to ask for some *modern* weapons. They might be sharp, but all that girl's got are some medieval stabbers and a homemade bow. Her arrows don't even have steel tips, just bronze, apparently melted down from old radiators! Kid hunts monsters on a student budget. Makes *us* look well equipped. You ever hear Bastion's description of that campground where the first definite sightings of her took place?" he asked.

"Yes, many times. Many, many times. And read all the wildly contradictory reports from the drunk lunatics who were there playing Vikings. Half of them thought they'd seen Legolas from the *Lord of the Rings* movies, right down to his fight moves; a bunch of others said it was his little sister. One guy insisted a gorgeous elf had been drinking with them the night before, but he wasn't sure who she really was because he'd done too many shrooms. Also, he tried to pull her ears off because they're serious re-enactors there, and the pointy tips weren't *period-appropriate.*"

Jones laughed, as if such unreliable witnesses were somehow *funny.*

"Did Birch ever learn anything beyond a bit of magic at those reenactment events?" he asked.

"Yeah. That he likes mead. He joined the club and has spent a couple weekends every summer since playing Viking with them. How have you avoided hearing all about this?"

He just looked at me. Right. Jones was very good at tuning completely out when Birch started babbling about anything unrelated to work. I occasionally envied that skill; while the kid had turned into a decent soldier, his ability to waffle on at *very* great length about his latest geek passion had to be endured to be believed.

"After his first event, he came back nerding out so hard it took two weeks to get him to talk about anything real again," I sighed. "He started working on learning Old Norse instead of Klingon, and every spring you have to dig through layers of *costuming projects* to get at anything in his office."

"Can't say I'm surprised. Getting to go Viking is probably almost as good as swinging a bat'leth around. Though, I mean, as *if.* Dude'd be Romulan, if anything."

We both just shook our heads for a minute.

"Look, there's no sign the girl's got significant Elsecomer tech," Jones said. "The Temperance River Giant, that snow dragon, the other kills we've seen... swords, spears, arrows. Sharp, but *primitive*."

My face screwed up. I *had* to catch her. It was vital, fundamental, absolutely necessary.

"Captain, Greenie hunts the same things we do. Girl's not an enemy. No one since you has come into the Box saying she irradianced them, so she must have gotten that under control. Also, nobody here wants to go up against anyone who could solo the things she's taken down with her sharp-but-crappy weapons."

"Our duty out here is to protect humanity," I snapped. "Regardless of whether the threat is a dragon or a supposedly hot elf girl!"

The look Jones gave me showed he thought her expected presence was already warping my thoughts.

"Yeah, and I think we can all *guess* which you'd rather wrassle."

The guys in the back seat laughed, and I rolled my eyes at the passing trees.

"So you really think the Green Lady's coming?" Hassan asked.

"Birch says the U is on spring break right now. His brother's a student, so he'd know. Her runs almost always line up with university vacations. I'm positive she's on her way."

"Girl probably *is* just like you, working on all her breaks. Gonna be miserable for the rest of us when you end up hitched," Jones said, like it was inevitable. "But I'll be ready to take over when your brain shuts off again."

"Yeah yeah. This time I'm going to catch her."

"Keep telling yourself that, dude. It's hope that gets us through."

I sighed and waved at a good place to park. He was probably right.

"Think this is as close as we're getting with the cars. Pull over here."

Jones parked on the side of the potholed road, and the other Jeeps and troop carrier followed. We had twenty-four people today, Birch's humans and my strangelings, and I had to make everyone tighten up their helmets and body armor before setting off into the woods, and make sure the guys carrying shields had them slung on correctly. Everyone had been enjoying the sun as much as me.

"We're checking into a little pack of unknown cryptids, so be on guard!" I told the troops once everyone had tightened up again. "We don't know what kind they are or what they're up to, but they're too close to the border! Shoot to kill, but if they run back home, we'll only pursue if they're bad ones."

Roberts took point. He was a good guy. Looked a bit like a werewolf stuck in "fuzzy but not totally monstrous form". His senses were acute enough that being indoors in a crowd was actively painful for him, but in the woods, he was in his element. Unfortunately for us, some of the cryptid packs knew about him and whenever they were out messing with things, the smart ones stationed somebody high in a tree, above the ground level wind currents.

These were some of the smart ones.

An earsplitting screech broke the woodland silence, and then a handful of fresh feces slammed into my shoulder, splashing.

Howlers.

It had to be howlers. God *fucking* damn, I hated howlers almost as much as they hated me. The cryptids were like large six-limbed lemurs. They hunted in packs, and they had it in for me specifically. I had no idea why. Any time their spotter saw us before we saw it, I got pelted with shit. And then they pulled out actual weapons, usually slings, and they were damn good with them.

"Shields!" I yelled. Over half the troop carries clear plexiglass shields, two-thirds the size riot police used to carry. They swung into a turtle formation I'd learned about in military history classes, partially covering us, and we moved forward in a tight group. I got a glimpse of the lookout and got a shot off before he disappeared, but I don't think I hit him.

The next ten minutes were a mess. We winged a couple of howlers and drove them off the ruined farm they'd been ransacking. They didn't get any great hits in on us, seemingly minimally armed today, but they more than made up for it with fresh shit thrown liberally at all of us. We drove them back to the inner Edgelands, though, and then tried figuring out what they'd been doing. It looked like they'd been trying to pull parts out of the old farm's well pump, a pretty weird thing for four-armed monkeys to try. They'd abandoned some tools when they fled, and the wrenches were good enough quality that we ended up taking them back to the cars with us. When everyone was clear, Birch tossed a grenade down the well to wreck whatever they'd been after.

We cleaned up in a little stream that ran by the farm, trying to get the filthy cryptid shit out of our uniforms before it dried. Then we patrolled until an hour before sunset without further encounters, swung out of the Edgelands and back onto real roads, and headed home. The streets honestly aren't in much better shape out there, but they at least don't have trees growing out of them.

We should have just stayed in the Edgelands overnight.

14

THE UNDERHILL RAILROAD

AISLING

I t was early afternoon when Rigs spun his van into a parking space outside my dad's place and blared the horn without even waiting for me to see him. Since he'd replaced the normal one with a speaker that blasted the *Mortal Kombat* theme at triple volume, it was unmissable. Today the van was black and had his musician road-trip facade in place, showing a gremlin spinning DJ gear on the side of it.

Rigs is some vague degree of cousin on my dad's side, but his mom was a cardiac surgeon from India and he takes after her: black hair, big brown eyes, and nerdy sort of cute. When his parents died in a redcap bombing, his Hindi grandmother, stuck in Minnesota since an unfortunately timed visit in early 2020, raised him. He'd gotten a lot of racist grief in school and decided to just embrace it and completely outdo everyone's stupid stereotypes about tech geekery. After we became friends, I beat up anyone who fucked with him, but he'd already set his course.

Coral was riding shotgun in her backwoods "survivalist" gear which, as usual, somehow looked like fetish wear on her. With her crimson hair, liquid curves, and succubus voice, just about everything does. She rolls out of bed looking like the femme fatale from some Golden Age of Hollywood film noir. We did a charity cosplay fundraiser once, and her Jessica Rabbit made five times what my Darth Fishnets did. Seeing the harassment she went through was half the reason I kept my illusion plain; if men treated me like *that*, I'd murder a hell of a lot more than she did. You wouldn't guess she spent every Sunday singing soprano for a Catholic choir in Duluth, but she was both the pride and scandal of every little old church lady there.

"Ready to *ride?*" Rigs said, pulling down his sunglasses and grinning at me. He'd glamoured his eyes solid black to fuck with me, and I jumped a couple inches as I slid into the seat behind them. I threw my pack in ahead of me and empty cans rolled away in a half dozen directions.

"How many of those caffeine shooters have you had?" I asked, a bit concerned.

"All of them!" he yelled. *"ALL OF THEM!!!"*

He squealed the wheels leaving the driveway and hit the stereo as we took off. A techno version of *Carmina Burana* blasted out our windows and I saw Aunt Thelma open her door and start shouting at us, but I was already too deafened to hear a word.

"Rigs hasn't slept," Coral commented when we were away, turning down the volume. "He's a teensy bit tweaked right now."

"Really?" I said. "No waaay. Never woulda noticed."

"Prepare ship for Ludicrous Speed!" he exclaimed, turning onto the Big Lake Road and flooring it. The van's shocks groaned. Magic flared and the windshield bloomed into an illusion of stars going to hyperspace and then tunneling into geometrical shapes... which then blurred into a plaid pattern.

"That better be an illusion you can see through!" Coral yelped as he cackled. "Your van is not *Spaceball One* and if we go to plaid, we'll just stay stuck in Northern Minnesota!"

"We might be safer sneaking past the military and Edgelands monsters than letting Rigs keep driving," I said, clutching the handle above my window.

"My crash is due in twenty-three minutes and seventeen point six seconds. Gonna snooze in back for a bit after we pick up the first canoe and Runner," he said, easing off on his manic speed and releasing the illusion. "I got a couple extra orders yesterday and was up all night working on a pair of decrepit X-Boxes. This might be the last run we fund like this, though. Had an interesting interview this week and might take a regular job."

"Department of Defense?" I asked. Rigs had just graduated and with his academic record, he'd been getting *offers*. Most of the country's civilian government had fallen apart, but the military still sort of held together.

"Nah, local place, Sterling Group, private security organization," he said. "Went in to talk to someone for unrelated reasons and ended up with a job offer. First place I've interviewed that didn't seem shadowed, and I could get good intel being there."

"It's that bad?" I asked quietly, glancing at Coral.

"Hail Hydra! Still haven't gotten a solid lead on what is actually going on, but it seems like that taint is faintly, like, everywhere," he said, grimacing. "I've been scanning all the places where I've interviewed. If you stay your course, you're gonna end up working somewhere our 'Squids' are influential. Saw some bugs and backdoors in various computer systems, but I didn't have good enough gear along to safely trace any without exposing myself."

"Dammit. I shouldn't be surprised. Have to carry on anyway, though."

"Someday I'll figure out the right questions to ask you," he said. "Then I'll actually be able to help."

"Were I able to open my mouth and make sounds come out of it to explain, I'd tell you two everything," I said.

"We both have monsters in our past," Coral said to me, reaching her hand back. "You don't leave their nests without scars."

I took her hand, and she squeezed mine.

"You guys are my family," she said. "Whatever it is, I'm with you."

Rigs nodded agreement. I squeezed Coral's hand back.

Ten miles outside Stinkwood, we picked up the canoe and trailer we'd come for, left by an Underhill Railroad sympathizer in an abandoned cabin's driveway. Rigs ran his hand along the side of the van and the particles he'd embedded in the paint job realigned themselves and suddenly we were driving a rusty brown van for *Bobbi's Bait & Tackle: Minnesota's Best Minnows, Leeches, and Nightcrawlers!* We traded seats and glamoured up with human versions of our Railroad personas in case anyone saw us. Then Rigs passed out on the passenger bench while I took the wheel.

The next stop was the ruined school where I'd dropped off Sara the night before. We pulled over on the side of the road, and Coral got out to "check the tires". A large dark form climbed into the canoe, just like the letter had instructed her to do. She looked shaky... and bigger. Coral exchanged a couple words with her and gave her another pack of the Radiance-fortified jerky, a bottle of water, and a loaf of bread. Then she pulled a tight boat cover with elastic edges over the canoe to keep Sara hidden. I shifted the van into drive and we pulled out and headed down the potholed road to old Highway 65, heading Southbound to St. Cloud.

Ten miles outside the city, we dropped the canoe, Sara, and Coral at another abandoned cabin. People near the taken Cities had to huddle together more than those of us who lived farther away; the Elsecomer's exclusion zone spawned ghostlands and monsters like nowhere else in the state. I started getting out of the van to help Coral with the canoe... and felt *him* when my foot was three inches from the soil.

"What's wrong?" Rigs asked, sitting up as he felt my flash of panic.

"Whoever's landbound down here is really coming into his magic now," I said. "The land's going to tell him I'm here the second I set foot on the ground, if it hasn't already. I think it's the fucker in Div 51 who keeps chasing us."

"Stay in the van until the last minute," he said. "Will he feel Coral and I?"

"You're not landbound like I am, up North," I said. "But we're all magically tied together, so... I don't know. It shouldn't be as extreme."

"Let me drive," he said. "I'm fine now. You can always jump out and run rabbit if it comes to that, lead him on a wild goose chase and then meet us on the way back North. We need to go buy the second canoe now anyway; that'll keep us moving."

"I'll stay here and get the runners ready," Coral said.

We nodded and took off.

15

INTRUDERS

Arthur

Ten minutes after we'd finished checking-in, while we were writing the day's incident reports, I felt *her* enter my patrol lands.

"Dammit, she *is* out there," I said, standing up and reaching for a jacket. "On the Mississippi, North of town. I bet she's getting ready to run the river now."

"Hart, *no,*" Jones said, sliding deeper into his chair. "Everyone is exhausted. We already had a crappy battle with cryptids today, and no one wants to go chase your will-o-wisp."

"Someone give Jones a swirlie," Black said, not looking up from her paperwork. "That pun was downright shitty."

"She's heading for the Elsecomers!" I exclaimed.

"Or visiting grandma," Jones said. "We don't know. It's late, we're tired, and I want a shower, not another fruitless chase through dark woods. I invoke the Greenie-Induced-Ridiculous-Lunacy override."

"Seconded," Birch said. "If we have to try catching her, let's get her on the way *out*, when she's more likely to have something incriminating and also it's not the end of a very long shift. We can deal with Captain's G.I.R.L. problems later."

There was nothing to do but grind my teeth. This was something I'd 100% agreed to two years ago in a non-crazed moment. The acronym was entirely on Jones, though.

"We could do an early patrol," Black said. "If she's overnighting somewhere, and canoeing, we could probably catch her before sunrise."

Birch groaned. He was decidedly not a "before sunrise" kind of person.

"A couple of us could just take basic gear and some motorcycles and go scout..." I said.

"Hart, go get a shower and some sleep. We'll go before dawn, okay?" Birch said. "Try to keep sane for nine hours. You can catch her in the morning."

"Yeah man, you wanna clean up before you try to wrassle the hot elf girl," Jones said. "Don't want to still be stinking like howler dung in case she really *is* as pretty as you."

Birch snickered. I shook my head disgustedly and headed for the showers, hoping with all my might that *something* would ensure she was still there in the morning.

What happened after that, I can't really say more than that I was going out of my mind and really didn't have any idea how my magic worked. I'd taken over a staff room as an office when the human guards moved out, and had the old shower room to myself. The water was running hot and I was scrubbing myself down with all the manic energy of extreme frustration. And all I could think about was that feeling of her magic touching my land and how every instinct in me was screaming to grab that scent and chase her down...

...and abruptly I felt a sort of lurching, and suddenly I was looking into a rusty old civilian van with two people in the front, kind of floating by it like I was a ghost or something. The driver, an Indian or Pakistani looking guy, was ordering something at a drive-thru window. In the front passenger seat was a blonde, her knees drawn up to her chest and showing through the holes in her jeans. She was practically vibrating with tension. Magic blazed through both of them, but his made me think of dark rooms full of servers and hers... she shone like a star, and the fae part of me wanted to wrap itself up in that light and roll around like it was catnip.

I didn't know if that was an improvement from going into a murderous rage every time I felt her nearby or not.

"Yes, I really do want a coconut rum butterscotch fudge shake," the guy was saying. "Real rum if you have it. I don't care if it's someone's personal flask. Use full portions of each of the sauces, then top it off with ice cream. Look, my friend's having a panic attack. This shit calms her down. I know it's disgusting! Just make the damn thing. Yeah, your homemade whiskey's fine."

I know exactly *where you are,* I thought, satisfaction flooding me as I recognized the old Dairy Queen on the edge of St. Cloud.

Her head snapped directly towards me, and the bluest eyes I'd ever seen opened wide.

You hunt me naked? her shocked voice said back to me, obviously somehow getting an eyeful, and I totally lost the vision.

I've never rinsed and dressed again as quickly in my life.

This is not *the poison figure of my nightmares. Nor the kid I saw up North... or was it? But I KNOW her. Who is she?*

Jones and Black were in the mess hall when I caught up with them, and tried describing what I'd seen.

They didn't exactly take me seriously.

"My man, you have *lost* it," Jones chortled. "Your nemesis drinks the whitest white girl shit ever? And you think she's actually maybe *not* evil and also oops by the way you probably magically flashed her? This obsession is *finally* paying off in entertainment value."

I gritted my teeth. Black tried and completely failed to keep a straight face.

Just hold her here, I prayed to whatever might answer something like me. *Just keep her here until I can catch her.*

16

RUNNING THE RIVER

AISLING

Twenty minutes after we pulled out of DQ, we picked up the second canoe, a heavy old aluminum junker, in trade for a working PS2 and some karaoke games. I hadn't felt that guy's eyes on me again, but I was jumpy as hell. Somehow it seemed like the land was out to get me.

About five minutes after we picked up the second boat, we got pulled over by the police.

"Whatcha doing wit dat boat dere?" the officer asked, peering into Rig's van. He didn't see a van, though. He saw a dirty old white pickup, the sides almost as much rust as steel, and two people inside who looked like middle aged white men, scruffy and paunchy.

"Gittin' ready for da Opener," Rigs said, laying on the Minnesotan accent extra heavy and giving the opening of fishing season its due as a major local holiday. Using illusions to play an old white guy and get away with things was practically a hobby for him. "Gunna be a good one!"

"Going on the Miss'ippi?" the officer asked.

"Nopers, just bought this here boat outta the local classifieds. Takin' 'er up Nort tomorrow, got a little cabin up by Leech Lake. Got a real sweet deal on the canoe, just needs some patchin' up and we'll be good all summer! We're visiting a buddy nearby to work on 'er, though, might needa test 'er out. Someting wrong on da river?"

"Well, you be real careful iffin you goes out there. Seen some Changed catfish this year, big 'nuff to swallow a man whole. And Div 51, them Monster Patrol guys, were out all day lookin' fer someone. And you lock that canoe up good, when you get yerselves home; some of those monster-people been swiping boats and runnin' down the river to the stolen Cities. Any of those Else-tainted folks get your boat, you'll be facing a fine or even jail yerselves. License and registration?"

"Yuppers, here ya go," Rigs said. "An' I 'preciate that warning, we'll be real careful-like. Think a bike lock on dat boat is 'nuff to keep away dem critter folks?"

"Some kinda chain, that'll do ya for. Lemme just call this in an' if it all checks out you all ken be on yer way."

The officer walked back to his car and radioed in the info on the card Rigs had given him.

"All good?" I asked him very quietly.

"Full fake persona," he said. "Paperwork and everything in the system. You doubt your technomancer?"

"Never," I said.

We sat and waited for a few minutes.

The officer ambled back.

"Yup, yer all good. Careful iffin ya go on the river in bad light. It's shoot on sight fer dem strangelings and we've had some real idiots out dere bein' spooky. You go out, be sure anyone looking can tell you're good pure human, got that?"

"You betcha. That's some good advice there."

"You have a good afternoon, Mr. Wijkowski."

"You too, officer, an' havva good Opener yerself."

We watched the cop pull away and breathed a sigh of relief.

"Dusty, this all sounds worse every minute," Rigs said quietly. "Do you think we should abort?"

I closed my eyes for a second, trying to feel for possible futures like my mother had taught me to do.

"No," I said. "This run is important. Don't know why, but... it changes things. Lines come together, Ways open. We need to go."

We drove south for a while, then slowed and killed the headlights. Rigs turned the van into the overgrown driveway where we'd dropped Coral and Sara. He drove right through the illusion of sapling trees he'd left up there, and we parked behind the collapsing garage of an abandoned house.

I stuffed my choker into the glove compartment and switched my personal illusion to that of the scruffy strangeling girl I wear when Conducting for the Railroad, and Rigs got out of the van. Coral came out and started helping him get the canoe off the trailer. I checked my reflection; Rue's angular face and bobcat-tufted ears stared back at me. Little claws tipped my fingers. Strangeling enough to reassure the Runners; human enough to look like I could pass with the right gloves and hat. Good.

"Everyone's here. I had the others scatter in different directions, just in case. Should I call them back yet?" Coral asked.

I'd pulled my personal energies in as tightly to my body as I could manage, and hesitated. We needed to check if we were clear, but I didn't want to use my magic like I normally would.

"Gimme a sec," Rigs said, and pulled an old FPV drone out of the back of the van and slipped goggles on to see through it. Of course, those things aren't supposed to work anymore, and using his magical wi-fi this close to the Elsecomers was a bad idea... but so was letting that guy stalking me get near us. I could feel his attention seeking me again already.

I tried not to think of the glimpse I'd caught of him, trying to scry me while apparently showering. Guy had no little bit of *Power* to him, but I wasn't exactly getting the impression he really had any idea what he was doing with it. He'd been exceedingly hot, too, with a body and antlers like some old pagan forest god. If he'd just hang out posing naked and quit trying to hunt me down, we'd be fine.

Or if he wanted to chase me down alone, when I didn't have a half-dozen people relying on me for protection...

The drone whirred to life and zipped away, straight up. Coral went down to the boats and distributed the food and blankets for the trip.

"Clear," Rigs said, as the drone floated back down to his outstretched hand. "At least in terms of Div 51. There's a couple water patrol boats out still, on the south side of the river, but if you glamour and hug the North bank, it should be okay. But, you know, keep your options open. Might need to use the backup plan."

I blanched.

"That could crack reality, open a ghostland even," I said. "I don't even know if I could hold that magic so long..."

"Reality's already broken," Rigs said harshly. "And once you're past St. Cloud, that's the edge of No-Man's Land. It's the eve of the spring equinox, so it's already a Between time. If you need to use that magic, *do* it."

I looked up at the sky. Breaking reality is what Mom's people had done. I didn't want to be one of them. And we'd be right on the Elsecomers' borders.

"Four kids," Rigs said to me. "Two of them babies. They deserve a chance at life. Get them *through*."

He was right.

I'm not failing another baby. Not like I failed my little brother.

I hopped down from the van and felt the antlered man's attention swing directly towards me. There was a feeling of frustration, though, like however much he wanted to chase us, he was locked up... as the strangelings who lived in the Box were every night.

Coral looked at us both, and I nodded. She turned her head to the sky and sang some old lines from a song about better places over a rainbow.

The runners had been waiting for that signal and came out of their hiding spots and met us by the water, at a little hidden launching place we keep clear enough to use. Rigs unhooked the trailer and covered and hid it, then took off, promising to stay wary. He organizes ops, but he's not a field guy. He was meeting someone in town to sell a couple more refurbished gaming consoles, the primary source of our income for running the Railroad. As his magic is mainly about controlling and repairing technology, it's pretty great in urban areas... and much less so in a monster infested wilderness.

Coral and I handled the actual river runs. We had six strangelings to transport that night. They gathered around in a circle, some distance from the water so our voices didn't carry. At least everyone except Sara was more or less normal sized, and she'd still fit in the canoe if she knelt instead of using the front seat.

"Okay everyone, welcome to the last stretch of your journey with the Underhill Railroad," I said quietly. "I go by Rue and that's Siren. Give me a nickname or just your first name to call you; I don't want to be able to answer questions if we get caught."

Four of the runners were a family. Jorge and Ramone and their tiny kids had eaten the meat from a strange pale bear, then started becoming something ursine themselves. It wasn't extreme, yet; they could still pass for human when bundled up for winter. Most of them looked okay, but the mother was too thin and her skin was sallow. The kids looked like Ewoks, too cute for words; they were one and three years old. Every time the parents looked at them and each other, you could see they didn't think they were going to make it.

The other two runners were Sara and a thirteen-year-old boy who looked part Native and called himself Grayjay. He had black hair streaked with copper and a feeling of awakening magic. The irises of his eyes had turned a golden orange like you see on some cats. He wore sunglasses to hide them, and because even the fading daylight seemed too bright for him.

Sara looked terrible, and she'd always been so *bright*. She'd become something like a hunchbacked bigfoot, and was probably a good eight feet tall. It was hard to tell because she was having trouble standing upright. Heavy black hair had sprouted all over her body, and her nose had retreated to two narrow skeletal slits.

I worried she'd go into the Hunger while we were in the boat, because it didn't look like the jerky had provided enough Radiance. We'd have to keep her some distance from the babies, just in case; every generation since the invasion has been born with more native to their bodies, and those in the Hunger can't feel anything but their desperate need to get more... from any source possible.

"I'll be Zahra now," she said. Lots of people change their names when they Cascade; I guess she wanted to do so as well. "And just let me know any way I can help."

"Are we likely to get caught?" the mother asked, holding her baby tight.

"Likely, no. But it's possible," I said. "We got stopped by a cop on the way here and questioned about the canoe we were trailering. He mentioned Division 51 - that's Strangeling Brigade, incarcerated people like us used as forced-labor monster hunters - were out looking for someone earlier. They came pretty close to us on our last run. There are also idiot rednecks out waiting to shoot anyone they think looks Else, and apparently monster catfish in the river. This is the most dangerous stretch of the run to freedom, and it's rare for it to go smoothly."

The parents pulled each other closer. The teenagers looked worried.

"If a monster attacks or someone shoots at us, we will do our best to protect you. I'm fast and a good fighter; if it comes to it, you guys run and I will put myself between you and the attacker. Siren might need to as well. Or policy is the younger you are, the more priority to get you through, because we aren't sure what happens to underage strangelings. Adults, you'd probably end up in Strangeling Brigade yourselves. So priority is the babies, Ramone since she's nursing, Jay, Zahra, Jorge, Siren, then me. So if Siren says run, you run like hell, and I will do my best to at least slow down whatever comes at us."

Everyone nodded, faces drawn.

"Siren and I both have a bit of magic that can make people look away from us," I said. "We're going to be using that until we're past the human lands, and again if Div 51 gets near us. Silence is very important when we have that going, so... do your best with the kids, okay? I can also call some fog to hide us, but we need to stay very close together if I do. With luck, we'll be in Strangelingtown by lunch tomorrow."

"I'll stand with you," Zahra said to me. "If we get attacked."

I nodded and gestured for her to get in the boat with me and take the front paddle. I really hoped she didn't recognize me. Jay got in the boat behind her, looking nervous and trying to hide it.

Coral and I pushed the boats out and then hopped into the canoes. Paddles dipped into dark water, and the current tugged our silent boats downstream. *Look-away* glamours whispered softly through the air around us.

The glamours were enough to get by the idiots with shotguns. They didn't do a damn thing to keep the landbound guy from tracking me, though, and we had one close call after another, as he seemed to somehow direct the patrols. Rigs didn't catch any radio calls, so it wasn't that. He just seemed to somehow direct his land's defenses against us.

As the canoes slipped under St. Cloud's bridges, I reached inside myself for the strange magic that had let me walk in and out of ghostlands. I breathed out, and mist swirled up from the water and out of the soft spaces between worlds. Coral twined some of her magic into mine, to tie us together, and we slipped down a river under stars that had never shone on Earth. Then fog closed around the canoes and night swallowed us.

17

HOLD HER

ARTHUR

I tried all evening to *see* the Green Lady again, but after the first hour all I got was shifting fog and water, sometimes an impression of a paddle and a wave of fear, and a sense that she was near but somehow also *elsewhere*. When she was at the closest point on the Mississippi to the Box, though, I *knew*, and I gripped my cell's bed with white-knuckled hands. It took every ounce of self-control I'd ever summoned to not run and shake Birch out of bed, and somehow get him to requisition an emergency services boat and chase her down.

I have to catch her tomorrow, I thought, my monster pacing in its darkness. *She knows now how clearly I'm sensing her, and won't be back.*

More than once I almost caught a clear look, and then she'd swear and the fog would pull itself over her again. I went to bed but tossed and turned, trying to figure out where she was from faint hints and glimpses of her surroundings. Most of that section of the river looks pretty similar, though, and the mist she moved through was almost like the edge of a ghostland.

I need to sleep, I finally thought, and forced myself to stop attempting to see where she was. *Tomorrow is my chance to chase her down.*

Eventually it worked. Kind of. But I woke up the second she set foot again on my patrol lands, and with my mind in the dreamy fog of half-waking, she didn't seem to feel my presence anymore.

The girl appeared to be a strangeling now, with bobcat ears and claws on her fingertips, but she was in the same threadbare clothes. She had half-collapsed on the Mississippi's bank on the edge of my patrol territory, less than half a mile from no-man's-land. She was shaking with exhaustion and could barely sit upright. Someone else was pulling her canoe up on shore and hiding it away.

"He's been trying to scry me all evening," she said to someone. "I can't even tell if he's watching or not right now. I've been holding fog around us the entire time and without calling land energies myself, it's too much."

"Should we go farther?" the other woman asked.

"Everyone's too chilled," the blonde answered. "And that herd of fanged horses hangs out another mile up. We can't reliably land if we go much further, in case they hunt us. I'll sleep with the boats. You guys go up to the cave and hide a fire. Think he's getting a lock on me because I'm land-bound too and there's a *frisson*. You guys keep some distance and hopefully you'll be okay."

"Here's a rations pack and a blanket," the woman I couldn't see clearly said. "Sleep well, Dusty. We'll make it, one way or another."

Dusty, I thought. *Why is someone who smuggles for the Elsecomers wearing rags and running a flooded river in canoes that should have been retired fifty years ago? The Elsecomers have the best of... everything.*

And yet, the threadbare girl was the Green Lady, I knew it beyond all shadow of a doubt.

The darkness in me growled, insisting I *must* catch her.

Even if she wasn't what I had thought, I needed answers.

Hold her hold her hold her, I thought to the land around her, not even sure why I was doing that. I knew exactly where she was, and there was an old access road that'd get us to her easily in the morning. If she was still there. *Hold her,* I thought again.

She made herself eat some trail food, then curled up under a canoe and passed out almost instantly.

Hold her, I thought, drifting away myself, and in my dreams I did exactly that. She fit sweet and warm in my arms, but when I tried to pull her closer they were willow roots, and wouldn't move from the sandbank. My frustration disturbed her, and she somehow sort of shook us both free of earthly tethers and we fell instead though starlight. Her mouth sought mine, and she pulled me to her and then...

And then a monster came hunting along the river bank, and her cold terror woke us both. I didn't care what time of godforsaken o'clock it was then, Div 51 was heading out.

18

THE BONE SNAKE

AISLING

W e were safe for the moment, but the moment wouldn't last.
You guys gotta get moving. Division 51 is closing on you, and the fog's going to burn off within twenty minutes of sunrise, Rigs said into my mind.

I looked down at the base of the cliff. Coils of bone-plated malice twitched in restless dreams, barely visible through a soup of pre-dawn fog. My breath hung in the air and frost glittered on the ground. I could just barely see our half-hidden canoes, tucked away under brush piles just past the monster. A snake with an armored body as thick as one of the riverbank's old cottonwoods had slithered between the cave and our canoes an hour earlier, following some prey it was hunting. Waking up to a monster swallowing a feral cow *ten feet away from me*, and freezing unmoving under the canoe until it fell asleep, had made this one of the longest nights of my life.

It interrupted some completely inappropriate but extremely hot dreams about the bastard hunting us, too. We'd been just about to...

Nope nope nope, not going there. This is what happens when I trade away my flipping batteries. Less than two days and I'm already out of my bloody mind.

I was stealthy enough to sneak past the monster and had done so as soon as it fell asleep. Coral *might* be as well. Our Runners, though? Not a chance.

In the distance, Jeep engines rumbled. Now Division 51 and the Strangeling Brigade of the army were closing in too. No doubt they were hunting the damn thing... or, more likely, us.

The bone serpent's still between us and the river, I answered. *It's sleeping off its kill, but restlessly. There's no way these guys can get past it without waking it up.*

Can you hunker down and let the soldiers kill it, then get to the river after they leave? Rigs asked.

They'll find the canoes, then look for us. And last time we ran into them, they had a tracker who chased us for ten miles. I can't glamour eight people against sight, smell, and sound while on the move, especially not with small children in the boats. And I don't feel any of that poison taint in the hunter's magic, but we can't risk the babies.

"Div 51's going to come in on an access road downriver from us," Coral whispered next to me. "If we can get them to engage the snake, they'll be too busy to chase us. We could run down the other side of that thing, get to the boats, and just hope the monster takes a long time to die. Might get us time to escape both threats. We're close to the border. If they cross it with weapons, an Elsecomer patrol will take care of them."

I nodded. That tentative feeling of possible futures I sometimes got agreed that was the best way through.

"Okay. We need the fog for cover and it's not as thick as I'd hoped for. It'll burn off with sunrise. That means we should hand off the snake to them as quickly as possible. Everyone's ready to go?"

The bone snake twitched and shifted. We all froze.

"We have to do this quickly," Coral whispered. "Everyone get ready to run."

The faces on the strangelings we were smuggling to freedom got even more drawn. The parents hugged their tiny kids tighter. Their toddler and baby had no idea what was going on. Zahra's oversized frame shook. Jay's orange eyes blinked back tears.

Their safety was on me.

"Give me the gun and two flares," I told Coral.

Flare guns were pretty much the upper limit of weaponry the Elsecomers let into their territory, and ours had once triggered a patrol. They were mildly sympathetic to the kids we were running and explained that they didn't care about low-tech stuff like bows and arrows, but nothing higher tech was allowed in their land. They'd spoken English, and neither of the pair sent to check us saw through my illusion or thought we were anything more than we appeared. Since then, we'd been caching the flare gun before crossing their exclusion zone's border, and had never triggered another patrol.

"I'll try to pull it towards Div 51, then find you on the river," I said. "If I can't do that, I'll get back to the van somehow, meet you there. You've just got to get past the border, and then you should be safe."

I shrugged on a quiver of bronze-tipped arrows and grabbed my bow and backpack. It was half full and basically had trail food in it at this point. Coral followed me a few steps outside the cave entrance.

"Going green?" she asked quietly. I nodded, and she gave me a quick hug. I was *done* with this shit. That guy wanted to push me, to pull me out of hiding? He was about to get a *real* good look at what I usually keep out of sight.

"Good luck," she said. "I'll get these guys through. Do whatever you have to. I'll see you soon."

"Yeah. Soon. I'll keep you updated. Good luck," I replied.

Halfway down the cliff I stopped and stripped off my clothes and shoes, packing them away into a drybag in my backpack, and dropped my smuggler persona's illusion. I called my armor in woodland stealth mode, and it spread over my body looking like faded green leather.

All in, now, I thought, rolling my neck and quietly bouncing up and down on my toes for a second. *Superhero time. No more holding back.*

I ghosted down the hill to the dirt river-front road at the bottom, careful not to slip on the frosty stones or dislodge any rocks. The enormous snake shivered again. Its head was so big I could stand up inside its mouth if it was striking.

Let's not think about that.

I could hear Jeeps less than a mile West of us and coming as fast as the overgrown road allowed. I ghosted past the snake in their direction, and about twenty feet from the snake's head, I pulled out the gun and two flares.

I flow like water and strike like fire, I prayed under my breath, while loading the first flare into the gun, *Still as stone and light as wind, dancing with the Tree and Stars Eternal.*

Ready? I sent to Coral, and got a mental thumbs-up.

I pointed the flare gun at the sky and pulled the trigger. The incendiary screamed up into the sky and bloomed into a miniature firework. I was pissed at Div 51 for coming after us, but I didn't want their enslaved strangelings caught completely unready to face this monster.

The giant snake jerked awake and opened eyes like portals to a realm of flame. Its head rose, eyes focused directly on me, weaving from side to side, closer to me with every movement.

I slammed the second flare into the gun and raised it like a duelist. The snake hissed at me and slid forward, the bone plates along its body clicking softly against each other.

"You chose a bad place to sleep," I said to the serpent, and shot it directly between the eyes.

It reared up and then slammed down in pursuit of me as I took off running towards the Jeeps. Behind me, at a volume only elf-ears would pick up, Coral was saying, "Go go go!" to the escapees.

I threw my awareness out around me into land-running mode, where I *know* every bit of land and life in a hundred yards of myself and the trees sing me wild songs of peace and warning, not hiding my power any longer. The giant snake cryptid was twenty yards behind me and gaining.

Somebody with similar magic up ahead felt me coming. Inexperienced, but with a feeling of nascent strength behind him. There he was, the guy who'd spied on me all evening, the ones the alien tribes called a traitor to the sidhe. He was pretty inept for all that, though; I really didn't think they had the full story.

Fumbling awareness swept out, trying to see what approached.

What's out there? asked a voice that tasted like wildwood honey, strong, masculine, but unsteady in the way of people new to mindspeech. It felt like a rhetorical question, like he didn't actually expect an answer.

Good morning! I sent cheerily back, partially just to see what he'd do, sending an image along with it of the giant creature chasing me. *Got you a thank-you present for all the harassment!*

"Weapons ready, NOW!" a tenor voice yelled in the fog ahead of me. Headlights flared in the fog and the Jeeps slowed.

I felt the snake coil behind me and put on a burst of speed just as it slammed forward. I leapt onto the hood of the foremost Jeep and bounced into a triple axis flip over the rest of the car, and right behind me, the snake's head smashed into the vehicle. Strangelings in prison-soldier uniforms bailed out sideways as the Jeep went flying. A grin stretched wide across my face as I dove into battle headspace, floating like a leaf on the wind through pure delicious chaos.

"It's the Green Lady!" a woman soldier's voice yelled over the din.

Guns sputtered to life around me and the snake threw itself up into striking position. A gigantic strangeling with striped red skin, at least 12 feet tall, jumped out of the back of a pickup, carrying a bazooka like a normal human would a shotgun. He planted himself like an action figure, focused utterly on the snake, and lifted the bazooka and shot a missile at the serpent's open mouth. It dodged aside at the last second, and the projectile missed and blew somewhere back in the forest. He shrugged and reloaded. Two other soldiers dove for me and I rolled directly between the giant's legs to escape.

A troop carrier, full of human soldiers, slid sideways as it braked faster than its momentum easily allowed. Right. Strangeling Brigade never patrolled alone - they're basically slaves, after all - but they always go in first. The carrier was now effectively blocking the road back the way they'd come from. I called a sword into my hand, spun, and slashed through three tires.

That ought to keep them all here for the fight.

"Boats on the river!" another man's voice yelled. Dammit, guess they'd had a riverfront scout already running along the bank. So much for the cover of fog. "She's using the snake as a distraction!"

Well, shit. They're getting smarter.

"Jones, lead on the snake! Roberts, boats! I'm pursuing Greenie!" yelled that tenor.

I pumped my arms and *ran*. The river went into a deep bend here around another sandstone cliff and I parkoured my way up it and to the top. I glanced down behind me and my heart just about stopped for a second. The guy pursuing was in a Strangling brigade uniform, with a muscled but agile frame, and he could move like me. A second glance as I hit the peak of the hill and I saw red-brown hair and short golden antlers, and the most exquisitely handsome face I'd ever seen on a man. Oh gods, he really was as hot as he'd been in his accidental sending. That questing land-sense flared out around him; I didn't know if I'd be able to lose him. If he was like me, my only advantage would be training.

And he'd no little bit of his own.

Active magic flared out from him, something verdant, primal, and deeply land-bound. I didn't recognize it at first, and then the next step I took, roots reached out of the soil and grabbed my legs. As fast as I was running, I went down hard, and it knocked the wind out of me. That was all it took for him to catch me.

A second later, I was on my back in the dirt and he was trying to pin and contain me.

I fought him. One ankle was thoroughly caught but the rest of me was kicking and punching for all I was worth. The guy was good, though, and had a lot more unarmed close-quarters grappling experience than I did; speed and agility are my best advantages and I try very hard to keep distance between myself and my opponents. And yeah, I could have pulled out a blade, but he wasn't pointing his gun at me and that whole enslaved labor thing... also let's be honest, I didn't have it in me to kill anyone *that* smoking hot. Because, let me just say, *damn.* Everything beautiful and masculine and dangerous I'd ever guessed at liking was *right* on top of me and, um, I couldn't entirely hate it.

Especially not after those damn dreams.

"You are *under arrest,*" he said through gritted teeth, trying to get a solid grip on me. His eyes flashed green, right above me, and something like faint gold smoke seemed to rise off his antlers. "For treason against humanity and trafficking with the Elsecomers!"

"For *what?* In your dreams!" I exclaimed. "And *stay out of mine!*"

He flushed bright red, and I twisted and rolled us over so I was on top, which, ah, didn't help. I finally got a good look at him, and it made me freeze in shock. He appeared every bit as sidhe as I was. I had seen no one like me in over ten years, except for that brief encounter with city guards telling us not to bring guns into their exclusion zone. His magic flared again, and it felt so exquisitely *right* against mine that I could have sobbed.

"You *are* like me," I breathed, and he rolled us and got me half-pinned again.

I tried to punch him in the head, but he twisted aside at the last second. Got some good clawing in as I pulled my hand back, though. He snarled at the pain and dropped his weight on top of me, and got my hands a second later. Golden magic swam through his eyes.

And here comes the whammy, I thought, pulling most of my mind back and away from it, and leaving some for him to catch. It's easier to counterpunch a glamour you know you can't resist if you pull most of yourself out of the way, and then give it a little bit of non-essential self. It's like letting an opponent grab your hand, then pulling them off balance with it.

"Stop fighting!" he snarled, trapping both my wrists together above my head. Oh hell, I'd had fantasies that went *just like this.* "I don't want to hurt you!"

Sidhe light blazed out from him, shining like a forest sun, wrapping me up in silk and luscious, vivid *life* magic.

Oh gods. Oh, very old gods of the woods and wilds, gods of the greening springtime...

I gasped, his light calling mine, the landbound magic in me very, very much liking the same in him, pushing aside all conscious thoughts about who we were (enemies, right?) and what we were supposed to be doing (fighting, dammit) into a golden fog of primal vernal lust.

My back arched, my body seeking a better angle against his. I saw the exact moment he realized he couldn't control the magic he'd just called up, and then he was dancing on its strings as much as I was.

I couldn't make myself care. Playing Maid of Spring with my delicious young Horned Lord suited me *just fine*, and his magic was just pushing our sensible objections out of the way of suddenly freed fae libidos. My unbound leg twined up around his, and I pulled him closer, laughing, and dismissed my helmet. He smiled like he planned to *take* every inch of my body. *Excellent.* I wriggled one hand free and pulled his head down to mine. The most luscious lips I'd ever seen brushed mine, setting me aflame, and then I pulled him in for a real kiss, opening my mind and magic to him. Inside me, I felt the deepest source of sidhe magic, the Tree that Grows Between Worlds, start opening its magic to flow up through me and over to him, so fresh, so new to all this. For a second he tried to fight it, and then instinct took over and he pulled me tight, kissing, *claiming*, branding himself into me.

Oh gods, the feel of him. His hands on me were warm, and strong, and steady. His eyes were all the green of the forest, with golden rays of light shining through, so warm and inviting, so familiar, like someone I had loved and lost and somehow forgotten, touching me like he already knew what I liked. His light reached out around me and I *opened* to it, welcoming him home. Every sharp, cynical defense mechanism that I keep wrapped up around my essential self started to peel away, like garments falling on a lover's floor. I wanted, *needed* his hands and lips everywhere his magic was touching.

The light thickened, deepened. I was free-falling through honey, everything warm and sweet and golden. I wanted to be naked, writhing, screaming for him. My hands were up his shirt and his lips were working down my neck, my armor melting away as his mouth headed for my breasts. His magic twined up around mine and I pulled him tighter, yearning for *more*. White flowers pushed up out of the soil around us, blooming, and I pulled my lover in against me like we could banish a lifetime apart with just a *little* more skin together.

Below our hilltop, there was a roar, a scream from the rocket launcher, and an explosion. The snake shrieked with a sound like the world ending. Wait, can snakes shriek? Well, this one could. Oh shit, there was a world out there. Dammit. I did *not* want it interrupting this.

The shrieking rapidly retreated as the serpent dove for the river. *Coral. The kids. The babies.*

I shook off the magic, swearing in frustration, and it snapped back against the antlered guy. He pulled back, blinking from the whiplash, trying to figure out what the hell was happening.

"DAMMIT," I said, called a short blade, and sliced through the root holding my foot and rolled him off me. "Let's pick that back up later, okay? Gotta go."

His eyes blazed at me as he tried to get control of his magic. He looked completely disoriented, and was having trouble getting to his feet. A wicked impulse took me, and I darted forward, kissed those luscious lips one more time, and ran for the river. He swore and I heard him behind me again a second later. Well. Not phased for long, that said something good. Inconvenient, but good.

I glanced through the trees and saw the giant had landed a hit; one of the monster's eyes was a smoking hole and its head was on fire. It threw its head into the water to put out the flames.

Coral, MOVE! I screamed at her, and felt her water magic twist the river's currents to speed the boats. They were almost around the bend, but waves from the impact of the snake flopping into the water hit their canoes and almost tipped them.

I ricocheted off tree trunks down the other side of the hill. The Div 51 guy lost a little ground on me; guess he hadn't done as much parkour and gymnastics. Out in the river, the Runners were trying to keep their boats upright in churning waves that threatened to swamp them. Chunks of late ice-flow smashed against the boats. The snake could swim, and it was bearing down on them quickly. The baby woke up and started wailing; her toddler sibling's voice joined it a second later.

The monster lifted its head out of the water and focused on their canoe.

Oh gods, no.

I shrugged my bow down into my hand, still running, and pulled three arrows out of my quiver. I aimed and loosed as fast as I could draw and release. It was an impossible shot, but one arrow hit the gaping eye hole and the serpent reared up again and shook its head in pain. Coral turned around in her boat and blasted it with a siren scream. The snake fell over backwards, but a twisting coil of its body hit the teenagers' canoe and sent them flying into the icy water. The wave almost swamped the family's canoe and the children's screams took on a frantic air.

Jay and Zahra resurfaced and grabbed at the flipped canoe. Its keel looked snapped but it had enough air under it to float.

Beach stones crunched under my feet and my pursuer's footsteps followed a second after me. How had he gained so much on me?

The snake righted itself in the water and redoubled its speed.

You want fast, beastie? I'll show you fast.

The snake was coming parallel to the shore now, the two canoes just slightly downstream.

I dipped into the magic of my mother's people and flashed across the water onto the snake's back, moving fast enough that the waves were essentially solid to me. From the corner of my eyes I saw Strangeling Brigade soldiers following on the river bank, moving considerably more quickly than I'd have expected. I shaped a long slim spear in my hands and leaped upwards. The spear drove down through the monster's burned eye socket and deep into its brain, and I ran a shiver of electric fire down the shaft and blade to finish the job.

But the flipping thing still didn't die. It shook like an earthquake, though, and I heard cries of terror as the second canoe flipped in the waves its coils sent up. Coral came screaming out of the water a second later and blasted it with another siren shriek, and I was flung into the depths. A coil hit me and everything went black.

19

RESCUES

ARTHUR

I wasn't losing it, I had lost it. Whatever "it" was, possibly my heart, probably my last grasp on sanity, and definitely whatever control I had over the magic blooming in me. I'd lost it... and I just wanted to throw it even farther away and go back to kissing the Green Lady on the bluff above the river.

Unfortunately, she had remembered we were supposed to be fighting when Bastion hit the snake with a rocket, driving the monster into the river. God, did she look pissed to be reminded; that made two of us. Then she did something to make my magic rebound on me and threw me off, completely disoriented by the sudden snap. She grinned and kissed me fast and hard, then took off running. *Dammit.* And I didn't care if I could barely stand, much less run; she wasn't escaping me again.

She focused completely on the snake, though, fear streaming off her like ribbons, and then children started screaming, little ones, in the boats. She pulled arrows from her quiver and shot at the snake *on the run*, hitting the burnt hole where Bastion had put a missile in its eye. Completely impossible. I'd almost caught up to her - and at that point, with a monster attacking children on the river, I don't even know what I'd have done - when she dove into some magic and *ran* so fast the waves were effectively solid for her. And I could almost, almost see how she'd done it, and yearned after that magic like part of me was starving.

A spear formed in her hand, and she stabbed into the burned eye-hole Bastion had blasted. The snake convulsed and threw her into the water. I pulled off my shoes and jacket and dove into the Mississippi.

"Help! Help, I can't hold on!" a woman screamed from mid-river. The aluminum canoe was upright again, but half swamped, and a woman was trying to hang onto her baby and get back into it. A toddler was already in the canoe, screaming his head off, and a man's arm scrambled at the other side of the boat. A large chunk of ice was heading straight towards them. Oh fuck.

Diving into ice water isn't fun. Your entire body clenches up, trying to fight back against it. But inside me the faery monster growled, and some kind of magic flared through my body and I could move through the pain of sudden freezing shock. That hunting awareness opened up, too, and I could feel my troops on the banks and the red-haired girl grabbing the Green Lady underwater and pulling her away. The kids gave up on their broken canoe and swam for the river bank. I caught up with the little family's canoe just as the ice chunk hit the boat and the mother lost her grip on the baby, numb hands unable to hold on. The child went under, and I went after it.

Nothing was visible in the murky water; I could hardly see my outstretched fingers, but I knew exactly where it was, the baby's magic sparking against mine. I grabbed it and we resurfaced, both of us gasping for breath. A button nose and big brown eyes looked up at me, fuzzy brown ears folded back. I grabbed the boat and caught the father's eyes and he steadied it while I put the baby in next to the toddler.

"Hold on to the baby!" I ordered, and the little one grabbed her and hugged his sibling tight. Both of them had the same teddy bear features, and I realized the parents weren't quite human either.

Strangelings. They're all strangelings, I realized, helping the freezing woman get back into the boat. Her lips were blue and her body was shaking violently. Fingers with short rough claws on their tips could hardly grip the side. A hole started to develop in my stomach, a suspicion that I'd gotten something completely wrong. Roberts joined us in the water, and with the father helping, we swam the canoe to shore.

A bit upriver from us, the pair from the broken boat were dragging themselves onto sand. My magic was saying they were both kids, even though one was huge, and they were my people, too. The red-haired girl and Green Lady were out on a tiny island in the river, just barely in sight; the latter was half-drowned and vomiting water onto the beach. She looked up, saw me, snarled, and magic flared as she vanished from sight.

Deep in my darkness, green eyes opened. A burst of hot possessiveness flashed through me.

Mine, my monster thought.

I started. Coherent thought from it? That almost never happened. But keeping these people alive was more urgent than catching her.

I have her scent, my monster said, more in impressions than actual words, tasting her magic and savoring it. *She won't escape me now.*

Seeing her was doing something to it, changing it. That energy off of the girl... it had been intoxicating, but it had woken something up in me too, and it stretched, hungry and restless.

Great. Another thing I don't understand and will probably screw up.

"We've got people going hypothermic on the river bank," Jones said into his radio. "Caught six of the people in the boats. Snake's down, Greenie and one other escaped. Get blankets and fire starting supplies over here asap. Four of the guys we caught are kids, two of them babies."

"Yes sir," a voice crackled back. "We'll bring food and thermoses."

Up the river, my people had reached the two kids and were pulling them out of their wet clothes and offering their own jackets in place of them. Bastion had the large girl, who was trembling with cold and what I worried might be the Hunger. His jacket was big even on her, but the only one out here that could possibly fit.

"Get the wet stuff off the babies, put them in your shirts," Jones said to the soldiers pulling the half-swamped canoe out of the water. "We gotta get 'em warm as fast as possible."

"Sir, I've got your jacket and boots," Hassan said, coming up to us and holding them out to me.

"Give her the jacket," I said, taking my shoes and nodding at the wife. Her husband was helping her out of the boat and she was having trouble, shaking so violently she stumbled repeatedly. God, the woman was *so* thin... she had almost no insulating body fat. When she was on shore, Hassan held up the jacket for privacy while they got her soaked shirt off, and then put my jacket right on her.

"Don't take my babies," she sobbed, sitting down in the sand. "All we did was eat something bad, 'cuz there wasn't anything else. Don't take my babies."

"Is running them to the Elsecomers better for them?" Jones asked.

"We aren't," the man said. "We're going to Strangelingtown. No one wants to go to the Elsecomers."

"Strangelingtown?" I asked, my stomach sinking again. "What's that?"

"Settlement for our kind," he answered, his voice anguished. "Deep in the Edgelands. The Underhill Railroad people say it's safe for us there. You're *one of us*. Why do you have to stop us?"

Oh shit. Fuck. What do I do now?

"Look, right now you guys are all going to die of hypothermia if you don't get warm right away," Jones said. "Let's prioritize. Then we'll figure out what to do with you. And you guys don't look like threats to humanity, but that girl in green is as dangerous as they come."

"She wasn't with us," the man said. "It was just Rue and Siren. I don't know where the elf girl came from."

"The Green Lady was with you the entire time," I growled. "I felt you. Eight people together, coming into my patrol lands."

The man just shook his head *no*, over and over.

"They've got a fire almost set up over there," Jones said. "Let's get you warm and then start figuring things out."

We pulled the canoe up further and then I helped the couple walk over to the protected spot my men were dragging driftwood to. Birch and another half dozen guys showed up with blankets and provisions. The wood was all damp and wasn't catching, until the boy who'd been with the giant girl focused on it and said something in a Native language, and then smoke rose in a little ribbon. A second later, flame sprouted and spread over the twigs and logs. He wobbled and almost fell over sideways. Birch righted him and made him sit on a log half embedded in the sand, and pulled a blanket over his shoulders. For maybe the next ten minutes, everything went quiet as the would-be escapees grabbed food and stuffed it into their mouths with the desperation of the deeply cold. Roberts and I joined them by the fire, trying to dry off, while Birch and Jones went down the beach trying to find the Green Lady and her comrade.

"No sign of them," Birch said, returning. "Kids, Captain? What's going on? These guys don't look like Elsecomer agents," he said, his voice dubious. Other people handed out coffee... well, warm drinks with a little caffeine in them, no one can afford much real coffee anymore, it grows too far away and the supply chains are too disrupted... and emergency rations.

"We aren't Elsecomer agents," the boy mumbled around a mouthful of rations. "We're just trying to get to freedom, so people like you don't murder us for having the wrong color eyes!"

"Nobody here wants to murder you," Birch said. "We're out here looking for a girl who smuggles for the Elsecomers. Why'd you people attack us if you're just running for freedom?"

Birch's radio abruptly sputtered, made an awful shrieking noise for a second, and then - considerably more clearly than our gear normally sounds - a voice spoke through it. Whoever was calling was using some kind of voice distortion, and I couldn't even tell gender from the call. Still, I *knew* it was the guy who'd broken into my team's radios the day I got irradianced.

"Underhill Railroad to Division 51. Am I talking to someone in charge?"

"Lieutenant Birch speaking, who is this?" he asked, raising an eyebrow at me.

"That's the guy who organized the run," the man with bear ears said quietly. "He was going to be nearby monitoring radio channels."

"Call me Tech Support. We aren't running anything to the Elsecomers," the voice said, and my people came closer to listen in. "We just get strangelings out of the human lands to somewhere safe, where they're no trouble for anyone."

"Yeah, well, we're down two vehicles now because you smugglers ran a giant snake into our patrol," Birch said. "Anything you want to say about that?"

"The girls thought you soldiers could handle a monster better than the toddlers," the voice said. Birch raised his eyebrows at me. Fuck. I mean, I couldn't fault that logic. "It fell asleep between the cave they slept in and the canoes. Siren took the runners while Slayer got the snake out of the way; everything else was incidental. And dude, you're the ones who were executing a pre-dawn raid on some innocents just trying to get to freedom."

"These guys weren't our targets," Birch said. "We're looking for the Green Lady. She's got Elsecomer-tech weapons and we want to know about them."

"Uh... shit. Look, I don't know much about her weapons," the guy on the radio said. There was a burst of static and something unintelligible. We all leaned in, focusing on his voice. There was another burst of static and it came semi-clear, if you listened closely. "Slayer's got some magic swords and armor. They were a gift and the giver is dead. The Underhill Railroad just runs strangelings to safety. We aren't working with the Elsecomers."

Everyone focused completely on his voice, trying to make it out. Somewhere in the distance, far away, a haunting voice started

singing "Fields of Gold." The radio crackled again, and... well, I
didn't think to guard my mind. I didn't even realize I should. The
song seeped into my thoughts like the warmth of a sunbeam, like a
west wind across fields of barley, into memories...

I closed my eyes. It was a perfect autumn Sunday, the last good
day before I started Changing, Indian summer at its finest. I'd spent
the afternoon fishing with my dad, and then gone home to Laurie
and my dog Buddy. I drank a creamy amber ale on the back porch
with them, and the foam rose thick on the top. The sunset dripped
honey over my world. Everything was good, sweet, simple. Our
future stretched ahead of us, so full of promise. It had been so long
since I'd felt *happy*, and content, and loved...

Somebody was trying to pull me away from the sweetness of the
memory. I didn't want to go, and clung to it.

"Captain! Captain! *Wake up!*" Birch was yelling at me from a
great distance. I ignored him. The dream was so much better than
my reality. "CAPTAIN!"

Warm coffee-substitute splashed directly into my face, and I
shook awake to find the Green Lady putting swords to both Birch's
and my throats. She was armored in something much heavier now,
only her eyes really visible through some sort of clear visor on
her helmet. Her partner was grabbing the strangeling escapees and
hustling them off to the aluminum canoe, still singing, her spell
twining out around everyone present. My people stood around,
oblivious, smiles on their faces and tears streaming down their
cheeks.

"Well, fuck," Birch said, glaring at me, an impossibly sharp
golden blade hovering just beyond his Adam's apple.

"Just let us get out of here and I won't hurt you guys," she said.
"You don't have to tell anyone you broke out of the glamour."

Birch froze, a shock of recognition running through him.

"Hildie?" he said, his eyes going wide. "You *are* the Green Lady?"

"Fucking *shut up*, Lutefiskr," the Green Lady growled. "Stop
now or I'll make sure you're blacklisted from ever getting the good

mead again. Also, let me remind you right now of the oath you took before I trained you."

Birch started swearing, long and low, in what was probably Klingon.

20

The Hunger

Aisling

*G*ods *fucking damn,* I thought, holding a sword to the
throat of a kid who'd stood in shield walls with me, one
I considered a friend. We'd assumed Helmut von der Laute
und Fiske was harmless, because it's not like anyone threatening
would name themselves for lutefisk, the world's stinkiest way to
prepare fish. He'd shone with magical talent and the group that
thought reenactment was a nice side hobby to things like alchemy
and witchcraft, well, we grabbed him right up. One night after
the fires burned low and the stick-jocks had passed out drunk,
because I worried about my friends and never wanted someone
mind-controlling them, Coral and I taught the crew how to resist
fae glamours. And dammit, Lutefiskr had been practicing, and I
was pretty sure I knew with whom.

*At least I have his magically bound word to not out me if he ever
figured out my undefined secret.*

The sidhe man who'd chased me earlier glared at me, frustration
and fury in his eyes, and gold stirred in their depths. His antlers
started glowing, Power swirling up from the land and into him.
Shit. No wonder he kept finding me; he was probably even more
landbound here than I was up North. Something about him felt

weirdly familiar, and the magic in me yearned towards him in a way I'd never felt.

I wish we could have just stayed up on that hill.

"*Meheleb va tiene hor,*" I said to him, and touched my blade gently to the skin of his throat. His eyes blazed. "And cut it out. I would love to pick back up where we left off, but I need to get these people to safety first. I'm not dealing with anyone in the stolen Cities, just taking these people to Strangelingtown. Zahra, keep moving."

"I can't," she said, dropping to her knees in the sand, halfway back to the canoe. She grabbed herself around her stomach, pinning her arms against her body. "Get the babies away from me! Get them away now!"

The mother and father looked at her in horror and fled for the canoe. Coral grabbed Jay and pulled him away from Zahra.

"She's going into the Hunger," the sidhe man said, still glaring at me. "The cold tipped her over the edge."

"Siren, go!" I called. "I'll figure something out."

She nodded, fear in her eyes, and pushed the boat into the Mississippi and leaped in. Gently, she let go of the glamour she'd cast on the soldiers, and dug her paddle violently into the water. Her magic grabbed the river's currents hard enough that the water practically grabbed the canoe and threw it out to the main current and away.

The antlered man's magic pulsed through his people, human and strangeling both, and they shook themselves awake, throwing off beloved memories to see me holding swords to both their officers' throats. Then I was outnumbered fifteen-to-one, with someone under my protection having a medical emergency fifteen yards away. The giant whose jacket Zahra was wearing cautiously got up and made his way over to her, moving slowly and watching me. He put his hands on her shoulders and seemed to steady her.

"Tech, I'm in a bit of a bind right now," I said aloud. "Can you make sure no one can call out until we sort out something here?"

"Roger, Slayer. I'll start prepping contingencies," he answered from Lutefiskr's radio, his voice perfectly clear again.

"You got any Radiant food for her?" I asked the antlered guy, trying not to get distracted by the way his wet clothes clung to *that body,* or think about how it had felt against mine. Looking at his face wasn't much better; if anyone ever asked me how my taste in guys ran, after today, I'd just sigh and describe him. He was slender where a man should be slender, broad where one should be broad, and muscled to tight definition. His build was light and agile, somewhere between a champion swimmer and soccer star. Angular jaw, high cheekbones, straight nose, high brow. Luscious lips, shaped by both humor and arrogance; eyes the green-gold of forest sunlight; golden tanned skin and reddish brown hair, cropped too short; and finally, delicate ears that tapered to sharp tips, just like mine.

Focus! I told myself.

"Radiant food?" the antlered guy asked, frowning at me. "Do you want a side of radioactive fries with that? *No,* we don't keep toxic waste on hand."

I looked at him. Dammit.

"Gods Between Worlds," I swore. "Why the hell did I hope there might be a brain behind a face like that?"

Lutefiskr choked on a laugh and the sidhe guy gave me the kind of look that says *your very existence offends me,* an expression I usually only inspire in cats.

"Look, I can treat her. Can we have a truce while I take care of her?" I asked them. "Or do you want to have to kill a teenage girl because you're too ignorant to take care of our people?"

21

THE CALL TO TRADE

ARTHUR

"**B**irch, you know her?" I asked, gritting my teeth to keep from grabbing the girl and either shaking or kissing her senseless.

"She doesn't look like that normally," he said. "I was *sure* the girl at Midsommer was human. She's the one who taught me to resist fae mind control."

"Midsommer?"

"Midsommer Fields," she said, glaring at both of us. "It's a living history festival. He didn't say he worked enslaving strangelings, or I wouldn't have taught him a damn thing!"

"What?" Birch said. "I don't! Hart runs this group."

She frowned at that, like she was trying to place a memory.

"Birch is my *partner*," I clarified, and a look of disappointment ran across her face before she quickly schooled her features neutral. What was that about? Birch bit his lips, looking at me like I'd said something both hilarious and horrifying. "We run this together."

"I can save Zahra, if you let me," the girl repeated, frustration twisting her face.

Serena stepped directly behind her and put a pistol to her head, and a dozen other guys leveled their guns at her. "I'll give you my parole not to attack as long as she needs me taking care of her."

"Your odds are very bad," Serena said to the girl.

"My armor can take bullet hits," she responded, her hands perfectly steady on her swords, "And these guys will be dead before I am."

"Drop the weapons and take off the armor as a sign of good will," Serena said. The elf girl looked at me, and I nodded.

"I ditch the weapons and armor and you'll let me take care of Zahra?" she clarified. "And get her food to manage the Hunger?"

There was food that could get people through the Hunger?

I clenched my jaw and nodded.

The Green Lady opened her hands, and both swords disintegrated into gold dust and disappeared. A second later her armor kind of folded in on itself and went back to the lighter leather variant. Her helmet vanished. Oh god, she *was* as beautiful as I'd thought. Her face was like a dream of wilderness given feminine form, every line as clean and elegant as a swan's wings. She had hair the pale blonde of birch wood, with eyelashes and brows the same color; her skin had that almost glowing translucence of alabaster; and her eyes were the vivid blue of an October sky. It was a strange, inhuman beauty, but I'd never seen anyone lovelier.

"I said, take off the armor," Serena ground out, cocking her gun against the girl's head.

"All of it?" she asked, her eyes daring me. I narrowed mine at her.

"Off. Now."

"If you say so..."

The rest of the armor sort of folded in on itself and vanished. She wasn't wearing a stitch underneath it. My brain shut off. Oh god. I had to close my eyes. She was slim and fit, and every line of her was perfect. Even the scars across her hip and thigh, from the claws of something *big*, just made her more attractive.

"Gah!" Birch yelled. "Don't give Naked Fucking Hildie an excuse!"

"This *is* your Viking friend?" I asked, eyes still squeezed tight. It didn't matter. The image of her had burned itself into my brain.

"Put some of the armor back on," Serena said, sounding like she'd swallowed a lemon.

"She's kind of... wild," Birch said, sounding like his eyes were screwed shut too. "She's gone into public battles with nothing but a helmet and shield, twice."

"Clothes. *Now,*" I said, kicking myself in every direction internally.

"*You* started this," she said.

And god, I wanted to continue it, no matter how terrible an idea it was.

But I heard a put-out sigh and then felt Serena ease off.

When I reopened my eyes, the girl was in something that looked like a tank top and jeans, still all green.

"How's that work?" I asked, desperately trying to find something neutral to say.

"Like magic," she said, daring me to contradict her. Pure Trouble, her, and god help me, but I wanted another taste. And if she was flirting like that, she did too. "I need to call for help to get the food Zahra needs. If you attack the people who come, our deal is off and I'll kill anyone who shoots them. Got it?"

I nodded. Birch did the same, a second behind me. The elf girl looked at me, and her face went deeply dubious.

"The tribes told me you're an Elsecomer traitor," she said, shocking me. *What tribes?* "But it's obvious you're a total noob with your magic, so I have doubts. Do you even know what we are?"

"I think after four years leading Division 51 I know a few things about strangelings," I said, a bit of growl in my voice. "People say *you're* a renegade Elsecomer."

"I'm a local, and I said what *we* are," she emphasized. "You and I."

"Strangelings? Yes," I repeated.

"You were born human?" she asked, taken aback. "With two human parents?"

"Um, yeah. You weren't?"

"Huh. Weird," she said, not answering. "Well, come on, I'll show you what to do."

And then she just completely ignored all the guns pointed at her and walked, back straight, over to the girl in the Hunger.

Birch and I exchanged glances and followed her.

The girl in green dropped to one knee in front of the giant and looked her over.

"Hey Zahra, how you doing?" she asked, her voice gentle. Some delicate magic flared out from her.

"Dusty?" the girl whimpered. Her pupils were tiny and hard shivers ran through her body. "I don't think I'm gonna make it."

"You can. You will," she answered. "We can get you through this, but some of it's going to be really strange. Think you can deal with that?"

The giant nodded, her head lolling a little.

"Okay. Just hold on a little longer. I'm going to call for help, see if I can get you some food that'll get you through the Hunger. And since I'm outed anyway, do you want the shape of your transformation changed? Sometimes I can mold Cascades, and yours feels malleable."

"I don't want to be a monster," the girl whimpered.

"None of us do," the Green Lady answered, sadness in her voice. "I can't stop you from turning into a giant. Might be able to make you more human looking. That okay?"

She nodded again, having difficulty with words. "I feel like I'm being made into the shape of people's fears."

"Then remember the shape of your own dreams," she said. "And we'll try to get you there instead."

Zahra nodded, apparently not able to speak again.

"Hold her," the girl in green said to Bastion. "She's not lost as long as she doesn't eat a sentient. I'm going to Call the Trade; don't shoot whoever shows up. It's probably going to be some kind of cryptid, to forewarn you, and it's going to take a bit of talking to make this work."

The last part she said looking at me. I glowered at her and nodded, still trying not to think about her naked. She stepped away from Zahra, drew in a deep breath, and then sang out a long musical line vaguely reminiscent of a call to prayer, yet wilder and more exotic, speaking not of duty but of opportunity. It ended on a questioning note.

For a minute there was silence, and then something awfully familiar sang back what sounded a lot like a formal response.

"Was that a *howler?*" Jones asked, shocked.

"It was one of the Dohoulani tribesmen," the girl responded. "Which is good. They're great scroungers, ought to be able find what we need if they don't have it on hand."

"We were in a gunfight with them yesterday," Birch said, looking spooked. Most of my men were holding their guns like they were ready to pull them up fast.

"You shoot *refugees?*" the girl asked, horrified.

"They're cryptid monsters invading Earth," I said, frowning at her, my stomach sinking again. "And our charge out here is to defend humanity."

"Sure, awesome," the girl said. "But the Dohoulani aren't a threat. Their homeworld was destroyed and their culture is too forest-oriented to make it in the taken cities. But they trade with Strangelingtown all the time, and regularly lead me to the bad monsters threatening the town and them. They're really great guides."

"They *throw shit at us* every time we run into them," Birch said. "Then shoot us with slings."

"For real?" she asked, both horrified and trying not to laugh. "Well, they thought you were a traitor. It's a misunderstanding. I'll see if I can sort that out."

"A *misunderstanding?*" I asked, aghast, and then a howler called down from the top of a tree right by us. Guns swung up towards and and the girl spun at us, and magic flared around her.

"Guns DOWN," she said, and holy fuck, suddenly she was a lot scarier than anything in the trees. "Shoot at them and *I will kill you all.*"

It should have pissed me off when she said that, not turned me on.

Serena went over and, trying to keep her hand from shaking, put a gun to the girl's head again. Rue, or Hildie, or Dusty, or whatever her name was, flashed her an annoyed glance.

"*Ameheli ti nuchoohala,*" the voice called down from the tree.

"*Ameheli oma t'nookala oochi ali,*" the Green Lady called back. "*Aieruska ili fa.*"

"*Meso fin daha. Shi'a r'hooka,*" the howler called down.

"*Shi'i nhia. Kaska oomana. Blaska dooma, michin. Engleeshka ozin.*"

"What's it saying?" Serena asked. "And what's that language?"

"Tradish. It's the galaxy's lingua franca. I'm telling Samouk that Hart isn't an Elsecomer traitor," she said, "Just a dumb human boy with pointy ears, who only speaks English."

Fantastic. Great. Good to know she thinks of me like that.

"*Gahoo alia Enzula,*" the howler said. "*Achabak oota. Eska wa?*"

"*Eili oosta, ana amoosha alen, kaska ootin.*"

A series of hoots came down then, and one echoed it from further away.

"They'll get the food, and they want to call in a matriarch who speaks English to negotiate with you," she said. "Are you willing to talk peace terms with them?"

"Holy shit, this is like First Contact stuff," Birch said, his eyes wide and eager.

"*That* would be way above our pay grade," I reminded him. "And communicating with Elsecomers is an automatic death sentence."

"Look, do you want them to keep pelting you with shit or not?" the girl asked. "Because if nothing else, we can get that to stop."

"Why do they do that, anyway?" Birch asked her.

"Because we Dohoulani doona tolerate traitors to dem who saved our people," said a clear voice with a peculiar accent. A purple and black howler stepped solemnly down from one of the tree trunks, appearing as if from nowhere. Her ruff was silver-white, and her face really did look like a lemur's, but she had lost half her teeth to age and lisped because of that. Her middle arms clutched a tiny baby against her chest. It suckled as we watched and stared at us with enormous eyes. One of her top arms clutched a cane, and she walked carefully forwards with it. "Or want anyting to do with dose who would betray the shi'i. Aisling, child of the Tree, true to the Compacts, what are you *doing* with dis one?"

The matriarch didn't even look at Serena, holding a gun to the girl's head, apparently finding her inconsequential.

"This is Captain Hart," Aisling said, as something in me recognized the howler had named her truly, making a gracefully formal gesture to me. "And he knows nothing of the sidhe or the Compacts between our peoples. He is human-born, and sworn to protect the Outlands from the monsters the Return has inflicted on Earth. It is ignorance, not malice, that made him the enemy of the Edgeland tribes."

"Hmph," the matriarch said, gesturing me over with her free hand. "Well, boy, lemme look at you den."

"Hart, this is Elder Matriarch Enzula, of the Windshook Tribe. Her people claim the treetops between here and the walls of the Freeport of Many Waters, all along the river's Southern bank."

Shit. I had a feeling my life was about to get *way* more complicated. I stepped forward, not exactly happily.

The howler elder stood about four feet tall on the ground, and I'm 6'3". She made an impatient little gesture just like my own grandmother used to, and I sighed and knelt on one knee to be on eye level with her. Satisfaction flashed in her eyes, and she focused completely on me.

"My second grandson will na ever use his lower left arm again," she said to me. "He, who was so clever with tools. And my great-granddaughter will limp for life. My people have dunna no harm to you or yours, but you hunt us like animals. Why?"

Oh fuck. Because we didn't even realize you were actually sentient? Shit.

"My unit is charged with protecting the human lands from monsters coming out of the Edgelands," I said. "We thought you to be more of the same."

The old howler examined me, and I was certain her critical eyes saw more than the physical.

"Aisling, dis boy is as shi'i as you, perhaps more," the matriarch chided. "Blood of the Hunter, if I am right."

"Okay, sure, so I'm a halfbreed," the elf girl said, shrugging and looking annoyed. "But he doesn't know *anything!*"

"You must teach him, den," Enzula declared, and stamped her walking stick on the ground to emphasize her words. "Dat will be de price of our assistance today."

"I have classes starting again Monday!" Aisling exclaimed. "And you guys always say I know jack shit anyway!"

"It is still more than him. Give him the time you can, now or later," the elder ordered her. "And *fix dis mess,* or any further Dohoulani blood spilled in the Edgelands will be on *your* hands."

"He lives in a *prison,*" Aisling said, utter dismay in her voice. "I'd be trapped."

"And human walls could hold you?" the matriarch asked, and a quick smile flickered across the girl's face. *"Go with him.* And sort out de mess binding both your minds and magic."

"The m-" Aisling said, her eyes widening, and her mind brushed against mine and... my monster's... and for a second I saw gleaming silver vines wound around and pinning him, and the same things twining across Aisling's mind. Then she closed her eyes and started swearing under her breath, at length and with great creativity. Finally, she gritted her teeth, set her shoulders, and said to the howler, "I accept your terms."

"Good," she said. "And if you cannot make peace or free yourself, whodo I tell?"

"The Underhill Railroad people I work with, of course," she said.
The Matriarch looked at her reprovingly.

"And who, with the actual power to save you?"

Aisling seemed to shrink in on herself.

"I've never met them," she said, and hesitated. The matriarch's
fingers tapped her cane. "My mother gave me three names she
thought would be safe, if they still... seem themselves."

"Yes?" the matriarch said, expectantly.

"Maddoc, or Ellith, or Morganna," she said reluctantly. "I don't
know if they're in the Freeport or even on Earth."

"Ahhh," said the matriarch, looking exactly like my grandmother
when she'd put some juicy pieces of gossip together to realize
something even more delicious was going on. "Dey are known. Yes.
De Blade of Light-on-Water, de Master of Whispers, and de Red
Raven Herself? Dey would be happy to bring a lost child home.
You have the Blade's eyes, you know, that same blue. He is most
often in the 'port, and de Lady Morganna keeps a residence dere."

"*I am not lost and I'm already home!*" Aisling said through
gritted teeth. "And I want nothing to do with the assholes who
fucked up my world!"

"You'lla never master your magic witout training," the elder
continued mercilessly. "And if you come from *dose* lines, you will
need some. Likely to end up stumbling out of de world and be lost
forever, if you have Maddoc's magic, and I dinka you might."

"I *can't* go to them," Aisling said. "My mother said shapeshifters
with mind-control magics have infiltrated them, and I don't know
if it's true, but I've no way to know if *anyone* there is who they say
they are."

"Is dat what has happened?" the Matriarch asked, looking
thoughtful. "Yesss, yes, I can see dat. Some bad stories I havva heard,
dat made no sense. But ze young Huntsman is a problem right now,
right here, and you dunna have the knowledge to train his gifts. An
elder will be needed, one wit de same magic, or Dat which Hunts
will consume him and hiz men, and a Wild Hunt loose on de land
will do far worse dan any simple monster."

Aisling hugged her arms around herself and tried to keep the tears flooding her eyes from being seen by any of us around her.

"What do you mean?" I asked, alarmed.

"De girl will tell you," the old female said, nodding authoritatively. "Come to me when you have better questions to ask. I lika human chocolates, de kind with cherries and rum."

Well, I guess I was dismissed then. I looked sideways and shared a *WTF was that?* look with Birch. The matriarch turned her back on me and started hobbling back to the tree she'd come from. A few feet from it, she paused, and turned back to us.

"You wanna hunt monsters?" she asked, as if it were an afterthought.

"That is what we're doing here," I answered, trying to keep the frustration out of my voice.

"Dere is a... bad pig. I do not know words for it. Big. Dat way," she said, pointing. "Five of your miles, I think. My grandson could guide you."

"And you want?" I asked, realizing how this was going.

"One less monster to hunt *my* people. And you to stop shooting at us, or throwing grenades down wells when we are just trying to secure parts to get our children clean water."

"We want our tools back too!" another howler voice yelled down from the tree.

"You'll stay in the Edgelands, then," I said. "And make no attempt to go out into the human lands."

The matriarch gave me a snaggle-toothed grin. I had a general feeling she'd just danced circles I couldn't even see around me.

"Until we have terms wit de humans, yes. Dat is acceptable. Darouk, bring down the food for de giant!"

A younger howler came down from the tree, one with a black and white pattern on its haunches that I thought I recognized, and handed something wrapped in leaves to Aisling. She took it, swallowing hard, and I finally realized how *young* she looked. Like, seventeen or eighteen at the oldest, and her expression said her world had just fallen apart.

"You wanna go hunt that pig?" the howler asked. "It's bigger than one of your jeeps. Good eating on that."

"Wait here," I said. "We need to handle the girl who's Changing first."

22

ALIEN TAKE-OUT

AISLING

I could barely make myself breathe.

Dusty... Rigs said in my head, *What the hell was all that?*

I'm fucked, I'm so fucked, they're going to find me and take me and...

Stop panicking. We'll figure it out. Why didn't you say anything? Those bindings the matriarch mentioned? Is this what you haven't been able to talk about?

I made myself take a deep breath and push the sudden terror aside.

I'm sorry. Yes. Part of it. Mom oathbound me not to talk about it unless someone already knows what I am and brings it up.

Dammit. I had figured she was something Else, but not details. Shit. Getting you away from the military isn't going to be easy.

I know. But it's Mom's people that scare me. The tribes will sell them my info in a hot second. Oh, and the bloody idiots just used my real name in front of human soldiers and I can't do a damned thing about it!

Everything that could go wrong was going wrong, and now I had to go to jail for a guy who was an idiot, an asshole, and also already taken. Oh yeah, and my mother had fucked up my mind over something to do with him. And the Dohoulani were going to give me up to the Elsecomers and then that side of the family would probably come kidnap me or something, because the refugee tribes are like the galaxy's worst gossips and there was *no way* my existence would stay secret now that they had "known names" to go with me.

And now I had to deal with delicate exhausting magic while people pointed guns at me and then let them take me away and maybe lock me up.

And it was my own fucking "foresight" that had told me to go down this path.

I took the package from Darouk. It was sort of a Dohoulani take-out box, made of large leaves soaked and dried into shape. Then I tried to push everything aside and take care of what was in front of me, because Zahra was going to die if the Hunger took her and we couldn't pull her back, and I didn't think I could take putting her down on top of everything else today. I gave the Elder a small bow, and she nodded and stepped back into the trees, disappearing moments later.

"What's in there?" the cat-headed soldier woman asked, nodding at the package. "God, that smells good."

"Dried mushrooms from a hotspot and jerky from something Radiant," I said, pulling open the leaves. "Mushrooms and meat both bioaccumulate Radiance, which fae bodies need. I'm going to take this over to Zahra now."

Zahra was pinned under Bastion's knee when I got back to them, foam on her lips and nothing but Hunger in her eyes. Tusks were visibly growing in the corners of her mouth.

"Shit, this is going to be messy," I said. "If you guys go hunt that monster pig, bring back a leg or something. She's likely to need a lot of bulk food as well as Radiance. I'm going to move quickly now to get some of this in her, don't shoot please."

"Do it," Hart said, nodding at the cat lady to step back. He kept watching me closely. I grabbed the largest dried mushroom in the package, took a breath, and darted forward into speed to get it in Zahra's mouth and away before she took my fingers off. I repeated the performance two more times, and a little bit of sentience started coming back into her eyes. It still looked like her body was inflating along with the tusks, though.

"What's happening to her?" Lutefiskr asked in horrified fascination.

"Her body's being reshaped by the Tree that Grows Between Worlds, the source of fae magic," I said. "Look with Sight, near that frequency I showed you for seeing glamours. If you're already totally colonized and can direct magical energy, there are windows when everything is malleable and can be shaped. By the way, this is probably going to knock her out, and maybe me too. I've got street clothes in a backpack under a weeping willow about two hundred yards downriver. If I have to go to prison I want to do it as Rue."

"Roberts, go get it," Hart said, and looked directly at me. "Show me what you're seeing."

Yesh master. I live to serve, I thought, pissed off at his high-handedness.

"Everything fae lives in symbiosis with the Tree," I said, and briefly shaped an armored claw on my right pointer finger, and pierced a little hole into my left pinkie. "Its sap flows in our all blood, but especially in sidhe blood."

I smeared mine onto the next mushroom.

"Sidhe? That's what you are?" Lutefiskr asked. I nodded. He turned sideways to Hart and said, "It's a term for mythological elves from Ireland and Scotland. Lucas named the Sith in *Star Wars* for them. They're, ah, mixed sorts, in the myths. But *epic.*"

"Pretty much," I said. "The best at everything, with the most awesome toys, deadly and beautiful beyond words, with a completely different morality than humans. They were also the first people from Earth to get off-world. Now they've come home."

"The Elsecomers? The Beautiful Monster type?" Lutefiskr said, eyes wide. I nodded and he swore. "And you're..."

"Local, okay?" I said. "And my mom died when I was fourteen. All the living family I know is human. But there's a... genetic component... to this Change. Your Hart probably has sidhe ancestors."

Lutefiskr looked like he wanted to object to something in that statement, but kept his mouth closed.

"The Elsecomers are cross-fertile with us?!?" Hart exclaimed, horrified.

"Yep," I said. "Possibly even more than with each other."

He swallowed hard, like he was trying to keep breakfast down.

"What are you doing?" Hart asked me.

"*'The sap of the Tree is the blood of the sidhe.'* Having my blood and magic inside her will help me shape the Change, make it less monstrous and, hopefully, less painful. Put your hand on my shoulder after I give her this. I'll have to mindspeak you."

I darted forward and got the bloody mushroom into Zahra's mouth. A brief shimmer of light ran over her as she swallowed, and a bit more of herself came back into her eyes.

"Remember the shape of your dreams," I said. "Choose to be more than others' fears."

Zahra's eyes closed, and a whimper escaped from her. Something seemed to roll through her body, under her skin, as if fighting back against my magic, and the heart of the light that makes me sidhe started burning, scintillating and dangerous.

"Choose, Zahra, choose the shape of what you'll become," I repeated, but I saw Hart notice the concern on my face. He didn't know what was going on, but could tell it was bad. I drew in a deep breath.

"Tech, we've got tainted magic," I said out loud. "Full Squid ink, I think. Skipped the checks last night because we were so busy hiding. You somewhere safe?"

Birch's radio crackled.

"I am, and Siren's ashore with the Runners making another fire. They're in a secure spot. Take what you need."

"Squid ink?" Hart asked softly.

"Contaminated Radiance," I said, and he frowned, obviously thinking all Radiance was a contaminant. "Everyone thinks it's humans versus Elsecomers out here, but there's someone else and they've got their own agenda. We call them Squids. They might be the faction infiltrating the sidhe, but we hardly know anything solid about them. Mostly they work through beglamoured agents who don't even realize what they're doing, or remember anything afterwards. We think they've been adding toxins to Radiance-contaminated food and distributing it experimentally; it was some charity rations that got Zahra. The Radiance starts a Change, but the contaminant makes it *bad*. This is the third case I've seen. Remember Zahra saying she felt like she was being turned into the shape of people's fears?"

He nodded, looking sickened.

"My troop has hunted things that felt similar," he said. I felt the restless magic in him too, wanting to shred and eradicate this. "Can you do anything?"

"Yeah," I said. "It's a sidhe thing, the reason we're called Shining Ones in folklore. If you burn bright enough against it, it can be purified, *if* the person affected chooses that. But it takes a lot of energy, that's why I checked my team was safe, in case I pull too much from them."

"Take what you need from me too," he said simply, and put his hand on my shoulder.

He touched me just down from my neck, his palm against bare skin. Strong hands, long fingers, calloused, steady. Dammit, why do the hot ones so often have to be gay? No, bi... even if that lust magic of his had been completely unintentional, and he was already in a relationship, he'd been *into* it. Dammit. I wanted those hands on *me*.

Focus, dammit!

"There might be a lightshow," I said. "And a minor Radiance Event. It's unpredictable."

"Birch, back up at least fifty feet and get the human soldiers out of the way," Hart said.

"He's probably okay," I said. "Already a practicing human mage. Usually means you've already found ways to ground magic without the Tree reshaping your body."

"Really?" Lutefiskr said. "Huh. Explains surviving some Radiance Events on the job."

"Go anyway," Hart said, and gestured to himself. "I don't want to risk you going through this."

Dammit dammit dammit. And they really care about each other.

"Okay, so put your hand on my shoulder. The first step comes from Norse myths," I said. "Like Odin, you've got to hang yourself upon the Tree, with one eye... well, perspective... in the Well of Memory and another gazing out from a high place, across all the worlds. Like this."

23

SCION OF THE TREE

ARTHUR

S he tipped her head back, closed her eyes, and her neck arched
long and swan-like up from cleanly defined collar bones. And
I'm going to have to admit, for a second, all I could really think
about was how her lips had felt against mine. She looked so *young,*
though, even if she didn't really act it. But she'd been out there
fighting things for at least five years... and the face that looked back
at me from the mirror every morning barely looked twenty...

*Dammit, she's half Elsecomer. Enemy of humanity. It doesn't
matter if she's of age or not.*

*She's hiding from the Elsecomers. Half human. She's fighting for
the survival and freedom of strangelings.*

She's mine. I don't care about any of the rest of it.

Except I did. *ARGH.* And my dirty-minded, hippy Nanna
would tell a different outrageous story every time someone asked
about Mom's father, so there *was* a big question mark over part of
my family's heritage.

Aisling's eyes caught mine and they were full of stars, as
bottomless as the marble-lined pool in our strange, changed
courtyard in the Box. Our courtyard, with its otherworldly tree,
whose sap I had just recently been drinking with William. The sap
that had finally made me start to feel *whole.*

The blood of the Tree waited in my veins like kerosene for a
match.

Wait, I started to say, but she was already rolling her shoulders and I felt her opening up to some kind of magic that I'd never felt, yet *knew* down to the marrow of my strangeling bones, and *needed* like I could die without it. Light bloomed around Aisling, a seed unfurling roots and leaves out of her heart... out of, I thought in a moment of odd poetry, out of the strange places love comes from.

Aisling reached out her arms and for a second I saw starlit branches supporting her as the Tree caught her, and an image of it blazed out around her, drawn in light, blinding, beautiful. The girl was crowned in stars and her feet danced in waters of mythic dreaming, her arms branches, her legs roots, the blood of the Tree of Worlds running strong through its chosen child.

Her mind touched mine, and our magic twined together and *ignited.* Light, blazing, brilliant, *Radiant,* poured through her, lighting her up like a sun on the riverbank. Bastion closed his eyes against it, blinded, but Zahra opened hers wide and light filled them, as if she were soaking it in. I saw the shadows running through her, spread through her body like poison tentacles, and a *wrath* rose in me like I'd never felt before. The monster inside me shook my depths, snarling at what it recognized as an inimical enemy.

Zahra roared, in rage and agony, overwhelmed as that light beat into the shadows filling her, burning them, and threw Bastion off of her. Oh god. She fell straight into *her* monster's grip, nothing sentient remaining in her eyes, shadows weaving all around her. I'd never seen anyone come back from Hunger this deep.

The Tree's light brightened, spilled into me. Stars floated like falling leaves down into the faery darkness in my core, illuminating for the first time what was imprisoned down there. Silver vines bound the great cat, pinned it and muzzled it. Light glinted on fangs a hands-breath long.

Aisling clapped her hands to the sides of Zahra's face, looking straight into her eyes.

"Sara Monique Little, now Zahra, I name *you.* Remember yourself!*"* she said in a voice of pure command. The monster froze. "Wake, and shape the form your soul was born to fill!"

Pure brilliant Radiance poured out of Aisling and into the giant. For a second it seemed the monster burned, incandescent, and then the wiry black hair all over her body fell away in ashes, the tusks melted back to barely more than regular teeth, and the almost skeletal nose regained human shape. She fell to the sand and convulsed, her spine straightening with each spasm. Strange markings blurred across her skin, red and white and black, and she screamed like agony was tearing her asunder. Inky black smoke rose from her mouth, condensing in the air above her.

Aisling went to her knees, gasping, not even enough energy left to keep standing.

Darkness twisted in the air above Zahra, its tendrils shaping into tentacles. They reached for Aisling.

Fierce, primal antipathy roused against it in me, everything fae and predatory coming to sword-point attention. Inside me, the great cat's snarl built. Its strength was visibly swelling as every falling petal of light landed on it. I was frozen, with no idea what to do. Its eyes caught mine, the same golden-green I see every morning in the mirror, and I knew beyond all doubt that for me, there would be no reshaping my monster.

For you, there will be no dream without the nightmare, its eyes seemed to tell me. *But I am strength, and I am power, and I am death to that creeping darkness.*

How? I asked.

Give me your hand.

I closed my eyes, and in my mind's eye, claws of light formed over my fingers, Radiant with the energy flowing through Aisling and I. The darkness hanging in the air moved for Aisling.

I moved faster.

Radiance blazed over my hand and golden claws tore into the darkness. Someone screamed, far away, and their magic shredded in the light of the eternal, blazing, unburnt Tree. The ink writhed, and embers snapped in the air until nothing of it remained.

The vision of the Tree grabbed me, flooding through me, and I saw its roots and branches and all the fine ways between probability and possibility and impossibility braiding through a suddenly illuminated world. The clawed hand at the end of my arm reached into that light, and power surged into me.

Oh god, the feel of that magic, like I'd been dying of thirst and suddenly collapsed into a river. I wasn't sure if it would save me or drown me. The faery monster in me gulped the light in with starved desperation, and I went to my knees, overwhelmed, seeing not the world but only this blazing flux of magic. Down in my darkness, knife-like teeth flashed and scraped at the silver bindings inside me, and the hand that was still mine went to my head as I screamed. I didn't know if I was tearing in two or coming back together. It felt like I was grounding out a lighting bolt, like that Tree Aisling spoke of had sent a root into me and found fertile ground that it would colonize completely. I tipped backwards and fell to the beach sand, burning up as though combusting. It was too much, far too much. It would rip me asunder; I couldn't handle it.

Inside me, the clawed paw at the end of my arm twisted and morphed into a fine boned hand, mine but... not. It caught the light pouring into me and twisted it up, deft, graceful, and wove a blazing blade of light from the wild energy, folding it back on itself over and over as if pattern welding it.

In the light of the blazing knife, the viney cage that held my monster illuminated. The monstrous cat rolled aside, and I got a glimpse of what he had been protecting. Antlers glowed gold in the darkness. There was a second flash, and I saw the elven face I see every morning in the mirror. Light flashed from the blade and a vine turned to ash. The sidhe boy inside angled the blade against another binding and something like lightning burned through me. That vine crumbled to blackness and ash.

That's me, I recognized with absolute certainty. *That's what I really lost when I was sixteen. The girlfriend who broke my heart was nothing compared to losing my own soul.*

That is Else, insisted the part of me that had been a soldier since leaving high school. *More Else than any monster I have ever fought.*

Another vine on the boy's cage charred to ash, and emerald-green eyes met mine, demanding. In the glare of the glowing blade in his hand, I saw his mouth had been sewn shut with the same silver vines. He reached that fine hand for mine, and I knew it was everything fae and wild and outside human control reaching for me. If I took that hand, everything I had done to hang onto my humanity, to stay in control and not let the magic steal away my essential self, could be lost.

Zahra rolled over and groaned. She opened her eyes in her large but mostly human face, and they were full of her own self, not a Hungering monster. Somehow she looked like a woman who had just gone through childbirth, exhaustion and triumph and awe mixed together in her expression.

I'm already far too Else for humanity, and the person I am could only have given her mercy, not a second chance. I can't take care of my people while staying so human I can't help them.

I reached inside and took that hand.

The world stopped burning. The Radiance flooding me was water, not fire, saturating parched and desperate ground. This wasn't being invaded, it was... accepting my birthright, the magic that should have been mine all along, that had been... stolen from me. Whose theft had broken me in two.

Some sort of ragged joy rang through me, and for a second my awareness flashed out through all the lands I patrol, that *other* way of seeing the world I'd caught glimpses of before suddenly crystallizing.

Then the other self inside me pulled forward, and I saw he was bound all over in the strange silver vines. One gagged his mouth, others tangled his antlers, and though he had some movement, both wrists were manacled. I touched one of those, and every bit of rage and despair and loss I'd felt at being sent to the Box came back to me. This... this was worse. This was essential self, confined and tortured.

In my hand I felt the hilt of the blade he'd made, and I knew as he placed it wordlessly there that I could shove it into his/ my heart and kill everything fae in me, burn out my magic and maybe even become human again. And oh god, I remembered that golden afternoon the siren had brought back, when things were simple and right and... easy, and my hand shook with how badly I wanted that back.

But the simple human soldier in that memory had no way to fight the darkness that had almost claimed Zahra, I thought. *And Aisling thinks it was from some research that's yet at an experimental stage.*

Foremost and final, my duty is to defend this world.

I grabbed the knife and started cutting vines.

24

THE BLADE OF LIGHT ON WATER

AISLING

The way the Tree's energies had poured through me left me feeling like a logging truck had run me over. My legs weren't quite responding and my brain was reeling. Whatever or whoever was behind that tainted magic had felt me blazing against it and fought back, *hard*. Other than being able to say it felt like whatever had gotten Coral's dad, I still wasn't sure what it actually was.

Inhuman. Old. Cold in a reptilian sort of way. And smart.

Please, please, don't let it be our worst theory.

I don't know how to save Coral if it is.

Zahra was on her side, eyes open, with the exultant expression of someone who'd just escaped hell and nut-punched every demon the way out. She looked like a nine foot tall African warrior woman, with *hair*. Lots of it. Vaguely tribal markings in red and black wove across her skin. She smiled at me, dragged her hand through the sand to give me a thumbs-up, and passed out.

Hart looked like the magic had hit harder him than her. I didn't understand why, though, because whatever magic had made claws of light form over his hand had been crazy-effective against that inky fog. His hands grasped at the river sand and his spine arched like he was convulsing. Shit, he almost looked like he was Cascading too, but that was... should be... impossible. The Tree's light flared over his body, though, blazing out his eyes and silently screaming mouth. Gold dust drifted off his antlers.

I had no idea what I'd done to him. *Nothing* intentionally. But the second he'd touched my Tree-aligned energies... oh fuck. He was a *strangeling*. Touching my magic today could have been his first contact with the Tree as it aligns to the sidhe. And the sidhe have a considerably different relationship with it than most.

What the hell is happening to him? I thought, frantically trying to figure it out. While I hesitated something changed. The energy steadied, grounded, started to flow somehow *right*. Then I felt another great pulse of Tree energy pass into and through him like a lightning bolt into his body. It reverberated out through his land-bond, peeling like thunder out across his land.

The Tree was claiming him, claiming him utterly, and announcing it to everyone with the ears to hear.

While we were right on the edge of the Elsecomers' no-man's-land.

There were people with exactly the pointy ears to hear, right down the river from us.

We need to get the fuck out of here, NOW.

But I couldn't even get to my feet. My nerves were buzzing like I was pure static electricity on the inside. I rolled over and started dragging myself to him, and then realized I didn't even know if touching him would be help or not.

Hart opened eyes that glittered like dark emeralds, and I was *certain* they had been a much lighter green before. He breathed deeply, and seemed to just savor the air's taste for a second. Then he looked at me. Old, wild magic stirred in his eyes, magnetic and fearsome and deeply fae. A little smile pulled at his mouth, and something simply deliciously male in his gaze said I was already his, inevitably his, and everything from this point forward was simply formalities.

Gods fucking damn, I thought. *His sense of timing sucks.*

No man had ever looked at me like that. I wanted to hiss and snarl back; I wanted to climb on top of him and let the world completely fuck off while I claimed him back.

The first impulse wanted to claw the second one to shreds.

I had absolutely no idea what to do.

Every radio on his troops suddenly squawked to life.

"Aircraft incoming!" Rigs' voice yelled through the walkie talkies, not bothering with masking distortions. "Hide them, hide Slayer and Hart, do it now!"

Humans don't have aircraft anymore.

There was a moment of horrified silence, then Birch yelled, "Do it!" and a second later his hands were under my arms and pulling me upright. We stumbled up above the flood line and he helped me get behind a fallen cottonwood log. A big black guy with bat ears helped Hart over it and next to me.

"Hide in the land magic," I whispered, drawing it up over me and letting my conscious mind spread out into it. Rigs grabbed at my magic and I dug my hands into the sandy bank to help him ground here. Thank the gods neither maneuver required much in terms of personal power; I was running on fumes.

Next to me Hart watched what I was doing and seemed to get it. He was fully landbound here, and that bond was conscious now. Hiding us in the forest's energies came to him as easily as if he were pulling a blanket over us.

My traitor id went straight to imagining what it would like to do with him under blankets.

Focus, I told myself. *We are in so much danger right now. No, it is* not *hot!*

"I feel them coming," Hart whispered to me, grabbing my hand. "They're almost here."

Shh, I answered. *I don't know if they can overhear this, but they'll definitely hear anything we say out loud. And the sidhe hardly ever have kids; if they see us, they'll take us.*

Something whooshed over the water, coming upriver and braking with a hard spin.

"**Human troopers,**" a melodic male voice said through some kind of perfectly clear megaphone, above and over the water, "**You are zero point three kilometers past the boundary of the Freeport's Exclusion Zone. Retreat or be vaporized.**"

Lutefiskr... *Birch*... did just about the bravest thing I'd ever seen anyone do. He stepped forward and answered.

"We're in the middle of a medical emergency," he said. "We didn't realize we'd crossed your border. We'll leave now."

"**Is your medical emergency what caused the disturbance in the land energies?**" the voice asked.

"Yeah, probably. I don't know anything about land energies," Birch answered, trying to keep his voice steady. Humans in the war had rarely survived direct encounters with the Beautiful Monsters.

I peeked through the roots of the fallen tree to see what was going on, and Hart, moving with complete silence, leaned over me, his body pressed against and over mine again. And oh hell, but the land-bound part of my magic pretty much purred and rubbed against his.

Oh, fuck *me,* I thought, and *Yes, do* went the uninhibited little idiot inside me.

Little quakes rippled out through the land energies again.

"**Lie. There it is again,**" said the chestnut-haired elf in the front of the weird hovercraft thing floating just above the water's edge. He was tall and his uniform looked like an officer's variant. Another four sidhe in white and silver uniforms stood behind them, guns right out of a sci-fi computer game held ready in their hands, and one other sat at the back of the craft. He had no weapons visible and wore simple dark clothes that looked somehow more like a karate *gi* than a uniform, and his black hair was streaked at the temples with white.

Silver magic flared around the team leader, and I felt him try to catch Birch's mind with his own. Birch grounded and sent magical shields spinning around himself, just like I'd taught him, and I felt Hart slip just a tiny bit of land energy to him. Silver glamours wafted over the lieutenant and spun away.

For a second, everyone just stared at each other.

"Well, hopefully your second-in-command will be more cooperative," the officer said, shrugging, and smoothly raised his weapon and fired. A bolt of light flashed out of its muzzle. Hart almost went over the fallen tree, but I grabbed him and pulled him back.

Five feet from Birch, the bolt stopped and hung fizzling in the air. Rigs' hand appeared first, and then the rest of him faded into view, wearing an elder Jedi's robes and definitely not looking like a his usual basement-dwelling nerd self. This Rigs was craggily elven, with blue-gray skin and black-light hair, with ears pointier than mine. I wondered if it was his vision of where his Cascade was heading; so far we'd managed his Change to keep him looking fully human.

Hart looked at me questioningly.

Illusion, I mouthed. The costume was a message to anyone with the eyes to see it.

"That is *sooo* cool," Rigs said to the sidhe officer. "Stun beam, right? This doesn't feel like it'd actually disintegrate anyone."

He shook his hand, and the beam dispersed into the air like dust in a sunray. I grounded harder for him, and his power quested out, tasting their technology.

" *That* was," the officer said, frowning, and tapped something on his gun and fired again. The new bolt was red, and it also froze and then dispersed into the air. Electricity cackled, and the guys on the boat jumped as their guns sparked and started smoking. One of them started swearing, words I remembered from when my mom once broke her thumb while helping with home repairs.

"Yeah, so, I can do that to your hovercraft too," Rigs said, as Hart's soldiers drew and aimed at the elves in the boat. "Division 51 and the Underhill Railroad just had a little argument, we've sorted things, and we're all going to head home now, okay? This had nothing to do with you and we'd like to keep it that way. I assume you'd rather not walk back to Minneapolis."

The man in the back of the boat laughed, the rich laugh of someone who could appreciate being unexpectedly bested. And then he disappeared, like, just winked out of existence. Something dark flickered by the farthest soldier, and he was abruptly on his knees, gasping like he'd taken a fist to the stomach, his gun a dozen feet away from him on the river bank. Another flicker, and the giant with Zahra was down, and another, and another. Light danced like sunlight on the river over weapons like mine, dulled or maybe baton shaped, appearing and disappearing as someone moved at speeds far beyond my fastest through the soldiers. I could almost see what he was doing, slipping in and out of the Tree's magic through depths I'd never plumbed. There was a music to it, a beauty, and I yearned for it like I'd never yearned for anything.

In under five seconds, the entirety of Division 51's soldiers were downed and disarmed, and Birch and Rigs both had golden swords at their throats.

Then I understood what Enzula had said about never mastering my magic without training.

"Finely done, young cousin," the weapons master said to Rigs, his eyes twinkling with good humor. "But perhaps overconfident. It isn't technology that makes the sidhe what we are."

Rigs tilted his head and looked at the elder as if unsurprised by the demonstration.

"Am I speaking to the Blade of Light on Water?" he asked, and the swordsman drew back slightly, surprised.

"Aye, you are, m'boy. And how would you know that?"

"Meheleb va tiene hor," Rigs answered. "I'm just trying to get my people out of here."

"You know sidhe words?" he asked softly. "And how would a local born child know those?"

"My cousin knew the son of one of your people," he said. "She learned a bit about the sidhe from his mother."

Well, that was as fine a bit of fae truth-twisting as I'd ever heard. Of course I'd known my little brother, for the half day or so he'd lived. Sudden tension ran through the sidhe man.

"Knew? And what happened to that son and mother?" he asked, his blade hovering closer to Rigs' throat. Then his eyes narrowed, and he turned his blade sideways and put the flat side of it right through the illusion, and sighed. His swords turned into a cloud of gold dust, then faded out of reality, just like mine do. He put his hands on his hips casually. Even without a blade at his throat, Birch looked like he wasn't even breathing.

"A redcap, and chronic iron poisoning from embedded shrapnel. Apparently it largely disabled her magic," Rigs said. "I never knew either, myself, though our town is small and I saw her at gatherings a few times. She looked human."

"And your cousin?"

"She's fae too, but can pass. Running a mission for the Underhill Railroad right now."

"Which is?"

"We run strangelings away from human authorities and down to a settlement in the middle of the Edgelands. These soldiers were trying to catch us because they thought we were smuggling for you Elsecomers, and our charges ended up in the water and hypothermic. The giant girl there is one of them. But we just worked out a temporary truce with these guys and got them talking to the local refugee tribes that so far they've been shooting at, so please don't kill them. They'll just be replaced with people who won't make any terms at all."

"Ah. Indeed. Though they've left our protection, we'd rather no one shot at the tribes," the sidhe man said. "I would speak with your cousin. A kinswoman of mine went missing in the hinterlands, before the Return. Knowing what happened to her would... ease my mind."

"She's terrified of the sidhe," Rigs said frankly. "Would you swear not to take her away without her consent, or do her harm, and the same for anyone she is with?"

"I would, if she'd spend an afternoon speaking with me. She goes to this Strangelingtown regularly?"

"Yes. I think she could meet you, alone, after this university term ends in a couple of months. Right now, her studies are somewhat overwhelming."

"I'll leave a communicator at the strangeling settlement, then," the sidhe man said. "Tell her to call and ask for Maddoc."

"I will," Rigs promised.

Maddoc looked at him for a minute and a little smile bent his mouth.

"This was nicely done. Canny. Promising. I have an old friend who I think might like an apprentice like you. Come yourself, and I'll connect you."

"I appreciate the offer, but have commitments," Rigs said, eyes wary. "Perhaps later."

The corner of the elder sidhe's mouth twitched wryly, and his eyes twinkled.

"Do the stars never call you, boy?" he asked. "Do the limits of human science sate your curiosity?"

Rigs' eyes went huge, and he sucked in his breath.

Fuck. How to hit my friend directly in the temptation. How had he known?

"I'll see you again," Maddoc said, grinning, and then winked away and reappeared in the back of the hovercraft. He made a little circular gesture with his hand and the officer sighed and it turned, lifted above tree level, and sped away. A second later, they were gone.

Birch's knees went out, and he sat straight down in the sand. I slumped against the fallen tree in relief and bumped directly against one of Hart's arms, knocking him slightly off balance and putting us in skin contact again. Green eyes caught mine, and my breath hitched. A little smile, too knowing, tugged at his mouth. His eyes said I was *his*.

And maybe, a tiny bit, I wanted to see how that fit.

"Slayer!" Rigs yelled. "Cut that the fuck out, I don't care how hot you think he is, I can feel what you two are doing to the land energies all the way to St. Cloud! Do you *want* the Elsecomers coming back?"

Hart gritted his teeth and shook his head. The fae wildness faded and his magic pulled back, and his body language... changed. He closed his eyes for a second, and when he opened them again, they were green-gold, not dark emerald.

Weird.

"I need to check my people," he said, giving me a look of pure frustration, then stood up and stepped over the fallen tree. He looked back, thought about offering me his hand, then reconsidered the wisdom of that. "And you *are* under arrest."

"Are we doing *that* again?" I asked, following him over the fallen tree, getting the impression he was more saying the first thing that came to mind and not something he really meant. "I said I'd come with you and teach you how to be sidhe. After that, if *I'm* not coming almost continuously, I'm heading back to classes."

Rigs' illusion slapped a hand over his eyes. Birch started laughing helplessly, like you do after a close call.

"These are going to be a long couple days," he said.

"He's neither unemployed nor a musician," Rigs said sympathetically to him. "And her relationships rarely last beyond concert afterparties."

"Oh, I know her from the SCA. She's infamous. Awesome cosplay, by the way," Birch said. "No lightsaber, though?"

"Haven't gotten one working yet, and this illusion was kind of slapped together," Rigs said. "Wouldn't want something I know is non-functional as part of it. I mean, we've got a prototype, and it cuts through just about anything, but you've got to be in full welder's gear to even turn it on. Sufficiently portable heat shielding is turning out to be a real bitch. We really need one for taking apart regenerating monsters, though."

"You're seriously trying to make one?"

"It'd be better than having to steal jackhammers at 4 a.m."

"Tech!" I snapped. "Op sec!"

"Slayer! Op sec! Don't sleep with the guy trying to arrest you!"

"Ahh, I'm just going to sexually harass him till he throws me out of his prison," I answered. Hart stopped where he was checking the guy who'd helped him hide, closed his eyes and his hands balled into fists. His soldier started laughing, and I overheard something like *M'dude, you're the one who wanted to catch her.*

"That's not how prison works," the cat-headed woman growled at me, limping over to join us.

"Have you tried?" I asked her, and she glared at me.

"We okay then?" Rigs asked. "I'm starving after spending that much magic. I'm gonna go get some fast food and find somewhere I can upload everything I scanned off those blasters and hovercraft. Lemme know when you need me to come pick you up."

"Will do. Good thinking, how you bargained with the elder."

"Hey, can't lose you. I'd have to deal with Siren's creepers myself," he said, shuddering. "Well, best of luck, I'm off."

"Yep," I said. "May the Force be with you."

Birch laughed, and did the Vulcan split fingered hand sign at him. Rigs' illusion grinned, signed it back, and faded out.

Zahra didn't look like she'd woken up yet, so I went and sat down next to Birch.

"That was really brave," I said quietly. "I appreciate it. And I'm not a home-wrecker; if you guys are exclusive, just say so and I'll leave him alone."

"Hart and I are not a couple!" he exclaimed, loud enough that everyone near us burst out laughing in that *oh my god we're still alive* way. "He meant *work partners!*"

"Oh," I said, grinning. "Well, then. I'm definitely going to try getting myself kicked out."

25

POLICIES

ARTHUR

My head was spinning, I felt like I was trying to think through two brains, and there was still so much magic sparking through my system I felt like I might simply float off into the sky. At least half my people were already rooting for the Green Lady, both her Underhill Railroad for free strangelings and her obvious intention to, at the very least, flirt incessantly with me for the next few days.

I wanted to do a lot more than flirt. How much of that was *me,* though, and how much was this magic twining through me?

My troops had been disabled without actual serious harm, just some strains and bruises, which was both a relief and possibly more intimidating than anything else the Elsecomers could have done. One guy, taking out an entire army troop without significantly injuring anyone, in under five seconds? Fuck. And the way his magic had felt while he did it, like a silver breeze moving across the riverbank... it called me. And from her expression, it had called Aisling even more.

Those Elsecomers were the same as the two of us. It screamed through my bones the second I saw them, that those... invaders... were *my people.* Every one of the Beautiful Monsters on that hovercraft thing had looked like her and me, but there was more to it than that. The connection to that Tree I'd seen, when the magic was flowing, ran through them strong and pure. And this... other self... down in me, that I'd started to free... he'd looked at them and

"Me? Nah. I just ate French fries and sat lookout while my friend did," she said, smiling brightly. "Last time it was just to get your patrol routes and schedule. Tech's doing a deeper dive now. He'll make sure we've got adequate blackmail on your superiors to buy my freedom, if it comes to that."

"Who are you *working* for?" Black asked.

"No one," the girl in green responded. "Or rather, the people we run. Free strangelings. We're just trying to do the right thing, and cells coordinate, but we're all independent. The Railroad takes care of the people nobody else protects."

"What do you mean?" Jones asked, walking over.

"Well, the Elsecomers don't need any help. You saw them. Humanity has its remnant armies, and you guys, and so on. So strangelings who want to stay free, and the refugee tribes who need trees and open spaces? That's our corner."

"What's with killing giants on the North Shore and all that?" he asked, considering her words.

"Gotta keep the monster hunters away from my people. And there's a little Mihooli tribe sitting on their nests right by where the Temperance River giant was hunting. They'd have been found and exterminated if all those military units went through there," she said, then grinned. "Also, the adrenaline rush is kind of what I live for. Cutting loose like that is a blast. Figured we'd have to cover the fight sounds anyway, so Tech brought a DJ setup and spun for the whole fight, under cover of silence glamours. It was fricken' awesome."

Dear god. They treat monster hunting like attending an underground rave?

A big grin spread over Jones' face as he saw my horrified expression.

"Can I join your team?" he asked her, watching me. "My man here makes all this feel like *work*."

Black glared at him so I didn't have to.

"Mihooli?" she asked.

"Owlies. 'Mihooli' is what they call themselves."

"You're fighting for *owlies?* They're like sky raccoons!" Serena hissed, scandalized.

"Don't say that to their faces! They've had an ongoing feud with the Rax for like ten years. But they're flipping awesome aerial reconnaissance and support," she answered. "Even if I have to listen to them bitch about my bad Tradish every time I talk to them."

"Your Tradish does suck!" the alien lemur hiding back in the trees said, finally peeking out again. His fur and ears were still pressed tight to his body in fear. "If you ever get to one of the big trade stations, you're going to be paying *extortionate* rates for anything you want, sounding like some mud planet yokel and disgracing your people."

"Yeah, yeah, whatever. You think I'm ever getting off-world?" she asked. "And how is your English so good, anyway?"

"Used to run a newsstand in the Freeport. Had one in the biggest refugee camp on Briargard, started another here after the evacuation," he said, climbing down. "Till the matriarch said our kids need trees and space. Talked to all kinds of humans and Changed there, and they didn't have any Tradish back then, so I picked up English."

"What do you mean, humans and Changed?" Serena asked. "And camps? Evacuation? Everyone in the cities died in the Broken Dawn."

"Did not. I think the Freeport had a twenty percent survival rate, something like that. Mostly very confused people who really want your leaders to get those truce papers signed so they can talk to their families outstate again. But I had a lotta regulars who were at least born human."

"What truce papers?" I asked, confused. I'd never heard a word about a potential truce. To my knowledge, no one had.

"The ones they offered a week after the main hostilities ended. Full text got printed in all our local news, in Tradish and English, didn't you see it? Seemed reasonable enough to me."

"Everyone here was kids or not born yet," Birch said. "And I've never heard anything about a truce or any communication from the Elsecomers at all. By the way, did you recognize anyone in the hovercraft? Was that some sort of elite unit?"

"Nah, though the old man could probably be considered one on his own; he used to train the lord of Briargard's personal guards and children in close range combat. That was just a city guard patrol and the Blade, who was probably with them for weapons training when they got the call to check things out. Most of the guards are bored to tears. They probably all jumped at the chance to get out of the walls."

"Bored? They stole our cities and destroyed our world and now they're *bored* with ruling?" Serena exclaimed.

"Ruling? The city there's a freeport. Nobody rules a freeport, it runs on rules developed for independent space stations. There's a city council, the spaceport authority, and security guarantors, and they work things out between them. Our matriarch was on the council for a few years, even had local-borns vote for her. She knows what's what. Most of the elves are just working security, or drinking and placing dumb bets. So, wanna go get that pig?"

"Spaceport?" Birch exclaimed. "So there *is* one! How do elves even have a spaceport anyway?"

"Can I explain the Elsecomer side of the Broken Dawn later, possibly somewhere with booze?" Aisling asked. "How and why the Elsecomers showed up here is a fairly long and weird story, and I'd rather get off this beach before they come back. Also, I'm starving. Did anyone grab my backpack? I need a granola bar."

Roberts picked it up from near his feet and looked at me.

"Search it first. Serena, if you please."

"It's just clothes, snacks, and twenty bucks," Aisling said, shrugging. "Oh, and a belt knife. I don't carry I.D. or anything like that on these runs."

Serena peered in and then cautiously pulled out a dry bag. Inside was exactly what she'd described - bare minimum gear, homemade leather moccasins, threadbare street clothes, and wilderness snacks. An old Bowie knife from probably the 1950s was the only bit of dangerous gear.

"Birch, you want to take this?" I asked, handing it over. The steel in it bit at my hand. Dammit, this magic flooding me was making me even more iron sensitive, and I already was the worst in the unit for that.

"Okay," he said, standing up and putting it on his belt. "I'll get it back to you at Midsommer Fields, Hildie."

"Sure," she agreed, totally assuming I was going to let her go, and grabbed the snack bar I tossed to her out of the air.

"Want to switch to street clothes now?" I asked.

"Later, when we're leaving the Edgelands," she said. "Don't want to wreck them if the pig hunt gets messy. If you're chilled you're welcome to the sweater, though. I haven't really gotten cold since I went after a snow dragon a few years back. That hunt did some weird shit to me. But hey, I can call myself a dragonslayer now."

"That where 'Slayer' comes from?" Jones asked.

"You bet!" she answered. It somehow didn't sound like the full truth. I thought I heard a sigh from my radio.

Her sweater was soft in my hands, though, and I *was* chilled. My clothes were still damp from river water and the escaping mother had taken my jacket. I hesitated, though, looking at it. It was just a homespun thing in a muted pine green, and looked like it'd be oversized on Aisling. I pulled it over my head, being careful to keep my antlers from tangling, and felt instantly warmer. It was probably the first civilian garment I'd put on in four years. Weird. Nice. And it smelled like *her.*

"You're going to be sitting in a Jeep under guard for that hunt," I said, trying to maintain some control while part of me wallowed purring, in the scent of her. She raised her eyebrows disbelievingly, but there was something else in her eyes too. "What?"

"Oh, just suspected I'd be warming you up eventually," she said, something almost possessive in her voice as she looked at me in her pullover. "Didn't think it'd be this fast."

Well, I walked right into that one.

She grinned at me, mischief dancing in her eyes, and more than a hint of after-battle *I want to drag you into the bushes and celebrate we're alive.*

Oh hell. I want that too.

My people were definitely placing bets on us.

"Let's go," I said, shaking my head. Bastion picked up the unconscious girl, and we started trudging back up the river bank. "Somebody call ahead and let them know who's coming with us, so no one freaks out and shoots. Are comms working again?"

"Yep, Captain, working fine," Rigs' voice came from Birch's radio. "Well, considering how crappy your gear is, anyway."

"Fucking hell, how long is he going to be in our systems?" I demanded.

"Long as you've got Slayer. Hey Birch, can I read your fanfic?"

"Sure, why not," he said, looking bemused. "Weren't you going to be digging up blackmail?"

"Yeah, that took like five minutes to find. Hoo *boy.* One of your superiors is running a porn studio with enlistee and prisoner actors, and everyone immediately above him is taking a cut of the profits. Those are funding all sorts of illegal or simply scandalous things on the side. Apparently they're making more from that than they actually get in local defense funding, especially off the G-Bat superhero parody series. They're gonna be RICH if we ever get internet back. Are your people taking part in that voluntarily? I mean, they look happy enough... Wow. Anyway, I really need to bleach my brain with some good old-fashioned Away Team smut right now."

"Are you for fucking real?" I demanded, as multiple members of my team, both human and strangeling, suddenly found the sky or their shoes very interesting.

Oh god. All those jokes Jones makes.

"Told ya I knew starlets," he said, shrugging.

"They had booze and mary jane," Roberts said. "Not just that crap beer substitute we get in the Box. Not all of us like being celibate, you know!"

I ground my teeth, unable to completely blame them.

"Celibate?" Aisling asked, horrified. "Tech, check my bands' tour schedules. I might need an emergency bang after all this."

"Like hell I will," her friend answered. "I'm still finding glitter in my van from the last time you had a 'bass lesson'."

My brain stuttered to a complete stop.

"Hart thinks the key to staying in full control of ourselves is living like monks and repressing every fae instinct," Black said, glancing pitying eyes in my direction. I wasn't hiding this at all, apparently. "Captain, everything is consensual. I monitor it. Corporal Bartles has a furry fetish and I agreed to let him lick my boots occasionally in exchange for veto rights over content."

What? Even Black was in on it?

"Repression is *not* how you manage a fae side," Aisling said, both horrified and trying not to laugh at me. "Unless that's what yours specifically needs, I suppose. How often do you guys turn into spree killers?"

Shit. The exact words I used to describe the monster inside me.

"Well, how do you manage it?" I demanded.

"Oh, banging musicians; hunting cryptids; and getting wasted on moonshine. My girlfriends and I get drunk, naked, and run down monsters in the woods and eat them raw every full moon or so," she answered, shrugging like those were all normal things and the last wasn't an image that was already burning its way through my brain and giving my fae side an entirely new set of *ideas.* "But basically you've got to eat enough Radiance and let your magic do its thing at least a bit, whatever that is. Trying to bottle it up will cause *explosions.*"

I took a deep breath, trying to relax my shoulders and loosen my hands out of the fists they'd formed.

"Were you coerced?" I asked the guys who'd shrugged.

"To make porn or to live in the Box and be celibate?" Jones asked. "And did you not wonder where the money for the new division tees and rec room TV came from last month?"

I closed my eyes and counted to ten.

"Oh shit, this must be why Bartles was asking me for racy Batman stories..." Birch muttered.

I stared at my people. This had been going on for years, right in front of my willfully oblivious eyes, and I'd kept myself from acknowledging it and dealing with the problem. I didn't even know what I *could* do to deal with it, if the set of names and ranks most likely responsible were running things.

What else am I missing?

"Let's go kill that fucking pig," I said.

26
ALONG THE RIVER

AISLING

Hart looked overwhelmed, and I didn't get the impression he normally let much phase him. My fingers twitched to twine through his but I had no idea if that would be welcome or not. His troop hefted their gear, though, and started limping back to where I'd disabled their trucks.

"You okay?" I asked Hart, and something flashed through his eyes then faded away. For a second he looked simply and completely lost. I wished I could kiss him again. What would a smile look like on his face?

"No," he said very quietly. His voice shook and I wasn't sure if it was with rage or despair or just frustration. "I have spent years turning a troop of humanity's castaways into the region's best monster hunting team, and today I find out that half of who we've been hunting are refugees. My own superiors are exploiting my people while also thinking we should die at each other's hands. I finally caught the girl who irradianced me, promptly lost control of my magic, and the first thing I did was make out with her. And, *incidentally*, I'm somehow like the people who broke the world."

"Irradianced you?" I asked, frowning.

He looked at me, exasperation in his eyes.

"Outside Grand Marais. Fighting wyverns."

"Captain Holt?"

Oh gods. The cute solider I thought I somehow killed was walking down the beach next to me.

"Used to be," he shrugged, but like a man trying to ignore a gaping wound. "Then I grew antlers and my C.O. told me I was dead."

"Oh gods. I am sorry. I am so, so sorry. And I have no idea how that happened. The shining thing isn't at all the same as molding Radiance in a strangeling. No one's ever just *seen* me and Changed."

"Yeah. Saw that, today."

He kicked the sand, and his shoulders sank again.

"Felt more like being a match next to a candle, I guess," he said softly. "There was a lot of that on the beach now too."

"Can I do... anything?"

"You already promised the Howlers you'd teach me how to live with this," he said.

I nodded, feeling like that was grossly inadequate. We walked in silence for another minute.

"It's a lot," I said. "Maybe you should all just up stakes and head for Strangelingtown?"

He stared into the distance, thinking.

"I can't," he said. "Too many people rely on us to protect them."

Yeah, I got that. Just abandoning my patrol lands would be beyond me too.

"I'm sorry," I said.

He shook his head and kept walking.

"The howler lady said we were bound magically," he said. "What did she mean?"

I hesitated.

"My mother made me forget something, *someone* I think, a few months before she died," I said, looking at the probable someone. Dear gods, he was handsome. Every line of his body, the way he moved, the curve of his lips, the way frustration flashed in his eyes when he looked at me. If I'd run into another kid with sidhe heritage back then, someone like this... I'd have been over the moon that someone else like me was out here. "Swore I'd be dead within a year if I didn't."

"When was that?"

"About ten years ago," I said. "I was fourteen."

Hart looked at me, confused, and gave me a once-over.

"Oh gods, don't judge my age by this face," I said. "Siren and Tech give me grief for looking like jailbait who couldn't buy her own beer every time I drop my illusions. Real-life me is a bitter grad student that no one cards."

"Real life you?" he asked softly.

"Dude, it's not like I could live like *this* and stay free," I said, waving at my face and body. "I wear an unobtrusive human face and work an underpaid job and drive a pickup that should have been scrapped thirty years ago. I'm in the wardrobe. Only time all *this* comes out is for hunts."

"You wear another face?" he said, shocked.

"Illusions!" I said, laughing a little. "No horror movie crap."

He went silent, his eyes wondering.

It was a bad idea. If we didn't work something out now... but then again, Birch already knew my human face anyway. And stupid as it was, I wanted him to see *me*.

"Okay," I said, and swiped my hand across my face and looked at him from my early teenage human seeming for a minute, then waved my hand across my face again and dismissed it. "I used to look like that."

Shock and recognition warred with confusion in his suddenly dark eyes, and no small quantity of grief and betrayal.

"...Ashley?" he asked, aching emotion in his voice.

"A lot of people mispronounce Aisling like that," I said. "When I was a kid, I rarely bothered correcting them. Only my family and the aliens who insisted on a true name call me Aisling now, though. Did you know me?"

"It's blurry. There was a girl... she broke up with me and I decided to be a different person. Orderly. Organized. Went into the military..."

He looked sick. Sudden fury shook his frame as that dark green energy flared over him again and then faded away.

"I'm sorry. I keep feeling like you're familiar too," I said glumly. "If I met you back then, and saw you were going to Change to be like me, I'd have wanted to know you. And my mother was... crazy paranoid, before she died. Wouldn't let me have friends or pets or anything. Bound me magically to forget something she thought would get me killed."

"Why?" he asked. "And you can tell when someone's going to Change?"

"She was dying, needed me to finish something for her, and didn't want me... distracted. Or fucking people up, who knows, she thought I was a walking Radiance Event when I was a kid. Maybe I was. Our magic was pretty different, and I never saw her shape a strangeling transformation," I said. "When people are about to Cascade... Usually I can tell. There's a kind of sparkliness. Then if they get a bit of Radiance, it'll go off like fireworks and they start Changing. There's a window when that energy is reshaping everything and I can mold it. That's why my team can still pass as humans. I caught them as the Changes were starting and slowed it waaay down and shaped them for hidden transformations and magic aptitude."

"Your tech guy looked pretty Else," he said, skeptical, his eyes golden-green again.

"The whole thing was illusion. In person he can pass, for now anyway. But people often have an idea where their Cascade will head. I guess he sees himself ending up something like that."

"Is it hard to maintain an illusion, and pass?" he asked, with everything he wasn't saying out loud aching behind those words.

I shrugged.

"Been doing it my whole life," I said. "Mom started when I was little, then I took it over once I was able. Helps to tie the magic to something solid, like a piece of jewelry. I wear a choker full of don't-notice-me glamours. That other face is more me than this is."

"Do you feel odd when you look in a mirror?" he asked, even quieter.

"No, because I don't," I said. "I never look at this face."

"*Never?*"

"Didn't say living in the wardrobe is all fun," I replied. "And as long as my mental image of myself is mostly human, I can be around human magic users without much suspicion."

"*That's* how you do it?" Birch asked, overhearing and joining us. I nodded.

"It's not *bad,* though, being sidhe," I said. "I get to be like the hard-drinking lovechild of the Flash and Buffy the Vampire Slayer. I'm flippin' awesome."

Dubious would just barely begin to describe the looks the two gave me then.

I gave them my biggest grin.

"Crazy Hildie, in a nutshell," Birch said, shaking his head.

"Show me another illusion," Hart said. "Something smaller."

He did want to learn. A wave of relief washed through me.

"It's usually best to start with mental influences, like *look away* glamours or *don't notice me* spells," I said, holding up my hand in front of me and closing it.

"He can do those already," Birch said dryly. "And let me say right now how much I've appreciated your training in warding away mental influences."

Hart flinched.

"Path to the Dark Side, dude," I said to Hart. "Gotta be careful with those."

"I *know,*" he said, light flashing in his eyes. "I don't *like* using that power. But it's the only way my people get any space or freedom."

"Fair enough," I said, shrugging. I knew I should care about humans more, but I spent so much time trying to keep strangelings from getting murdered by them that sometimes it felt a bit abstract.

I opened my hand. A white moth sat on my palm. At first glance it was just a cabbage moth, at second, Pictish swirls decorated its wings in silver. The morning sun shone through them, translucent, glowing, and it twitched and took a second to pause and groom its fuzzy antennas. Hart held out his hand and put it under mine, touching my fingers from below. Everything in me sat up and quivered again, and I had to close my eyes for a second. When I opened them again, the moth had crawled into Hart's palm as he took over the illusion, and emerald eyes glittered at me above it. His fingers caressed mine and my brain froze. A touch of a smile pulled at his lips, and the moth jumped into the sky and fluttered away.

"Interesting," was all he said, then pulled out his radio and called ahead that he was bringing in two captives and a cryptid, and not to shoot any of them.

"I am *not* your captive," I told him when he put the radio down.

He grinned at me and his face lit up. My heart skipped a beat. Nothing I'd been imagining held even a candle to the reality of him smiling.

"And yet, I've caught you," he said, and that smile got even brighter.

And dammit, he might have.

27

REPAIRS

ARTHUR

O h, Aisling's face when I told her I'd caught her. She was *pissed.* But tempted, too. It took her from being unearthly beautiful to a real woman, one I wanted to see sweaty and moaning.

This is a kink that's going to get me in trouble, I tried to tell my inner self, to no use whatsoever. The fae part of me, that had recognized her, was yearning for her almost as much as he was enraged that she could forget him, magic or no.

She didn't chose to leave me, she was forced. What am I, that just seeing her again would trigger my Change? What were we?

"Captain!" one of my troops who'd stayed to fix the personnel carrier called from where she'd been sitting lookout. "Everything okay? Some guy's been on our radios telling us that if we hurt the people you're bringing in we'll never have another electronic work for us. Holy fuck, did you actually catch *her?*"

I looked at Aisling, grinned, and wanted to say yes, but reconsidered the wisdom of that. She looked back at me, eyes sparking with temper.

"You didn't *catch* me, I gave you my parole," she snapped.

"Just technically, Lopez. She's consulting with us for a bit," I said. "Jones was right, she's not an enemy. Knows a lot we don't. How are repairs coming?"

"Crappy. She sliced three tires on the carrier beyond repair, and we've only got one spare. And your Jeep is trashed. Whole front is smashed, the engine is probably totaled, and the front axle is broken."

Well fuck. Div 51 is at the bottom of the supply chain. It could take months to get a replacement.

"Do you have anyone with smithing magics?" Aisling asked.

"Say what?" Lopez answered, blinking.

"Smithing magics. Fae, but can handle iron," she answered. "Good at metalworking, mining, and so on."

"That's possible?" I said. "I mean, I know trolls and giants have less trouble with it than the rest of us..."

"Yeah, one of my team is a smith and works as an auto mechanic for his day job," Aisling answered.

"Day job?" Serena asked, taken aback. "You have day jobs?"

"Well, *we're* not getting free food and housing and equipment," she answered, shrugging, as if that was what incarcerated life was all about. "Of course we've got day jobs, or classes, or both. We hunt monsters and guide Runners on long weekends and school holidays."

"Your whole team can pass for human," Serena said, staring, "And lives in the world and doesn't go on rampages."

"Yep," Aisling said, and then grinned insolently at me. "And I can discreetly solo stone giants that you lot need multiple military units to take down."

The monster inside me seemed to both purr and growl at that.

She likes aggravating me too, I thought, part of me dreading it and part of me grinning in anticipation.

"Team, gather up!" I called out to everyone who'd both stayed with the vehicles and who was coming in from the river, and we took a few minutes to bring everyone up to speed on where we were at, what the Underhill Railroad was actually doing, and that we had a tentative truce with them and the Dohoulani.

"Captain, this all sounds... bad," Jorgensen, said. He was a private in Birch's team and liked keeping things simple.

I nodded.

"The whole situation's bad," I said. "Birch, can you explain why this at least solves some problems for us?"

He told everyone about the termination policies, and how getting people out to Strangelingtown could save them from having to shoot their own comrades-in-arms. We're a tight team; a lot of eyes widened in horror when he explained that.

"Fuuuck," Jorgensen said. "I don't want a different captain, better to have someone already Changed than another who turns redcap when he gets pissed off."

Aha, so that's how Jorgensen ended up stuck in our unit.

He was solid, but tended to take things very literally. Couldn't say I was entirely surprised he angered people who couldn't work around that. Redcaps transformations happened almost exclusively to people with fascist tendencies, "master race" types who had little patience for things like a touch of autism.

"Yeah, and I much prefer being second in command to being in charge, and I think we can all agree on that," Birch said, to a round of heads nodding. "So let's make the best of this. Anyone know where the tools we took from the howlers yesterday are?"

Jorgensen shrugged and ambled away to get them from the troop carrier.

The howler Aisling had called Darouk came down from the tree he'd been waiting in, examined the tools, and asked if he could call his uncle to come take them. I gestured *go ahead*, and he ululated something up to the trees. About half a minute later, a smaller brown and grey howler cautiously crept down and joined us. He took the wrenches, dropped them into a shoulder bag, and pointed at the sliced up tires and at Aisling and said something incomprehensible.

Listening to them speak their strange language tickled my brain weirdly, like part of me was trying *really* hard to figure it out.

"Faza wants to know if your tech guy can fix a molecular fuser," Darouk said. "He worked in the starport when they were first converting it from an airfield. They kept using some of the old trucks for the first five years, and they had tires like this. But the fuser we tried smuggling out got broken when it went through the city shields."

"We can try," Aisling said. "Go get it. Tech would be happy to have a shot at fixing it through me."

"How's that work?" I asked.

"We've been practicing together for ten years and our immediate group is a bondnet, so we can work some magic through each other. He and I are like third cousins or something so it's easiest for the two of us. Siren and I can share a bit too, but not as well."

"So he's getting into our radios because you're here?"

"More or less. He was able to ground his projection enough to stop those blaster bolts because I was nearby."

God, we're in so much trouble. Contact with bloody Elsecomers!

"You know, none of that would have been *necessary* if you have just stopped and explained things instead of trashing my vehicles and running a monster into our patrol."

She looked at me, and her eyes flashed.

"Stop and talk to the slave labor prison group that gets driven in first against cryptids because they're the most disposable soldiers in the state? You guys hid how you were operating too well. We found no reason to think you'd do more than kill us on the spot!"

"You had canoes full of kids!" I exclaimed. "Why would you assume we'd shoot?"

"*Because* we had boats full of kids, and because the locals know we're using the river! We got stopped by the sheriff just for pulling canoes on the way here! And we had to sneak past two different 'citizen patrols' of guys just hanging out in boats with their guns ready to shoot anyone who looked 'off' to their idiot eyes."

"What? Yeah, and *I* had anything to do with that!"

"When did you know I was in your lands?" she demanded. "Early last night, when you started spying on me? You had to have had time to organize a raid and come directly for me."

I froze. Why was this relevant?

Hold her, I thought again.

"...yes."

"Did you will the land to hold me in place?"

Ahhh fuck.

"What do you mean?"

"Did you wish very hard for me to be pinned in place, and did you put magic behind it?"

"What would that have to do with anything?"

She looked like she wanted to combust.

Damn she's hot when she's pissed off, my other self thought, and I deeply wished the rest of me disagreed.

"Fucking noob," she ground out. "That snake was your own damn fault!"

"What?"

"I can't believe I let you catch me!"

"I don't understand!"

"It's just like when you willed the tree roots to grab me! Exactly the same! You're tied to the land, and it's responding to your magic."

"That's... a thing?"

That's my thing, the fae voice in me thought smugly.

"Oh my fucking gods," Aisling said. She slumped and looked at me like she had no idea where to even start.

We should will the trees to catch her again, my fae voice said. *It would be hilarious. Or you could ask her about that fog she cloaked herself in.*

"So that fog you called had nothing to do with a ghostlands monster suddenly showing up on the river bank?" I asked her.

She bit her lip, and those big blue eyes went wide.

Suddenly she didn't look cocky or overconfident at all anymore.

"I... don't know," she said after a pause. "Boats kept almost finding us. I had to get the kids *through.*"

Faza very hesitantly came over and handed Aisling what looked more or less like a small electric drill, minus the bit, in an odd alien aesthetic. She took it, her movements jerky, and I could feel her reaching out to mindspeak her partner.

You just want me trapped in that magic with her again, I replied to the fae voice inside me. He nodded, some bittersweet longing swamping him, and sent me another flash of kissing her on the hillside. Dammit.

She's scared. Terrified of being trapped, I thought, *and she doesn't know if a clueless idiot like me is worth getting trapped for.*

I got trapped for her, thought my fae voice.

"This will take a minute," Aisling said, and sat down heavily. "Watch if you want to. Can I borrow a radio?"

"Sure," Birch said. "Why though, when you can mindspeak like that?"

"Just keeps communication tidier, when Tech's working through me. And I'm running on empty. Darouk, to be clear, the usual price?"

"We're fucked for hiding you anyway, if the sidhe find out," the alien said. "But what did you mean they have been infiltrated? Is that something we should worry about?"

"My mother was an advance scout sent here before the Broken Dawn," she said, her shoulders drooping. "But she was really in counterintelligence, and hunting down some faction that had infiltrated her people. She thought they were already on Earth... and influential in human leadership circles."

Holy shit. Well, that explains a lot.

"She told me her people were being sabotaged from within, and she had found evidence that some of their leaders had been killed and replaced with doubles," she continued. "When their world fell and the retreat to Earth happened so far ahead of schedule, she took that as confirmation of all her worst fears."

Birch and Jones glanced at each other, consternation in their eyes.

"Shortly before the Dawn she was in a building the redcaps blew up. My dad pulled her out and got her to a hospital; it was how they met. The triage unit didn't get all the steel shrapnel in her body, leaving her only able to use magic and mind-speech if she was touching someone. When she'd finally recovered and was planning to make a run for the Freeport, she got pregnant with me. Got cancer later, leukemia from the slow iron poisoning. She was wildly paranoid at the end, so I'm not sure how good her intel really was. We've run into things like she described the infiltrators doing, though, so currently I'm assuming she was onto something real." Aisling shrugged like she really didn't know.

"Like what?" Darouk asked.

"When you were with the sidhe, did your people - the most vulnerable of them, the most easily disappeared - did they lose children sometimes?"

Darouk froze and his eyes went wide enough to see the pale yellow beyond his large irises.

"My cousin's nephew," he said quietly. "Two months before the retreat. He was just learning to walk when he disappeared, no signs of a struggle, nothing unusual, no body. And... that happened. In the camps. No one had any idea what was going on, but littles disappeared, one or two every month. Refugee camps, though... such places always have problems."

"Out here, it's the strangeling kids," Aisling sighed. "The ones too young to be on their own, and too small to be of use as prison labor. That's why the Underhill Railroad runs them to safety."

"Strangeling kids don't make it," Serena said, frowning. "Kids who Change can't deal with their monstrous impulses."

"Kids deal with Changing considerably better than adults do," Aisling said. "More mental flexibility, they're already pretending to be other things half the time. But if they get caught, they disappear into a 'testing' system. Ashes are eventually returned to their families. I've looked at such ashes under a microscope, though. It was just wood ash, not even animal remains."

"That can't be right," I said, feeling golden claws scraping inside me again, like the monster cat saw a hint of his enemy. "There's a ton of documentation. Even most adults can barely deal with Changing."

"Because you don't have *strategies* for it," she said. "But two-thirds of the people we run to Strangelingtown are kids, and as long as they get Radiant food and a support network, most do fine.

Most of the adults there now arrived as teens. By the way, when you're deciding who needs to 'die' and head there, give priority to anyone with childcare, medical, or educational backgrounds, because the town is still like half kids."

"Fuuuck..." Birch said.

"Sorry to interrupt," Aisling's tech guy said through the radio, "But I've got my first sale in forty-five minutes and need to get this thing fixed and schematics saved before then."

"Yep," Aisling said. "Let's do this."

She closed her eyes and blue light flared around her hands and through the alien gizmo as if taking a very detailed internal scan of it. A second later, she raised her right hand and an intricate schematic of the thing started drawing itself in the air around her fingers.

"Darouk, what's this bit do?" she asked. He looked at Faza and translated the question. The other howler gave a fairly long and technical description and Darouk blinked a few times and tried to figure out how to put that into English.

"Uh... short version, if you feed similar material to what you're patching into the hopper, it can synthesize missing molecules. Mostly the tool is just meant to knit the molecules around cracks and breaks back together though, that's just for when too much was lost."

"So it's kind of like a little handheld Star Trek replicator?" Birch asked.

"More like a combo welder and 3D printer for repairs, I think," Aisling said.

"Ooh, Robb is going to love this," Tech said. "Okay, got the schematic. Let's fix this baby. Slayer, you recovered enough?"

"Guess we'll find out," she said, and put both hands back on the tool. Blue light seeped through her fingers, sparkling and crackling, but some of it seemed to kind of fizzle, too.

Help her, the fae voice inside me demanded, and I put a hand on her shoulder. For a second I saw as my other self did, lines of light outlining a world somehow bottomlessly deep, and bits of that light converged on my hand and swirled into Aisling. She took it gratefully, and a second later the blue light flashed white and I got a sense of completion.

"Original energy flows restored," Tech said. "And schematics on the way to our best engineer. Good doing business with you, now I've gotta run."

"Later, Tech," Aisling said, sounding tired. She handed Darouk the tool and put a hand up on mine to hold it in place. Something I'd barely even remembered I could feel swept through me, something warm. "Good luck."

"What's he doing?" Birch asked.

"He fixes old electronics and we sell them to fund the Railroad, our budget for gas money and used canoes and stuff," she said.

"With the schematics."

"Oh, some of the gremlins are pretty good at figuring out Elsecomer tech," she said. "They're working on creating our own versions."

"Gremlins?"

"Technomancers. Strangelings with magic that works mostly on technology. They organize the Railroad."

"Why?"

"Because they're pretty good at vetting people without getting caught."

"No, I mean why are you trying to figure out Elsecomer tech? You guys must be a tiny organization with virtually no resources."

She shrugged.

"Well, we're running people now, but we're not going to run forever. We've got ideas. This is *our world*, and damned if we're going to lie down and let it be taken from us forever."

I squeezed her fingers a little, agreeing with the sentiment, and she looked up at me, all huge blue eyes, and then looked at her hand entwined with mine and slumped and stared at it.

"I'm wiped," she said. "Can I nap for twenty minutes while you guys fix the tires?"

I squeezed her fingers again, and she sighed and squeezed them back. A grin threatened to break out across my face, but I restrained it and reluctantly let go of her hand. She sighed, let herself slip down to the ground right under where she'd been sitting, put her backpack under her head, and was asleep by her second breath.

"Is she okay, do you think?" I asked Birch.

"Using magic takes a physical toll," he said. "Never seen anyone toss around as much as she has today. Didn't sound like she got much rest, either, with that snake camped under a cave full of toddlers. So, I guess you like her?"

"What?" I said.

"Well, you seem to keep trying to give her flowers," he answered dryly, and I looked around and saw that once again the area around us had suddenly greened and bloomed with early spring wildflowers. Hot blood rushed to my face and my people snickered.

"Let's go see if we can fix the trucks," I said, and we went off to start repairs, four-armed alien mechanic in the lead.

28

DISPOSAL DUTY

CONNOR

About thirty-six hours after getting eaten alive, I stumbled into work a couple hours before my shift started, so hungover I could barely walk. The Freeport's residents, both alien and local, knew how to *party*. I hadn't been sober since I crowd-surfed my way off the catwalk at the end of Danielle's show. The rest of the night had been *fantastic*, and the party just kept going and going.

Things were good until this morning. The hangover was probably more from how much I'd drank to be able to sleep than the actual partying. Every time I had closed my eyes, the devouring darkness inside the monster catfish engulfed me again. But that morning after, my head was throbbing, my body ached everywhere, and even the thought of breakfast was enough to make my gorge rise.

Or maybe that's the lingering catfish smell. I can't believe how persistent that crap is!

The day began about how I'd expected, which is why I'd made myself come in a couple hours before mid-shift swipes in. Someone from Diplo yelled at me for at least an hour while my head pounded and I made vaguely apologetic noises. I scribbled out some BS for a late incident report and put in a requisition order for a new uniform. Then I got to endure a series of both terrible jokes and head-shaking lectures from every damn colleague I ran into.

That stupid robot fish on the Fail Trophy sang to me while I changed into my uniform. This time the song was *Take Me to the Water.*

When I finally got to my desk, there was a small envelope on it, sealed with a wax stamp showing a triskelion made of three running legs. *Father.* Hadn't seen him for a couple years. I sliced the top open with my duty blade.

Saw the clip, it said. *Good fighting, son.*

There was no signature. There didn't need to be, with the seal. I sighed and tossed the note in a desk drawer. He still held out hope I'd "come to my senses" and go back to him and all his politics and maneuvering. Thought we could build another Briargard, somewhere Out There, and wanted me to help. Or at least provide a well-connected grandchild if I remained too broken and useless for anything else.

Not a chance, I thought. *Briargard is dead, let her rest in peace.*

At three p.m., I headed down the hall for shift assembly. It sounded like morning shift had some excitement in the Edgelands a few hours earlier, but when I walked into the room I got thrown right into punishment duty and didn't hear anything about it.

"Who's the Fishballs Fail Queen this month?" Captain Bhairton called out at shift assembly. "Oh right, *Connor.* Nice of you to show up today, McMann! We've got a nasty one and I want to hand it to someone deserving."

I groaned. I remained convinced the reek of evil fish still clung to me, and, "a nasty one" wouldn't likely do anything to improve that.

And *for the record,* I wasn't scheduled to come in the previous day, because I knew I'd be recovering from the show's afterparty; I might have walked out before writing a report the night I got swallowed, but gods damn it, I *earned* that!

"Sir, with all due respect, I already got eaten alive by one mutated Earth monster this week..." I said. Best to leave the hangover still chewing at me unmentioned.

"Yep, I know. Even an *honorary* Raven is supposed to be more competent than that, oh 'Hero of Briargard'. So here's the info. Go do full forensic scans on the dead giant snake that just washed up against the Mississippi intake on the city walls. Determine if it's any sort of threat or if whatever killed it might be one itself. When that's done, oversee disposal as quickly as possible, because it's starting to stink."

Hero of Briargard. Gods Between, I was sick of that epithet. How can you be a hero of a place that doesn't exist anymore? If anything, I was an unwilling and maimed survivor; hero wasn't *at all* the right word. Heroes actually save something; all I did was buy my world a couple extra hours. And for them, I gave *everything...* and failed.

But this job was my main reason to keep getting out of bed, so I just sighed and held out my arm for the captain to tap. The relevant info flowed over to my duty vambrace and I glanced at the screen projecting up from it, then double checked what I'd read.

"Sir, is this accurate? I didn't think Earth supported megafauna like this?"

"It didn't before the Return! Apparently it does now. Just think what might die against the city walls in ten years! We could *all* be smelling these things before you even get sent out to clean up."

The thought of ten more years on this lunatic planet made me want to retch, recent drunken commitments to finally make a life here be damned. Well, that might have been the hangover. I didn't *hate* this place, it just... wasn't home, and I didn't think it ever could be. Living trapped in a madhouse city full of a few dozen species of aliens, Changed survivors from when the Freeport of Many Waters was the human Twin Cities, and sidhe fighters on forced extended shore leave was *not* how I'd hoped to live my life. I mean, the nightlife was fantastic, no complaints there, and I'd used to adore visiting this kind of place... but the city was *never* quiet. Briargard had been civilized, beautiful, and elegant. She was the sidhe's second homeworld, shaped from creation to our own tastes. Losing her was devastating.

But at least this assignment would get me outside the city walls, if just barely, and that was something.

Rellen looked at me as I stopped back by my desk.

Gee, think he'll be up for monster corpse disposal duty?

"So... I'm way behind on my paperwork and only in for a half shift today..." he started.

Sure you are.

"More secret training with Maddoc?" I asked, my voice innocent. He flashed me an annoyed glance.

"Nah. Going out with some friends visiting from Byzance. And I don't want to stink."

"I'll be fine. You can stay nice and fresh for your date tonight."

"*Date* is a strong word. It's just some friends and their sexy, eligible, single friends hanging out..."

"The hot pediatrician's going to be there?"

"She'll say yes to a real date eventually! I can *feel* it."

"Hope springs eternal! Keep telling yourself that."

"Sooner or later!" he said brightly, then his shoulders drooped. "...but it might be later."

Rellen was a hard-working, insightful Investigator. He had a talent for seeing directly to the heart of a matter and finding exactly what buttons to push to get people to react, often strongly. Unfortunately, that was a better skill for interrogations than dating, and if there was a department romance fail trophy, it'd live stuck to *his* locker.

I sighed, waved a token farewell, and went down to Gear to get the monster forensics kit. I checked out a Guard floatie bike, swung on, and headed out to the river intake on the city's fortifications. A big, stinky dead thing was waiting for me.

It was kind of like coming to Earth all over again.

The hangover had faded to the point my stomach could handle something, though, so about a third of the way there I stopped for some coffee and pastries at one of my favorite sidewalk cafes. The usual team was in and I joked with them a bit, picking up a jabiree fruit turnover and a couple of baklava triangles. Baba's Cantine did a mix of Middle Eastern human foods and Briargard nostalgics. All of it was delicious. Everyone had seen the video of me getting eaten and made a point of congratulating me on surviving, and asked if the river would be usable again. I said I didn't know, but I hoped so, and the staff cheered.

A delicate, magenta-haired boy behind the counter grabbed a local events magazine with a shot from Danielle's runway show on the cover, me shining bright in her mirror ball outfit, and had me sign the picture for him. Then we talked hair care and tricks for getting that perfect crisp cateye until my iced latte was ready.

So *okay*, maybe the city had become a *little* bit home, and maybe I've gone a *tiny* bit local.

Twenty minutes after breakfast, I was at the city's fortified river intake. The stench of something large and very dead curled my nose as soon as I pulled into the parking lot. A pair of giant strangelings, each about twice the height of a tall human and wearing Sanitation uniforms, waved me over to an entry gate.

"Ho ho, they sent an actual knight?" one boomed. "What'd you do to get stuck on shit duty like this?"

For the record, "knight" isn't a rank we actually use, but it's what the former humans around here tend to call us foreign sidhe fighters. Nobody argues. It's at least a word with good connotations to them.

"Got swallowed by an evil catfish two nights ago," I said, and he winced and laughed. "I think the assumption is that I still stink from that, so how much worse can we make it?"

"Yeah, this is a nasty one. Tells a pretty crazy story though! Somebody used an actual bazooka on this bad boy! And it is *covered* in bullet holes. But it's also got what looks like magic damage and... well, you'll see. I'm Jenkins and this is Crawford."

"Probably that prison labor group in the outer Edgelands took it down then," I said. "What are they called again? And I'm Guardsman McMann."

"Strangeling Brigade, and if we ever get peace terms and can get them out of prison, lemme tell you, I'm enlisting. This ain't the first kill of theirs we've found, and they've been getting pretty damn good over the last couple years."

We walked out on the other side of the fortification. The sky was blue and cottonwoods waved barely-budding branches in the breeze coming across the waters. It'd have been lovely if not for the reeking, rotting monster. The river intake workers had pulled the snake corpse out of the water and up onto the bank. It was *huge*. The top of its head, tipped on its side, came up to my belly. A charred and gaping hole was all that remained of its left eye, and part of an arrow stuck out of the hole.

"Whoa, looks like it was a battle and a half to take this down. Let me scan it and see if we can figure out how the fight went."

I pulled out the forensics scanner and walked the length of the serpent, being sure to get everything, and took a couple tissue samples from various open wounds, then hit "send" and waited for results to come back.

"Hey, once you've got the forensics done, you mind if we call our own guy to clean up the body?" Jenkins asked.

"Long as it doesn't stink up the city and you're not doing anything criminal with it, we couldn't care less," I answered honestly. "What are you thinking?"

"Clean it down to the bones and then use them to decorate my buddy's bar," he said. "This skull would *make* the place."

"Awesome. I want to see it when you've got it up."

"Ha!" the giant boomed. "Be hilarious to see a pretty little elf in there. Dunno that anyone who took part in the invasion would really be welcome, though."

"Well, 'luckily', I was in a coma for all that. Gave my all trying to hold Briargard, and it wasn't enough, but frankly I did my damnedest to go down with the ship. Woke up here a year after the hostilities ended."

"Could make an exception in that case. Have to talk to my buddy. You like coal brews?"

"Are they alcoholic?"

"You better believe it."

"That's really the only standard I have left."

My wrist dinged.

"Results are in. Let's see... good call on the bazooka. Chemical analysis on the eye indicates a portable rocket launcher; bet a big guy like you was carrying it," I reported. "And the lump in its gut is an entire cow! Bullets from at least fifteen different small arms, two bronze arrowheads, looks like impacts on the face from both a magnesium burn and a car grill, and you're right about magic damage. The scales show sonic distortions! Huh, this can't be right. I need another look at the burned eye."

There was no way anyone out there should have sidhe weapons, yet the scan was showing the killing strike came from something probably spear-like with nano-tech sharpness, the blade's edge a molecule wide and able to cut nearly anything. What's more, it had cauterized the edges, something sidhe blades can typically do. I pulled on disposable gloves, took a deep breath, and pulled the wound open. Yep. That definitely looked like one of our weapons had made the cut. I pulled out the arrow. It was handmade with goose feathers and knife marks on the shaft, not military issue of any sort. The tip was bronze and didn't bother me at all.

"Fuuuuck. I need to make a call, gimme a sec," I said to Jenkins and Crawford, stepping back from the snake and closing my eyes.

Maddoc? I called out to my mentor. He's well above the city guard chain of command, but these wounds could be implying a mess just as far above the Guard's pay grade. *Do you have a second? We may have a security breach.*

I got an impression of an eyebrow raised at me, and a second later he teleported in next to me, a tumbler full of whiskey in his hand. He'd had *despair* issues since losing his daughter, Derdriu, ten years ago, and today didn't look like a good one.

His free hand went straight to covering his nose as he inhaled with no time to steel himself against the snake's stench.

"Ugh, warn a man, m'boy!" he exclaimed. "What the hell is this?"

"Giant snake that just washed up on the river intake gates, sir," Jenkins explained. "Floated in about an hour ago, going to guess it's been dead three or four days."

"Forensics say it died this morning, actually. Some of the weirdling monsters rot fast. It looks like it was in a battle with a military unit, probably the Strangeling Brigade that patrols the outer five miles of the Edgelands," I explained, and switched from English to the sidhe language. "But the killing strike looks like it was from a bound sidhe weapon. Do we have anyone out there?"

Maddoc looked at the snake and its many wounds, and had me pull open the killing wound again. His face went still and serious. Then his eyes narrowed, and he swore, almost admiringly.

"Well, that dokkalfar boy was better than I thought he was," he said, then grinned, and something floated through his eyes like it does when he's assessing possible futures. "Let's fight fire with fire. Connor, come with me."

"My guard bike's down in the parking lot..." I said in English.

"It's safe here," Crawford said. "We'll make sure the next shift knows about it if you take a while."

"I appreciate it."

"Hey," Jenkins said, "You find the guys who killed this thing, if they're not an enemy, tell 'em if they ever get the chance to come over to the Caves Bar in St. Paul, and tell us the story about taking down this monster!"

I gave the giants a grin and quick salute, and Maddoc teleported himself and me over to the lobby of a military building that monitors the Edgelands around the city. It's rather empty, as the humans know quite well by now to keep away and have given up encroaching on our buffer zone, and had a disused air.

"I'll be right back," Maddoc said, and blinked out again.

29

THE FERMI PARADOX

ARTHUR

The two howlers... Dohoulani... disassembled the 6x6 troop transport's tires and then used what *must* be the galaxy's handiest repair gadget to patch up the tire and even the wheel's deeply scored hub. That needed some extra steel, in the form of some bolts from our tool kit, fed in through the tool's hopper. It all took a while, but at least we wouldn't end up down a troop transport until we could bring new wheels back from St. Cloud. They even managed to rig up a salvaged air compressor and inflate the tires.

I got an emergency blanket out of the back of my trashed Jeep and put it over Aisling. She mumbled something and pulled it up tight.

Not my type, I told myself sternly. *Much too wild.*

Absolutely and completely my type, my fae side replied. *Even if loving her got me completely screwed last time. Fierce. Untamed. And remember how she flipped over the Jeep's hood? Athletic and flexible. Just think of the positions we could get her in now that we aren't kids...*

I closed my eyes and swore at him, then looked around for a distraction.

About then, Darouk suggested something to his elder, got hit on his muzzle with a wrench, and backed off, rubbing his nose and smarting from the rebuke.

"What's he saying?" I asked the younger Dohoulani as the older one grumbled and tried to get the tool into a corner where it barely fit. Apparently, "crusty old mechanic" isn't a role confined to humans.

"Oh, Faza's just bitching about crazy sidhe kids. Reckless, flashy, prone to breaking everything. Aisling is pretty typical, for all she's avoiding her people. Amazing any of you survive."

I thought about myself in my early teens, before the binding was put on me, and couldn't disagree.

"So, you said the sidhe don't actually rule the stolen cities, but yet somehow they're the Elsecomer leaders, too?" Birch asked, joining us.

"Well, Many Waters is a freeport, but most other sidhe-run cities are closed and run on different rules. I dunno know how those work. Freeports are more interesting, anyway, probably that's why the old ones like them. They've seen everything and got bored. Weird to have freeports on a planet, but they seem to make it work. Mostly."

"So what's it like in there?"

"Crazy. City's manic, never sleeps. Whole thing's under climate controls, so it never gets cold like out here. There are pubs and cafes and restaurants spilling out onto half the streets and roofs, music everywhere, street markets day and night... miss those, it was so easy to get something when you needed it. Little starships come in and out all the time, big ones a few times a month... used to think I'd ship out someday. Wanted to find my way Out There, maybe tell some stories myself instead of just selling other people's..."

His words trailed off, and he looked at the ground. Guess his life wasn't going as planned, either.

"The sidhe are characters out of our old myths," Birch said. "How'd they end up traveling space?"

"Oh, they mostly don't use starships for that. I mean, they have them now, some of the best. But they can step through underspace with their magic. The rules of normal time and space kind of break around them. They've got some fifth dimensional transit network they call the Tree that Grows Between Worlds. Gates into it look like enormous trees, usually, and time and space distort around them. They've got a weird relationship with this Tree, but you'd have to ask one of them about it. Not sure if it's biomedical or religious or what."

A huge Tree, that distorts time and space... I thought of the vast tree in the Box's courtyard, and a shiver ran through me.

"Think Aisling could explain it?"

He snorted and made a sound like a laugh.

"I'm sure she'll try. Kid barely speaks her people's language or even Tradish, and it sounds like her mother, who should have trained her, was crippled and wildly paranoid. She and her friends just figure things out in terms of human sci-fi and fantasy, or those movies with superheroes. Good kids, but *sweet Ancestors* do they need an education."

"Fifth dimensional? What's that mean?" I asked.

"Not sure," he answered. "Transcending or bypassing normal time and space, popping through otherworlds and alternate realities... I've heard explanations but none entirely made sense."

"What about what she said about infiltrators and lost kids?" Birch asked.

"Dunno. The sidhe are the only reason any of my people are alive, though. So even if they've been infiltrated by hostiles, they gave their world and over half their fighters to save the people of our star cluster, and we'll never forget that."

"What do you mean?" I asked.

"When they first left Earth, the sidhe built themselves a new homeworld, Briargard. They terraformed it from a barren rock into one of the most beautiful worlds in the galaxy. It was in a star cluster further out the galaxy's arm than Earth, about four hundred light years from here, with a sky full of brilliant nebulae. A bunch of the other stars there had inhabited worlds, my people's among them. Some of us had starships, but most of us kept to our traditions and stayed home. The sidhe don't need anywhere central because they can just step into underspace and walk the Tree's branches to other worlds, so being in the middle of nowhere was fine. Then the World Eaters came."

"...World Eaters?" Birch asked.

Some feeling of dread, like this was something I somehow already knew, washed over me.

"Machines, artificial life, a horde of synthetics ranging in size from microbots to moon-sized ships. Some idiots out there built them and got destroyed by them long, long ago. Now they're loose and have a virus' mindless need to reproduce themselves. They eat planets, prefer ones with molten cores and carbon-based life because they use those components to build new ones of their kind. Briargard was the last world in our cluster to fall, and the sidhe had brought as many refugees from the other worlds there as the environment could support. When they were overwhelmed, they opened Ways through the Tree and brought us here. We think opening all those Gates simultaneously sort of... cracked reality, here."

"Holy fuck," Birch said. "They broke the local space-time continuum, you mean."

"Almost *everything* went wrong with the war and then the evacuation," Darouk said. "The fact any of us survived came down to terrible sacrifices on the part of the sidhe. Like Connor, the youngest guy in the Freeport guard, he used to have some of the strongest shielding magic the sidhe ever produced. He burned it out and put himself into a coma for two years guarding the last open Gate. The rest of the Shields died hours before he fell. Our tribe's alive because he *held*."

Damn. I glanced at Aisling, still asleep, and thought of the kind of magic that'd take.

"If she's too bonkers, by the way, Connor's chronically single. Don't know why, everyone adores him. Could really use someone stable in his life, get him to drink a bit less. Not sure he's any saner than her, but he at least knows what's what."

Birch's face went bright red with the effort of not laughing.

"I think Captain's more into girls," Birch said.

No, no, that's flexible, my fae side said, and I remembered a bit more about how wild I'd been before he was bound. I hadn't dated exclusively girls. I hadn't dated "exclusively" anyone. Oh god.

Yeah, if I'd been able to kill myself, I'd probably have done it about when you joined that youth church and committed yourself to that re-virginity nonsense and saving yourself for marriage, my fae voice said very dryly.

I winced internally.

"Oh, that's fine, Connor spends half his weekends dressed as one," Darouk said helpfully. "He's been 'Queen of Pride' more than once. It's a ceremonial position for a big local holiday in the city."

"Earth's invaders kept *Gay Pride* going?" Birch asked in total disbelief.

"It's a party, and like I said, they're bored," the alien answered, shrugging. "And sidhe seem to hook up with whoever they like, I'm not sure gender actually matters much to them. Or species. Our tabloids *love* them."

"Our *alien overlords* are alcoholic pansexual paparazzi-bait?" Birch asked, disbelieving, and saw my face and couldn't keep that laughter in any longer. He glanced over at Aisling. "Are *they* all adrenaline junkies too?"

"Eh, enough of them. To be fair, most settle down after a couple hundred years."

"Why Earth?" I asked, wondering why the hell a six-limbed lemur would think I needed a drunken alien drag queen in my life... and wanting to change the subject as fast as possible. "I mean, why did they come here?"

"They registered it as their planet when they first got off-world, which is the privilege of whatever culture first gets off their home planet. Put it on a no-go list so it wouldn't be interfered with,"

Darouk answered. "Wanted to give the other locals time to develop themselves, see if they became anything interesting. But then humans trashed the place, killed off half of all other life-forms, and had the world on course for a climate-change induced death spiral... The galactic courts sided with the sidhe when they said they needed to reclaim their homeworld. Habitable worlds are precious beyond everything else; if a populace is wrecking theirs, which happens now and then, they forfeit their rights to local sovereignty. And we've simply lost too many worlds."

That all makes sense, I thought, my stomach twisting.

"Well shit," Birch said. "This explains the Fermi Paradox."

"The what?" I asked.

"Humans used to think that there must be a bunch of other inhabited worlds and intelligent species out in space, but none of them contacted us. Given the probabilities, it seemed a paradox."

"The sidhe could have, like, made contact *before* invading," I said.

"They did," Darouk said. "But this world had no unified leadership, and every country responded differently. As I understand it, your country's last full-term leader tried to get some sort of massive bribe. When the sidhe wouldn't negotiate one, he threw a huge tantrum aimed at, like, *everyone*, and eventually turned into a redcap and overthrew his own former government. Then some of his own dumber followers nuked the capitol with him in it. Apparently, the troll transformation magic was based on folkloric redcaps just because that guy's followers wore red hats and were so obnoxious."

"Oh. Damn. Guess I can see that," Birch said. "My parents *loathed* that guy."

"Yeah," I said. "My dad would just be stoic about criticizing the former American government, but my mom would swear a blue streak about their greed and incompetence wrecking the world, leaving us with a pandemic, the redcap war, and an alien invasion... all while the shops were running out of contraceptives."

"Wow, there's a birds and the bees talk," Birch said. "My dad just told me I came from a six-pack of Leinies' and a weekend of home leave."

"Wonder how far back your sidhe blood is," Darouk said to me. "Bet it's on your mom's side. It's a shame no one taught you. Never heard of anyone shifting like this, so we all assumed you must be an exiled traitor after we first saw you chasing Aisling."

"That why you all quit trying so hard to kill us?" Birch asked dryly.

"Well, if someone were to get exiled instead of killed, it'd probably be because of family connections. We couldn't risk it."

Oh god, I thought. *What if I do have family amongst the Elsecomers?*

Even the voice inside me went quiet and pensive at that thought.

30

SURVEILLANCE
FOOTAGE

CONNOR

M addoc returned twenty minutes later, Morganna's strangeling ward in tow. Sveta raised a pierced eyebrow at me, obviously as clueless as I was about what was going on, and I shrugged. Her lips narrowed. Guess she was still pissed over how I'd seduced the *completely inappropriate* guy she was flirting with a month earlier. She had some weird bias about only wanting to date totally straight guys, so the fact he'd ended up in bed with me just *proved* how wrong he was for her.

She hadn't been exactly grateful for my help, though. Even after I told her I saved her from one of the worst lays ever!

Oh well. If I'm supposed to play big brother, the least I can do is protect my kid sister from inconsiderate lovers. And that guy was SO dull in the sack. Maybe that's not how human brothers protect their sisters, though? Hmm. Hard to tell. Sveta does have a lot of baggage from her birth culture.

She's so weird.

Maddoc led us into a room full of scanners and screens, and I saw her fingers twitch with temptation. Her short lavender hair moved like a sea anemone, as if swirled by currents that affected no one else.

Sveta almost looked sidhe, with pointy ears like we have and a Tree connection stronger than most of the Changed. She's petite, though, smaller than most of us, but in that way that indicates a temper held under compression. Didn't have our type of over-the-top beauty, but rather the kind of pugnacious punk cute that could cause even more trouble. I once told her she looked like a cartoon pixie who'd fallen in with a bad crowd, and she called me a *goluboi suka* and tased me in the stomach. She spoke our language now, with only a hint of a Russian accent. That... and her thug background... mainly came out when she spoke English.

"There's a boy like you out in the hinterlands," Maddoc said casually to her, speaking our language, and she stilled like a cat seeing a mouse's tail. Oh gods, she was going to be awful. "Met him this morning when we went to check a border incursion. I need you to find him now."

He turned to a technician who'd stepped up to help us.

"Callum, we need footage of this morning's encounter, and pull up all relevant satellite and sensor footage from that area going back to an hour before sunrise."

"Yes, sir," the technician said, and hit play on the skimmer's footage of Maddoc and four Guards encountering Strangeling Brigade. Maddoc activated some privacy protocols, and the tech stepped away. On screen, someone very large was unconscious on the beach, and the group's leader said they were having a medical emergency.

"You think the snake had something to do with people ending up in the water?" I asked, and Maddoc nodded.

"They're hiding something," Sveta said. "Trying to keep your attention away from something. Zoom out."

"There are tracks in the sand," I said. "Like they half dragged some people away from the unconscious giant, up to the tree line. You can see it still crumbling there."

"Let me take the replay controls," Sveta said.

"Watch the whole thing first," Maddoc said.

"Did that human soldier just shrug off Lieutenant Ziglos' truth-compel?" I asked, surprised, and my mentor nodded. "How'd he learn how to do that?"

"Something we should have asked, no doubt," Maddoc sighed. "Watch."

Ziglos went to stun the soldier, and a hand formed from the thin air between him and the human, and then a young guy, not sidhe but definitely elven, faded into view behind it, his skin slate-blue and his hair the colors of deep space nebulae, wearing robes straight out of a human sci-fi classic.

And Sveta went completely still.

"Ha!" I laughed, seeing his outfit. "The guy's an illusion, right?"

"How did you know?" Maddoc asked, surprised.

"His costume's from an old human movie; it'd be a message to anyone who'd seen it. This grumpy old wizard gets an entire army to focus on him while his people flee. They blow everything around him to smithereens. Then he just brushes some dust off his shoulder and infuriates them even more. Once his team is out of there, it turns out the wizard was a projection and he was never even actually there."

Sveta nodded agreement, watching the dark elf fritz out the guardsmen's guns and threaten to disable their skimmer. She started smiling, a hunter's grin spreading across her face.

"You have the guns, yes? I can get a taste of his magic from one," she said. "Will help with tracking."

A second later, Maddoc had disabled the troops and had blades to the throats of the human officer and the young elf, who promptly apologized for intruding on our lands *in our language.* Then he described what was likely Maddoc's daughter as the person who'd taught his cousin.

"Pause," Sveta said, and some ridiculously high tech goggles slipped over her eyes. Something subtle crackled in the air around her for a second, and her hair twitched in another unseen breeze. "We monitor and archive local news. This will just take a second."

Electricity crackled over her, sparking through her hair like one of those weird contained lightning bulbs some humans liked to decorate with in films from the 1980s.

"Cross-referencing child deaths in outstate Minnesota for the last twenty years with redcap attacks. Got him. Putting up extra privacy shielding now."

I blinked. Even Maddoc, who'd obviously brought her in for exactly this, looked taken aback, but a second later sound from the rest of the room disappeared and we understood why the search had gone so fast.

"James Maddoc Lingren, son of Deirdre and Tomas Lingren, killed by a nurse who had a redcap transformation in the maternity ward. It ate his mother's arm while she was still partially tranquilized from the C-section. It got three other infants and the hospital security guard. The baby's thirteen-year-old sister killed the troll with a scalpel, but it was too late. The mother never really recovered, and passed six months later."

Maddoc's knees buckled, and I caught him, then grabbed a chair with my free hand and pulled it over for him. He dropped his head between his knees and tried to catch his breath.

"Talk about technical truths," I said. "The strangeling boy is fae enough to avoid outright lying."

Sveta dismissed her goggles and blinked at us, then regret flashed across her face.

"Callum, can you grab some water for Maddoc?" she said, her tone deeply apologetic, dropping the shielding. "I'm so sorry. Everything's electric and inhuman when I'm in the data. I should have spoken... better."

The sister? I mindspoke Sveta. *Go back in and find everything on her. And look for anything interesting on the Underhill Railroad and Strangeling Brigade, especially the guy who resisted Ziglos' glamour.*

"Can I have access to the computers here and this morning's videos? I'll just put everything together at once," she said. Maddoc nodded, and took the water from Callum and drank it, then looked at it in disgust.

"I'll be back in five minutes," he said, and blinked away, no doubt to somewhere with whiskey.

Sveta nodded and her goggles slipped back on. A second later, she was completely lost in her magic. I sat down in Maddoc's abandoned chair and wished I could have a shot or two myself.

31

ALIEN PICNICS

ARTHUR

"So, why do you hide her?" Birch asked Darouk, glancing over at Aisling's still-sleeping form. Flowers bloomed all around her, and she looked like a delicate elven princess from a book of fairy tales. An exhausted and rather bruised one; her encounter with the snake had left marks. I wanted to go get under the blanket with her, lie down next to her and keep her warm. I wanted her to open those big blue eyes and pull me down for another kiss...

No. Bad libido. Getting involved with her would be a terrible idea.

"Lotta monsters out here, weirdlings that come out of the fog, or assholes leaving the Freeport," he said. "After she drops off Runners in Strangelingtown, we lead her to the worst of them. Might be daft as fuck, but she's damn good at killing things, real sidhe there. We support her team with salvage we find out here, helps keep them running. But she's only here a couple times a year, and the monsters show up more often than that. Be good to have an ally who's actually around."

"Assholes leaving the Freeport?" I asked. "What do you mean?"

"Freeports are supposed to be *space stations*," he said. "They can only enforce their own laws, and people from treaty-signatory nations must be able to come and go freely. It's part of their legal package. Wild places. Great for trade. But... dodgy, too. Because they don't have border terms with their neighbors, that's you, they can't enforce border terms on anyone wanting to leave. And when you step out of the city gates, you aren't instantly spaced. All they can do is say that this is a barbarian primitive world and no high technology is allowed past the city walls. So that stops the big game hunters who want to take out guns, but not the sorts that want to go tear up sentients with their bare teeth. And those of us who leave aren't entitled to any protection anymore."

Well, isn't that great.

Faza, Bastion, and a couple of the more mechanical guys almost had the wheels back on the truck.

"This makes a lot of sense," Birch said. "We appreciate the explanation."

"Anything we should know about this 'bad pig' you want us to hunt?" I asked.

Darouk shrugged.

"It's big, dumb, and it chased some guys trying to get a field ready. Broke a bunch of farming gear. Keep your trucks well away from it! Attacks anything it sees, though I don't think it has very good vision. And we aren't certain, but it might teleport, or move oddly anyway. I'm not sure 'pig' is the right word, but it looks a bit like a very large, shaggy boar. Has a horn on its head as long as my arm."

"A horn? Like a pig unicorn?" Birch exclaimed.

"Let's see if Birch can ride it!" Black said, overhearing that. "If he can, *I'll* call it a unicorn."

"Fucking monsters. Totally par for the course out here," I said, pointedly ignoring her. "Writing incident reports about fighting unicorn pigs will definitely be the frosting on the cake of today."

"Is it an alien from the Freeport?" Birch asked.

"Nah, came out of the fog," Darouk said, shrugging.

"Bloody ghostlands. How do they work into the invasion?"

"No idea. Not sure the sidhe even know about them. They were really confused by the Sochan Effect too, didn't expect that at all, or the sheer scale of deaths when they arrived. First few months on Earth were a bloody mess."

"Sochan Effect?" I asked.

"Changing. Cascading. I've heard some theories that all the Gates caused it, but I don't think anyone actually knows."

"This sounds like everything around the invasion of Earth was one big clusterfuck," Birch said.

"Yup," the four-armed alien monkey said, shrugging again. "Pretty much. Honestly, Aisling's story about internal sabotage explains a *lot* of things."

Faza hooted something to Darouk.

"He says he'll see if there's any hope for the Jeep, but it's probably beyond repair."

On second inspection, with the working alien tool, Faza thought it might be fixable but would take a while. Their "bad pig" wasn't threatening anything immediately and everyone was hungry, so we started another fire and the troop pulled out lunch rations. Some of our better hunters went out and got a pair of rabbits, and Roberts found some wild leeks. Two of the human guys found a pond with cattails and pulled up some tubers. Putting it all in a soup pot, together with some dry buckwheat, cooked up a solid lunch.

Aisling continued to sleep, but Zahra woke up. She showed minimal signs of further Hunger, but was deeply disoriented, like she was coming out of dreams more vivid than reality. Bastion sat down with her and started trying to explain what had happened. There was a bit of food left in the package Aisling had traded for, and he made sure she finished it. She was dazed, though, as Changing often leaves people, and Bastion made sure she was taking things slowly.

Birch and his aide Thomson, who was also into languages and had been working on Old Norse with him, made extra portions for the two Dohoulani and then sat down with Darouk and started taking notes for a basic Tradish phrase book. Faza howled out an order for something he needed. A few more Dohoulani showed up, carrying tools and parts and yet more food. They were all relieved to have basic peace terms and curious about us, and it turned into a bit of a picnic. They brought their own food, too, some of it Radiant, and the strangelings on the team went from cautious nibbles to

OMG I had no idea this was what I was craving... and then started relaxing like I had after drinking William's fermented sap.

It was surprisingly enjoyable. The aliens didn't differentiate between our human and strangeling members at all. A lot of them had some basic English, especially the younger ones, and having even weird aliens treat us like we were just *people* was disconcerting but... nice. I joined Birch and Thomson for a bit, because it really was completely obvious we weren't going to be shooting at these guys anymore and that they were totally and absolutely civilians. Also, they told us about a lot of other refugee groups in the Edgelands, some we'd thought were monsters, many we'd had watch us but never directly encountered, and all of them used this Tradish language to communicate with each other. Even better, there were some extreme basics that used hand signs, and we made sure everyone in the group learned the half dozen essential ones Darouk showed us.

Aisling's color got better, and I woke her up and made sure she ate something. She still looked exhausted when she sat up, but she glanced around at the picnic and a smile spread across her face.

There might be hope for you, she said into my mind, and I glimpsed that same desperate protectiveness towards her people that I feel for mine.

Accurate intel makes all the difference, I said, and she smiled and I made myself step away before I dragged her off into the bushes. I saw her eyes twinkle. My fae side just stared at her, yearning and angry and desperate, remembering a kiss that tasted like bonfires in the snow and clear blue eyes like pools into which he'd fallen... and both found and lost himself.

Completely obviously, she had no such memory.

She checked on Zahra, and I couldn't avoid overhearing most of their conversation. The giant girl was sitting on the ground against a fallen tree, eyes closed, stunned like a bird who'd flown into a window.

"You managing, Zahra?" I heard Aisling ask quietly, and the girl blinked at her.

"Dusty?" she asked, confusion twisting her face when she opened her eyes. "How do you have Dusty's voice?"

"Just... hush, okay?" Aisling said, wincing. "No names, so we can't answer questions, remember?"

"Is this... is this what you really are?"

"Ask the big philosophical questions, why don't you?" she responded, and flopped down with her back against the fallen tree next to Zahra. "I dunno. I mean, I don't think I'm *fake* the rest of the time, you know. Just... different. Part of me's in the wardrobe, part *is* the wardrobe. Sucks, but it is what it is. Keeps my family safer."

The giant girl blinked, trying to reconcile the Green Lady with whoever *Dusty* was.

"Damn. No wonder you never hesitated to take us running backcountry. My mom thought you were the *worst* babysitter ever when I told her about that. Wanted to brain you with her frying pan."

Zahra knows her, knows her in her human life, I thought, a little stunned and briefly, wildly jealous. *Knows where she lives and what she does and who she loves, and has for years.*

"And she let me watch you again after that?" Aisling asked, grinning sideways.

"You think I told her before *years* had passed?" the giant laughed. "Do I look suicidal?"

"I'll check on her," Aisling said. "Keep yourself intact and give me a few years, and I'll try and get you back in touch with your family. I'm going to do everything I can to get Changes treated as a medical issue. Just have to jump through all the right academic hoops first."

"Vicki got exposed too," Zahra said quietly. "Do you know if she Changed?"

"She was going into quarantine with the rest of your team," Aisling said. "When I get home, I'll go in and make sure they're clean of that tainted magic. I think she'll Cascade eventually, but I put a choke on it for now. Dunno how long it will hold."

"They'll let you into the holding tank?"

"One deputy is a cousin and thinks I'm the village witch. He'll let me in, or Siren will make everyone zone out and we'll walk in while they're oblivious. It's doable."

"Okay."

"You look awesome, by the way. Love the direction you went with your Change. Mrs. Rowan's going to squee so hard over your hair."

The girl examined her now-huge hand, spreading her fingers.

"Guess you never realize how much the stories we love *matter,* until push comes to shove and someone tells you to find the shape of your dreams. You know that movie you found got me through ninth grade? Afro-futurism. *Damn.* Dreamed of being one of those kick-ass warrior women every night. And now through... this. I hope, anyway."

"Yeah. I think about Gandalf's speech to Frodo and living through difficult times a lot, that no one would choose them but here we are, cope and deal."

Zahra looked at Aisling and shook her head.

"Still Dusty Books, queen of nerds, even when you look like a fragile little snowbell," she said. "I can't reconcile this face with that rust bucket you clonk around in. *Top Model Middle Earth* drives that junker?! I wasn't even sure the pickup bed would hold me when I climbed into it, or if it'd just disintegrate underneath me! What were you thinking, though, bringing your cousins along?"

"Their mom went on another bender, and they set things on fire if left unsupervised. Got them dumped on me right before I was supposed to meet you," Aisling answered, making a face. "They want to be eyes and ears for the Railroad now, though. And we need people who can do that."

"Do they... know, about this? About you?"

"No. None of my family does."

"Mine must all think I'm a monster now," Zahra said, tears welling in her eyes.

"The day I realized I was a monster was the day I became myself," Aisling said, trying to look like she wasn't papering over a giant unhealed wound. "I just choose to be a useful monster."

"When was that?"

"Remember the rat goblin siege?" she sighed. "Think you'd have been in early grade school then."

Zahra stared.

"They said some of the corpses looked like a combine mowed over them," she said. "And others were killed with a single precise strike. You were already the Green Lady then, with the blades and armor?"

"No," Aisling said quietly, staring off into the distance. "I was a scared fourteen year old with a dead baby brother and a mom dying of untreatable leukemia. I got a butcher knife from my aunt's kitchen and went out and made sure I wouldn't ever be too slow again."

"You run kids down the Railroad in your brother's memory."

"Couldn't save him. Maybe I can save you. Or give you a chance to save yourself, anyway. I can't really do more than try and clear out the crap my people are responsible for; the rest is up to you. You're on your path. When your opportunity comes, *grab it,* and don't hold back."

The giant girl looked at her hands again, stretching her fingers.

"Well. At least no one's going to call me *little* again."

Zahra yawned. Her fingers went to the pendant at her throat, on a chain that barely fit around her neck now.

"Bastion said we're going to hunt a pig unicorn later," she said. "I always wanted to see a unicorn. But... not like this."

Things rarely come to us as we'd wish, I thought, looking at Aisling and trying very hard not to fall for her.

"Rest some more," Aisling told her. "We're not going anywhere for the next few hours."

Zahra nodded again, curled up, and went back to sleep.

Aisling went over and helped with repairs for a bit. She herself was *useless* on that front, having apparently no mechanical aptitude

for anything beyond breaking shit, which we got to hear about at
some length from her tech friend. He somehow connected an old
tablet computer one of the aliens brought to a working webcam at
her mechanic friend's place. He was a big jovial guy who introduced
himself with a cheerful, "Hi, I'm Bob!" and he could completely
pass as human too. He explained parts of the engine function the
aliens didn't understand, making it clear that an essential part of the
repair process would be keeping Aisling from touching anything.
Eventually Tech found a pdf of a Jeep manual and somehow sent it
to the tablet and then there was a bit of a mess about translating it.
He was at least able to work through Aisling and tell us what was
broken in the electrical systems.

The pair couldn't do anything for the steel parts, and Bob
couldn't work through her like Tech could. She was more iron
sensitive than even me, and couldn't do any magic directly on iron
or steel. The molecular fuser came through, though, and the team
got the axle back together. Having Bastion physically lift the Jeep
up and hold parts in place helped enough that Bob told him they
could open their own garage together, someday when we all ended
up in Edgelands exile. Bastion laughed and said that sounded good.

I shivered when he said that. It had an edge of foretelling to it.

Everyone involved wanted their own "sci-fi duct tape" by the
time half of the repairs were done. Tech told us his friend had
already said he was putting everything else aside until he'd worked
out a reasonable facsimile of it.

Aisling yawned and went back to her backpack and blanket and
passed out again. A mixed team of my guys and the aliens started
working on the broken parts of the engine. It looked like they were
actually going to fix it.

"This is so fucking awesome," Birch said, beaming at our team
working with the alien mechanics. "Like all my Trekkie dreams
come true."

"Trek was a lot... tidier," I said, thinking about the massive
amount of trouble we'd be in if brass ever caught even a whisper of
this.

"Yeah, but let's be *real*. There was no way Earth was ever heading towards a future that orderly."

I sighed, and didn't even try to argue.

PART 3

ACROSS THE BORDERS

32

INFILTRATED

CONNOR

I could smell a faint hint of whiskey when he returned, somewhat more than five minutes later, but Maddoc didn't come back either drunk or alone.

"Sir, welcome to the Freeport of Many Waters," I said, jumping to my feet for Commander Daire of the Red Ravens, one of Maddoc's oldest friends, when he teleported in with my mentor. Hadn't realized he was on Earth currently. He was tall, with sandy hair and hazel eyes, and his every movement screamed *experienced warrior*. He was one of the old Earthborn, who'd ridden with the Celts in their ancient heyday, and he and Maddoc had been comrades in arms since they fought the Romans.

"Commairge!" he exclaimed, holding his arms wide for me. "You're looking considerably more sober than I'd expect, after getting eaten alive like that."

"Connor now," I said, my head throbbing as I wondered if every single person in the entire world knew about that by now. "And today's turning out interesting enough to be dry for. How have you been, sir?"

"Good, good," he answered. "Might be an end in sight for the Kzephian Civil War, conditional on the elimination of the one faction absolutely everyone else hates, but I'm off the front for a bit now and was stopping by to visit Maddoc. Faron said to tell you he loves the care packages, and to put more of those 'Girl Scout' cookies in the next one."

I grinned, making a mental note to remember to hit up the enterprising little Mihooli girls who ran cookie sales... and a minor protection racket... in my neighborhood.

"So, what brings you back to Earth?" I asked.

"We've got ten, maybe eleven, new Earthborn kids for the Convocation this winter, and I'm going back on youth evaluations and mentoring for a few years," he said. "Been getting a look at them before the gathering, and am off to confirm if a human-born girl on the West Coast is ours. You'll be there this year?"

"So many? Really?" I said. That was as many kids as Briargard had produced in her entire final century, myself included, and that would be just from the first five years on Earth.

"The Return did good things for our people's fertility, at least," he answered, grinning. Guess it was something. "Though half the kids have a human parent, so that's a factor."

"Rí Morganna is hosting this Convocation and the Many Waters guards will be on security," I said. "I'm hoping to be part of the contingent."

"She's off in Europe making arrangements this week," Maddoc said. "Or I'd have asked her to join us."

"You can go whenever you want, you know," Daire told me. "Your father would always make sure there's space for you with his party."

I just shook my head *no*. That wasn't me, not anymore.

Something electric crackled in the air around Sveta, and Maddoc put up his hand.

"Got them," Sveta said, shaking her goggles away, and paused, looking at Commander Daire.

"Daire, this is Svetlana Ivanova Sebrova, Morganna's strangeling ward, who is probably one of Stoyven's people," Maddoc said, and I jolted. That made sense. I'd met the abrasive old dokkalfar once, before Briargard fell; he'd designed the starship Faron served on and was widely considered one of the galaxy's most brilliant weaponsmiths. Most of his magic revolved around technology, too. To my knowledge, though, there were only three dokkalfar left alive. "We may have just found another like her, and... perhaps some answers about what happened to Derdriu. Sveta, this is Commander Daire of the Red Ravens."

"My greetings, sir," she said, triumph in her eyes. "And I've indeed found a bit. We need a secure room."

Callum gestured for us to follow him, and a minute later we followed him to a small conference room with a projector setup at one end. He made a small bow, offered to bring coffee, and left.

"Secure, *moy hopa*," Sveta snorted, and there were popping sounds from the light, light switch, and something inside the projector. Daire blinked, and Maddoc swore softly.

"Is that from..." Daire started to ask, and Maddoc shook his head.

"Classified," he said. "The kids here are too young to know about it."

"I know the sidhe have been infiltrated," Sveta said, putting up some surprisingly complex security wards, and I startled.

Maddoc looked at me, worried.

"Your systems are filthy with bugs and recorders," she continued, oblivious. "I have to check everything I use, *every* time I use your systems, because the bugs keep getting replaced when I take them out."

"What?" I said, and Daire made a calming gesture.

"Not all our... bad luck... from the last century has been entirely ill fortune," he said, not saying *sabotage* aloud.

A fist could have slammed into my throat, and it would have hit more gently.

Briargard. The Shields. My lovers. All the other children of my generation. My mother. My magic, my people, my world. Our losses, our stumbling retreat. Our disaster of an invasion here on Earth, where everything that could go wrong did so.

That wild light I'd felt on the battlefield two nights earlier started to slip out of me again.

"Connor, control your breathing," Maddoc said, and a lifetime of training made me obey him.

"How *long...*" I asked, when I was breathing almost normally again.

"Since before you were born, though it intensified over the last fifty years," Maddoc sighed. "We don't know who, still, and that isn't why we're here now. This is part of why I made you go through our basic Intelligence training ten years ago, though, even if you didn't want to stick with it."

I didn't stick with it because half my remaining magic is empathy and fertility stuff, and I'd have been getting pillow assignments if I stayed a moment longer. Thanks, but never again.

"Why didn't anyone tell me?" I demanded.

"Because your choices carry consequences," Daire answered calmly. "Commairge Sciatho an Briargard would have been entitled to this information. Connor of the local guard is not. Are you certain he should be here, Maddoc?"

"He's bound up in this," Maddoc said. "I Saw it. And I may need to send an agent into the outlands for this matter. He's had training for that, and can pass as a human better than just about anyone else we have here. Sveta, go ahead."

I sat back, choking on all of it.

"Commairge... Connor. You were wounded, almost beyond hope of survival," Daire said, putting a hand on my shoulder. "And you're still recovering. No one holds any of it against you. And no one is asking you to give more, or wants you hurt again."

Callum knocked and came in with a tray of coffee fixings and mugs, bowed, and left again.

After a second, I nodded. My breaths came in and out raggedly still, and the remnants of my hangover were helping nothing, but I grabbed a coffee and made myself drink. If only on the warm mug, I could refocus for the moment.

33

TRANSGRESSING BOUNDARIES

AISLING

S trong arms wrapped around me and lifted me off the ground, and I snuggled into their warmth. Gods between, whoever had just picked me up smelled *good,* and people so rarely did. I breathed in the scent of his skin, honey and oak leaves and clean maleness. He froze, and I heard Hart swear softly under his breath.

Oh. *Him.* Mr. "I've captured you." Dammit. Who was getting hotter by the moment, what with actually listening to me and fixing problematic bits when he realized what they were. Seeing him befriend people under my protection did... weird things... to me. I'd wanted to run off into the bushes with him, too.

I briefly considered sending him the mental image I'd had of licking my way down his body, starting from his neck, directly in kissing distance right now, and regretfully decided that was a *terrible* idea.

"I can walk," I said out loud, and his arms squeezed tighter for a second. He just looked at me, and carried me over and put me down in the back seat of a Jeep, then got in next to me.

"You've overdone it," Hart said. "And Darouk was just telling me about some sidhe guy in the city who ended up in a coma from spending too much magic. Just take it easy."

I tried stretching, and my body *objected.*

"Owww..." I groaned.

"Snake hit you pretty hard," Hart said. "You look like you're half black and blue."

"Arg. Dammit. I knew that'd get bad. Was going to have a girl in Strangelingtown help with that."

"What do you mean?"

"She's got healing magic. Laying on of hands kind of stuff. Used to work with my team occasionally and I helped her with her Cascade, but she needed to Change too much to stay out in the human lands."

"Healing hands are a thing?" Hart asked, frowning, and looked at his hands. Magic sort of pulsed.

"You've got no idea what you can and can't do, do you?" I sighed. "Go ahead and try, if you want to."

He kind of bit his lower lip and seemed to think about it, then his eyes glittered dark green and he reached for me. Warm fingers touched the skin under my jaw and on my left arm, and heat seemed to seep out of them and into me, his magic soaking into me like warm honey. I gasped in pain, because accelerated healing *hurts,* especially when the healer doesn't know what they're doing, and he made a little concerned noise and readjusted something.

A wave of luscious sexual need swept over my body, every inch of my skin waking up hot and wanting.

Not pulling him down to me took about as much willpower as I've ever used in my life.

"Hart... stop. Now," I said through gritted teeth, not actually wanting him to stop *at all.* He pulled his hands away, blinking confused golden-green eyes at me.

"But it was working!"

"Yeah, well, you can go learn to differentiate between *get better* and *feel good* magic on *somebody else,* okay?!? Because healing and lust magics are not the same thing! Or fuck, at least properly introduce yourself and take me somewhere with a bit of privacy!"

Jones leaned his head against the steering wheel and started laughing helplessly. Birch looked at us and shook his head in slow disbelief. Hart's face went *bright* red.

"M'dude hasn't been able to think a coherent thought when you're in twenty miles of him for the last three years, girl," Jones said, leaning back and looking at us. "Don't expect too much of him when you're right in arm's reach."

Hart put his head in his hands in despair and swore. Jones laughed, and the Jeep lurched forward. Darouk made one of those crazy arboreal leaps Dohoulani can do and grabbed onto the front passenger roll bar, and pointed the direction we needed to go. The other Jeep and troop carrier chugged to life behind us, and we were off.

A few minutes later, Hart looked up at me. His face was still crimson.

"Arthur Hart," he said, holding out his hand for me to shake.

I looked at him for a second, shook my head ruefully, then took it.

"Aisling, but my friends call me Dusty," I said, since Zahra had used my nickname anyway.

"I'm sorry," he said. "About... that."

"Well, the bruises *are* feeling better," I answered. "And the rest... has potential, okay?"

Poor guy blushed again, and mumbled something I couldn't make out. I felt a second's deep relief that I'd come into my magic as a kid and teenager, not at an age when self control and dignity meant much to me.

"Arthur," I said, and he glanced over at me. I shrugged a little and smiled. "Your name suits you."

He caught my gaze for a second, sighed almost wistfully, and looked out at the woods.

Our Jeep rumbled into a bit of darker forest where the trees were already leafed out and formed almost a tunnel around us. The temperature dropped sharply as the sun disappeared, and the clamor of spring birdsong went silent. Little bits of mist seeped between the trees, and I saw pale mushrooms along the roadside and growing in shelves out of some of the silver-barked trees. The air smelled... different, like the wind was coming off distant ice.

Something startled and looked at me through the fog, and I caught a glimpse of the kind of antlers not seen on Earth for ten thousand years.

"STOP!" I yelled, jumping half up. "Stop, we're driving into a ghostland!"

Jones swore and skidded into a brake. The cars behind us did the same, and Jones waved frantically at them to back up. All three vehicles reversed and screeched backwards until we were back in sunlight.

I let out a breath.

"How did you know?" Birch asked. "Other than the sun going behind some clouds..."

"I go in and out of ghostlands now and then to explore," I said. "Had to hide from monsters in them a couple times too. The edges are like... places where the boundaries between worlds get soft. But there's never sunshine, it's always a bit misty, and you see mushrooms all over. And those trees were all birches, and it's too far South here for birchwoods. Also, saw a megaloceros, an extinct Ice Age deer. Bit of a hint. I feel some magic stuff too, but it's harder to describe."

"Huh."

"If you're in the edge at night, a lot of those mushrooms are bioluminescent. It's pretty cool. I should run back in and harvest some."

"What? Why?"

"Because a bunch of those were edibles, and they're about as high Radiance as you can get. Zahra might need more, and I bet you have other people going into the Hunger now and then too, right?"

Arthur considered, then nodded.

"Darouk, call your tribesmen and check if they've seen the ghostland and know a route around the edge," he said. "Birch,

Jones, pull out maps and see if there's a better way. Troops! Any of you know edible mushrooms?"

"I know some," a dark blond guy said, getting out of the troop transport. "Used to go out picking with my Ukrainian grandma."

"Okay, Sokolov, come with us," Arthur said.

"He shouldn't handle them directly," I said to Arthur. "FYI. He's had a bit too much Radiance already."

"Shit," the soldier said.

"Div 51 hazard," Birch sighed. "We've all been over-exposed. Grab some disposable gloves out of the first aid kit."

I glanced over the human troops, examining them with my magic. It was true. Most of them had a bit of that sparkliness people got when they were one moderate Exposure Event from Cascading.

"So, we'll want to run a string or rope in with us to be safe," I said. "Or set a magical anchor to follow back out. Basically, think of ghostland exploration like going diving in dark waters; you want to have something to show you the way back out. You don't have to come, though. I can be in and out in a couple of minutes."

Arthur *looked* at me.

"What do you use to find your way back out?" he asked.

"My bondnet, and I've developed a general sense of direction in there. I think what that Elsecomer weapons master was doing earlier was sort of skimming in and out of something like a ghostland. Wish I had an idea how he did that."

"Maddoc's a Navigator," Darouk said. "One of the best at using that system the sidhe travel through. You want to learn that stuff, *go to him.*"

I just shook my head and gathered up the blanket I'd woken up in. One of his troopers threw Hart a bundle of thin rope, tied in a figure eight to keep from tangling, and he started unwrapping it.

"How do we do this?" he asked.

"Either tie that to the Jeep or have someone hold this end," I said. He pulled a couple feet out and made a half hitch knot around the Jeep's front roll bar. "We'll walk in, I'll harvest some mushrooms and put them on the blanket, and Sokolov here can confirm they're edibles he recognizes. You keep your gun ready and stand watch."

Arthur nodded.

"Captain, let me take the rope, keep your hands free," Sokolov said, pulling on some latex gloves, and Arthur passed it over.

"Okay," I said, and closed my eyes and mentally mapped the space around me, noting the magical signatures of Birch and the strangelings around us, and the land and the trees and the soft space between worlds here...

"What the *fuck* are you doing?" Arthur growled at me, and I opened my eyes to see him sparking gold and looking pissed and territorial again.

Good gods he's hot. Why the fuck couldn't we just have stayed up on that hill?

"Oh, get over yourself," I said, and grabbed his hand and pulled him into a mental connection, trying not to think about how delicious his energies felt against mine, how perfectly his body had fit against me. "Look, I'm mapping where we are and who we're with so if we somehow get lost I can shift us back here. I don't *need* a rope, that's just a backup."

He took a deep breath and *looked* through me at what I was seeing.

"This is... a little like when I'm scanning for monsters," he said, frowning, and released my hand. "Ah, I need to back off on this."

"Dude's hopeless," I heard Jones say quietly to someone. "And this is hilarious."

I opened my eyes, and the woodland floor around us was awash in blooms. Arthur was blushing bright red again.

Nobody had ever given me so many flowers. It was sweet, really.

"Birch, what time is it?" I asked, trying not to embarrass Arthur any more.

"About four," he said. "Twenty minutes?"

"Sounds good. If we're not back in twenty, tug the rope and try to call me mentally," I said. "Time can get wonky in the ghostlands. One tug is a welfare check, two means come back, three is emergency and come here, okay?"

"Yup, got it," Birch said.

With a sigh, I turned and faced the way into the ghostland, finding that place of balance in my core. I closed my eyes and stepped forward. Arthur's hand landed on my shoulder and when I glanced at him, saw his other hand was on his soldier's arm. Two more steps in, fog billowed around us and all sounds from his troops and vehicles disappeared. Three steps beyond that, it faded enough to see birch trees around us again, and that ice-scented wind sighed through them. Nine steps in, and I could clearly see the patches of mushrooms covering the trees and forest floor.

Fog swirled between white trees. Everywhere we looked, mushrooms sprouted from fallen logs and trunks and the earth itself. No birds sang; nothing sounded at all, except the sighing of the wind through the small leaves on the trees and an occasional drip of water falling.

"That wind smells... weird," Sokolov whispered. "Like, too clean."

I nodded, and answered quietly, "I think it smells like a glacier. Some ghostlands I've gone into linked to an Earth that never left the Ice Age. So, eyes open for megafauna. You guys keep watch and I'll pick mushrooms as fast as I can."

"Pretty sure those are chanterelles over there and the ones coming out of that log are oyster mushrooms," Sokolov said. "Babushka loved them."

I folded the blanket to make a carrying basket or sorts, shaped a little harvesting knife from my bound weapon, and started picking.

34

THE HALL OF THE MATRONS

ARTHUR

T he weirding birchwood was the spookiest place I'd ever been. Large stones lay scattered between the trees, so covered in moss and lichen you could hardly tell what they were. Aisling gathered mushrooms with swift efficiency, keeping her wits about her, but something was off. We were intruding in the domain of ancients, and both the monster and the emerald-eyed boy inside me paced within their cage of cracking bindings, feeling something I could make no sense of.

I scanned again for monsters, risking both magically opening up to whatever was out there *and* the moon-eyed idiot inside me sending Aisling more flowers, and felt nothing. Yet, there was something. Some intelligence of the lost forest watched us, so primal and diffuse I could barely even feel it.

"Check this batch," Aisling said, placing the blanket full of gathered mushrooms by Sokolov's feet. He knelt, nervously glancing up and around, then started examining them. "I'm going to go grab the boletes over by the big boulder, then we'll get out of here."

"Why double check everything?" I asked my soldier, scanning the trees.

"Because all mushrooms are edible *once*," he said, "But sometimes deadly ones come up near the safe ones, and can look similar. You want to eat wild mushrooms regularly, from types that aren't extremely distinctive, you *double check them.*"

His hands skimmed through the mushrooms, tipping them over and examining the stem and underside of every cap.

"I'm not sure about this one..." he started to say, looking up at Aisling, then, barely breathing the words, "...oh god in heaven, protect us."

Fog swirled around Aisling and solidified into huge feline shapes, one atop the boulder near where she was kneeling. Two flanked her, blocking her way back to us. They hadn't been hiding in the fog. The mist itself took shape and became great pale cats with heavy ruffs and golden-green eyes and teeth like long knives. The monster inside me went completely still at seeing embodied creatures identical to itself.

So did Aisling.

The large sabertooth on top of the rock yawned lazily, showing off fangs at least six inches long. She looked at me, expectantly, with gold-green eyes were far more intelligent than a beast's.

Put down the gun, the fae voice in my head said urgently. *Put down your gun and get your soldier out of here.*

The cat nearest Aisling sneezed and then put his chin down right on her shoulder. Its huge teeth pressed into her vulnerable skin. He chuffed, almost like he was laughing at us.

"Sokolov, I want you to carefully and slowly gather up that blanket and follow the rope back," I said, very gently putting my gun down. "Tie it off to my gun first, please. I don't think they're going to attack, but *don't come back for us.* You got that?"

He nodded slightly and did as I instructed, and running the rope through his fingers, stepped backwards and away. Fog swirled, and he faded and vanished from view.

Out of the mist beyond where he'd disappeared, a huge white stag stepped forward, easily nine feet tall at the shoulder, golden palmate antlers spreading back from his head in a vast, ivy-tangled crown.

Irish Elk, some trivia-hoarding corner of my mind whispered. *Extinct since the Ice Age.*

Lord of the Wildwood, some other internal voice said, and I found myself dropping to one knee in a graceful sort of obeisance I'd never even seen. The great deer huffed, its nose inches from my face, and I looked up into dark emerald eyes glimmering with all the forest's ancient secrets. Millennia spun in their depths, ice coming and retreating, stars wheeling cold through the sky, comets blazing through the night and lights I couldn't understand dazzling up from Earth to meet them.

And inside me, the bound parts of me screamed against their confinement.

"Help me," I whispered to the ancient one, the voices of the spirits inside me speaking directly through my lips. It snorted, and hot breath blew against my face.

"That may take a more delicate hand than my father's," said the girl atop the great deer's back, sliding down to stand before me. I don't know if I somehow hadn't seen her or if she hadn't been there. She was sidhe, and looked young, but her eyes were deep and ancient, the same dark emerald as the deer's, and her hair fell in reddish-brown waves to the small of her back. Her bone structure was European, but her skin was nut brown, like you see in depictions of prehistoric people. Small antlers, like a female reindeer's, sprouted from her forehead. Her clothes were sewn skins, primitive, decorated with swirling designs of shells and beads, and she carried a bow and arrows on her back.

She reached out and touched my cheek, looking at me like she was seeing the lines of someone beloved in my face, exactly how Grandma Holt used to look at me when remembering her husband. But it was my mother I saw in the huntress' smile and eyes.

"Well, come along then," she said, and waved for Aisling to join us. She was scratching the neck of the young male sabertooth that had been pinning her, and it was purring hard enough its neck was visibly vibrating. When she tried to stand it leaned into her harder and she almost fell over. My monster made a little jealous growl. The large sabertooth on top of the rock chuffed something, and the smaller one made a complaining sort of noise and let Aisling go. Then the large one leaped fluidly down, and sauntered over to the girl and me. Aisling followed, her movements as spare and graceful as a cat herself.

We followed them around the rock, and fog billowed white for a second. When it faded, we were walking into a circular clearing through a stone gate like the trilithons at Stonehenge. Night fell as we stepped forward. A huge cauldron boiled in the center of the space, pale blue flames flickering around its round belly and steam rising to join with the fog. Beyond it, at what I somehow knew was the North side of the clearing, a large skin tent sat amongst the roots of a vast, gnarled tree. Pale mushrooms sprouted between cracks in its bark, and small golden apples hung from its tangled branches. The tent was made of rough skins, thick fur still on them, and its entry was framed by an arch of mammoth tusks.

A slender hand pulled the skin door open and warmth and firelight and women's laughter spilled out. The woman who opened the door was dressed like a lady of the classical world, but her garment's fabric was not linen or wool but something otherworldly fine. A crown of seabirds and starlight wove across her brow. Her hair tumbled in curls like golden sunshine down to her knees, and her smile of welcome dazzled with its brilliance.

The horned lady kissed the starlit queen on her cheeks and led us into the room beyond her. It wasn't the rough stone age camp I expected, though, but a cottage inside, with toddlers' playthings scattered across the floor around a large loom, and knitting and spinning projects on practically every surface not already taken up by cats. A round kitchen table waited for us. Apple turnovers fresh from the oven sat on a central platter, and the fragrance of mulled cider warmed the air.

In the back of the room, a woman with blue-black skin and silver-streaked hair, somehow smooth and young but ancient beyond all measure, worked to detangle a very unhappy kitten from a knotted mess of gray yarn. When she moved, the shadows on her skin went transparent, and pale, bare bone shone through. Behind her in the darkness, a shrouded woman nursed a baby.

Welcoming us into the room was another woman, this one with pale blond braids hanging down each shoulder. Pink blossoms bloomed in her hair. She wore an oversized Scandinavian sweater and faded bluejeans dusted in animal hair, and poured steaming hot cider into mugs and cheerily waved us into seats. I had a feeling the muddy farm boots next to the door were hers. She smelled of ripe apples and horses.

Aisling has her hair and cheekbones, I thought. One glance and you knew they were kin. They could almost be sisters, but for the long ages dwelling in her ancestor's eyes.

Every ear I could see came to points.

"Welcome to the *Dísarsálr,* the Hall of the Matrons, children of our children," the Nordic woman said with a wide smile, putting cinnamon sticks into each mug.

"And bearers of the children that will be," the crowned woman said, looking at Aisling.

"You took your time getting here!" said the wildwood girl. "We expected you years ago. But I see you were entangled."

"Quite a mess, truly," the Nordic woman said.

"Grief does terrible things to the mind," the queen said. "Unfortunate, that."

"It can hone a weapon into something deadly, though," said the girl in skins, setting her bow down by the door.

"We have need of such weapons," said the queen, sitting and sipping from her glass. "Serpents slither amongst our people; worlds are wracked with mothers' wailing."

"Eat, drink!" the farmwife said. "You will need your strength."

Aisling looked at the apple turnovers and steaming cider, and hesitated.

"You're fae already, child," her forebear said, smiling, "And your ancestors ate and drank plenty of these. How do you think the sidhe came to be?"

"The boldest, the bravest, went into the mists and wilderness," the huntress said. "And ate the fruits of the Great Tree, igniting starstuff in their bones. It was *Shining Ones* who came back from the lost spaces between the trees."

"I was there when your grandfather was given the apples of gold," the queen said to Aisling. "The Blade like Light on Water, with grief in his heart and stars in his soul. Well done was that deed, a needful thing to bring us here."

In the back of the room, an almost inaudible sob escaped the nursing mother.

Aisling picked up the mug in front of her and inhaled the steam rising from it. A slow smile spread across her face, and she drank, then sighed and sank back into her chair. Color flooded back into her face, and vitality into her body.

"There aren't enough sidhe," the queen said, looking at me, then her. "Not to face down the tide, not to save our people. We need allies."

"A spark was needed, to awaken dormant bloodlines," the farmwife said to Aisling. "To kindle the memory of my kind, and build them a bridge back to the world: blood of my blood crossed with that from beyond, water to waken seeds long sleeping."

"Who are you?" Aisling asked the three.

"Who am I? Only a simple orchard keeper," the farmwife answered. "The youngest of Ivaldi's elder children, whose daughters tended a farm below the linden trees."

"Who am I? Only a lady, once, of a fallen world," said the woman crowned in stars, and looked at both of us. "Grandmother of your child-to-be."

"Who am I? Only the Wildwood's daughter, who stole the Hunt lord's horses and then his heart," said the girl in skins, and looked at me, grinning with my mother's smile. "Keeper of our oldest Ways."

I reached over and took a turnovers, took a bite, and washed it down with a drink of cider. It felt like drinking William's magic sap hooch, but... so much *more*. Gold flooded into everything hungry and aching in me. Across the table, Aisling took a pastry too and started eating.

"And what would you have of us?" she asked the women when it was finished and her mug was empty.

"Do the right thing," said the farmwife. "Tend your land and people, that they may thrive."

"Do the necessary thing," said the queen, and looked at me. "Lead and guide them."

"Do the hard thing," said the huntress, and put her hand on Aisling's. *"Keep going,* even blind, alone in darkness, when all has failed and fallen. Trust to that hope which kindles when despair has fallen deepest; *protect it at all costs.* And when you make the kill, take the Serpent's head *and* heart."

"Last time, we only took her head," said the queen, muscles working in her jaw. "It wasn't enough. Scatter the remains *widely.*"

"Give the heart to burning cold," said the farmwife. "My girlfriend will help you; she liked how you handled the winter dragon. She's been a bit lost, though, you'll have to find her first. Went skiing by Mimir's Well and hasn't come back."

"Give the head to fire," said the huntress. "And the body too. Separately. Let sacred waters take the ashes."

"Keep a tooth," the queen said. "To prove your kill."

"The Serpent?" I asked, feeling completely clueless. "Another big snake?"

"She takes many shapes," said the farmwife, grabbing an apple and munching on it. "You'll hear about her sooner or later. She's been sliming all over everything."

"She stole my life and little child," the queen said, her voice cold. "Vengeance comes due."

"Now *we* hunt her," said the Huntress, smiling with a predator's grin. "And will use such weapons as come to hand."

"Once they're cleaned up and honed a bit, of course," the farmwife said, and glanced towards the back of the room and the woman detangling the yarn-ensnared kitten. "How's that coming?"

"Done," the black-haired woman said, and I saw it wasn't gray yarn in her fingers, it was silver vines. The kitten jumped down from her lap, freed, and firelight sparkled on fangs that hung below its chin. Bones shone through her skin as the dark woman looked behind her. The shadowed mother rose with her baby, holding the child with her right arm because her left was missing. Aisling startled and half fell out of her chair.

"...Mom?" she whispered, tears filling her eyes, and the shrouded woman looked at her with sorrow. Milky, dead eyes turned blindly towards us. Her lips didn't move, but we heard her words.

"From my bonds, from my bindings, from my chains on hearts and minds, be unfettered, be unbound... be freed," she said, and the silver vines inside us turned to mist and spun shadows into the brightening air. Aisling went to her knees, hands to her chest, and I felt myself falling.

Things went black for a while.

35

DISCOVERED

CONNOR

Sveta nodded, and a projection illuminated the air above the table, showing a map of Many Waters and the buffer zone around it.

"At six-thirty this morning, an hour before sunrise, we had some proximity alarms go off on our outermost boundary, right on the Mississippi river. It appeared to be the monster patrol group that acts as a shield against weirdlings exiting the Edgelands, and as they promptly engaged with a gigantic snake, we didn't pay it much attention - they were just doing their jobs, nothing unusual."

"I just came from doing forensics on the snake," I said, putting the entire *sabotage* thing forcibly aside. "Which washed up here a couple hours ago. Everything was normal for one of their kills, except for two bronze-tipped arrows stuck in it and a slice into its eye socket from what looked like a sidhe nanotech weapon."

Daire raised his eyebrows at Maddoc.

"Yes, we finally got some answers about Derdriu, though nothing was said about someone getting her armaments, or how that would even be possible. Forgive me, Svetlana, I know you kept speaking, but I didn't hear a word after you said a troll ate my little girl's arm. There's a dokkalfar kid out there, though, or a strangeling kid with similar abilities. He said his cousin knew her, so either they somehow got Derdriu's blades or the boy has imitated our technology somehow. Keep going."

Stoyven's people were known for circumventing the commonly understood laws of nature and pulling impossible technology out of almost thin air, so either theory made sense. Nanotech armor and weapons generally return to their maker when their bearer dies, but Derdriu's never had. It was the last thread of hope Maddoc had held onto for his daughter, even after he felt her light go out. The technology was of dokkalfar design, though, so perhaps a young one of their people could have done... something.

"The snake fight started here, and the creature ran into our outermost buffer zone. They pursued," Sveta said, gesturing at the satellite image. "The people on duty kept some basic tracking on it, but it wasn't until some weird magic started going off that anyone really paid any attention."

"About forty-five minutes after they first engaged it, some kind of magical fireworks went off downriver from there, just inside our lands," Maddoc said. "Some of it felt like ancient earthly magic, I'd have said coming from a landbound sidhe if that wasn't something lost to us. Really *weird* Tree magic, too, with a completely different flavor to it, more like what the alfar life-shapers used to wield. Still not sure what it was. I was at morning training with the Guard, and went out on a skimmer with them to check it out. Sveta, play that footage first."

The little video we'd already seen started playing."

"Remind me to make another note that Ziglo should *never* get promoted out of the Guard," Daire said dryly, watching it. "Does he not realize we're trying to make peace with the outlands? We're never going to get even basic terms if our own people are this damn stupid and trigger-happy."

"It was just a stun bolt," Maddoc sighed. "But I don't disagree."

On screen, the dark elven boy complimented the guards' weapons, then broke them all.

"Epona's hooves," Daire said, eyes widening. "I want him. Stoyven's going to *really* want him."

"He's not part of Strangeling Brigade, that's the odd thing," Maddoc said. "Sounded more like he's part of a Guardian-style organization taking care of refugee victims of the Sochan Effect. We've allowed small settlements of them to grow in the Edgelands, most halfway between the Freeport and the edge of our buffer zone. Strangelingtown is the largest. People who Change out in the human world are killed, or imprisoned and enslaved, so we've turned a blind eye. The refugee tribes who've left the Freeport seem to have good relations there."

"Why'd the boy defend the soldiers?" Daire asked. "For the sake of the giant girl there?"

"No," Sveta said. "For the sake of his cousin, the one terrified of the sidhe, who's hiding behind that fallen tree behind them, off to the side there. You can see her eyes peeking through the roots now and then. He's just there to distract you."

Sveta paused the playback and zoomed in. There was definitely someone back there. Maddoc blinked and swore.

"I mapped the space before taking out the soldiers. There was no one else there."

"There were two people back there," Sveta said. "The Underhill Railroad agent and the real leader of Strangeling Brigade. They set off those fireworks in the land magic, collapsed, and their people pulled them back there just before you arrived. Aerial surveillance got all of it. That landbound magic you say the sidhe lost, was it good for hiding people?"

"Superb," Daire said. "Brennos and I used to... Ahem. Never mind. If you're landbound and don't want someone to see you, they won't see you unless they're far more skilled than you are and actively looking."

"It's amazing you two survived yourselves long enough to grow old and respectable," Maddoc said, his voice very dry, and Daire grinned and nodded his head in complete agreement.

"Can someone landbound tell when someone else with magic is coming into their territory?" Sveta asked. "Especially if the other person perhaps is landbound as well, somewhere else?"

"Oh yes," Daire said. "Makes you want to take off screaming and drive a rival out of your land with your teeth and nails. I remember Brennos running naked into a blizzard once."

"He would," Maddoc said. "Who was it?"

"Bethanna of the Wildwood, stealing his horses. She got them, too, and rather more, when they had to wait out the blizzard in a cave together. The pair spent the next thousand years arguing over whether she'd actually stolen them or he gave them to her as a courting gift. Either way, a few months later, she rode up on his favorite horse, belly already rounded, and put a spear to his throat. *Marriage,* she said, *Or war.* And he jumped up right behind her, grinning like a maniac, and off they rode to arrange the rites. It was amazing the wedding itself didn't devolve into a battle, putting *those* two clans together for three days."

"Ahh. Of course," Maddoc answered. I wondered if Faron knew that story; his unit was usually under Brennos' command. To be fair, all the sidhe forces in Kzephian space were under Brennos' command. The Firebirds were just a bit more directly so. I'd heard of Bethanna, too; the ancient had never remarried after her death. "Continue playing."

We watched the rest of the clip in silence.

"So Maddoc says you found what happened to Derdriu?" Daire asked Sveta. She waved, and a series of newspaper headlines and photos flashed across the projection.

"About ten years ago, in a little town about two hundred kilometers North of here, an overworked maternity nurse underwent a redcap transformation... while on duty. The new troll ate four infants, including a James Maddoc Lingren, the hospital security guard, and the arm of a mother, one Deirdre Lingren," she said. "She had just had a Cesarean and was still immobilized. She was saved from the troll when her thirteen-year-old daughter sliced its throat open with a surgical scalpel, but died of supposed leukemia six months later. The symptoms resemble chronic iron poisoning, however, and may have been misdiagnosed."

"Daughter?" Maddoc said, startled, like his grief had kept him from hearing that earlier.

"One Aisling Sorcha Lingren," Sveta replied, and Maddoc went completely still. "Who sounds completely bonkers, and I kind of want to go work with her. Was Derdriu good at illusions?"

"Excellent," Daire said, glancing with concerned eyes at his frozen friend. "It was part of what made her such a good Intelligence agent."

"Well, Aisling lives under an illusion full time," she said, and some grainy photos of a plain, intelligent looking human girl came up. She was pale blonde with blue eyes and braids, and clothes that spoke of rural poverty, but there was something magnetic about her. "She must have some great obfuscation glamours going to get away with everything she does. I've got her school *and* police records here. Her first citation, she was nine years old and ran down some sort of cryptid with a newspaper delivery horse. Brained it with the newspapers and then stabbed it to death with a pocketknife. Got cited for endangering the horse."

Daire laughed.

I don't think Maddoc had even blinked yet. I grabbed a cup of coffee and filled it halfway up, and held out my hand to Daire. He glanced at Maddoc with pitying eyes, and reached into his friend's pocket to pull out a flask of whiskey. I finished filling the mug and handed it to my mentor. Fumbling fingers grabbed it, and he took a long drink.

"Five years later, a couple months after her mother's death, she went from being homeschooled to going to a public school for the first time since 4th grade. A forest troll chased some kids who'd been smoking in the woods into the building, and this scrawny little girl did a backflip off its face, nut-punched it, and led it directly into an ambush some older boys set up with the school's fire axes. I suspect she'd already met the dokkalfar boy then, because they said they'd been instructed to get the axes and be ready for her by a voice on the school's otherwise non-functional intercom. Then there are a few further citations for underage drinking, public brawling, and indecent exposure at some amateur night that got raided *and* later at a living history festival. She showed up for some kind of public Viking reenactment wargame wearing nothing but her shield and helmet. Her file also has a semi-stern warning about breaking longshoremen's bones, from last summer after a trio of them tried forcing her friend into a nightclub's back room."

"Oh gods," Daire chuckled, "She sounds like some of the old Earthborn, back when we were young."

"Indecent exposure? What's that?" Maddoc asked, looking like he might be in at least mild shock and grabbing onto some random thing he didn't understand while he dealt with the larger issues.

"Human prudery. Apparently, this is considered 'unacceptable behavior'."

A picture flashed on the screen of the girl in a very abbreviated sci-fi dark lord costume, basically the cloak and chest piece over fishnets and cheap black lingerie, holding a costume helmet and suggestively licking a red toy laser sword.

Not bad, I thought. *Has potential.*

"Congrats, Maddoc. You've got two of them," Daire said, looking at me. My mentor looked like he needed more whiskey. I swallowed a giggle.

"Shenanigans aside, she's done very well academically," Sveta continued.

A graduation picture flashed, the blonde and a mixed-race boy, part Indian or Pakistani, grinning at the camera in well-worn traditional hats and gowns. He looked like he could have been the un-Changed brother of the dark elf boy on the beach, so that was probably his human seeming.

"She was co-valedictorians with one Steven Bharat Riksby, nickname Rigs, apparently a third cousin on the human side, and both of them got full ride scholarships to the University of Minnesota Duluth campus. She did biology and chemistry, he did computers, engineering, repairs, software. He's known for being able to fix just about anything electronic. He just graduated; she's got a semester to go on her Master's degree."

"What's she studying?" Daire asked.

"Well, here's where it gets interesting. Her undergrad work was ambitious; she did a dual major in Elsecomer Studies and Biology, with a minor in veterinary medicine and a lot of chemistry classes. Now she's writing a master's thesis on ferrous poisons and cryptids, and seeking a post-grad internship at the kind of military science sites people don't come out of."

"*Ferrous poisons?*" Maddoc said, staring. "What the hell is she doing?"

"That gets us into her moonlighting," Sveta said, obviously enjoying this. "The summer before she started university, our girl joined a group that goes binge-drinking in historic costumes, with a bit of sword fighting and such on the side. They're called Northshield, the remnant local branch of an American historical reenactment group called the Society for Creative Anachronism. The first event she went to got hit by a redcap slave raid riding in from the Bakken oil fields, where they have a large base. It sounds like the main band of fighters got drawn off on a wild goose chase, and then about forty of those things hit the non-combatants and children left behind."

"Good gods. How'd she escape?" Daire asked.

"She didn't. Official records say she got hit over the head and woke up concussed in the woods after the raid. The concussion appears to have been real; she had a follow-up check on it a couple days later. Unofficially, that day was the first time in six years the so-called 'Green Lady of the North' showed up, the Northwoods' own mysterious protector, who first appeared two years after the Return. Apparently kept the area around Duluth clear of bad cryptids. She, or rather Derdriu's successor, is still operating, and took down an eight meter tall, man-eating stone giant earlier this week, up on the cliffs of Lake Superior. Half the state's monster hunters were about to go after it, and it looks like she took it down alone, or possibly with a small support team. She's known for moving impossibly fast and slicing things up with inhumanly sharp blades, usually a spear or two swords. Sound familiar?"

He tried to hide it, but the cup in Maddoc's hands shook.

"Anyway, the redcap raid. She killed over two dozen trolls in about as many minutes and held the slave convoy at a bridge long enough for the camp warband to catch up. Witnesses said it involved explosions and flying motorcycles. Then she disappeared, and 'human' Aisling showed up concussed. The camp kids said 'Legolas' little sister' saved them."

Daire and Maddoc frowned, puzzled.

"He's from another human movie," I said. "Blond fantasy elf, pretty and very deadly."

"So, here's where things start to tie together a bit. A couple years after the raid, the human boy who was on the river bank, Lieutenant Birch of Minnesota Guards Division 51, joined the history group, probably looking for info on the Green Lady. There's a subset of the club that practices magic and old pagan religions, though that isn't officially part of what the group does. Anyway, he promptly joined *them*, not the fighters. He got into that later, but to a lesser degree. One 'Alfhilde of the Mead Horn' - club members create 'historic style' names for themselves - was by then firmly established as part of that clique. She also fights, sometimes naked! And apparently they train each other at gatherings."

"Alfhilde is old Norse for 'elf battle'," Maddoc said. "They know what she is."

"Well, whoever gave her the name knows," Sveta said. "Most people just call her by her nicknames, though: Crazy Hildie, Naked Fuckin' Hildie, or Hildie the Boozer."

Definitely sounded like a young sidhe. Daire was having a very hard time not laughing at his old friend. Maddoc rubbed his forehead. The pained expression on his face was one I was *very* familiar with, but a spark of hope lit in me that maybe this could pull him back to caring about the world again.

"Get any footage of her without the glamour?" I asked.

"Yes," she said. "She's given Strangeling Brigade her parole to let her take care of the giant girl. Seems to be trying to work out some sort of alliance with them. This is from a couple hours ago."

The picture changed to her and the giant girl from the beach, twice her size, leaning against a fallen log and chatting quietly. Aisling was white-blonde, pale as sunlight on spring snow, and *beautiful* even for a sidhe. For a second I just stared, then someone walked by in a human army uniform and I realized one of our people, lost and at best half-trained, was in the clutches of an enemy military. My fingers went white-knuckled on the tabletop.

"Kid's got your eyes," Daire said to Maddoc. "And you can certainly see her grandmother in her frame."

Aisling's eyes caught on someone, and frustration and wariness and what might have been attraction flashed across her face.

"Strangeling Brigade has a reputation even in the Freeport as excellent soldiers, though," I said, shaking myself. "The Sanitation workers with the dead snake were telling me they want to enlist if we ever get peace terms. And their leader ended up with a bunch of magicians?"

"Aha, but Birch's just the team leader on paper," Sveta said. "Meet Captain Arthur Hart, who theoretically leads just the incarcerated strangeling part of the team, and technically is the junior member after losing all rank when he Changed."

The projection screen changed, and a still photo of a young human soldier flashed, then was replaced by a lower resolution one of a somewhat similar looking sidhe man about my age. I blinked, and had to hold back a sigh. He was gorgeous, from his green eyes to his defined jaw. Wildwood antlers rose from his forehead. Makeup artists would weep with joy over his lips and cheekbones. His hair was cut too short, and he wore a human military uniform trimmed in orange. Command presence practically radiated off him, but there was something... lost... in his eyes too.

Daire and Maddoc sat up straight and just stared at the screen.

"So, Arthur Hart, born Holt, age twenty-six. He pre-enlisted in the Minnesota Guard at sixteen and went active duty as soon as he graduated high school. Been a soldier for nine years now, mostly in active combat zones or hunting monsters. He spent a couple years with one of the few remnant national American units, the Army Rangers, fighting trolls and redcaps out West. Glowing commendations and battlefield promotions all over his record. He and a handful of other soldiers got trapped behind redcap lines for two months when he was nineteen. Their officer got killed the first day, and the others picked him to lead them. They then rode deep into redcap territory, stole and improvised weapons and explosives, and took out at least a dozen redcap camps and stores of pre-Return munitions, freeing every human slave they could along the way. He went in with five guys, returned with over two hundred people. Details are classified, but I'll get them. Command put him in an officer training course the day after they got out. The first part he did by distance learning, then he finished back here in Minnesota. Excelled again. Guy was going places."

Sveta sighed like that hit close to home for her, then continued.

"About a year after graduating, he woke up with a headache and sore spots on his forehead, Cascading. Got incarcerated in the state's maximum security strangeling jail and changed his name, like many strangelings do. It appears he was basically in full military command there within the week, and the Division has become a respectable force in the time since then. Mainly, they patrol the territory just beyond our security zone, but they get sent all over the state for monster hunts, and usually end up at least unofficially leading them. Their motto is *'Strangeling Brigade Goes in First'* - used to be because they were the most expendable, now it's because they're the best."

"Didn't everyone think a sidhe transformation was impossible?" I asked, and the elders both nodded.

"His human face looked a lot like both his parents' photos, so it's unlikely he's a lost half-blood," Sveta said. "He's also got two younger brothers who've shown no signs of Cascading, who look very similar to him pre-Change. However, there's no paternal name on his mother's birth certificate."

"Well fuuuck," Daire said, leaning back and chewing on his lip. "But for now, let's assume it *is* possible, or that sidhe blood from somewhere back in his family line woke up. Sometimes it'd skip a generation or two, back when we crossed with humans more often. And now we have not one but two of our own kids, working for the other side?"

"Maybe, maybe not. All they really do is hunt monsters," Sveta said. "So, Hart's been obsessed with catching 'the Green Lady' for years. He Changed in September 2044, and it sounds like an encounter with her may have irradianced him. Late December, Division 51 went after a cryptid monster, a bad one. Here's a photo."

Something like a long white Chinese dragon appeared on the projector, first attacking a crowd of fleeing humans and then, in a different picture, as a frozen corpse in the snow.

"That's a Sylothon," Daire said, shocked. "One got to Earth?"

"Sort of. Maybe," Maddoc answered, looking exhausted. "I remember that one. It got into the starport in the cargo hold of a ship that ought to have been hauling something completely different. Then it somehow mind-controlled a baggage handler into driving it to the city gates, ate him, and fled into the hinterlands. Seemed to have a lot of magic those things have never shown before."

"They're known for hunting sidhe, right?" Sveta asked, and Daire and Maddoc both nodded grimly. "Well, this one fixated on Hart. Was almost suicidal about trying to get him, even let his giant tear a leg off it while trying to reach him. Strangeling Brigade had barely had casualties from when he took over till then, and then he lost seven troopers in two days to it. They were hunting it well outside the Edgelands, chasing it up almost to Duluth, when apparently it caught a different scent."

"Aisling," Maddoc said, looking sick.

"Right in her hometown, yes, where she was visiting family for winter holidays. And then three weeks later 'the Green Lady' killed it in front of a school bus full of kids that it was about to devour, up by the Canadian border. Used bronze arrows coated in what appear to have been a mix of ground car rust and blood, probably her own, a combination which seemed to have been wildly poisonous to the snow dragon. She disappeared then, but Div 51 tracked her backwards and it looked like she had spent those weeks on skis, hunting it as it hunted her, through the swamps and the deep cold. I don't know how she survived the weather, much less the dragon; it was down to minus fifty for over a week."

Some newspaper clippings and photos from the aftermath flashed through the projection.

"Witnesses on the bus said their rescuer was an elf made of snow and ice, and that she got clawed badly enough in the last fight no one thought she'd make it. But a couple of days later, Aisling went back to classes with a doctor's note that she'd been sick after getting chilled, and local news credited the Green Lady with killing some kind of mutated wolf a couple weeks later. And Hart there developed the beginnings of an obsession with catching her, which apparently bloomed into what his people think is outright madness every time she runs strangeling escapees through his patrol lands. Which she was doing last night."

"Sounds just like Brennos, back when Bethanna was tormenting him," Daire said, chuckling a little. "Poor kid's probably been going out of his mind, with no idea why."

"How'd you find all that about Hart?" I asked. "Thought you hated going through the old human computer systems?"

"I do. They are inefficient, cobbled-together crap buckets. However, after tracking the satellite footage of the boats back to where they launched, I found the vehicle that dropped off the Underhill Railroad people, then followed it to its current position. The van was full of better than average human tech, much of it with wireless capabilities that shouldn't work at all... and thus weren't particularly well secured. It's in St. Cloud right now, near the prison Strangeling Brigade lives in. Riksby hacked their servers and went through everything a couple hours ago, and had already collated all the data on Hart," Sveta said, grinning like a shark. "So I hacked *him* and took it."

"What's he doing now?" Daire asked.

"Apparently they fund this 'Underhill Railroad' mainly by repairing console gaming systems damaged in the invasion's EMPs. They sell them to gamers and collectors. He's meeting some now."

"Is he going to know you hacked him?" Daire asked, raising an eyebrow.

Sveta shrugged, unconcerned.

"If he can learn enough Russian to read 'Your wifi security sucks, noob', then yes, he might figure it out. I left the message on the background of every screen in the van."

Maddoc looked at her and sighed. I suddenly felt some pity for the old ones who take the time to teach the young of elvenkind.

"Did you get much about the Underhill Railroad?" Daire asked.

"Not yet," she said, eyes sparkling. "His security *is* good enough that there's little mentioning it in his portable setup. I'll hit him at home later."

"What are they doing now?" I asked, thinking I was seeing the beginnings of a courtship dance much like Daire had described his old friend going through.

"They're on their way to hunt a giant pig for the Dohoulani. Spent the whole day trying to fix the vehicles Aisling broke this morning. Have some tribesmen helping them out now; sounds like they worked out some basic peace terms. They had some trouble with the road though and seem stuck at the moment. Signal's weird and scratchy, and fog is obscuring the aerial view, but they aren't going anywhere."

36

OATHBOUND

AISLING

S ilver vines drew back, gray fog parted, and I was a kid again, fourteen years old. I skipped through the front door of the farmhouse I grew up in, dropping my backpack on the floor and kicking my muddy shoes off by the door.

"Aunt Dahlia sent fresh eggs!" I called. "And cornbread muffins! Trey threw a cat at my head, but I caught it before it clawed me. Then he got sent to the barn for 20 minutes and I was supposed to be helping him with his math homework, so I went through his answers and made sure everything was wrong!"

There was silence, and then a tiny bit of the cloud of rage and grief waiting for me in the dining room slipped out of my mother.

She found the letters. I knew before I even stepped into the room with her and saw the stack of envelopes, an open one in her shaking hands. Tears streaked down her gaunt cheeks.

Oh gods, no. No no nooo. They were hidden!

"Aisling. Sorcha. Lingren. *What have you done?*"

"It's just... it's just a boy, Mom! I met a boy I like and we write letters, that's all! We only see each other at Knowledge Bowl meets. We aren't... we haven't even had a date or anything!"

"If it's nothing," she growled, her voice unrecognizable, "Why are you hiding these from me? Why do you have them sent to your grandmother's address? And if... this boy... is putting things like this into writing, *what are* you *putting on paper for anyone to find?* You're going to get yourself killed! You're going to get that boy killed, just like poor Samantha, and maybe the whole family if hunters find us! Do you not understand how important my mission is? *If I fail, we are all going to die."*

I looked at her, at the stump of her arm and the patchy hair chemo was quickly destroying, at the grief and madness that haunted her eyes.

"I know, Mom. I know. It's okay. We're all going to die. You aren't going to complete your mission," I said, and she sucked in her breath. "You can't. You're too sick and it's too late. So whatever, it's all pointless! If I want to like a boy before it all falls apart, so what? I found somebody like me and maybe for a little while I won't be alone, before it all ends!"

"A boy like you? *Like you?* Is that what this picture means?"

She pulled out the drawing Arthur had sent me, sketched in colored pencil on lined notebook paper and rather well done. He held me against his chest but facing forward, my head just under his chin, the antlers I saw in his energy already tines upon his forehead and our pointed ears fully visible. The edge of the paper was soft from being handled.

"He's still human on the outside," I said. "Still passing. It's okay."

"Okay? *Okay?* It's okay to Irradiance some poor random boy and Change him just because you like him?"

"I'm not Changing him! I saw the magic in him the first time I saw him at Knowledge Bowl! He's already got some kind of elf blood and it's going to express on its own sooner or later. It was... it was like we already knew each other, like from another life or something. And he can already glamour a little so by the time he really Cascades he'll be able to do illusions and keep himself safe. I'm showing him what to do, so he's ready!"

"Mother of Stars," she swore, closing her eyes. "You're going to trigger him Changing and get him killed just like Samantha."

"I didn't trigger Samantha!" I sobbed. "She just Changed! I only tried to be there for her!"

"Your childhood best friend. The boy you're in love with. The flipping racoons you used to think were cool!" she exclaimed. "I don't know why the Tree's magic becomes a contagion through you, but you can't do this to people! Aisling, you *can't do this!*"

"I didn't, Mom, I didn't! *Your* people did this to us. They're the ones who broke the world. We wouldn't all *be* irradianced if you hadn't invaded! You think I'm fucked up, you ever think that might be why?"

She sucked in a breath.

"This world was tipping into a death spiral when we came. If the polar regions had melted, they'd have released so much methane the climate changes would have turned it into an inferno like Venus! We didn't break the world, we saved it!"

"*Great job.* Well done! So your daughter's a mutant and everyone I love turns into a monster - well, where do you think I *got* that from???"

Her eyes tipped up, and I saw the vision come on her, some foreseeing of a possible future.

"This ends," she said, when it was over, and Radiance glittered at her fingers.

"*No!*" I cried. "No, Mom, no! Those are mine!"

She picked up the stack of letters, leaving one empty envelope to the side, and gold light glittered across them and they disintegrated into glittering ashes that disappeared before they even reached the table.

"Forget him, Aisling," my mother said, standing up, losing her glamours and reminding me she was one of the Beautiful Monsters of the invasion. She glanced at the remaining envelope and the return address in the upper corner. "Forget him, swear it to me, or I will go to this address and kill the boy I find there."

"No. No. Please, *no*, leave him alone."

"*Swear to me.*"

"Mom, he's just a boy! He never hurt you, he never hurt me, he never hurt anyone!"

"Swear, or *he dies.*"

"Mommy, no," I sobbed, slipping to the floor. "I love him."

She closed her eyes and her posture went grim and lethal. Gold dust shivered into the air around her hand, forming a long slender saber. The tip prodded my chin, forcing me to look up at her. This wasn't my mom. This was the spy from the invaders, the ones who'd destroy everything to achieve their goals.

"Swear you will forget him. Swear you will take over my mission when I fall. Swear to me. Now. Or I will go to this address and leave it a slaughterhouse."

"...I'll... I'll forget Arthur," I whispered, feeling like my soul was leaving my body. Sidhe magic clamped down around me, vining into my mind, into my heart, tearing me apart.

"Swear to continue my mission," she demanded. "Swear to find my partner and return him to Ellith, or Morganna, or Maddoc, if they seem themselves. Swear to dedicate your life, your education, your career, to this cause... until the deed is done."

Numbness crept into me as my memories tore away. I was seeing Arthur across the classroom, magic blooming through his energy, our eyes meeting for the first time and my heart leaping, and then that was gone. I was kissing him behind the school buses, and then I was holding nothing. I was pouring my heart into another letter, and then my hands and mind and heart were empty.

It wasn't a boyfriend I lost. It was myself.

"I swear to continue your mission and find your partner," I said, my voice flat.

"Swear this to the Tree, not to me. Swear by your name, by the Blood of the Tree, and by the magic within you."

I Saw the end of that path, the road ahead of me, the silent blackness awaiting at its end. The mission was not survivable. Success was perhaps possible, but for me, all that waited at the end was darkness.

"I swear to the Tree, I will complete your mission. I swear by my name. I swear by the Blood of the Tree. I swear by the magic within me," I said, feeling the bindings wrap tight around my soul.

She nodded, sharply. The hard resolution in her eyes swam in a sea of grief.

A napkin was the only piece of paper within reach. She told me to write "It's over. Goodbye," and sign it. I did. I didn't know or care who it was for.

"Go to your room and study," she said. I nodded, numb, and picked up my backpack and went. I was going to have to work a lot harder; the Way in front of me was going to need an impeccable background in hard science to get me where it needed me to go.

Behind me, I heard car keys jingle, and then she went out the door.

My cousin Trey came over after school the next day, hell-bent on revenge and continuing our usual round of pranks and shenanigans. I closed the window and wouldn't talk to him; he was just a distraction. A couple days later, I heard him screaming at my mom, and her telling him that this was the way things had to be. He came and yelled at me then, shaking me and telling me to snap out of it, but I told him he was distracting me and to leave me alone, I had to study.

Eventually, he did. Eventually, he quit trying to come back.

Mom died three months later. I was already lost, emotionally broken. I couldn't even cry until a month after her funeral, when her bindings on me started loosening. Dad couldn't manage homeschooling me alone, or understand the strange fog I was lost in, and I went back to a public school. Steve Riksby was waiting for me in eighth grade algebra, and Saw me for what I was the second I walked into class. His magic chimed against the weirding power in me, tuned almost the same as the stuff my mother could never make sense of, and he was smarter than anyone I'd ever met. After class, he invited me to join his D&D group.

This is part of the Way forward, the oath-bound voice in me said. Rigs knew he was heading for a Change, and with my strange magic saying the same thing, we slowly figured how to both hide and slow a Cascade. A couple months later, we helped the seniors take down a troll that got into the school, and I discovered my heart might be fucked up and half numb, but that made me fearless. Even better, I could still *feel* the sweet rush of adrenaline, and through that eventually learn emotions again, to care for friends and family. I could laugh and love my people and pretend sidhe magic hadn't eviscerated me.

37

Embodied

Fae Arthur

I stretched my fingers, breathing into my lungs and fully feeling the solid weight of flesh around my spirit for the first time in... so long. I didn't even open my eyes at first, just marveling at being in a body, and the body actually *fitting* me, like it never had when I was a child and mostly human. I rolled my neck, flexed my shoulders, and breathed deep.

A campfire burned in front of me, and its smoke smelled of applewood. Distant ice chilled the wind. The scents of fog and mushrooms hung in the air. The fire's warmth kissed my skin, and I shivered at the simple pleasure of it all.

"Savoring, grandson?" asked the Wildwood's daughter, across the fire from me. I opened my eyes and saw its light flickering orange and gold over her. The Hall of the Matrons was gone, but we sat in the hollow below the great apple tree where it had been. A small campfire burned in the middle of the clearing. The great cats had returned, and lounged around the hollow and on the vast roots around us. The wild part of me purred to be with pack and kin.

Aisling lay on a skin beside the fire, trapped in dreams. Tears ran silently down her cheeks.

"She didn't remember me," I said softly, wanting to lie down beside her and hating myself for that impulse. Dear gods, that girl had broken my heart. We'd talked about everything, seeing each other at occasional academic meets but mostly pouring our hearts into letter after letter. Both of us felt we knew each other already, the day we met; we'd both had the same nightmare of dying under a sky boiling with technological monsters, and our spirits rising to meet a blazing light in the sky even as it sputtered and fell. We wrote each other almost every day. Finally, we had someone with whom we could put all the weirdness into words, the magic and the grief both. We argued, a *lot*, but it was just how we flirted. I'd been hers and she'd been mine since the first moment our eyes met.

And she left me in one scribbled line on the back of a napkin.

A woman had come to me, I remembered, found me walking the dog in the woods near my parents' house. I was sixteen. She looked like an older, dark-haired version my girl, the one I wrote letters with, that I'd only kissed once but was madly in love with. She said her daughter was in danger, that she'd discovered a threat to her life, and asked me if I would help her protect Aisling. Of course I said yes; I swore it even on the magic blooming within me. And then... and then... she said *I* was what endangered her daughter, that I was going to get her killed, and handed me that scribbled message. When she threw the bindings and glamours on me, then, I didn't even resist. The vines swallowed me, and I let them.

And even after that, I loved my girl still.

But I was also choking on rage over what I'd gone through because of her, how I had been trapped and broken. And it all mattered so little to her she had completely forgotten me. Ten years I'd spent trapped and screaming, and she didn't even recognize me. Magic or no, it was unforgivable.

"Her mother made her choose between your life and her memories of you," the wild girl said, poking a stick into the fire. My whole body clenched up around that, choking me. Sparks shot up into the air, sparkling and dying away into the night. "Aisling chose your life. What her mother did to your magic, she did to her daughter's memories and heart, and the child has far too much empathy to come out of that undamaged. She won't be entirely well, when she wakes, and likely not for some while. Have patience."

"Why? Why would her mother do all that?" I asked, the question coming straight up from the kid I'd been then. "Was I so terrible?"

"It had little to do with you. The situation is far more dire than anyone breathing realizes. And more likely than not, you'd not have been able to hide your Change," the girl sighed. "And Aisling would have come for you, no matter where you were imprisoned. Then you'd both have ended up in our enemies' bellies, and they'd have been strengthened that much more."

"The missing children she talked about?"

"Yes," she said. "And that is the least of what they do, and are capable of. They will want her. The Serpent is the mother of monsters, and seeks always to make better ones. She will want Aisling with a voracious hunger, when her people learn a daughter of Ithuinn can shape the strangeling magic."

"And I need to protect her?"

"Perhaps. As much as you can," she said, her voice grim. "Mostly, we hope you will give her something to fight her way back to after darkness takes her. That will happen, that *must* happen; it is the only way we foresee to get within striking distance of our enemy, and *the Serpent must die.* Most will think Aisling dead, but we will guide her as we can, and send allies her way as possible; hold faith while she is gone. If it goes badly... we will let you know, somehow. You will need to protect her people, and your own. Her fight... far too much of it will be a long, solitary way. It's up to you if you wish to be lovers, of course. I hope you'll at least be allies. I hope she may return from the darkness when her hunt is done."

She sighed deeply and poked the fire with a stick.

This plan sounds terrible.

I don't think she likes it, either.

And just as obviously, she sees no better option.

"What, no words from you about grandchildren?" I said dryly, to change the subject, and she laughed.

"My kinswomen have hopes," she said. "Of course I would love it if you were to have a great brood of little long-toothed kittens, and send them to my husband to make him crazy. Ahh, but seeing his eyes in your face made me miss him."

"He's not... here?"

"He walks yet in the world," she said, voice tight with longing. "I was ancient already when he was young. We had our time together. When I went into shadow, he went into starlight. Tell him, if you remember this, that he has mourned too long, and should live again."

"How would I know him?" I asked, bewildered.

"It's not my side of the family who bonded with the spirit cats," she said, leaning into the one behind her, who purred. "Fond as I have become of them. And for all *you* take after me, what you think of as your human side takes after *him*."

"I don't understand."

"I know. And you won't for some while. You have the magic of two primordial bloodlines in your veins, from tribes who spent millennia feuding... small wonder your spirit split along the lines it did. But now I have you here between worlds, and you must learn what it means to be blood of the Wildwood. The girl is safe; come run with me, and I will show you. Leave your shoes and uniform here. Such things are not fit for where we are going."

"The cats?"

"Will protect her. It's not just my friends from the Matron's Hall hoping for the continuation of their lines. And hopefully my husband can teach you to manage their magic, eventually."

The cat who'd gotten Aisling to scratch him earlier yawned and hopped down from the root he was lounging on and sauntered over to her prone body, flopped down next to her, and licked her tear-stained face with his tongue. He somehow looked smaller, younger. The spirit in me started growling again, and then the beast looked at me, crossed his eyes, stuck his tongue out, and wiggled in against Aisling like a little kid.

And the monster in me just sat down, completely floored.

"Come along," said the greenwood's daughter, laughing, and I followed her into the night. It opened before her, breathing mysteries. And what I did and saw there... well.

The forest has its secrets, and not all are meant to be shared.

38

THE ORCHARD

AISLING

For a second I thought I'd woken up back at the U's Vet Med barn, smelling old traces of horses, but the air was stiller than anywhere living. Silence hung like a physical presence in the windless air. I stood up, wondering how I'd gotten wherever I was. Definitely nowhere built by lowest-bid contractors, anyway. A little paper note fell off me. I *was* in a barn, but one that made the Hall of the Rohirrim in *The Lord of the Rings* films look minimalist. Constructed in a circular fashion, it had an open center and oculus in the roof. All around me, elaborately carved wood beams and pillars decorated entirely in ancient Norse and earlier Scandinavian styles rose to the opening. The construction mixed dark, ancient timbers and sleek glossy elements even more elegantly technological than I had seen on the Elsecomer patrol.

I picked up the little paper that had fallen off of me and saw words written in a runic script I didn't recognize. Blinking, I watched the letters scramble and rewrite themselves in English. Or maybe my brain did that, I don't know.

Rest and recover, it said. *Scream if you need to. No one will hear. You're outside time and have my old home to yourself. You'll find apples to eat, herbs for tea, and a bed in the cottage by the orchard. Take as long as you need. When you're ready, sit down at the bench again and will yourself to leave.*

P.S. Please gather windfall apples for the horses. You probably won't see them, but there's a place at the edge of their field to leave treats.

The hole inside me opened again, releasing everything I'd been too messed up to feel for the last ten years. My back thumped into an elaborately carved stall door, and I slid to the floor, realizing trying to control this flood was impossible and pointless and probably bad for me anyway.

I did scream, and weep, and take every advantage of the solitude.

Eventually, I got up and found a bucket and shovel and went to find an external mess to clean up. If there were horses that came here, at least occasionally, there would be manure too.

The barn was huge and more beautiful than I'd ever thought such a building might ever be. It had been hand-built entirely of ancient wood, almost every inch of the timbers carved in startlingly elegant Norse knotwork. Some things were labeled, like old names next to stalls or what I had to guess were prescriptions or treatment notes, faded and yellowed, too fragile to touch. A fine layer of dust coated every surface. One room I went past looked like a medical lab straight out of one of the more recent Trek shows, but with the same elegant aesthetics as the ancient parts of the place. I peered in through the window, wondering what everything inside had been used for. I touched pillars made from trees vaster than any I'd seen back in my world, and marveled at the beauty of their carvings.

They must have built this place before they went star-faring, I thought. *Long before. And then upgraded things like the medical rooms as their level of science advanced.*

The place was most certainly abandoned by whatever sidhe or elves had once used it, though. I followed my nose and found stalls with open doors and long-dried droppings in them, and mucked stalls and hauled out long-dried droppings until my arms were as sore as my heart. It helped. There was some kind of elaborate composting system outside that I didn't understand, so I just added the old straw and manure to the first section, unsure if the normal processes of decomposition were even in effect.

Outside was a wonderland. Light snow dusted everything, and no tracks disturbed it. A frosty fog diffused the delicate sunlight, which sparkled and glittered through golden air. Hoarfrost clung to every branch and post and fence, to the roofs and walls and windows of the buildings. The silence was deep and long and even footsteps trained for stealth seemed loud against it.

Gods Between, I thought, looking around, *But this place would be beautiful in spring, full of people and animals, bees buzzing and birdsong ringing from the blooming trees.*

I found the orchard, bare and leafless. The trees were triple the size of normal apples, their branches bare and gaunt and black, and one in the center of the orchard was even larger than that, beyond even the size of an ancient oak. Golden fruits hung from twisting branches, and lay scattered across the ground. I found a basket in a little outbuilding full of orchardist's tools, and started gathering windfalls. After a while I began crying again, kneeling in the snow amongst the frozen apples, their scent wafting fragrant through the frost.

My mother, I thought. *My mother did that to me. To us.*

My mother is doing that to me still. Her bonds on me are gone; my oath to fulfill her mission remains. As does the darkness waiting at its end.

My mother rests in Hela's keeping, in the silent dark, with the baby I was too slow to save, still missing her arm. I didn't think that's where the sidhe are supposed to go after things end.

The apples were cold and hard with frost, but sweet still. Some smelled partially fermented, but none were rotten.

Do the right thing. Do the necessary thing. Do the hard thing.

Is the hard thing down in Hela's realm, below the world tree, where serpents gnaw its roots?

I picked up the basket of fallen apples and walked back to the edge of the pasture. There was a long wooden manger, and I poured the fruit into it. I whistled a few times, the call we used for horses back in 4H club. Only silence answered me. In the distance, at the edge of visibility, steam drifted into the sky, as if rising from a hot pool. Nothing else moved. I returned the basket to the shed it came from and went and found the cottage my ancestress had mentioned. It was as beautiful as the rest of the farm, and made with the same ancient elegance. Inside it was equally unused, and covered in a fine layer of dust.

Tea. There were herbs outside. Tea would make this better.

Most of the kitchen was the high-tech stuff like in the barn, and I had no idea how to use it. There was a little ceremonial looking hearth, though, with a round-bottomed cauldron like I'd used while reenactment camping. I found running water, built a little fire, and hung the cauldron over the flames. Then I went back outside and cut a bit of creeping chamomile from under the snow, its frozen flowers still blooming, and went back in. Both mugs and honey were in the cupboards, and I set up a cup and checked the water. Looked like it'd be a while yet before the water boiled.

There were rags and cleaning supplies under the counter.

If you can't fix something, clean something, Aunt Dahlia's voice echoed in my head. My normal preference is to stab something, but lacking any options along those lines, I started wiping down the place. It was too nice to be in this condition.

The Matronae are out for blood, I thought. *And will use the weapons at hand. Like a pair of idiots who wandered into their realm thinking to grab some medicinal mushrooms and just leave.*

Dear gods, I've gotten Arthur so fucked over.

That entire line of thought still hurt too much.

Back up. Try to figure out the big picture, the whole thing.

I mulled it over, trying to think beyond my own pain.

The Matronae *are out for blood. This... isn't something minor. It isn't something Mom hallucinated in her grief at losing the baby. The matrons of the sidhe and some old Norse powers are united in this. Even Hela was helping. "Worlds are wracked with mothers' wailing." This is... the missing kids. At the least. At the very, very least.*

The starlit queen's words came back to me. *"There aren't enough sidhe, not to face down the tide, not to save our people. We need allies."*

A shiver ran through my whole body. How was I supposed to bring in more allies? The only group I really worked with was the Underhill Railroad, which was basically a network of tech nerds and small-time smugglers. Our main allies were sympathetic librarians who looked the other way when we hid fliers in the paranormal section, and we had a few people good at backwoods guiding. Not exactly an army, no matter our ambitions to make things better. We could barely even get by know-nothing groups like Division 51.

Gods, Arthur. What am I going to do?

I wondered where he was and what the Matronae had him doing. The Strangeling Brigade captain was plenty attractive in his own right, but so utterly the opposite of the dark flame of a boy I'd known. What had my mother done to him, to change that untamed creature from someone who raced wild deer and went running in thunderstorms into the discipline-obsessed soldier he was now? He had been more fae than anyone I'd ever met, then, with more magic already awake than anyone not yet Changed really should have had.

I met him at a regional academic trivia meet when I was thirteen. Knowledge Bowl was something my dad had out-argued my mom I be allowed to do, even though I was homeschooling then. I felt Arthur's power before I even saw him. He was filling in on his friend's team because one of the regulars had moved and they hadn't found a replacement yet. When he walked into the room, I caught my first glimpse of what "sexy" meant. He hadn't Changed, but I could see he would. My heart jumped into my throat when I somehow realized he was going to be *like me*. He was almost two years older than me, had hair longer than mine, and wasn't really into "nerd clubs". He didn't like to be indoors long, but he loved reading about history, particularly military history involving rebellions and insurgencies, and his friend couldn't have competed if their team was short too many people. When the questions veered into his topics, he absolutely dominated the room. Then they turned to science, and I jumped in and demolished his team's lead.

The final question of our set was, "What animal was 'Heorot', the hall where Beowulf fought Grendel in ancient British literature, named for?" I looked at the nascent antlers glimmering in his energy body and, grinning like a maniac at his completely clueless expression, answered *A hart, a mature European Red Deer stag*, some random factoid I knew from one of Dad's natural history books. Then I mindspoke him, to see if he could hear me... and to gloat. His eyes met mine, and a fire ignited that had never entirely gone out.

He found me in the hallway after the competition, demanding to know how I'd done that. I whispered to him that he'd better figure that out before he Changed, and he pushed me against the wall and maybe I should have been afraid, but my body was fluttering in a way I'd never felt before... and anyway, I was sidhe and he wasn't, yet; I could take him. I gave him glimpse of my magic, and let him know that.

I saw the exact second fear of being outed turned into attraction, as he realized he didn't intimidate me.

"You're kind of not bad," he told me as I scowled at him. "Maybe a bit deliciously Else yourself, even with those braids. Wanna join my harem?"

He had a girlfriend already. And a boyfriend, who also had another boyfriend of his own and who was sometimes up for "playing". He sang in a little garage band and had "groupies". And when I asked, shocked, if those people all knew about each other, his face screwed up with an effort not to laugh at my naivete.

"I absolutely will *not* join your ridiculous little pod of deviants," I answered him, more tempted than I would ever admit. "Thank you, but I have *some* self respect!"

He smiled, too knowing, and said I'd be his before the year was over.

And things proceeded from there.

He stayed in Knowledge Bowl. We saw each other at meets, and started writing letters, competitive as hell but drawn to each other like magnets. I was certain my mother wouldn't approve, and just as much so that my dad's mother *would*, so used Gram's address. Writing him got me through the grief of Jamie's death and the fear of my mother's illness, and it opened up a future I could actually *hope* for too. I kept the letters in a box hidden behind a loose bit of wall in my room. Eight months after meeting, he was "abruptly single" and deeply frustrated, following some accidental bit of magic that had spooked him out of dating too-easily-beglamoured humans. I kissed him behind the buses at the last meet of the school year, and fell harder than I had ever guessed was possible.

It was my first kiss. My weirdling package of magical "gifts" included a degree of empathy that made being around most people... difficult... then, and never mind intimacy. The bindings on me had at least numbed *that* for the last ten years. But Arthur, oh Arthur... there was this pure clean fierceness to him, a touch of untamable wilderness, and it intoxicated me like nothing had before or since.

Kissing my wild boy was like riding lightning.

I was fourteen, and I knew when his lips met mine that he had been right; I would love him always. Part of me was convinced I already had, somehow, that my soul had known his for lifetimes.

My hands clenched up on the rag I was wiping down the cupboards with. His younger self had *known*, as big a dingbat teenage jerk as he'd been. Part of me was just *his,* beyond all argument, even still.

I had no idea what to do with that.

Was part of him also simply *mine?*

I thought about the morning on the river.

Rather importantly, was he going to keep trying to arrest me when we got out of here?

Gods. What an idiot. What a pair of idiots.

I remembered thinking back then that if he was as sidhe as I expected, and survived Changing, it'd probably be a few hundred years before he even thought about settling down with just one lover. I sighed and smacked my head repeatedly against the cupboard I was working on.

This is going to be a mess.

If I was free, and remembering all this, I could probably assume he was, too. And the boy he'd been... wouldn't have been inclined to forgive being dumped via a note hastily scrawled on a napkin, magical compulsions or no. Getting punished for someone else's sins by being glamoured into being a straight, discipline-worshiping soldier... even if he did still find me attractive... was probably unforgivable. Completely unforgivable.

Gods damn it all.

I wanted to kiss him again. I wanted to look him in the eyes and know him and have him know me and pull him to me and do everything I didn't even imagined was possible when I first met him. Ha. Look at how the tables had turned... after banging half the Northland's worst musicians, trying to scratch an itch that never got satisfied in the least commitment-necessary way possible, it was pretty much *me* who was the promiscuous sexual deviant now.

Sigh.

Even if he had tried to arrest me, I liked the guy he'd grown into. Who'd have guessed my wild fae boy had that kind of responsible steadiness hiding anywhere in him?

I wanted to be held in his arms, warm and wanted.

He'd be nice to wake up next to.

If he was even willing to look at me after all this.

If he didn't keep trying to arrest and trap me.

If I could even manage an actual relationship.

Frankly, I have doubts.

I sighed, finished wiping down the cupboards, washed out the cloth, and hung it to dry.

Eventually, my tea was ready. I drank it and watched flames dance in the hearth. More memories came back, parts of myself I'd lost, griefs I'd never been able to process, and I wept until I fell asleep by the fire.

Three days and nights I stayed there, mourning, recovering, cleaning whatever was in front of me, the heavy silence my only companion. Every morning the manger was empty and I refilled it with windfall apples, but I never saw any signs of tracks or hoofprints; it seemed to simply empty itself. Perhaps there was some kind of teleportation magic on the manger, like whatever had brought me here. There was no sign of where the apples might be going.

When I could think about things without instantly breaking down again, I added a pouch to my armor, put some apples in it in case I didn't find any other food before leaving the ghostland, and silently said my farewells to this forgotten place. I went back to the bench I'd woken up on and sat down. I looked around one last time, wondering if I would ever get to come here again.

And then, far down one of the barn's halls, hooves clattered at the other end of the barn and a horse whinnied, desperate and demanding.

39

ETERNITY'S SHORE

FAE ARTHUR

W e left the forest behind us, hours later, and stepped onto a hillside strewn with glacier-scarred rocks. Water lapped the beaches of a moonlit lake, the reflected light dancing across it like a road up to the Milky Way. It was as vast as the distant glacier that fed it. Only the slightest breeze rippled the surface, and stars above burned colder and brighter across the sky than the mortal world had ever seen. On the shore, a campfire burned, its light a tiny puddle in the darkness.

"Follow me," said the Wildwood's daughter, and stepped directly into a tree. For a second I saw a flashing of light through its roots, and then through those entwined with its neighbor, and through shrubs and brambles and smaller trees all the way down to the shore by the distant flame. I followed her, stepping forward through the roots of the forest and out onto the strand.

Round stones crunched beneath my feet and the antlered man and great cat by the fire looked up at us. A grin spread across his face, making me think again of my mother. He looked like me, sidhe but older, like a human in his late thirties but weathered, with antlers like an elk's. Behind him, a boat lay pulled high on shore, a lapstrake thing with almond-shaped eyes carved into the prow. It was bleached and weathered, possibly beyond all seaworthiness. The rope tying it to a cedar on the shore was frayed as though centuries had passed since it was knotted.

"You came," he said, and stood. Metal clanked at his ankle, and a chain snaked from it into the heart of the fire.

"My son," said the Wildwood's daughter, walking to him and giving him a kiss of greeting.

"Mother," he said, embracing her, then turned and opened his arms to me. "And a grandson. Finally. Be welcome at my fire."

"What is this place?" I asked, my heart wanting to break open or into pieces simultaneously as he wrapped those arms around me. We were kin, beyond all doubt; the magic burning me up was a steady flame in him, tended carefully and skillfully.

"Eternity's shore," he said. "Someday, soon I hope, I will board that boat and ride the moon's road until the stars above and below become one."

"And then?"

"Home," said the Wildwood's daughter. "We will go home, to the fires of our people."

The great cat yawned, like such an idea bored him terribly.

"Yes, I know," said the man. "The cats wish to return to the world, not go beyond it. They fought by the sides of my father's ancestors when the Enemy first came, and his tribe continued to share souls with them even after their physical extinction."

"We are sidhe," said my ancestress. "The defense of life itself is our first and final mission. The Wildwood tribe tended the greening land, its forests and tundras and the wildernesses of the world. Those with hooves were our kin and sacred companions. We were Earthbound, all of us, too much to leave this world as others did."

"The Cat tribe was not so bound," the man said, stroking his companion beast's fur. "They delighted in exploring, and the entertainments of humanity, and war."

"Well, they were very good at war, anyway," the woman said. "*Liking* perhaps overstates things."

"Father savors nothing more than a good campaign," the man said wryly, and his mother rolled her eyes. "He just tried to keep that side of himself discreetly away from his wife."

She shook her head, smiled ruefully, and did not disagree.

"Who is the enemy you spoke of?" I asked.

"Ah, them," he said, and stared into the fire for a minute. "My whole childhood and youth we fought them, and eventually thought we had defeated and eradicated them. They live by lies and illusion, though, and we were wrong."

"The stars sent their forebears here, off-course and disabled," the woman said, and held a hand to the far horizon. A light flared above it, arching across the sky like a meteor. It approached us, coming in fast, and passed low enough overhead that we could see the huge burning starship at the heart of the blaze. There was a flash of light on the beach, and a small group of inhuman beings suddenly appeared, coughing from smoke inhalation. Terrible wounds wracked their bodies.

"Are those aliens?" I asked.

"They were," the Wildwood's daughter answered. One looked up at us, and suddenly a cleaner, older version of him appeared across the fire from us. He looked rather like if you exaggerated all the sidhe features out of us and left humanity entirely behind.

"There are two common ways to colonize planets beyond your own," the alien said, taking a seat on a driftwood log. "One may introduce the building blocks of life from your homeworld to a barren rock, and with luck and skill and the blessing of the Tree, it may bloom."

He stretched his hands towards the fire and I saw he had only four fingers on each, and a sleek smoothness that was unnervingly inhuman.

"Some species adapt not a world but themselves," the Wildwood's daughter said. "Most often the fluid, changeable children of air or water. They might even come to a world that has already birthed life, and make themselves a part of it. Sometimes that works, sometimes it does not."

At the edge of the horizon, the burning ship slammed into the glacier. A blazing light brighter than the sun blew from it as it vaporized both ice and the bedrock below it, and even the illusion's brightness made me turn my head aside. A spectral shock wave tore apart the world a second later, and I squeezed my eyes shut against the purely illusionary debris.

"The prisoners on that ship were the second kind," the alien said. "But they had melded themselves with a race that was attempting to take apart and reassemble life from its component blocks. Crimes beyond measure did they commit, and we fought them almost onto our own end. We thought them finally defeated."

"That doesn't look like it went so well," I said, staring at the crash still burning in the distance.

"It did not," he said. "We guardians were driven to the edge of extinction in battling them. Our ship was bound for the planet your people call Venus, there to imprison the last remnants of their kind in a world and climate they could just *barely* survive. We *almost* made it there."

"When was this?"

"Around 13,000 local years ago," he sighed. "We lost control of the ship, but trying to minimize damage until the end, we crashed it into a glacier in a place you know as Greenland. Had we landed in the ocean, the tidal waves would have destroyed all the lands along the Atlantic's shore; on land, and the dust cloud would have sent an already frozen world into winter beyond what life on Earth could survive. As it was, the Younger Dryas Impact made the Ice Age last another thousand years beyond when perhaps it should have."

"The prisoners of that ship did not precisely survive," the horned man said. "But the building blocks of their mutable, binding genetic material were scattered across the world, and especially the North Atlantic. The hungry ghosts of those prisoners have haunted this world since then."

"Giants and monsters were born of their traces," the wildwood's daughter said. "Things that stalked the dark, gibbering with hunger and impulses alien to this world. And humanity... humanity was *changed.*"

"From time immemorial, primate man had stayed a simple *part* of their lands," the horned man said, firelight gleaming in his eyes. "Following the herds and the seasons, using stone tools and warming their tents with bow-kindled flame. They were hunters and prey both, and there was, at least, a simple sustainability to that life."

"When the stars bled on Earth, other impulses awoke in humanity," the alien said. "Greed, lust for power, ambition for *more.*"

"Well, ambition is not wrong in itself," the antlered man said.

"The Tree that Grows Between Worlds pushes always to expand the boundaries of the possible," the Wildwood's daughter said, putting up a hand to forestall what sounded like a very old argument. "It is, most fundamentally, the impulse to *live,* and life in great diversity sprouts wherever it takes root."

"Wherever life is born, so too is a connection to the Tree," said the alien. "And like all living things, it must have an immune system. When life blooms into sentience, the Tree opens ways for potential defenders to attune to it beyond what is commonly possible. When that ship crashed here, it created a great need for such. My people were spent, but the Tree led humans to us, ones chosen to take on our guardian mantle. We shared our essence with them, that *our* lines not be entirely lost."

"They weren't exactly enthusiastic about the locally available options," the antlered man said, grinning. "Humanity has the strong potential to become the rats and pigeons of the galaxy, to hear them talk. Excessively adaptable, energetic, and as short-lived as they are short-sighted."

"In the sidhe, we perfected their better traits," the alien said stiffly, and the antlered man guffawed. "And if you could come to decent terms with your cousin species, there might be hope for humanity too. Provided, of course, you both survive the coming years."

"We already had shamans and magicians here," the Wildwood's daughter said, sighing at them both. "The Elders taught us to walk the Tree's starry paths, and travel to worlds beyond our own. Some of humanity's worst mistakes are attributable to *us* bringing ideas home, to be honest."

"What do you mean?" I asked.

"Agriculture, first and foremost," the antlered man grinned. "Our people are rather known for liking a bit to drink. We got some human allies to plant grains and malt them, after seeing others do such out Beyond, and ferment them as they already did with wild honey. One thing led to another, though, and, well... My grandfather had quite the rant about lousy idiots bringing things as terrible as *civilization* and its bastard step-child, *religion*, to his perfectly good world."

"Humanity would have had no hope of the stars without such," the alien said, and the antlered man leaned forward, grinning, to argue more.

"So," the wildwood's daughter said, putting up hands to stop them both again. "We have tried to imprison the enemy. We have tried to eradicate them. We have even, at times, attempted peace marriages with them."

I blinked.

"Well, they merged with humanity, much as the sidhe did," the alien said. "Your peoples have too much in common, honestly."

"But if we are an immune response, they are a poison," the antlered man said, his eyes hard.

"Poison is always a matter of dosage," the woman answered. "What kills in concentration may become medicine in dilution. Some of the best of the sidhe have the others' blood in their veins. Perhaps the problem's solution will lie in that direction."

"Speculation only. Enough of this. Time stretches long but grows yet short," said the antlered man, and gestured at the ancient boat and the chain bound to his ankle. "Grandson, you know me now, and my truth is this: I have been bound too long to this shore."

He looked at the other two, and both nodded.

"When the time comes, do what must be done, with my deepest gratitude. Our bloodline walks the world again and my duties pass now to you and yours. I have lingered here too long, far too long, and would sail free across the waters. Your strike will be a mercy; remember that."

"I... what?" I said, alarmed.

He put one arm on my shoulder and looked me straight in the eyes.

"There is no way back for me," he said. "I can only go forward. That boat is my only way off this shore, and I must take it before it rots and I fade to nothing. What binds me yet here... *that thing is not me*. This stupid chain doesn't even work as a puppet string anymore. That... it will never recover. I cannot return. Anything else is the enemy's lies."

"I... understand, sir," I said, even though I really didn't.

"Then go with my blessing," he said, and embraced me. He grinned. "I think you'll do just fine, son of my daughter! Not an easy road ahead, but one that will be worth the tale. Take my father to drink crow-dark brew at the pub with no name, someday, and share a toast to my memory."

All my confusion must have shown on my face.

"Oh, just tell him that. He knows where it is," he laughed, standing and pulling me to my feet. "Well. One last thing, then. Some mysteries the women of the Wildwood can teach, but not all, as I could not initiate you into their magics. Take on my legacy, son of my line, and be one with the wilderness."

I blinked at him. He leaned his head against mine, and magic glowed in his eyes. He shook his head, and his antlers struck mine. Sudden fury billowed through me, and I pulled in a great breath to bellow back a challenge to him. He stepped back, a sardonic smile on his face.

"Well, go on then," he said, and blew hot air into my face. *"Battle."*

A second later, every trace of humanity in me was gone.

40

ELVENSTEEDS

AISLING

For a second, I froze. Then everything that had endured ten years of 4H just to get near horses, and did a vet-med minor to improve my cryptobiology dissection skills, recognized the life-or-death quality of that desperate neigh. My feet were running while my mind was still stuck on, *Huh! There really are horses here!*

But "horse" was an entirely inadequate word for the shining creature rearing at the end of the hall. The stallion gleamed like old silver, lustrous and dark, with a subtle pattern like tiger stripes covering his body. The longest mane and tail I'd ever seen floated around him. He neighed again, spinning back to the exit, and gold dust flared like when I summon my weapons. A saddle and bit-less bridle appeared on him, more elegant than anything I'd ever seen.

Elvensteed. As fine a horse as myth could dream, I thought as my hands pulled me up into a saddle covered in Norse knotwork, and my legs swung into the stirrups. It took him two strides to get out of the barn. Then powerful muscles bunched beneath me and I barely got a grip before he launched himself forward.

My gods, the way he *moved.* I am sidhe, born and trained, able to step outside normal time and space and, for brief flashes, move as if neither really constrains me. But until getting in that saddle, I never knew what *speed* really meant.

Worlds flashed by us, and I mean that literally. One had three suns in the sky, another a dozen moons. I felt my magic stretch with each stride of those incredible legs, feeling *almost, almost* how he was doing it. Then the horse grabbed my magic and sped up again, until the space we raced through became pure blur. The... density... of whatever we were traveling through eventually changed, and the horse slowed enough I could make out our surroundings again. Black volcanic stacks surrounded us, an inky river flowing past, its stones as dark as the cliffs. An ocean pounded into a monochrome shore behind us.

We clattered into a pool and behind the waterfall flowing into it, down a blue-lit glacial cave and then across a bridge that seemed as thin as a sword blade, rainbows glittering in the pattern-welded texture of whatever composed it. A vast oak tree, larger than any I'd ever seen, spread broad limbs wide across a field before us, and I had just enough time to glimpse the hollow between its roots before we dove through it and into the space between worlds. Then it wasn't sparks flying from the stallion's hooves but *stars*, falling into infinity from the golden bridge we flashed across. Then we were out another hollow tree, this one almost entirely dead, entering a dim and icy world. Cold gray fog wrapped around us, still and somehow far *heavier* than mere water vapor, and ice echoed beneath the silver's hooves.

The stallion slowed, his movements going wary, and whickered softly.

Another horse answered, even more quietly, but with urgency in her voice. The hair on the back of my neck stood up. Something was here with us, hidden by fog, something inhuman, something coldly predatory.

It was hunting the horses.

Dim light hung as leaden as the fog. I glimpsed the herd through a billow in the mist, all of them armored and circled together, defending something pale and prone in their midst. Their heads lowered and turned as whatever was out there circled them, looking for one more vulnerable than the rest.

Like the one completely outside their ring.

The silver's ears pinned back, and a shiver of eagerness ran through him. Gold light shimmered again, and fine horse armor covered him.

Whatever hid in the fog was hunting *us* now.

Well, I thought, the irony of doing it from horseback not lost on me, *not my first rodeo.*

The silver flicked an ear to me and somehow I knew what he wanted. I slipped soundlessly down from the saddle, armoring up myself and forming a spear in my hand. I ghosted after him as he stomped hard and neighed a challenge.

The fog billowed heavily again, and I could barely see the end of my weapon. Then there was a brief window through which I caught a glimpse of something tiger-sized, sleek muscles twisting under grey amphibian skin as it stalked us. Then the fog thickened again, and it was gone. I closed my eyes, realizing they were useless, and *listened.*

A scuff, a heavy breath, a claw clicking against the ice... five yards ahead of me and to the right, focused on the stallion.

Go, I told myself, and shaped the end of my spear into a sweeping blade like a naginata's, then launched myself forward. I caught the beast in the rear haunch as it spun for me, hamstringing its left hind leg. I barely ducked below a barbed tail as it swung over my head. The creature turned a lamprey's face to me, its mouth a horror-pit of teeth, a mane of writhing tentacles surrounding its head, and it spun on its five remaining good legs.

Oh shit.

The spear spun to dust and twin swords formed in my hands, and I dove towards the monster instead of away, as it obviously expected. I stabbed one blade between its ribs and sliced a clawed front foot clean off with the other, and then rolled under it as it tried to pounce on me. I stabbed backwards, knowing it had turned as fast as me, and rolled forward again. It was right behind me. That tail swung again, and the end took me right in the stomach. The barbs skittered off my armor, but the impact sent me flying backwards and knocked the breath right out of me.

The monster stalked towards me, barely a swirl in the mist, as I gasped and choked and tried to get upright. It stopped, claws inches from my feet, drool dripping towards my knees, and a long tongue reached out of its mouth, savoring the taste of my fear. I reshaped my left blade into a shield, and slowly pulled myself up and snarled back at it. Its muscles tensed, easing back to a pouncing position. The foot I'd cut off was visibly regenerating.

Its focus was entirely on me, fixated, like mountain lions get.

A neigh of pure fury split the silence, and an armored black hoof cracked open the monster's head. Lightning crackled around another set of hooves and a spotted grey smashed into the monster, electrocuting it, and then a flame-red mare joined him and actual fire blazed over the corpse. I rolled and got the hell out of their way.

Take the head and the heart, I thought, and when the horses were done turning the thing that had hunted them into a gooey puddle. My sword bit through its neck and I tossed the head one way, then shaped claws on my armor and dug into its chest to find a still-pumping heart. I sliced it free and pulled it out. I placed it on the ice in front of the red mare, and flame leapt up from it hot enough to leave only ashes behind.

I started to slip down to my knees, reaction hitting me, but the dark silver was back, and as soon as he had my attention, he looked back into the fog and pinned his ears back. So there were more. We had to move.

And then he nudged me towards what the herd had been guarding.

She was pure white, pale as snow, but there was an opalescent, almost crystalline quality to her coat that I'd never seen on a horse. Her belly was twice the size of any other's here. She looked like she'd been in hard labor for far too long, and sweat streaked her sides. But she struggled to her feet, and let me pet her and encourage her, and then she nudged the pouch at my waist.

I blinked, remembering I had apples there, and pulled one out. She took it almost delicately between her teeth, chewed briefly, and when she swallowed it, sudden vitality swept over her and she surged to her feet.

She looked me right in my eyes. Hers were green as moss and full of desperation.

Home, I swear she begged, almost mindspeaking me. *Let me give birth at home.*

The dark silver was back next to me, and sidled up for me to get back in his saddle. I hesitated, thinking of how *far* we'd come, and he stamped an impatient hoof.

On the other hand, every place along the way had seemed a better place to give birth than this Gigeresque murk. I pulled myself up and swung into the saddle.

The stallion spun back the way we'd come from, and the red and spotted grey took up defensive positions around the pregnant mare, and then the rest of the herd fell in behind and around them. Some magic shivered over them, warband magic I wasn't familiar with, and the herd moved out as one. These horses, these elvensteeds, every one of them had was trained for war and riding in formation, and even with only one clueless rider along with them, it showed.

Deep in the fog, another predator called, not a wolf's howl but the kind of primal hoot you hear in nature documentaries about the beasts of the savanna night, a descant cackle that made a shiver run through my whole body. Another animal answered, to the right and behind us, and then a third, off to our left.

The dying tree loomed out of the fog, and magic rippled through the herd, uniting them. The silver grabbed my magic again, weaving it around and through his herd. The horses thundered into the hollow of the Tree, and we leaped into the blackness of utter sensory deprivation. For a long, long moment there was nothing, barely even us. Then light glimmered, the hint of a Way, and we turned to it and it blazed open before us. Hooves sparked stars, and we shifted into a rippling nebula of undefined possibilities, running towards a chosen set of probabilities that would devolve into such a cascading Now as creates a world. This time the silver went slowly enough to show me what he was doing, and how *I* could do it.

It was like a key finding a hidden lock in my soul.

Time and space slowed, condensed into a single infinitesimal point, and that point held the seed of all potential. Roots stretched out from it, and sprouts, rhizomes spreading to everywhere and everywhen, into every imaginable reality. Buds swelled and bloomed, the impossible becoming the improbable becoming the likely becoming the real. The magic within me met those spreading roots and entwined with them. The Ways between Worlds unfurled through and before me, and nebulae streamed out like mycelia. The roots twined and twisted into a bridge that shimmered like a rainbow, and the herd pounded onto the new Way.

We skipped, like a stone on a pond, out of one set of probabilities that had condensed into a reality towards another, dipping into the primal unformed with every step. The herd broke into a canter and then a gallop. The glittering colors melded until the road glowed golden, and behind us the dying Tree gave up the ghost and crumbled away. Dust billowed into the womb of night, not ash but *spores,* I somehow knew, and in their light I caught a glimpse of the vast impossible space around us, planets and nebulae and galaxies wheeling past, all entangled by bridges of golden light that stretched like neurons between the stars...

Home, the horses seemed to say, and the light I'd felt every time I ate one of the apples on the abandoned farm... I mean, there wasn't really anything else, it was all I'd been eating... shivered inside me and I found my arms stretching out and my head tilting back and the magic in me bloomed out around us. The Way we ran on turned into twisting vines that *reached reached reached* out towards not just the deserted farm but into me, into an entire unimagined heritage hidden in my veins.

I had an impression of vast, tangled branches, and briefly of running through a stream as warm as blood. The herd neighed in triumph, like trumpets heralding glory, and the Tree opened again. We spilled out into fragile spring sunlight and a grove beginning to bud and blossom. We cantered out of the ancient apple tree at the heart of the abandoned orchard, the sun broke through the clouds, and frost melted from greening grass.

The herd spilled out into the light, and I could finally really *see* them. Their beauty took my breath away. The elvensteeds were as like to mortal horses as sidhe are to humans, every line of their bodies flowing and perfect. They bounced into the orchard like foals into a meadow, prancing and frolicking, and then started grabbing windfall apples and eating as if they'd been starving.

A sound of some extreme relief came from the white mare, and she dropped to the ground directly where she exited the Tree. Contractions rippled across her stomach. As far along as she was, I half expected to see little hooves any second, but she pushed and pushed and the foal didn't come.

And didn't come.

I got her a bucket of water, and washed the gore from the monster in the frozen fog off my hands and arms, knowing what I'd have to do and trying to get as clean as I could. I couldn't find anything I recognized as towels, but there were blankets aplenty. I took half a dozen from the cottage back to the orchard with me, propping open a gate to the meadow for any horses who wanted to leave the orchard. They seemed content where they were, or concerned for the white mare, and stayed nearby, not directly by her but keeping an eye on us. I fed her more apples, and gave her water from the bucket, then told her what I had to do, hoping she would understand me. I knew what was needed from my vet med classes, but hadn't ever done it myself, and usually the horse should be sedated first.

"Your baby might be backward," I said. "I'm going to see if we can get the little one into the right position."

Then I gritted my teeth, slathered water over my arm, and reached in to check. The foal wasn't backwards, thankfully, but his front legs were bent like he was leaping, not straight like they needed to be. It was awkward - *so* awkward - but I pushed the foal back in and get a hand under those front forelegs to straighten them out. About two seconds after I got the baby lined up properly, a contraction spasmed over the white's belly and a sopping wet little black colt practically fell out on top of me.

Oh, he was beautiful, in that awkward baby way, all uncoordinated legs and fuzzy hair sticking in every direction. His mother licked his face while I dried him with blankets, and in short order he teetered up onto shaky legs and started to nurse. Once he could walk, the herd moved out to the pasture, dancing as much as trotting, then burst forward into a joyous gallop around the meadow and back.

I had thoughts about just staying on the ancient farm and taking care of the horses and just saying *screw it* to everything else in my life. Too tempting. I went back to the cottage, cleaned up in the tub there, and fell asleep for a few hours. In my dreams, I rode horses across golden bridges, and a multiverse opened before me, worlds beyond worlds, aching to be explored.

Even in the dream I wept, knowing how unlikely a future like that was.

41

PREDATOR AND PREY

FAE ARTHUR

I bellowed, and slammed my vast, palmate antlers against the other stag's. They caught together and our hooves dug deep into the lichen-covered ground as we struggled and groaned against each other. The fragrant scent of my herd's does filled my flaring nostrils, intoxicating and engorging me. When this pretender was driven away, they would be mine to claim again, mine by right of battle in the way most old and true. They stamped and snorted in eagerness, the estrous as heavy upon them as the rut was on me. I threw my weight forward and the other stag lost ground against me, once and again, and again, until he was quivering with fatigue. He pulled away, defeated, and I bugled my conquest across the steppes. When he had fled sufficient distance, I heaved my way back to my harem. Raw lust pounded through my body and I mounted them until satiation and exhaustion lay so heavy on me I could barely stand on my shaking feet.

Our herd would have strong fawns in the spring.

I would not live to see them.

The scimitar-toothed cats came early in the night, before I had recovered. I trumpeted groggily at the predators, and my herd fled while the cats surrounded me. Starlight glinted on shining fangs, and I shook my antlers at them. A brash cub dove for my hind legs, and my hoof opened his hide from neck to foreleg. Another cat came at my side, and I swept my antlers sideways to gore him, but he danced away at the last second. The movement gave the pack matriarch the opening she wanted, and she clawed her way onto my back and dug dagger-like fangs into my spine.

I fell, and my blood seeped out into the tundra moss.

My mother's pack feasted on the great elk's corpse, then, and I grew strong in her womb. In the spring I was born in a bone-strewn cave, and learned to hunt first rodents, and then deer, and then all the megafauna of the Doggerland steppes. I was sleek and strong and clever; I had my pick of mates and lovers. Our kind was already rare, but the life we had was sweet.

When a strange, dirty wind blew in a straight line across the steppe, it brought storms and cold behind it, but we were fit and adaptable. A dark, bitter winter followed, colder than any in my life. In the depths of the dark months, *they* rose from the waves, hulking shapes with no true definition beyond their glassy fangs and claws. Before their ravenous ferocity, my pack of top predators became just more hunted prey. Where the monsters passed, corpses rotted on the snow, slaughtered but barely eaten, and all who could hide themselves did so.

When the sun finally returned and drove *them* back to the sea, the mammoths were gone, and the woolly rhinos, and the elk with their wide-spreading antlers, and over half my pack. We were skin and bones by then, and hunted prey only cubs would have sought before. Starvation's sharp ferocity drove us to desperation.

It drove us to the camp by the shore, where a pack of fur-clad humans hacked at a dead whale. The sea had washed it up on the beach, strange slice marks from the battle that killed it covering its body. Humans were not particularly worthwhile prey to us, but the fat whale was a *prize*.

We advanced, growling warning, and they pulled out their strange projectile claws... but backed away, cussing and swearing, all but one. He stood straight and tall, with a long black mane and ears more typical of wilder creatures than primate kind. Some odd light slipped through him, and a voice like I had never heard spoke in my mind.

Brother, he said to me, and something opened inside myself that I had never guessed at existing. *Hunt with me, and we will share this meat. When the dark again rises, we will fight those creatures side by side.*

That was interesting. I had found nothing the little primate packs did *interesting* before, so I sat down and cleaned my claws and considered it. The two half-grown cubs hunting with me cocked their heads to the side and followed my lead.

How? I thought back, and he sent me an image of a Tree vaster than the starry sky. Light seeped from it into the living, and it radiance coated his weapons and tore mortal holes into the very creature that had slain the rest of my pack. The thought of such light slicking my claws and fangs pleased me, and our bargain was struck immediately. Him, I took for my own hunting partner; the cubs with me formed their own bonds with his children. Two surviving females from another pack joined us later, and two women like my not-quite-human. They shared their blood with us, shining stuff full of the sap of that luminous Tree, and we shared our kills with them. Their eyes changed, matching ours, feline pupils the stamp of our compact to mark them across generations.

When *they* returned, in the deep dark after midwinter, we met them with weapons and claws sheathed in raw Radiance, and drove them back to the sea. They fought, then fled before us. We killed many, very many, but never *enough*. Always, more came.

The ocean is vast, and its shores long. My life stretched into summers beyond counting, living and fighting and exploring and hunting, as did that of my two-legged brother. Very few cubs came to us, and the slaughtering monsters too often attacked far from where we were. In a few generations, the vast beasts of the tundra who had fed his people and mine were almost gone, and in their hunger, humans hunted the remnant populations to extinction.

One night, a new demon came to us. She looked like one of the females of my brother's people, and her call drew him and all with him down to the shore. I smelled her though, the undercurrent of aquatic rot the same scent as the monsters bore, and sat on him even as he fought me to go to her. Crazed under her power, he drove a knife into me himself, and with my last breaths, I followed him to the shore and dragged her guts down to the sand. She fell back into the waves, her body broken, and my brother saw what he had done. He screamed his grief up to uncaring stars, but I was dying.

I do not wish to leave this world empty of my people, I spoke to him.

Stay, then, brother, with me, he said. *Share my life and my soul and my body.*

And so I did, and my packmates did as well, with their chosen ones, as one by one we succumbed to inevitable fate. In his time, my brother fell as well, and his people took his body into the Tree. We joined the packs that hunt beyond the stars, then, for a while at least. Then the sweetness of life called us back to a womb and milk and living, again and again, until I finally awoke as an antlered sidhe boy, curled between roots at the base of a great tree.

We have been together that long? I asked what the other me thought of as his monster. My "human" side was beginning to wake up again, and I felt his confusion and fear of losing control. I didn't care, though; tonight was mine. The great cat purred, and I felt his desire to run free through the woods. I grinned, elated to share that again, and gave myself to the night.

42

WILD THINGS IN THE DARKNESS

AISLING

Before I opened my eyes, I could tell I was lying on my side by a campfire. The farm and horses were gone, and I somehow *knew* I could not get back to them on my own. Tears started running down my face, and I choked back more sobs, not sure where I was. Then a very solid cat snuggled in against me, purring and radiating heat like a small oven. For a minute I just petted it, feeling both lost and oddly comforted. Its fur didn't feel quite like any other cat I'd ever touched. It bumped me for head rubs, and I felt the fangs hanging down below its chin.

My eyes snapped open. It wasn't a housecat; it was a fat cub of the faery sabertooths, and it appeared to be laughing at my surprise. It had eyes like tropical seas and was otherwise a gold-tinged white, and had that extreme fluffy cuteness of animals that grow up to be top-of-the-food-chain predators.

I glanced around and saw I was in a little hollow between the roots of the enormous apple tree we'd seen behind the Hall of the Matrons, which appeared to be gone now. The rest of the pack of faery sabertooths lounged around us, apparently amused by the antics of their little one. I sat up and it crawled into my lap, flopped over, and started begging for belly rubs. Definitely a little boy. Every kind of trouble glinted in those gemlike eyes.

What a cutie, I thought as he started batting his oversized paws at me.

There was no sign of Arthur, but his shoes and shirt and my sweater were on the ground next to me. The big cats seemed to be guarding me and waiting, so I obliged the cub. He swatted at my hand and wrestled my fingers and I wondered who his mother was, thinking if there was an utterly exhausted looking cat here, it would be her.

The cub was on his back in my arms, growling at the hand tickling him, when the wild thing entered the darkness beyond the firelight. He paused just beyond where I could see anything, and a wave of some emotion hit me like a physical shock, so intense I could barely begin to decipher it.

Oh fuck, I thought. *My empathy isn't dulled anymore.*

My mother, and I guess many sidhe, could see emotions around people like colors or textures in the air. Feeling other people's emotions as if they were your own was a more delicate and rarer gift... or curse... and it had made a good bit of my childhood hellish. The one blessing of the time under my mother's spell was that I wasn't *reactive* to emotions like that anymore; I felt them like a breeze on my skin, not a knife in my guts.

"Arthur?" I called softly. The cub wriggled out of my arms and tumbled on clumsy baby feet out of the firelight, and I saw a glint of gold light on antlers as he knelt. Around me the great cats stretched and stood, then ambled down the roots and away. The cub danced back into the light for a second, sneezed at me, and melted away into the darkness with his pack.

What stepped out of the night, once we were alone, was most definitely *not* the mostly human army soldier who'd tried arresting me on the riverfront. He was shirtless and barefoot, and firelight glinted on sleek muscles. Nothing in the way he moved was pretending to be at all human anymore.

My heart just about stopped, then started beating overtime. The hunter stalked me, his balance perfect, poised... predatory. Old Wild Night might have simply stood up on two legs. This wasn't the army captain, this was something that had haunted the dark beyond the firelight since early humans first sought to huddle in that fragile safety.

Panic stepped into the light with him, billowing out from him in clouds.

Run, something inside me demanded. *RUN!*

Instinct told me the wild thing in front of me would like it very, very much if I fled from him... and in this ghost-haunted wood, there would be no escaping. A shiver ran through me, impossible to suppress, and I hugged my knees to my chest to keep my legs from simply taking off beneath me.

I hunt monsters for fun. This... this one frightened me.

For perhaps a minute, he just stood there, waiting for me to do something, anything, as terror gibbered through me. I tried to find my way back to that icy core I'd found hunting the winter dragon years earlier, the place of crystalline clarity far beyond mere emotional numbness. A simple thing, an awareness of what was me and what wasn't, not magic but *will* alone.

Run. Run. RUN.

His eyes glinted at me.

Flee!

You will be hunted, prey. My prey.

Like hell *I will,* I thought, gritting my teeth as the storm of his magic tore at me.

Run from me.

Run!

Surrender to the inevitable.

The inevitable?

The *inevitable?*

Fuck. That. Shit.

Aha. There it was, beyond all magics and glamours and empathic curses. Just me, right at my core, a stubborn clarity about what I was and what I was willing to be.

"Is there a point to this?" I asked him, as the moment stretched, tilting my head sideways.

The wild thing grinned, and his panic magic disappeared as swiftly as it had manifested. I glared at him and the grin got wider.

"Is the guy from the riverbank still in there?" I asked him, getting to my feet.

Do I need to call armor? Weapons? I don't want to hurt him.

He cocked his head sideways and stepped closer to me, inhumanly graceful, like everything dangerous and masculine and fae condensed into a shape directly out of both my most breathless and terrifying fantasies.

"Do you want him to be, when you could run into the night with *me?*"

The wild boy had indeed survived.

My wild boy was most definitely not a boy anymore.

A breath caught in my throat, and he was right in front of me. His lust magic hit me as hard as the panic had, just as intense and far more insidious. I gasped. My clothes were suddenly too tight on my aching skin, my armor painful against hard nipples. A hot, desperate *need* slammed through me to meet this wild thing with wildness of my own, to let him take me, to make me a plaything to use at his merciless leisure.

So I guess he is holding a grudge.

His eyes glowed gold with the amount of magic he was throwing at me.

Being his plaything sounded *fantastic.*

I tried to remember some reason I shouldn't want that. Nothing came to mind.

His fingers brushed my cheek, and a shiver ran through my whole body, helpless, hypnotized, *wanting.*

A gasp escaped me, and satisfaction filled his eyes.

Oh hell. *I'm going to have a major willpower fail in very short order.*

A smile tugged those arrogant lips. He *knew.*

I mean, I resist fear all the time. It's been years since I was *totally* numb, and anyway, fear is part of the adrenaline experience. Sex, though, just isn't something I'm really inclined to say *no* to, assuming it didn't have too many strings attached, especially not what would absolutely be the most mindbendingly hot sex of my life. And whatever was going on with Arthur right now, he was still the most delicious man I'd ever met.

Resist this the same way as the fear, I tried to tell myself, closing my eyes and trying to control my breathing. *Old cold ice, clear as the deep winter's sky. Ice in my heart, in my veins, in my body.*

Strong fingers touched my jaw, gently, and tilted my head up to meet his eyes. All thoughts of cold evaporated as he pulled me to him. Worlds of loss and regret, frustration and fury swam in those emerald depths, more powerful even than the lust magic, and there was nothing in me icy enough to meet those with frost.

"You *forgot* me," he said, pulsing his magic through my body again. With his skin touching mine it was ten times worse. I already wanted him. No one had ever kissed me like he did. I looked into his eyes and saw someone badly, deeply lost, and in desperate need to control *something* after so long helpless.

That was a bad thing, right? I had a reason to resist, didn't I? I mean, I could give him that. It wasn't exactly like I disagreed.

Under the raging mess of his emotions, there was still love. He was trying to hide it, but it sang like a bass note under every chord. He didn't want to, but he *cared.* If I said no and made him believe it, he'd leave. Probably into the mist, and never come back.

And too much of me wanted to give us a chance, no matter how short my future was likely to be.

Lord of the Wildwood, his magic chanted, the words running through my mind like a prayer, wanting me to let go and be as primally female for him as this wild thing was elementally male. I locked my knees to keep from collapsing in front of him, to worship him with my mouth and let him take me every way he wanted. A moan choked in my throat, imagining the taste of him, the feel, how thoroughly he would fill me. I could barely think beyond the hot pulse pounding through my body. on

"Take your clothes off," he breathed against my cheek, gold light filling his eyes, and I was nude before I could even consider it, my

armor evaporating away. A breeze blew through the forest and I
felt it across every inch of my overheated skin, the heat of him a
magnetic pull to it. A line of sweat ran down one breast, and I felt
every microsecond of its progression. "You come to me *naked*."

HIs fingers brushed down my breast, my hip, my thigh, and an
inferno ignited where they touched me.

"I didn't bring Hart in here for him to be lost entirely," I
whispered back, while I could still say anything.

"That inhibited, unimaginative asshole," the sidhe man in front
of me snarled, pulling back. "Do you know what I've been through,
locked in the back of that stupid, prudish head? Do you know the
utterly boring shit he fantasizes about? Do you know how she made
him power the bindings on me? No. We're not going to discuss
that. Touch yourself when I talk to you."

I gasped, losing another inch of self control. Obedient fingers
followed too-welcome orders, one hand heading south as the other
went to my breast. Something hot and satisfied in his gaze made me
want to preen for him, to peacock, to remind him *I* was desirable,
not just magicked. That he wanted me too.

Because he did. No matter how much he hated doing so.

He shook his head from side to side, as if fighting something, and
dark determination glittered in his eyes. His pants strained at the
front, barely containing him. He stepped back, and in a single fluid,
unbelted his trousers and let them fall to his feet. He stepped out
of them and stretched, every muscle long and sleek and perfect.

My mouth went completely dry.

"You can have him back," the wild thing said, one hand grabbing
the hair at the nape of my neck and pulling my throat bare for him.
I felt his breath against it. His other hand caressed an aching breast,
a thumb rubbing circles against my nipple, and I could have wept
with relief and gladness, "If you take *me* first."

I tried to think of a downside to that.

My wild boy still wanted me.

And, Gods Between Worlds, I wanted *him*.

I nodded, beyond words, and pulled his lips down to mine. He smiled in triumph as our lips met, and pulled me tight against him. I sobbed in relief, abandoning all resistance to his magic. It swept me under like a tsunami, and...

...and I have *no* regrets about letting go.

43

SOMETHING TO SHARE

ARTHUR

T he night in the forest was a long green blur, interspersed with moments of a kind of fierce wild joy I hadn't known I could even feel. I started coming back to myself when we first glimpsed the fire in the distance, under the vast apple tree where we'd left Aisling. My fae side, still in command, was exultant from the night running in the forest. He was tired, but not yet ready to cede control again.

My body moved so perfectly with him piloting it, light and poised and exquisitely balanced, somehow aware of everything around it. The forest around him might have been just another part of himself.

I wondered if we'd be switching back and forth like this for the rest of our lives.

We'll have to find something we agree on, he thought, *Something we can share. Reintegration into one person might still be possible.*

Aisling looked up from beyond the fire. Some little bundle squirmed in her arms, and a flash out of time hit me, a foreseeing or a glimpse of fate or I don't know what.

My wife, with our child in her arms, I thought, overwhelmed with sudden warmth and the knowledge that so much of what I'd wanted from life was still, maybe, possible. The sabertooth cub I'd mistaken for a baby tumbled out of her lap and tripped over to me. The faery cat in me purred at the little one who might someday share a life with our son. I picked him up and held him to my heart for a long minute while the little creature licked my face and tried wrestling me. The biggest cat chuffed, though, and he squirmed away and disappeared into the foggy darkness with the rest of the pride.

I looked up at Aisling, staring uncertainly into the night around me. She looked brittle, with reddened eyes and an exhausted set to her shoulders.

I wanted to go to her, and put my arms around her and hold her until all those tears were forgotten, then kiss her until she couldn't breathe.

She abandoned us! She forgot us! She left us to that witch's mercy! My other self screamed, trying not to want that glimpse of domestic contentment as badly as I did, as angry at my desire for something normal as at all he'd lost for her sake. *She'd run. She doesn't have it in her to stick around. She couldn't deal with what we really are.*

I thought of her jumping on the head of a giant snake to get a better angle for her spear, and doubted that.

We'll see, he thought grimly.

Dark power billowed out of him, something learned in the night, and I saw the whites of Aisling's eyes as she fought panic so hard she had to grip her own knees to keep from fleeing.

She held, though, glaring at me. My other self grinned in grudging admiration, and let the fear magic go.

"Is the guy from the riverbank still in there?" Aisling asked him, getting to her feet, and my heart thumped and warmed again.

Mine, he thought, snarling at me. *She was mine first and she'll be mine first again.*

The lust magic I'd accidentally hit Aisling with when trying to heal her bruises ignited again, and I saw her almost fall to her knees when that whammy hit. I could see instantly that she wouldn't throw this magic off. Our girl, for better or for worse, was a lot better at fighting fear than temptation. I felt... ah. There was a feedback aspect to this magic. Some of what hit her, hit me.

And I could absolutely drown in it. In her.

Oh god, but it felt good. Not just ensorcelling her body, but using magic, letting it flow, not holding back. Not fearing. Taking control and letting the energy rip.

I saw the control points, the strings of magic I had bound around her body. They could be plucked, pulled... I could play her body like a harp.

I set my hands and struck the strings.

Her skin flushed and breathing sped up. A trickle of sweat ran down her cheek.

Huge blue eyes looked into mine, needy, vulnerable, seeing me... Changed, Else, antlered *me*... and still wanting.

Oh hell, that was *hot*.

How much was using this magic on her affecting me as well? Because I'd never needed a woman so badly. And it had been so long, so many years alone.

I wondered if, under her bluster and snarky cheerfulness, she was as lonely as I was.

He told her to get naked and her armor was gone before the words finished leaving my mouth.

And oh god, the glimpse I'd gotten of her before had *nothing* on the slow perusal of her form my other self was approvingly making. She was exquisite, light and graceful as a sapling, but her muscles were defined and the scars of monster hunts decorated her skin.

Fighter. Huntress. Mate, the three sides of me thought, approving.

She was resisting my glamours, but in a pro forma sort of way, like she thought she probably should but wasn't actually invested in freeing herself. It felt as though she had no actual interest in escaping.

Because Aisling was *mine.*

And she knew it. Even with all that challenge in her eyes.

I couldn't tell you which of us thought that. It just felt... fundamental.

She didn't really actually want to fight this at all. It was written, clear as day in her energy, how much this did it for her.

I could... I could do anything I wanted with her, my faery self thought, stunned.

And he'd had a lot of time to think about what *anything* might entail.

We can't risk getting her pregnant while we're living in a prison! I yelled at him, getting a glimpse of what he was contemplating and unable to keep any other control of the situation.

She isn't fertile now, he answered coolly, showing me how to tell, and how the old magic of our line could affect arousal and fertility, and her breathing sped up under his touch. A little smile tugged on our mouth.

How many spirits in here just talked about grandchildren? I demanded, and felt a grudging acknowledgment of my point.

He considered her, thinking of everything he could do to that slender body, while she almost hyperventilated with the effort to hold on to something of herself.

Do YOU have a way to provide for and protect a baby?

There was a feeling of him going utterly still for a second.

Aisling gasped under our touch, trying to hide it.

Well, he said, an anticipatory grin forming on my face, *there's a LOT we can do without chancing that. Follow along, let's see if we can get you into things a bit more interesting than those bland suburban girls you were glamoured to fetishize.*

He pulled our pants off, and Aisling bit her lower lip, eyes going wide.

I might have been as beglamoured as she was by that point, and just nodded numbly along with her as she agreed to his terms for eventually getting me back in the pilot seat. She pulled my head down to hers, her tongue licking into my mouth, and smiled as she came to me.

Our magic swept unimpeded through her eager body as we kissed her willing lips and thrust demanding fingers into her liquid core.

"Open your legs for me," he demanded, and her neck arched as she gasped. Oh god. I could fall so hard for her. Did she feel anything like this?

Open your mind for me, I added, nuzzling in against hers, and I saw the shadows of fear she'd felt that I'd never forgive her for what her mother had done. She thought it likely that I'd never want her again, when she'd had the thought that, in spite of everything, she might love me forever. For a second, I was in control as my other self froze wordless inside me.

But it didn't last.

It's lust I want right now, not love, he snarled, making her moan when he grabbed one of her sleek breasts and flicked his thumb against her nipple.

I'm cool with that, she sent back to me, and opened her mind to her own set of thoughts about what she'd like to do with me. Because my hated Elseness? Was doing it for her. An image from her blasted into my mind of her hands on my antlers, holding me down and directing me.

Not Else to me. A man of my people, she said. *Someone like me. Delicious. Sexy. Desirable. Am I, to you?*

She had to ask, after all this? And oh gods, but she had her own ideas for what she wanted to do with my body, things she was whispering to me that I didn't even know people did... the girl in my arms now was most definitely not the easily shocked teenager I'd known ten years ago. And, like, nothing in her was objecting to all this. We had a free hand.

Thank the gods, both parts of me thought, our dread and eagerness mingling.

Yes, I answered, everything in me agreeing.

She's with me, my other self thought, shocked, delighted, scanning through her fantasies. She likes the hunt and the playing.

"Apologize," he whispered in her ear, feeling her own need to do that. *Beg my forgiveness.*

She turned huge blue eyes to me, asking what I wanted. I pulled her to me and kissed her deeply for a minute, then my other self took over again, and gave her a hard smile.

On your knees. With your mouth.

What? I said to him, *You can't say things like that...*

She grinned, confirming he absolutely could. I saw then how hard the greenwood magic was riding her, feeling her *need* to get me inside her any and every way we could manage. Her hands went to my hips and a second later she dropped to her knees in front of us and I lost all ability to object to much anything at all. She certainly wasn't complaining, except that her own body was on fire, unquenched, and she might go mad if she wasn't touched back soon.

Good, he thought. *I've had plenty of time sitting in the dark going crazy.*

This felt... oh god, this *felt.* I might not be in control but every bit of sensation was hitting me, so much *more* than anything else I'd ever done. I'd had *one* relationship after getting bound, more or less forgetting the ones I'd had before, and Laurie and I had both been "saving ourselves" and had no idea what to do when we did eventually end up in bed. And about the time we started figuring it out, I Changed.

I... I want to do something like this to Aisling, I thought, wondering if I could break her brain like she was breaking mine, imagining demanding hands grabbing my antlers and steering like she wanted to, and groaned at both the thought and what she was doing with her tongue right then.

Let her burn a bit more, my other self thought mercilessly, and our fingers reached for her pointed ears. She moaned helplessly as I caressed her, finding the little hidden nerve bundles in the tips.

Are my ears that sensitive? I wondered, losing myself in what she was projecting, wanting to feel the same thing.

Let's find out, he said, and pulled us down to the bedding.

Then he completely took over again, and introduced us, with almost sadistic slowness, to how much pleasure a sidhe body could withstand, to how much my new form could *feel*. The boundaries between who was who blurred until I wasn't sure who was giving orders and who was helplessly, eagerly obeying. And when I was as into it as our girl was, as lost in the wild ecstasy, he let me, inch by shuddering inch, back into my own body.

Or I think he did, because I wasn't really sure where he ended and I began by then.

44

RAVEN POTENTIAL

"So, back to our smugglers," Sveta said. "Have to start with some satellite footage."

The projection switched to an aerial view over the Mississippi. A red circle lit up around two tiny boats slipping into the river at late dusk. A second later, they faded away, and were lost in an odd fog. That happened repeatedly. The last time it happened, I thought I glimpsed pale, serpentine coils in the water behind them.

The footage followed them down the river past St. Cloud until a bit after midnight, by the running time stamp, when they pulled up on shore right by the border of our restricted lands. Sveta had enhanced our local aerial surveillance beyond what I'd realized was possible. We could get a pretty good look at everyone getting out of the boats.

"So as you can see, this is right on our border, probably a place the smugglers think is safe from both us and the monster patrol. There's two 'Conductors' from the Railroad, Siren and Rue - Rue's our girl Aisling in yet another seeming - a pair of teenagers, and a couple with a baby and toddler. They hide the canoes and Aisling stays under one, then the rest go up to a cave in the cliff there to spend the night. But a few hours later..."

In the footage, a familiar oversized serpent followed a feral cow into the flood zone below the cliff, ate it, and promptly laid down and fell asleep between the refugees and their canoes. Once it was asleep, Aisling rolled out from under her canoe and fled straight up to the others.

"Sequana's sweet waters," Daire said, laughing. "Those poor people must have been cursing every god they could name."

"Total *pizdets*, yes. And it gets better," Sveta says. "The landbound boy could feel her out there. She even blamed him for somehow calling the snake to hold her in place later."

"Oh yeah, back when we could landbind, that was a thing," Daire said.

The footage switched back to a high satellite view, showing the headlights of a small military convoy heading almost directly towards the cave.

"So, stuck between a rock and a hard place, watch how your granddaughter solves problems," Sveta said to Maddoc. He kind of started at the word "granddaughter."

The strangeling girl with tufted ears and clawed hands slipped out of the cave, moving like she'd been born part of the night. Halfway down the rock wall she dropped her glamour, pulled off her human clothes, and green sidhe nano-armor unfolded over her body. The pattern was odd, not one I'd seen before, more like something a movie elf would wear than the armor of the starborn sidhe. She packed her street clothes into her backpack, pulled out a small gun, and shrugged the pack back on.

"Well, I suppose that could have been Derdriu's armor," Maddoc sighed. "Odd form to it, though."

"Killing the snake with a gun that small seems unlikely," Daire said dubiously.

"Oh, she's not even going to try," Sveta answered. *"Watch* this crazy lunatic."

The girl slipped down to stand much too close to the snake's head, then shot off a distress flare from the pistol into the air. She stood there calmly reloading as it awoke and began slithering towards her. Maddoc's eyes widened in horror. She raised the gun again, shot it right between its eyes, and took off running directly towards the approaching Jeeps.

"I don't think this kid's ending up in Siobhan's class," Daire said dryly.

At the Convocations, when young sidhe are fully brought into society, Siobhan generally ends up mentoring the sane and civilized kids. Daire gets... the *other* ones. Like me. Back then, I'd been "promising", though, not broken, with all the invincible cockiness of the very young.

The boy I'd been would have thought this girl was *fantastic.*

She ran the snake directly into Hart's patrol and did some sort of aerial gymnastic flip off the hood of his Jeep right before the monster smashed into his vehicle. A second later, she shredded the tires of their troop transport and fled up a cliff, Hart bare meters behind her. Daire started laughing, almost helplessly, and Maddoc glared at him.

"No, no," he said, holding up a hand. "It's that I was just telling Brennos a week ago that I didn't think any of the new Earthborn kids really had Raven potential. They're all too over-protected and cautious. This is like watching an insane young Macha all over again, back when she had all the *go* and none of the know-how."

Maddoc glanced at the projection like it was giving him a raging headache, one he expected to get much worse, and waved his hand like, *You've got a point.*

Magic flared from the antlered man, and every exposed root and tree branch around the girl in green reached for her.

"Holy..." Daire said, choking, as the boy's magic flared again and suddenly the two young sidhe weren't fighting, they were twining their limbs together, every movement suddenly coordinated and beautiful, kissing in the forest loam. A circle of vegetation around them greened and bloomed. I closed my eyes, my broken magic aching in me like a lost limb. This was *old* sidhe magic.

Then there was an explosion, and the footage zoomed out enough to show a hit on the snake, then back in to the young sidhe. The girl pushed Hart off her, obviously swearing. She used a bound sword to slice herself free, kissed him again fast, and took off running for the river. For a second he just blinked, stunned, then pursued again.

I would have too. She was worth chasing.

"That poor boy," Daire chuckled. "He's got absolutely no clue what his magic is doing to him. If he's really one of ours, it seems like the Wildwood line bred true. Looks a bit like Hrinn, but he's barely even been responsive for the last thirty years; doesn't even make any of his escapes from the care home anymore. Heard they have to feed him through a tube half the time now. Given his state, there's no way he could have recently fathered a child."

Seconds later, the girl flashed across the water and on top of the snake's head. She leaped vertically and stabbed a spear down through its eye.

"I think she learned how to fight from human action movies," I said, not seeing a good way out of this battle. "I mean, what the hell sort of exit plan does she even have here?"

"Very likely," Sveta said. "Given that Riksby spent the afternoon reading Star Trek fan-fic and they've been best friends since eighth grade. School records note the two of them were the biggest nerds in their class, though she somehow managed to *also* get a reputation as a violent thug."

The snake spasmed and smacked Aisling with a coil. She went limp and fell into the water. The red-haired strangeling she worked with dove after her.

"Who's the other girl?" Daire asked, seeing her pull Aisling back to the surface and apparently glamour them both unnoticeable, given that they went directly past soldiers who didn't see them.

"She goes by 'Siren' and is some kind of water fae, but passes as human. She can glamour with her voice, and has some sort of sonic attack as well. Let's skip ahead, you can see. Works as a musician. It looks like this team faked a new I.D. for her about eight years ago, but I'll figure out who she was originally. Might take some time. A lot of local records are only on paper now."

The footage skipped forward to Div 51's soldiers and the strangeling runners trying to warm up at a beach campfire. This part had some audio, low-tech radio communication as Riksby's magic took over Strangeling Brigade's radios. Even better, he kept it open to listen in after he stopped talking, and we monitor and record those frequencies.

"I like this little team, raw as they are," Daire said. "The dokkalfar boy just ran a nigh perfect distraction to open people up for the siren's glamour. What's happening to the giant girl?"

The redhead and five of the refugees made it into the surviving canoe and fled, leaving Aisling behind with swords at the officers' throats. I took a moment to pity the poor lieutenant who'd had sidhe blades at his throat twice in under an hour.

"Damned if I know," Maddoc said. "She didn't have any of that fur when I saw her, and was passed out, but otherwise looked okay. Certainly wasn't a ravening monster."

"She's going into the Hunger. Outside the sidhe cities, the Sochan Effect is still spreading," Sveta said, trying to hide how pissed she was at that bit of conqueror's ignorance. She'd Changed in her early teens and ended up on the street when her family threw her out. The years before Morganna took her in... hadn't been kind.

"Many people who Change become inconsolably ravenous while it happens," she said, "And eat anything and anyone around them then. I've never heard of a treatment for it, so I don't know what Aisling is talking about here."

Pistol to her head, Aisling sang out the Call to Trade. In very short order, it was answered.

"The Edgeland tribes know we had lost children and told no one here?" Maddoc exclaimed. A minute later he added, "And she knows *my name* and hid when I was mere steps away from her?!?"

"Listen to the way she phrased that, though," Daire said. "Maddoc, or Ellith, or Morganna, *if they seem themselves*. And it sounds like Derdriu glamoured both her and the soldier."

"*Shape-shifters with mind-control magics?*" I said a few seconds later, dread twisting my stomach. "Might be good to call Ellith and find out exactly what Derdriu was working on when she disappeared. This sounds like she didn't stop doing spy shit, even in hiding."

"And perhaps she had good reason to stay away," Sveta said. "Given how much crap from your infiltrators I keep finding. I don't understand why the Rí won't let me go after them. Anyway, we're almost to where the fireworks go off. I have to admit I'm not sure what I'm seeing."

Morganna's not letting you go after them because they're good enough to fuck up the galaxy's most elite fighting force, and you're a damn kid, I thought, and realized with dismay that Daire and Maddoc were thinking the exact same thing about me. And my heart cracked a little as I looked at my life and realized they might be right.

"*...wounded, almost beyond hope of survival...no one is asking you to give more, or wants you hurt again...*"

Am I that fragile?

Aisling started feeding the monster mushrooms covered in her own blood, and it actually seemed to stabilize the girl. Then she said something about Norse mythology and the elders frowned like this was really weird to them too, tipped her head back and spread out her arms and light slipped out of her, almost shaping an image of the Tree that Grows Between Worlds, almost, and then Hart put a hand on her shoulder and it flared into him and light blazed up like a sun rising on the river. It poured through them and into the warping strangeling girl, and she screamed silently and convulsed as the wiry hair burned off her and her spine straightened out. Some sort of dark fog that seemed to move under its own power rose from her mouth, and Aisling went to her knees, her magic spent. Gold light formed a shape like a lion's paw over Hart's hand and he shredded the odd black smoke.

Daire choked on his coffee and almost dropped the mug.

"That's not Wildwood magic," he said as Maddoc thumped on his back. "Oh, fucking hell. Maybe he *is* Hrinn's... gods know how that'd be possible, though."

Something went wrong, impossible to tell what from the footage. Hart threw himself away from Aisling - or was thrown - and lay on the beach sand looking straight up at the aerial. It looked like he was burning up from the inside, the Tree's light blazing out from his mouth and eyes and glowing antlers.

Sveta zoomed in, enhancing the footage well beyond what was normally possible. The giantess was still large, but no longer monstrous.

"What the hell was all that?" Daire asked, staring. "I've never seen any sidhe use the Tree like that."

"Stoyven's people were Norse, right?" I asked. "Because with the way she called on a Viking god and then did that... and if her cousin's turning into something like him..."

"The alfar who didn't go starfaring with the sidhe married into human lines," Daire said. "Died off otherwise, but we've got two human-born kids in Stockholm and Reykjavik, and they're both a bit different too."

"Lingren's a Swedish family name," Sveta said. "Means *linden tree*. If her magic works like this, her studies on cryptids make a lot more sense."

The light around the soldier turned from gold to emerald green and then soaked out of him and into the surrounding land. The aerial footage showed a flush of green spill out across the landscape, centered on him.

Daire groaned, seeing it.

"Well, that'd explain why it felt like someone doing a land-claiming ritual," Maddoc said, shaking his head. "Thought I think it's more that he's *being* claimed than doing any claiming."

"This is a disaster," Daire said. "A child of ours who's an enemy soldier, that landbound, right on our border?"

Not an enemy, I thought, thinking of that lostness in his eyes. *Not really. Not yet. Give him a chance.*

Radios squawked again, the dark elf boy shouting for the soldiers to hide the two young sidhe. Neither could even walk at that point and needed to be dragged into hiding. But a second after they were behind the fallen tree, some magic spread over them both and they virtually disappeared from the screen.

"We've seen the bit where the Guard's there," Sveta said, fast forwarding. "The sidhe kids come out of hiding as soon as you're gone, ineptly flirt with and aggravate each other for a bit, then go off with Hart's team and their new Dohoulani guide. They plan to hunt a monster pig back outside our borders, but end up stuck on car repairs well into the afternoon. Interestingly, the human commander actually pulled rank and told Hart not to write up a damn thing about running into a sidhe patrol, saying any action against the Elsecomers is pointless and they need to focus purely on containing the weirdling monsters."

"Well, that's something," Daire said, looking like he was trying to figure out how to deal with this situation. "Sounds like *he's* a smart kid, anyway."

"Aisling apparently intends to teach Hart how to be sidhe," Sveta continued, "And given that she described it as like getting to be the hard-drinking lovechild of the Flash and Buffy the Vampire Slayer, that ought to be an interesting education! Poor boy."

"Who?" Daire asked, confused, and I just started laughing.

"They're a bunch of human pop-culture superheroes," I said. "I want in on these lessons."

Maddoc rubbed his forehead like he was in serious pain.

"We need to bring them in," he said. "But I just gave my word I wouldn't take the dokkalfar boy's cousin if she talked to me. And it would be hard to avoid that, were I introducing her to sidhe society."

"Hart's pledged to an enemy military that won't even discuss truce terms with us," Daire answered, tapping a finger on the table. "And dammit, he's exactly what I was hoping to find with the new Earthborn kids."

"He's in a prison labor brigade," I reminded Daire. "He might pretend to, but he's not really serving freely."

"Yeah..." Sveta said. "One more thing."

She played a clip of Lieutenant Birch telling everyone on the beach that they needed to fake the deaths of some of their soldiers because none of them were even supposed to live over five years after Changing.

"Gods of our forebears," Daire swore. "I had no idea things were such a mess here on Earth. How long ago did you say Hart Changed?"

"It'll be five years this fall," Sveta said.

Daire leaned back, looking pensive.

"So he's got a little time, but not much," he said. "And a policy that's been ignored can be revived at the drop of a hat. One mistake and he's likely to be killed by his own superiors."

45
WARM

AISLING

O nly a tiny tendril of smoke was wafting up from the campfire by the time Arthur had fully come back to himself. We were spooning in a tangled pile next to it, our minds as entwined as our limbs. He was slowly nibbling on one of my over-sensitized ears and sliding a slow, possessive hand down my hip. It wasn't exactly morning, here in this weirding place, but the fog had turned a lighter color.

I could barely move, I was so spent. We'd done pretty much everything you can do without risking pregnancy (much; I'd had to explain to the idiot halfway through the night that birth control was a thing and I was on it) or having props or toys on hand.

Dear gods. I'll never be able to resist his lust glamours, knowing something like this could follow.

Good, Arthur thought, purring possessively into my mind. I wasn't sure which voice that came from; the last few hours had made it pretty clear there were at least two or three in there, the soldier and my wild boy and something more primal than either. That sounded like it might have come from all of them.

Oh well. I wasn't exactly feeling like I'd *lost* a battle.

Someday I'm going to top you just as hard, I sent back to him, and felt him smile into my hair.

You're welcome to try, he replied, anticipating.

"You'll have to wait until my muscles work again," I sighed, snuggling into him. "Right now I feel like a puddle of wet noodles. You back together?"

"Mmm," he hummed, pulling me around to face him. "Can we do all that again if I say no?"

I grabbed one of his antlers and pulled him down to kiss me. The last couple hours had more than shown that whatever they were made of, it wasn't insensitive horn, and a lot of his magic flowed through them. Having them manhandled was most definitely one of his kink points.

"I should probably apologize for all that," he said a minute later.

"Well, you told me pretty clearly how one goes about asking forgiveness," I said, and smiled. "So you can just head south and spell your apology letter by letter..."

"I didn't overdo glamouring you?" he asked, very quietly. Ah. right. The thing that had made him abandon his teenage 'harem' before we first kissed.

"I am still perfectly capable of seeing everything aggravating about you, and only intend to worship your body situationally," I answered, gazing into his eyes to let him know I was still myself.

He sighed, satisfied, and pulled me closer. I half heard the echo of another voice inside his mind, somehow both pleased and grumbling.

"So what's going on in there?" I asked, kind of tapping his forehead. He sighed again, much less contented, and made himself sit up. My body protested, vociferously, but I did the same.

"Your mother's glamours and bindings split my personality, somehow," he said. "Like she grabbed everything fae and magical... and not whitebread straight... and bound it up deep inside me, then patched together everything inclined towards discipline and order and left that running things. And I also seem to have a spirit cat like the ones who were here last night somehow part of me; I've thought of it as my monster for the last four years."

I thought about it, chewing on my lip, then shrugged.

"Okay."

He looked at me, totally nonplussed.

"*Okay?* That's all you have to say?"

"Well, obviously I wish this hadn't happened to you, and I'm horribly sorry I didn't hide our letters to each other better; I thought they were safe in the broken wall. I'm sorry about everything you've been through, and I'm incredibly glad you survived it all. But if you're asking if I'm going to freak out about you having multiple personalities or something, nah. I'll just think of it as a low maintenance threesome. And I have plenty of my own issues to inflict on you."

He looked at me like I was the crazy one.

"*Low maintenance?* Really?"

"Well, only two people's worth of laundry and cooking, anyway. But I always wanted to try a threesome and have had the worst luck with making one actually happen."

He shook his head ruefully.

"It didn't... disturb you?" he asked. Oh gods, the vulnerability in his eyes. My body protested as I moved over to straddle his lap. I put both my hands under his jaw and made him look directly into my eyes.

"That *rocked my world.* That was flipping amazing. Everyone in there," I tapped the side of his head again, "Was incredible, and I can't wait to do all this again, because *wow.*"

He leaned into me, and relief rolled off him like a wave. I pulled his lips to mine and kissed him long and slow, savoring the moment and the taste of him.

"I thought you might be too furious to ever look at me again," I said eventually, running a hand down his cheek.

He winced a little, then laughed and his eyes went dark green. My faery lover looked out at me.

"Almost," he said, his eyes and hands running over me like I was beautiful. "But it's hard to abandon a view like this."

"Mmm, same. This all suits you," I said, grabbing an antler and pulling him in for a kiss again, feeling his pleasure wash over me when I did that. "I like your Changes very, very much. If you asked me to be part of some ridiculous harem now, I might say yes."

He blinked, then laughed, remembering.

"Hart," he said. "I took the name you gave me, that day."

Then his face went stricken and his shoulders shook. I wrapped my arms up around him, trying to soothe my lover.

"I've been so lost," he whispered, his 'human' self back in his voice. "I hated all this Elseness so much."

I hugged him tight to me and held him for a minute, then gently kissed his antlers, and his ears, and across his face, telling him without words how beloved it all was to me.

He tipped me back onto the skins again and his mouth and magic opened to mine and we explored what we'd become a little more. Adults. Lovers. Openly fae, at least with each other. He looked like he could possibly be convinced to get used to all this. He went for my ears again and my brain shut off a bit.

"I have no idea where we take things from here," he said when I was curled up purring against him again.

"We're in a terrible mess," I agreed with him, eventually, not actually minding right then. "But we found each other again, and that's something."

He smiled. Then we were kissing again, and that turned into somewhat more, and there were no more words between us for a while. We kind of snoozed for a bit, afterwards, warm and content to be together, not knowing when we might have a chance again at time this simple.

Eventually, he pulled me in against his chest, and I cuddled in, enjoying the afterglow.

"So what's this make us?" he asked, petting my hair as I lay half on his chest.

I shrugged, wondering about that myself.

"Relationships... haven't really been a thing for me," I said. "I've just been doing friendships and flings, one night stands mostly. The binding on me made feeling much beyond adrenaline and endorphins difficult for a long time, then I worked up to friendships and such, but... I know I'm going to be a mess for a while. Making something work... it's going to be new territory for me."

"But you might stand to at least think of having a boyfriend? As a start?"

"Maybe if he stops trying to arrest me," I said, smiling.

Something glittered in his eyes.

"I don't know, having you in cuffs has potential," he said. "Naughty little smugglers sneaking into my land ought to be *punished.*"

I glared at him, trying not to grin.

"Scarves or soft ropes *only.* Cuffs give me iron burns."

Arthur held me tighter for a minute, kissed me again, then sighed and started looking around for his clothes.

"I don't get the impression that last night did more than scratch the surface of my other self's kinks," he said, looking like he both dreaded and anticipated finding out more. Mmm. Me too. "I wasn't by any means straight when I was younger and I don't think ten years in chains did anything to inhibit him."

"Guess we'll need a safe word," I replied, finding his shirt. "Apples, maybe?"

"You don't seem very disturbed."

"Bisexual band groupie, remember? I've done every member of *Jackalopes on Speed,* and those guys named their band well. Thirty seconds and *done.* Weird half minute though! So, you happen to play any instruments?"

Emerald green glittered in his eyes for a second, and he grinned wickedly.

"What?" I asked, reluctantly calling armor back on and wishing I had some actual clothes. The armor works, but it's not exactly *comfy.*

"Just your body," he smirked, and I threw his t-shirt at his head.

There were still two apples in my pouch and I munched on one while Arthur got dressed. He looked at me, seemed to wonder if that was a good idea, and then sat down next to me and had the other. Some magic in the fruit sparkled through me, revitalizing, and I got up and ran through a few stretches and then some katas.

"You studied karate?" Arthur asked, recognizing them. Light shimmered over his antlers with every bite he took; I wondered if he realized it. They were still covered in velvet but seemed to be taking on more definition.

"To second *dan* black belt. Taught my hometown teenagers class for a couple years," I said.

"I got to brown belt before joining the military full time," he said. "You had some moves that definitely weren't learned in a dojo, though."

"My mom taught me a sidhe fighting style when I was a kid," I said. "And I've learned to imitate a ton of fights from movies, even a bit of Drunken Monkey. That's fun, good in bar fights. I did gymnastics from when I was three to fourteen, so use that here and there. Needed an excuse for being too coordinated for my age. My coach was *so* frustrated that Olympics aren't a thing anymore. Not that I'd have competed, but it was nice to hear."

"Aha, so that's why you're so flexible."

We both contemplated the pretzels he'd twisted me into over the course of the night.

"You have any idea how we can make something work?" I asked.

"Nope, but we will," he said, no doubt at all in his voice.

"I'm not really entirely free," I said apologetically.

"That hunt?" he asked, and I nodded.

"Well, the way we're living, any of us could die tomorrow," he said, sighing. "Let's make the best of what time we get."

It was as good a plan as I'd ever had.

"Okay. Ready to go?" I asked.

"Sure. I'm beyond lost, though."

I pointed. The exit was clear as day in my mind.

"That way, with a couple twists and turns. I feel it, don't worry. Hopefully we can bend time to get us out shortly after your soldier."

"That's a thing?"

"Does space in here seem solid and normal to you? Time's the same. Will and focused intent can bend them, same as any magic."

He stood up, stretched a little himself, and pulled my sweater back on. I held my hand out for him, he took it, and we followed my sense saying *go that way* directly back to his gun, still lying on the earth where he'd left it. The moss around it looked faintly burnt everywhere the steel wasn't covered in rubber dip or hockey stick tape, and Arthur swore when he touched it. He looked at it for a second, pulled the sweater sleeve down and used it to pick up the weapon.

"I'm always more iron sensitive after being in a ghostland too," I told him, and he nodded grimly. He didn't have any non-steel weapons, after all, and being out in the Edgelands without arms was a bad idea.

I put my hand in his and pulled him into a link with me to share magic.

"Think of your soldier as we last saw him. Ok. Got him. Go!"

I closed my eyes, navigating entirely by instinct, and pushed him forward, still holding on. Space and time swirled like mist around us, and I pulled us along the connection binding Arthur to his man. I heard panicked voices raised in argument, Rigs' among them on a radio, and then sunlight hit us and dry leaves crunched under our feet as we stepped back into the mortal world.

Arthur's team looked up at us, relief flooding their faces, and my bondnet connections lit up. Something *shifted* in the ghostland. I spun on instinct, looking behind me, and the fog we'd wandered into billowed and pulled back as if sucked away. I almost, almost saw the sabertooth matriarch and the little cub beside her in the fog, toothy grins hanging in the air like huge Cheshire Cats, and then spring sunlight streamed down and lit the empty road ahead of us.

"Woohoo!" I yelled, pumping a fist. "Take *that,* four-dimensional physics!"

46

BACK IN DAYLIGHT

ARTHUR

There was a second of confusion and everyone went silent, probably not least at seeing us come out holding hands. Jones raised an eyebrow and I grinned a little and shrugged.

"Captain, arc you okay?" Serena asked.

I thought about it, and nodded.

"She broke the time space-continuum again, didn't she," her tech guy's voice said from Birch's radio. "How long were you in there?"

"Couple days," I answered. "Or maybe lifetimes. Time was weird. Out here?"

"About a minute since Sokolov got back," Birch said, staring. "What happened in there?"

"Weird vision quest shit," Aisling said dismissively. "We're fine. Gods, I need some real world food to ground me like *now*. Is my backpack still in the Jeep?"

My people looked even more confused, and no little bit concerned.

"You sure you're okay?" Birch asked. "You're both moving kinda *off.*"

I tried to think of a way to answer that.

"Gods damn it, Slayer, you already shagged him, didn't you," the voice from the radio demanded. "Do you have even a single ounce of willpower in that minuscule murder hobo brain of yours?"

"Nope!" she said cheerfully, pulling out her backpack to dig through it for snacks. "Speaking of which, don't we have some sort of ambulatory bacon to go collect? I'm starving. Captain Handholds here kept me up *all* night."

Oh god. She was as bad as my other self, and people could hear *her.*

My other self grinned like she was making him proud.

I tried to think of something to say to all the troops now staring at me, and ended up just kind of shrugging.

"Slayer, you are a fucking *imbecile*," Tech said, as Jones, trying very hard to keep a straight face, discreetly reached over and fist-bumped me. "You have been halfway arrested and are on a *run*, not doing a concert afterparty!"

"I know! It was awesome. All I had to deal with was Arthur completely losing control, not a single dumbass with a hand puppet. And it's been almost five days for me and I haven't had a thing but magic apples to eat. Incidentally, I might be tripping. I can see everyone's potential magic sparkling around them, even the human guys. Think if I poked it, it'd trigger."

There was a moment of horrified, face-palming silence. She found a bag of hazelnuts and started munching on them.

"Well, I'm out, you guys can keep her," Tech said. "You want to lock her up with you? I could use a break from this nonsense."

She laughed and offered me the bag. I smiled and took a handful of nuts.

"Oh, don't worry, he says something like that at least once a month," she said, grinning, and giving me a glimpse of how her unit operated - not a general army troop, but one of those little specialist operations where everyone was practically family, and gave each other a similar level of grief.

"Show me what you're seeing," I said, walking over and running a hand along the nape of her neck, and mindlinked her as if we'd done it every day of our lives. She turned a brilliant smile to me and let me see what her magic was showing her. Light sparkled across my people, through me and out through the land I was bound to. It looked like a wild tangle of branches and roots, with flowers buds all over the branches, probably the incipient magic she was seeing.

I saw the lines my magic had taken when I pulled my people into the hunting bond, before when I had lost control to the faery cat inside me, and he purred like he was saying *Mine. My pack.*

Deep roots reached down from me, into my patrol lands, and the same sort reached from her into the lands North of us, and... those roots had begun twining together.

I looked at her, trying to check if I could see in the same way, and found my vision of such let me see broadly along the same lines, if without quite the level of precision. Aisling blazed like starlight given human form, her magic more beautiful even than her face, and I fell even harder for her.

Dusty, what the hell are you doing? I heard her partner ask her, and felt him freeze and swear when I gave him a little wave.

Just making sure our next run goes more smoothly than this, she said blandly. *I might have to run off in the middle of the night to pay passage tolls next time I'm Conducting, by the way.*

I laughed, thinking that had potential.

She's teaching me how to be sidhe, like she promised, I sent to him, feeling the "bondnet" she had described. It was... really interesting. Comms that never broke down or lost range would be *really* handy. *She's safe with me.*

Your minds feel different, he said, looking at us and considering. *More open, and more fae. Those bindings?*

Removed in the ghostland, I said. *Aisling's likely to be having trouble with wild empathy for a while, I was warned.*

I felt him nod and make a note of that. Damn. The feel of his mind was something else: precise, organized, brilliant.

"This telepathy thing your team does," I said out loud. "How intrusive is that? Can you keep your thoughts to yourselves or are you all broadcasting to each other all the time?"

"We all isolate at will," she said. "And a guy left the net a couple of years ago, when he decided he needed to travel and 'find himself'. It's not a trap. There's a learning curve when you're new to it, and major shocks often make you project to the group. Bob dropped an engine block on his foot last week and we all heard him swearing about it. And I've been known to overreact to team members panicking; some longshoremen cornered Siren in the back room of a bar last spring and I broke 3 ribs and an arm getting her out. I mean, she could have taken them, but it might have outed her."

"Ouch," Birch said. "How did you recover fast enough to fight at Midsommer?"

"Didn't say they were *my* bones," she said, grinning. "Hey, you've been studying Norse myths, right?"

Birch looked a bit surprised and nodded. He had a just about photographic memory for his various random passions, so asking him made sense.

"Any idea who 'an orchard keeper, the youngest of Ivaldi's elder children' would be?" she asked.

"Idunna is described like that, the goddess who tended the golden apples of immortality for the Aesir gods," he said. "Though sometimes she's referred to as a Vanir or an elf-maid."

"Huh," she said. "Thought so. And Ivaldi?"

"He was either a dark elf or a dwarf, depending on the translation," he said. "His sons were some of the great craftsmen of mythology, made Freyr's ship and Odin's spear and Sif's hair. Were the apples you ate golden?"

"Mmmhmm. She'd made some into turnovers and hot cider. Delicious. I was worried about eating them but she said we were fae already and our ancestors ate plenty of them; I got the impression eating the fruits of the Tree might be what made them sidhe in the first place."

"The Matron who took me out into the night showed me some things along those lines, too," I said. "Talked about prehistoric people taking on Radiance intentionally for... reasons. Something with fighting monsters from the sea. It's all blurry and dream-like, though."

"That was the antlered girl?" Aisling asked. "You look like her, you know."

"She called me grandson," I admitted. "She talked about stuff from the end of the last Ice Age, though, so I'm going to guess there would be some 'greats' in there. Taught me some stuff about how my magic works."

"Well, you having some idea what you're doing would be a relief to everyone around you," Birch said. "Getting back to the apples, aren't you a little concerned about what eating apples of immortality might do to you?"

Aisling shrugged.

"Sidhe live until something kills us, most often our own stupidity," she said, unworried, and Darouk had a coughing fit over on the hood of my Jeep. "I think my mom was at least five hundred or so, though she was vague about it. Wasn't sure of the time conversion to Earth years. Visited Earth during the Renaissance, anyway. And her parents were far older and still alive, though she never told me much about them. Said her father fought the Romans when they invaded Wales, and that her mother was named in Celtic myth."

"You're serious," I said, blinking.

"They don't have a lot of kids, as the flip side of that," she said, grabbing more nuts. "The apples *did* do something to me, though. I'm seeing, like, energy flows moving through people a lot more clearly. I think I could trigger a magic Cascade without an actual transformation, or only very minor visible Changes. There's a... hmm, a trigger point I didn't see before, and it's in most of your human guys."

"Where were you, if they separated the Captain from you?" Serena asked.

Aisling considered the question.

"A... *farm* seems an inadequate word. Agricultural research station? Yeah. Like an abandoned elven agricultural research station. But Norse, not Celtic. Well, the parts that weren't totally sci-fi, anyway. Maybe Idunna's orchard. And a lot of the buildings looked like they were built in the Bronze Age but retrofitted to starfaring standards, with tech I had no idea how to use. Figuring out the kitchen and bathroom took some doing. Weird place."

"What did you do there?"

"Erg. Mostly scream at my mother, remember the stuff she'd bound me to forget, scream some more, and scrub every surface in sight. Then some horses showed up, and I had to help one with a stuck birthing."

Serena blinked.

"I did a vet-med minor," Aisling said, unconcerned. "I hadn't actually had my arm shoulder-deep in a horse before, but I knew what to do. And the foal was *totally adorable*. But after I cleaned up, when he was doing okay, I took a nap and woke up back where Arthur found me. Which is probably for the best, because I was having fantasies of saying 'fuck it all' to real life and just staying with the horses. Most exquisite animals I've ever seen, more like a dream of what an equine could be than anything you'd ever believe could actually be alive."

She sighed regretfully and reached for a water bottle.

"Redneck nerd," Tech's voice said from the radio. "You guys know anything about monster catfish in the river? Or fish-men? Siren's telling me Strangelingtown had some attack last night. They're circling in the water nearby. She barely got the canoe past them. Some of them seem wounded and they're *hungry*."

"Read reports, but Div 51 hasn't run into them yet," Birch said. "Wounds from them tend to get infected. The ones with barbed tentacles sometimes have poison in the hooks, and it can be either Radiant or somehow mutagenic, no one's sure. It's bad though, might be your Squid ink. Guy in St. Cloud got bit and lost half his leg, but they thought he was recovering. Then he grew catfish whiskers and tried to eat a nurse. They shot him in the hospital hallway. Had to amputate two of the nurse's fingers to make sure she didn't Change too."

"*Okay* then. I'm going to go source some antibiotics and possibly holy water. Slayer, might need you to run them down. The Healer got hit when she was treating a kid on the riverbank, and she's in a bad way. Siren's going fishing now, wants to slaughter the lot. She says they all smell like her dad did the night we first found her."

Aisling's face went pale.

"She need help?" Darouk asked, perking up. "Sunscratcher Tribe lost a daughter to those fish last week. They'd be happy to assist."

"That would be great," Tech said. "Call them in."

The alien tipped his head back and barked out two extremely loud hoots, then ululated a long musical line I could somehow *almost* make sense of. Miles away, another voice picked it up and repeated it, and another far beyond that. I faintly heard one even further, and a minute later a different line was howled back. Darouk hooted three times, and then said, "They're on their way to her."

"You said Captain lost control," Jones said. "Which is something he's been hella freaked about doing. But you're both okay?"

"He needed to work through some stuff. Letting him take it out on me sounded better than any of the other alternatives for handling it," she said, shaking herself, and gave me a wicked, afterglow-filled grin. "And I don't think he regrets not getting me to panic and run from him *too* much, though for someone with no weapons or armor on him, he sure tried."

Oh. Yeah. She could have pulled blades on me any time she felt like, I thought.

She didn't, though, my fae self sighed, glowing. *She wanted me to catch her.*

"You're going to owe me money soon," Jones said to Birch, who just looked incredulous.

"We're losing daylight," I said. "Let's go hunt a unicorn. Or a pig. Or whatever the Edgelands have decided to spew on us today."

"At least they aren't tossing literal shit at us anymore," Jones said, shrugging. "Let's go."

I took my girl's hand in mine, and off we went to hunt a monster.

47

EXFILTRATION PLANS

CONNOR

"**D**o you want to talk to the pair?" Sveta asked, and the projection went back to an aerial view, apparently a live one now, and zoomed down the river to a little settlement just a bit up a tributary flowing into the Mississippi. A group of mixed strangelings, most very young, and alien tribesmen, mostly Dohoulani, were on the riverbank armed with a weird array of primitive weapons.

The redhead who'd been with Aisling walked into the water and sang, her magic sweeping out from her, *calling*. Seconds later, a godawful familiar blobby black shape charged out of the water, whiskers trying to grab and hold her. She flipped twin kukri style daggers into her hands, dodged sideways, fast as a fish herself, and guts spilled out as she opened its side from gills to pelvic fin. Three people behind her dove in with spears. Two others grabbed it with hooked poles and pulled the catfish-man out of the water, then dragged the twitching body over to a stack of them.

I tried to hide a grin. There was just nothing in me that felt the least bit bad about killing those horrendous things. Good on the villagers for taking care of them.

"Siren is still in Strangelingtown, in our territory," Sveta said with a wolfish grin. "I imagine her team would like her to come rejoin them. Be a shame if anything delayed that, no?"

Maddoc leaned forward, and Daire put his hand over his friend's to stop him.

"We've got commitments for the next couple of days," Daire said. "Maddoc's going to be jumping me around to see the new Earthborn kids that'll be at the Convocation. If we cancel or delay, there will be questions; if *we're* being spied on, someone will go looking for answers. However..."

He looked at me.

"Ahh..." Maddoc said. "Well, that explains why the way forwards showed he was needed. Sveta, I need you to check if the forensic results on that snake have been seen by anyone but Connor."

She paused, and electric light glowed in her eyes for a second.

"They have not been."

"Alter the results showing a sidhe weapon was used to say normal steel caused the injuries."

"Yes, sir. Done."

"Connor, do you know where the exfiltration kit you used when I last sent you out is? Visualize it. Good. I'll be right back."

Maddoc teleported out and came back with a backpack in a local style. It'd been over a year since I'd last gone out in the human world, but all the clothes and I.D. in there should work fine.

"Sveta, I need you on support for him," Maddoc said. "Have you used the sort of comms equipment we have in here?"

"Yes, all of it."

"Good. And keep this quiet. When it's time, I'll let family know about her. Now, Connor..."

"I know, I know, you need me to look like an idiot incompetent you're putting on punishment detail, *again*," I sighed. "Nothing new."

"Line to Captain Bhairton, please, Sveta," Maddoc said.

A second later, a line opened up.

"Weaponsmaster? How may I assist?" my supervisor's voice said.

"I'll be requisitioning Connor for a few days," Maddoc said, sounding pissed. "He's obviously in no state to be guarding the city, so I think he shall guard my cat while I'm away. He's to stay in my quarters. The liquor cabinets will be locked, and he won't need any visitors stopping by. My feline companion will be happy to tell him everything he needs to know about wasting people's time."

Maddoc's "feline companion" was an infamously awful little ball of spite and arrogance that loved only him. The cat was a torn and matted ball of blood and wounds when Maddoc found him half-dead in an alley and nursed him back to health, back while I was in the coma. After that, everyone else was a waste of air, an opinion Horrid (I named him; Maddoc calls something unpronounceable in Welsh, but everyone else, including *I swear* the cat, feels my version fits better) believed strongly. He liked looking you straight in the eye and vomiting, hit-and-run attacks to draw blood on your ankles, and making you watch him lick your blood off his claws. And if you took your shoes off, he'd leave you special *gifts* in them. Everyone in the Guard knew not to cat-sit for the old man.

So Maddoc frequently assigned Horrid-care as a punishment, since the old man somehow *always* knew when I was fucking up.

There was a sigh from the captain.

"Yes, sir, understood. My gratitude for letting me know."

I put my head against the table and hit it with my forehead. Daire clapped me on the back and laughed.

Twenty minutes later, I was pulling a special exfiltration slicer bike out of a hidden storage garage in the Edgelands, a few kilometers beyond the city's borders. It's got all kind of nifty camouflage and spy stuff built into it, can be disguised as an old human motorcycle with the push of a button, and handles like a dream. I loved that bike. Even better, I was *outside.* The sky was blue, birds were singing out their hearts to the springtime, and the only other sounds were the river gurgling and the wind in the treetops. It was heavenly.

"Rules of engagement?" Maddoc asked, using his teacher voice.

"Don't get caught, don't be seen, and don't fall in love with the target," I replied with a grin.

"That'll do," he said. Then he paused for longer than he needed to, looking at me. Some of that eeriness of the old ones flowed over him, the sort that reminds me that while we might be related to humans, our kind has drifted a long way from those roots.

"Connor..." Maddoc said, looking at me with serious eyes.

"You Saw something?"

"Just a feeling that your road home will be... convoluted. But it's better if you go than if you don't. And if you have to break some rules, do it. Just find out what we need to bring those younglings in."

I nodded, and Maddoc clapped my shoulder and blinked away.

48

THROUGH THE WOODS

ARTHUR

W e piled into the Jeeps and personnel carrier. Zhara was looking more with it and Bastion was still watching over her. Sokolov had checked the rest of the mushrooms and handed the improvised bag of them up to Bastion, in case she needed any, and I took it as a good sign when she made a face and said she'd prefer coffee.

I waved Aisling over to my Jeep, and she got in the back with me while Birch and Jones got in front, Jones driving. Birch looked at the two of us and shook his head in total disbelief.

"Crazy Hildie, Captain? Really?" he asked. "Thought you'd like 'em sane."

I glanced at Aisling, wondering how she'd take that. Sudden tension tightened her shoulders, and I wondered briefly if that warning about loss of empathic control meant loss of emotional control too.

I like them able to do the splits both ways, I sent to her, including a very explicit memory from the night before. She laughed a little, reassured.

"Why Lutefiskr," she said, batting her eyelashes at him, "Are you saying you need some full-contact heavy weapons remedials?"

He shuddered and shook his head emphatically *no*. Jones shifted the Jeep into drive and pulled out, much more slowly than last time. We drove onto an empty dirt road where the fog had been. We all held our breaths, but everything remained normal.

"Captain has said his standards were at 'willing civvie'," Jones said to Birch, letting out a relieved sigh when the road remained clear of mist, and glanced at Aisling. "But girl, you get my man to relax a bit, our whole troop will forgive three years of him going loony every time you were nearby."

I tried to repress a smile.

"It's part of being landbound, I think," she said. "Having you guys come up around Duluth aggravates the hell out of me too. Tech actually took away my water balloon slingshot and won't give it back."

Water balloon slingshot? Oh god, maybe she is too crazy for me.

"I *threw it away* as soon as I left the hill!" Tech's voice crackled from the radio. "And my hand stank just from touching it! Your lab skills seriously suffer when you're hanging out with Be... I mean Weaslemaster."

"This I gotta hear," Jones said. "Your team's had to deal with you going bonkers too?"

"Oh... maybe a bit," she said, giving me a rueful look.

Well, maybe our crazies are compatible.

"So whenever Div 51's up by Duluth, they take turns sitting on me and keeping me from doing anything too dumb and impulsive. Except one time, the responsible team members had work or classes and that left, ahem, Weaslemaster. Yes, he was high when we picked our call signs. His strangeling power is talking to rodents, and he says he's our team healer, but really all he does is administer painkillers..."

"By which she means pot," Tech broke in, and Jones guffawed.

"Ah man, could have used some for Captain when he was frothing at the mouth..." he said. I rolled my eyes at him.

"So, you guys were up in Duluth looking for the East End Ripper, I think. Even though I had *already killed and buried it.*

Long story short, Weez tried to calm me down, but he partook of his own medicines while administering them. Five pot brownies later, we had stink bomb balloons and were setting up to bombard your camp from the cliffs above it. Which at the time I thought was a gentle way to say, 'Get off my lawn,' but Tech disagreed..."

"Oh my god, you guys were the totally high kids getting bitched out by their friend?" Birch said, choking on laughter. "Captain was sure someone was watching us and sent Roberts out to look. He came back saying some stoned idiots had been planning to bombard the camp with stink bombs, but some considerably more responsible friend showed up, yelled at them about hate crimes, broke the balloons with a stick, and dragged them away by their ears?"

"I've had finer moments," she said, smothering a grin. "Spent the rest of the night digging up the Ripper and left its head by the camp entrance around dawn. Gods Between, did we stink by morning."

This is what I'm into? I thought. My fae side nodded happily, laughing at me, and I sighed internally. *She saw me at my worst and didn't run. Apparently, I shouldn't expect any common sense whatsoever.*

A howler call echoed through the trees.

"That way," Darouk said, pointing. "There's an old driveway, but it's too overgrown for the cars."

Jones leaned around and looked at me.

"Think it's an ambush, Captain?"

Darouk snorted.

"The Matriarch would kill anyone who did that now," he said. "Probably with her own hands."

"What?" Birch said, startled. "Why? We've had one short negotiation."

Aisling shook her head, looking at him like we'd been totally suckered.

"You're about to find out why I wear a human glamour and don't let the tribes know who I am in daily life," she said dryly.

"Which is 'a gross-a abdication of responsibility'," Darouk said, imitating the Matriarch's voice.

"Whatevs," she said, waving a hand dismissively. "I'm still in school, with double the credit load anyone sane takes. I don't have time, bandwidth, or legal knowledge to adjudicate every inter-tribal tiff you guys can't sort out on your own."

"Uh, what?" I said, getting a glimpse of why the Matriarch had looked at me like she'd won our discussion of terms.

"An... effect, I guess, of sidhe being bound to the Tree that Grows Between Worlds is that we are bound also to its great... cause, I guess you could say: the diversification of thriving life throughout the worlds, in a very big picture sort of way," she said. "And we live a long time and supposedly some wisdom eventually comes along with that. The sidhe are widely viewed as an ethical neutral party, if utterly ruthless; make of that what you will. So you'd better either make it *very* clear that all you intend to do for the tribes is hunt monsters, or be prepared to arbitrate all their weirdest disputes."

"Like what?" Birch asked, curious, while I swore internally.

"For example, how to divvy up dumpster diving rights between owlies and sentient raccoons in a little town up North," she said. "With full gang warfare over it on the table, involving actual guns, poison blow darts, and garbage bins rigged with IEDs."

"You're serious," Jones said, trying to keep a straight face.

"Rax now get the town dump Tuesday through Saturday, and Monday morning dumpsters. Owlies get to scavenge the dump Mondays and have dumpster rights the rest of the week. Sunday they have a market and trade. Weaslemaster and Tech mostly worked out details while Siren kept everyone calm; I just broke up brawls. And I'm not allowed to buy moonshine from the Rax anymore, to prevent favoritism."

"Your town has moonshiner *raccoons?*" Jones asked, barely holding it together, and Aisling nodded, grinning.

"There *is* a general consensus that you could eventually make a great Raven if you ever got any training," Darouk said to her. She shuddered, but her shoulders slumped too.

"Raven?" I asked, that odd feeling of recognition hitting me again, and a strange yearning.

"Military elite," Darouk said as Jones parked the Jeep. "Maddoc's one, no one else on that boat was good enough."

"Yeah," Aisling said, her voice bleak, "You need someone to conquer a planet in like three days, they're the ones to go to."

"Wasn't three days!" Jones exclaimed. "People were fighting for over a year!"

"The Elsecomers took what they wanted in three days," Aisling said. "Humans argued about it for the following year, but Earth was lost in three days, and we here haven't gotten an inch of taken ground back."

It was true. We were barely holding the line against the redcaps and random monsters. To my knowledge, no one had tried taking on the Elsecomers again since that first year.

"What'd your mom say about the invasion?" I asked Aisling.

"That they only even let us argue because they didn't actually want to kill us all."

"Whoa," Jones said.

"Could always accept those truce terms," Darouk said, shrugging. "Given how sick of being stuck in cities everyone is, you've got some negotiating power now. Otherwise, the tribes in the buffer zone are already sending word to relatives in the city that we've got our own sidhe out here now, and it'll be safer to come out."

Wait, what?!

"Nah, don't freak out," Darouk said, seeing my expression. "Just means we can do this all civilized-like now. You can tell us what the deal is with the lunatic humans and what to avoid, and we can pull monsters coming after us into your ambushes, or guide you like we're doing now. Makes it better for everyone."

"Yeah, until our brass finds out we're making deals with Elsecomers and executes all of us," Jones said dryly.

"Just get to the buffer zone, and we'll guide you the rest of the way to Strangelingtown," he said, shrugging. "Too many kids alone there. They need adults and defenders. You don't have to keep living in a prison."

Jones looked way too tempted by that.

I felt way too tempted by that.

"Let's see how well the new food treatment stabilizes our more erratic people," I said. "And we've got a lot of territory under our protection, not just the Edgeland borders."

"Um, weird question," Tech said suddenly from the radio. "Can any of your guys read Russian?"

Aisling frowned.

"Something wrong?" she asked.

"Yeah. Just got back to my van, and the background on my screens has all been changed to a message in Cyrillic."

Shit. That didn't sound good.

"Didn't your soldier say he had a Ukrainian grandma?" Aisling said.

I waved at the other vehicles to pull over and called for him. "Sokolov?" I asked. "Any chance you read Russian?"

"I know the alphabet," he said. "My family got out just before the Russian invasion turned into the first redcap war. Only learned it so we could read old family documents."

"Do your best," I told him.

Aisling shook her hands, put them together, and then spread them apart, shaping a picture frame. Illusionary light glimmered, and a couple lines of foreign text.

"Um... I don't know most of this. But that word is 'wifi' and that one says 'noob'."

"Oh fuck," Tech said. "Some of my gear has wifi capabilities. It only works with magic though. That shouldn't be an issue."

"No," Aisling said. "It only works for *us* with magic. I'd assume the people jamming wireless signals can bypass the blocks."

"But why would *Elsecomers* leave a message in Russian?" Sokolov asked.

No one had an answer for that.

A Dohoulani howled out something urgent from one of the trees, and somehow I *knew* he was saying their monster was close. In the woods at two o'clock from us, a few hundred yards back, a tree crashed over.

"We need to set that aside for the moment," I said. "Think we've found our unicorn pig. Let's park a quarter mile up, where the cars can turn around if they need to and they're some distance from that thing."

"I'll, um, go run diagnostics," Tech said, and the radio went silent.

Well, whatever was going on with apparent Russian hackers, there wasn't a damn thing *I* could do about it. The vehicles chugged forward again.

49

To Hunt a Unicorn

AISLING

There was a sudden wisp of fog in front of the Jeep, and then we slammed into a hairy boulder. We'd been going about twelve miles-per-hour, so the impact wasn't terrible, but I smacked into the back of Birch's seat and he bounced off the dashboard.

What the fuck? I was still thinking when the boulder bellowed. I had a second to see four feet of arching horn before it caught the front of the Jeep. It heaved and flipped us sideways off the road. I grabbed Birch by the collar of his jacket and flashed into speed for a second, shaping a shield around us and hitting the ground rolling. Arthur and Jones leaped free of the car, and then the creature started just *going to town* on it. Two more impacts and it looked like a landslide had crushed it.

"Bad pig!" Darouk yelled, a bit late. "Bad pig!"

I don't think sci-fi duct tape is going to handle repairs now, I thought, as the shaggy beast slammed its horn *through* the engine and flung the Jeep onto its side. It teetered for a second and tipped over upside down.

The creature was shaped like a wild boar the size of a utility van, with a patterned gray and white hide. A horn like a rhino's jutted out the middle of its head. The thing was slab on top of slab of muscle, and its yarn-like hair hung in dreadlocks almost a foot long.

"We just fixed that car!" Birch whispered, outraged, going flat in the underbrush next to me. "It took all afternoon!"

Dohoulani voices whooped through the treetops at deafening volume. The monster bellowed in response and stomped the front of the Jeep like it was flattening a pop can. One of the tires burst under the pressure and the creature redoubled its attack at the sound, impaling a door on its horn a minute later, then sending it flying. It caught on a tree limb twenty feet up, barely missing Darouk. He screamed in panic and leaped away, and all his tribesmen started *howling*.

I gritted my teeth and willed proper armor on, with ear protection.

"Everybody out of the vehicles except drivers!" Arthur ordered into the back of the troop carrier, voice low but carrying. "Drivers, I want you to back away slowly. We'll try to keep the pig's attention."

"That thing ain't no pig," Jones said, belly crawling up next to Birch and I.

"It *is* kinda a unicorn, though," Birch whispered. "Medieval Europeans misunderstood traveler's accounts of Asian and African animals, and thus the unicorn myth was born. But I think this is a *woolly* rhinoceros, out of that Ice Age ghostland!"

"*Elasmotherium sibiricum*," I whispered back. "Related but bigger, went extinct earlier, and only had one horn."

Both men blinked at me.

"I did a prehistoric biology course," I said defensively. "And my family didn't have many kids' books, so my dad read to me about science. He liked books about the Ice Age. Shit, it's eyeing the troop carrier. I'm gonna go tank it."

"*Tank it?*" Birch asked. "Did you learn team tactics from *computer games?*"

"Yep!" I said, starting to pull myself upright while Jones just laughed under his breath.

"*Aisling!*" Arthur snapped at me, keeping his voice down. He pulled on leather gloves and took a sub-machine gun one of the human troopers handed him. "We have *guns!* Stay put so you don't catch crossfire!"

The rhino's head swung up directly at him.

"Ready weapons!" he called, looking it straight in the eye, and raised his own. "FIRE!"

Gunfire broke out all along the roadside where his soldiers had taken position. I grabbed my head in sudden agony and tripled the ear protection. A ricocheting bullet slammed into a tree next to me and I called a large shield with my bound weapons, forming it to cover Jones and Birch as well.

For a minute everything was just noise. We couldn't see anything behind the shield. When the gunfire finally sputtered off, we peeked over the edge of it.

"Fuckin' hell," Jones whispered. "Did that fucker take a single hit?"

There was a final sharp snap of gunfire. Light flared, a bullet smacked into something hard about a yard out from the cryptid, and then ricocheted into the gravel near its feet.

"It's shielding," Birch breathed. "Damn thing's a magical."

The damn thing snorted and pawed the ground, huffing aggressively at the troop carrier.

Gold dust rose from Arthur's antlers, and his eyes started glowing emerald green. He very deliberately switched on the safety of his firearm and handed it to the private next to him, then drew his belt knife and grinned like a hunting cat.

"God dammit," Jones groaned. "Twice in one *week?* I'm not *made* for this shit."

Are you, Aisling? my faery lover's voice asked, teasing.

You betcha, I answered, and felt the great cat spirit bonded to him purr against my mind. I laughed, feeling *wonderful* as the woods woke around me through his landbond, and rolled my shoulders. My shield disintegrated into dust and reformed as an eight foot boar spear in my hand.

I slipped into speed and dashed in, slashing at the rhino's hamstrings, but it bellowed and shielded. It stomped, and a blast wave rolled out horizontally from it. It sent me flying and knocked everyone flat on their backs, except Arthur who leaped straight up like a cat and avoided the wave. The troop carrier rocked sideways and almost tipped over. Seeing that movement, the rhino focused forward and charged.

Another burst of speed and I got the driver, halfway out the door already, out of the way and behind a group of his compatriots and Zahra. The big red giant grabbed the rhino by its horn and tried to throw it sideways. The driver of the second Jeep spun his car around and hit the gas.

Struggling against Bastion, the rhino's eye caught mine. Stars wheeled in them, and silver leaves shook in an otherworldly breeze.

"We can't kill it!" I yelled. "Arthur, it's Tree-bound, like us!"

He gave me a look of utter disbelief, like I'd just *deeply* offended his inner feline.

"Okay, what then?"

"Aren't unicorns traditionally tamed with a virgin?" Black called. "Birch!"

"I've been in the SCA for three years!" he yelled back. "Not applicable."

"Anyone?"

Shit, I really do not know what to do with a violent, nearsighted magical tank that I can't just kill...

"Sorry, Aisling," Arthur grinned. "But my troop's apparently half porn stars..."

Jones snickered, and the rhino redoubled its efforts.

Arthur's magic pulsed and suddenly two dozen minds lit up around me as he pulled everyone into a warband net, something my mother had mentioned once, like a bondnet but usually temporary.

All those minds and wants and needs and fears and *emotions* washed over me like flash flood. The entirely inadequate defenses I'd put up around my wounded empathy broke like a dam under the onslaught.

TERROR bloodlust connection resignation WONDER love amazement pride camaraderie despair eagerness fear discovery JOY fear dread exhilaration

Oh gods, it was too much.

This is magic, real magic, like I always dreamed, someone thought.

Goddamit I'm too old for this shit, someone else thought, reveling in it nonetheless.

Kill kill kill. Fucking hell I love these moments!

We're all doomed, everyone here is going to end up a strangeling.

This is amazing!

That thing's going to smash us all.

My pack, my people. We HUNT!

...I'm losing myself...

I'm already lost...

We're never coming back from this.

Too much *too much TOO MUCH.*

I yanked myself forcibly out of the warband net and rolled aside, trying to get into some cover while I pulled myself back together.

Zahra's hands grabbed my shoulders and pulled me behind a tree. She wasn't one of Arthur's people; he hadn't pulled her in.

"Dusty, what's happening?" she whispered.

Oh gods, my head hurts.

"He made a warband net," I answered, my words slurring. "Too... much... for me. I've got empath magic, but it's... broken."

She put her hand on my shoulder, and looked up at the fight. Arthur was on the rhino's shoulder and ineffectively trying to stab a knife through its extremely thick fur. Bastion had it by the horn and was trying to wrestle it down. The rest of the troop had knives or some spears they'd pulled out of the troop carrier and were darting in and back like a hunting pack. The rhino's shields didn't seem to do so well against attacks from so many directions.

Some booming sound came from the rhino and a dome of light flared out from it, burning Bastion's hands and blowing all the attacking troops away from it. Arthur did another impossible flip up into the air and came down like a cat pouncing, but just before he landed, the rhino smacked its head sideways and sent him flying into a late-lingering bank of snow in the road's old ditch.

The rhino bellowed, about to charge the troop carrier again... and trample a half dozen people sprawling in its way. Zahra leaped to her feet and ran for it.

"Stop!" she cried to it, putting herself in front of it, hands up and gentling. "Stop! We aren't enemies. Stop attacking random things. We'll stop attacking you."

I saw Arthur blink like he'd been stunned, but he didn't look like he was in too much pain. He started pulling himself up on his elbows.

The rhino snorted and shook itself, leaning in to charge again. Zahra closed her eyes, steadying herself.

"Grab your moment," she whispered. "Don't hold back."

The rhino dug its toes into the gravel road, and lurched forward. Zahra dug her feet into the ground and set her shoulders. Her hands grabbed its horn and muscles rippled in her arms.

The rhino strained against her, shaking, and light flared as it tried something magical again. Zahra didn't fight it, but let its magic somehow flow into her.

"You're not the white unicorn I dreamed of," she growled, wrestling it downwards. Her feet dug furrows into the road as it pushed her back. "And I'm not some delicate princess to lure you into my lap."

It shook its head violently, and she barely managed to keep her grip. Her arms trembled with the effort of holding on.

"But, you'll do for me, if I'll do for you."

It thundered at her, digging hooved toes into the grave, trying to swing its head sideways.

"You need better eyes and someone to help you in this world, and I need a *friend*."

Every muscle in her new body strained. The troop carrier was only two yards behind her.

"I'll take care of you. You're magic and I am too. Come on, Uni-Tanky, give me an inch. We can *do* this."

Her feet were pushing against the carrier. If she kept holding, it'd push her under the truck and then knock it over on top of her.

The same light that'd washed over Zahra when we were reshaping her Cascade glittered again, in her eyes and at her fingers. The rhino huffed in surprise and eased back. It shook its head and its ears went back, then forwards again, as if it were listening to her speak.

She just bonded with it, I thought, pushing myself upright. *She did it. The maiden tamed her unicorn.*

Zahra dropped to her knees in front of it and started sobbing with joy. It pushed its head against her lap like a pet begging for scratches.

Then it kind of shuffled its back legs sideways, rotating around Zahra in an arc until its rump brushed the troop carrier. It sort of shrugged... and hip-checked the troop carrier, *hard.* The vehicle groaned and lifted off the ground until only the passenger side tires were still touching dirt.

Uni-Tanky gave a shake like a horse scattering flies, and the truck tipped over and slid sideways into the ditch.

Birch started swearing, cursing the creature's ancestors all the way back to our Ice Age.

The rhino gave a contented sigh and flipped its tail happily.

Over in the opposite ditch, Arthur dropped back into snow and started laughing his ass off.

50

AGGRAVATING

ARTHUR

I just laid in damp snow laughing, absolutely *flying* on how exhilarating it had been to fight with all three sides of me working in unison. The rhino was off being comforted - and kept away from all people and vehicles - while the giant girl fed it fresh greens. The warband net had sort of evaporated with the rhino's shock wave, and we were all purely individuals in our own heads again. Aisling limped over, put her hands on her hips, and looked down at me like I was a flaming idiot.

I hadn't had a woman give me that look since I was engaged. It was a helluva turn-on.

"Get down here," I said, and my hand snaked out and grabbed her ankle and pulled it out from under her. She made a funny squeaky noise and fell on her butt in the snow next to me.

"Arthur!" she said, as I rolled over and pinned her, then pulled her into a kiss. "Are you drunk on magic?"

"So what if I am?" I asked, flying still. "That was *incredible.*"

"Yup, the captain's totally lost it today," Jones said, some distance away.

Arg. Dammit. We need privacy for everything I want to do with her. Have to get her out of here.

"You should run from me," I told Aisling, grinning down at her. "You can have one last chance to escape. Then you're mine."

"Yours?" she asked, her eyes going wide.

"*Mine,*" I answered, grinning and kissing her again. Oh god, I wanted to spend my life aggravating this woman. Her eyes sparked at me, and she did something with her hips and threw me off her.

Yes. Good. She'll run, we'll have sex in the woods, and then she'll head home and we'll do this again on her next long weekend.

She did a twist and flip and was on her feet, and I rolled to mine, eager to go.

"You think you can just say I'm yours and make it so?" she said, temper in her voice, and something shaky I didn't expect.

Everyone was watching us. She *must* realize I needed a bit of an excuse to escape my troops.

"Last chance," I said, grinning wider. "Run now, or I'll have to take you back to the Box, tie you to my bed, and keep you there until I've tamed you."

Her chin jutted forward like she was grinding her teeth. Wait, she couldn't possibly think I was *serious?* "Tame" is the last thing I wanted her to be. She stepped closer to me, and I grinned and wiggled my eyebrows at her.

"And what about Zahra?" she asked, glancing at the giant girl.

"What about her?" I asked, not thinking about my answer. "We'll take care of her. She'll be great with Strangeling Brigade."

Run from me, I told her, feeling magic gathering through the spring-kissed land, snapping in the air between us.

But she pulled back. She clenched her jaw and both sadness and temper flickered through her eyes before giving way to resolve.

Wait, what? What'd I say?

"Nope," she said, "I get my Runners *through.*"

Her hand kind of flickered. I barely felt the impact on the side of my neck.

No, dammit, flashed through my mind, and then the lights went out.

The blood came back to my brain about a minute later, and I woke up to the sound of Jones laughing his ass off, and most of the troop along with him.

"Can I join the bet?" Black was asking Birch. "I want to put money down on Captain choking to death on his own boot."

"What... what happened?" I managed to get out. My legs weren't quite connecting yet.

"The pointy-eared alien chick got you with a Vulcan neck pinch," Birch chortled. "Which you totally *deserved*. Magic-drunk, beyond any doubt!"

"She hit you with a brachial stun straight out of a SHARPS course," Black said, trying and failing to keep a straight face. "That's 'Sexual Health and Rape Prevention Strategies' by the way, a self-defense class for girls dealing with jerk men who don't respect their boundaries. Then she yelled, 'No, I will *not* join your pod of deviants!', and asked Zahra if she still wanted to go to Strangelingtown. The girl nodded, and they jumped up on the back of that rhino. A sudden patch of mist opened and they disappeared into it. How are you feeling?"

Like a fucking idiot. Like I just screwed up the first good thing to happen since I Changed, I thought, trying to sit up. Ow. I rubbed my neck.

"That is... a *way*... with women you have," Jones said, trying not to laugh directly at my face. He offered me a hand up. I sighed and took it.

"I just... I just wanted her to run back into the woods with me," I said, my words slurring a bit.

"Well, your years without even flirting are *showing*, m'dude."

I managed to get back to my feet with his help. She was gone, not in my patrol lands anymore. I didn't anticipate how hard the feeling of loss would hit me.

"Let's go home," I said, my shoulders slumping, and turned and started walking back to the trucks. Jones clapped me on the shoulder.

"She'll be back, Captain," he said. "And I think as long as you don't jail her people, she'll give you another chance."

"Why?" I asked bitterly. "What could I actually offer a woman? I'm a monster serving a life sentence in a prison labor unit."

"She ran for the kid's sake," he said. "If it was just her, you'd probably be eating your teeth and begging forgiveness right now. She'll be back. Women with tempers like that don't just fade out and disappear, they hunt you down and make you apologize for everything you've ever done wrong, point by point by point."

"That experience talking?"

"*Oh* yeah."

I sighed. Jones was probably right, and at least now I knew she wasn't an enemy. Even if she blocked me mentally, one way or another, I could probably reach her. Eventually.

It might be better to let that temper cool a bit first, though.

My troops picked themselves up and we trudged over to the troop carrier to see how much damage it had taken.

51

OUTLANDS

CONNOR

The exfiltration bike needed a thorough check before I took it out, having sat in storage for over a year. I really didn't want my gear breaking down in case I had to run from... oh, who *knows*. Out in the human world, the possibilities ranged from the local army to random monsters to mobs of angry exes convinced I'd turned their boyfriends gay.

I checked my human clothes and kit, and reviewed my ID data. I'd glamour up and change at a hidden station near the edge of the security zone, once I was past all the refugee aliens in the Edgelands. Finally, I checked in with my short punk support team.

Ready to go, Sveta, I sent. *Got coordinates and info ready?*

Five minutes, she sent back, her mind completely focused on something else. *Stay put.*

I sighed, set my bike to standby, and sat down against a tree. The sky was cloudless and rosy with the setting sun's light. A ship had just left the starport, and a golden trail of condensing vapor marked its path up to Beyond.

They were welcome to it. I had fresh air on my face and birds singing their souls into the twilight. On Briargard, I'd have felt the flows of all the life around me, been able to slip into an awareness completely in tune with my world, feel when things were wrong and when everything sang in harmony, wind and trees and waters all together. Here... I knew the music played, but my ears could catch only faint hints of it.

Even those faint strains were exquisite, if still alien to me. They were clearer than last time I'd been out, though, so that was... something.

Mount up and be ready to accelerate fast, Sveta said. *My cloaking field is only four meters wide.*

What?! I sent back, throwing myself up onto the bike.

A barely audible scream of displaced air was approaching at speed from above me. Oh gods. She must have shot herself vertically over the main city shields, following that spaceship out, and was now coming in imitating debris falling from it. I slammed the accelerator and angled to intercept.

Ahead of me on the river, water suddenly displaced into a deep dome around something invisible. Sveta must have braked with her stabilizing shields. Dear gods, that was *insanely* dangerous. Where had she learned to fly like that? She accelerated directly out and away upriver, leaving only a tiny wake in the water for me to track her progress.

"*Sveta, what in the bleeding hells are you doing out here?*" I yelled as I slipped into her cloaking field.

She was wearing goggles styled like human antiques but for the glow of a heads-up-display and what looked like a bomber jacket in the same style. The little lunatic didn't answer, just threw me a thumbs up. She grinned more happily than I'd ever seen her and gunned her bike to twice the speed anyone sane would fly.

I gritted my teeth and clung to her tail. It wasn't easy, and I'd had high-speed chase training and aerial experience from before my magic broke. If I'd only had the pursuit skills I'd gotten as a city guard, I don't think I could have kept up with her.

Which is probably the point, the little bandit.

Finally she slowed and pulled her bike up under the ruins of an old bridge. I slid in after her.

"What the hell are you doing?" I shouted as soon as we could hear each other. "You're supposed to be on support for me! At *home*, where it's safe!"

"There are others like me out here," she said. "I'm not letting the village idiot make first contact."

"*Sveta!*"

"Keep your voice down, we're right around the bend from the strangeling settlement. They're still fishing. Aisling should arrive shortly, if she hasn't gotten herself lost in the mist."

"What?!"

"I left some things out of my report to the elders," she said, shrugging like that was nothing new. "Maddoc's granddaughter is probably a Navigator, doing things like an old-times beginner. I need a Navigator. And I need you to look ahead into possible futures right now, and tell me if I'm on the track that takes down our infiltrators."

"You can't be out here, you're a... a... filmmaker! You're a behind-the-desk person!"

"I'm the Red Raven's ward," she said, perfectly calm. "You think Morganna would raise someone helpless?"

Oh fuck. Oh bloody fuck. Why did I never see that?

"Are you Intelligence already?" I asked, horrified. Sveta was *way* too young for that.

"Well, I'm smarter than *you*," she answered smugly. "Confirm, or don't, what I feel in the branching futures."

I closed my eyes and felt through the Tree for possible futures. And she was right. Straight as an arrow, the Tree showed the way that led to survival.

Inconveniently, it *also* showed I should let her lead on this.

"Fuck! Fuckity fuck fuck!" I said. "I see it. About the possible future, not being smarter than me."

"That's because you're a walking Dunning-Kruger Effect," she said. "Look it up. So, go in open or stealthy? I say openly. There are a dozen Dohoulani Sunscatchers there already, and that tribe credits its survival to you holding Briargard's last Gate. I suggest you spend some hero credit and let them introduce you to Strangelingtown as such."

I stared at her.

I *loathed* being introduced as a hero.

It was not, however, that bad a plan.

"Bloody hell. Outlands runs are supposed to be *quiet,*" I finally said. "Is Hart about to show up too, or just Aisling?"

"This is the Edgelands, not the Outlands. It's just Aisling coming, so you don't have to worry about local military yet. She and Hart are already on the way to the perfect young sidhe relationship: they've fallen madly in love and broken up violently in less than a day! She'll likely arrive in a terrible mood."

Fan-fucking-*tastic.*

"Where is she now?"

"I didn't have an Eye capable of following where she went," she said. "Don't worry, I've got a special one that can track Navigators with me now. She's already gone in and out of a fold in reality and timed it well enough that days inside passed, and only about a minute out here, so I assume she's okay."

That isn't a MINOR navigator talent.

Maddoc is going to kill us both.

"Sveta! I can't hide that from her own grandfather!"

"I refer you again to the branching probabilities," she said coolly.

The ones that say let her lead on this.

I'm a dead man walking.

I closed my eyes and swore.

"So, I'm going to introduce myself as a bit of a free agent," she said cheerfully, knowing she'd won this round. "And you're going to be out here because you owe me a favor."

"I don't owe you!"

"How much time of mine have we wasted while you try being the big brother I don't want or need? You *do* owe me."

Why would she resent that I tried to make her feel welcome? I wondered, flabbergasted.

"I'm not going to argue about something this pointless! But this is blackmail."

She gave me another wide grin.

"No, I'm not wasting the *actual* blackmail material I've got on you. Yet. But I might suggest that I'm doing so. Play along if I do. Let's go."

Wait, what? I thought, staring at her. *She might not think of me as her big brother, but I sure feel like I've got a kid sister.*

She gunned her bike again, and I followed.

52

RIDE TO THE RESCUE

AISLING

M ist or no, I could hardly see I was crying so hard.

Why do men have to be so stupid? *Why would he think Zahra should go to prison?*

And I have just horribly over-reacted to something I'm not completely certain Arthur was serious about?

"Dusty, are we lost?" Zahra whispered to me.

Fog swirled all around us, tasting again of distant glaciers. The huge rhino we were riding snorted.

"No," I said, seeking Coral down the bonds between us. Dimensions rippled, and I felt bloodlust and panic and do-or-die determination from her.

"That way," I said, pointing, though external direction didn't truly matter, just movement. "Go! Fast!"

Zahra squeezed her legs and made a little clucking sound, and the rhino ambled forwards, building speed. Inside me, I saw the Tree the elvensteeds had traveled, and the roots around its hollow twisted and uncurled through me, weaving into a road in front of us.

Mist shredded into daylight, and we saw Coral standing alone, facing down a monstrous man-fish half again the size of the rhino. The two figures mirrored each other's every movement. Darkness flared around the creature, and something like light through deep water around her. She looked minuscule before it. Behind her, three kids and a Dohoulani spearman were trying to pull a screaming boy with a shredded leg away from the shore. Another half dozen fish-men were trying to trap them in a pincer formation before they escaped, while villagers further back threw stones and shot ineffective arrows at the monsters.

"*Come home, lostling,*" the huge fish-man crooned to Coral. "*Join us and feast. Masters will welcome a lost daughter.*"

Coral snarled, and her hands tightened on her knives.

Zahra gulped, steadying herself. I felt the fear run through her like it was my own.

"You ate my father," Coral said, an odd light rippling over her. "I'd rather die."

A gurgling hiss rose from the catfish-men.

"*Then I will devour your magic and make it my own.*"

Coral was going into the peaceful place, I saw, readying herself to fight with everything she had.

No one had seen us.

Zahra's knuckles went white with terror as she clenched her fists into the rhino's hair, and her eyes clenched closed as she nerved herself up. She let go of the rhino's fur and crossed her wrists across her chest, like one of the warrior-women from her favorite movie. Her breath shuddered as she drew it in.

"... *forever,*" Zahra whispered to herself.

She leaned forward and squeezed her legs against Uni-Tanky's sides.

We lurched towards the shore. A battle scream erupted from her throat, and the rhino lowered its head and charged. Its horn started to glow, some white-hot magic shimmering through it. We slammed through the pincer line and into the big one before it could reorient. I cartwheeled off and sliced the tentacle arms off the smaller one next to it before it could react, and spun into speed against the next one and the one beyond it.

The big catfish-man was impaled on the rhino's horn and shrieking. The rhino bellowed, and the fish burned from within. Blazing light spilled through its horn and into the monster, incinerating it. I sliced through the neck of the next fish and kicked its head into the face of the one trying to spear me. Coral flung herself into the other side of the pincer, putting herself between the fish-men and the kids.

I whirled sideways, shaping my blades into a longer spear. But before I could even stab forward, a beam like a red laser took it through the back of the head. Each half fell sideways as it sliced in two lengthwise. The beam moved smoothly sideways and straight down the line of other fish-men, and they fell into twitching pieces.

"Looked like you could use a hand," the Elsecomer elf who'd just shot them said casually. He was sitting on something like a floating speeder bike, twenty feet away over the water. His silvery white uniform and curly blond hair shone in the golden sunlight, and his eyes glinted like aquamarines. His hand on his weapon was dead steady, and the faintest aura of sidhe light shone around him.

"Damn, is it ever satisfying to just shoot these bloody things," he said, grinning widely. My heart just about stopped, then started thumping wildly. My brain completely froze.

Arthur had been deadly handsome. This guy was *beautiful,* like some god-touched Renaissance artist had painted him out of purest light, like some fairy-tale prince from an old ballad.

His smaller partner took out the fish-men in the other half of the pincer with the same kind of laser. She looked more like a cyberpunk pixie, one who held grudges.

"Connor!" howled the closest Dohoulani tribesman, and launched itself from the bank into six-limbed monkey hug around him. He laughed, embraced the alien back, and said something in its language. It made a hooting chuckle and howled something deafening up to the trees, then yelled in Tradish at the shore, "The Hero of Briargard has come to our rescue!"

The sidhe found me, was all I could think. *They found me. I'm fucked.*

It's a damn good thing no further fish-men attacked, because I couldn't even make myself move to close my mouth.

53

LANDBOUND

CONNOR

We heard the screams before we saw the villagers, and blasted around the bend in the river just in time to see a huge furry rhinoceros, of all things, slam horn-first into the largest fish-man. Aisling vaulted off its back and a smaller monster catfish's head was falling before her feet even touched the ground. Light flared around her, blazing, reaching out and grabbing Sveta and me. My gun was in my hand and a beam from it was slicing fish-men in half before I even stopped to consider if I should... or the lectures I'd gotten from Diplo earlier that afternoon.

Oh well. My bad.

I couldn't have pulled my finger off the trigger even if I'd wanted to.

Landbound. She's a land binder, and I just got pulled into her magic, I thought distractedly, holding my laser steady as it bit through the last fish-man on my side of the big one. Around me, all that music I could barely sense before suddenly sang out, and I *knew* with deep fatalism that whoever and whatever she might be didn't matter. At least a part of me would be *hers* for the rest of my life.

So that's *what it feels like.*

In the back of my mind, I felt the lights of the other Shields of Briargard snuff out again, one after another, *holding*, loyal to their last breaths as they followed me into the sky one last time. The fight was hopeless, and it hadn't mattered at all. While their landbound leader held, they would too.

So it is, to be sidhe, my father had said, trying to explain to me in my grief.

I finally understood.

Sveta, who shouldn't have even *owned* a blaster, was cutting down the other side of the fish-men's pincer formation, looking even more maniacally happy. I couldn't even tell if she'd gotten bound up too or was just enjoying the chaos.

Probably both.

I looked at Aisling.

Her eyes met mine.

The world stopped.

I fell into the wild blue of Northern lakes and drowned there.

Oh, I thought, sudden senseless happiness bubbling through me. *There you are.*

"Looked like you could use a hand," I said to her, trying to keep my voice smooth and not go straight to my knees and pledge fealty or undying love or anything else equally ridiculous.

She stared back at me, eyes filling with unabashed horror. Her jaw dropped open and gaped. Terror froze her completely stiff.

Oh.

Dear.

That is not the response I was hoping for.

Sveta glanced over at us and cracked up laughing.

"Finally!" she called to me. *"Finally,* someone reacts to you the way I should have!"

"Connor!" Jainek of the Sunscratcher tribe howled, and made one of those great Dohoulani leaps out to my bike and embraced me. I hugged him back. He'd been little when Briargard fell, and his tribe was one of the last through the Gate I shielded.

Well, Sveta's plot to use my "hero credit" was on track.

"Slayer, close your mouth. We're both fucked," the redhead told her friend. "But right now we have wounded."

Aisling shook herself, snapped her mouth shut, and glanced with still horrified eyes from me to the kid screaming on the shore. I could see exposed bone, and black streaks were visibly climbing up his leg from the wounds.

"We have a mutual enemy," Sveta said to the girls, kicking her bike in closer, "And I'm blackmailing the blond twit, he will not expose you. We can help each other, *da?*"

"Wounded first, then we'll talk," Aisling said, looking at her and seeing more than her physical appearance. "You're a technomancer? Are you the Russian who hacked Rigs?"

"*Da.* Sveta Ivanova, from Moscow. I do security audits for the Freeport, saw footage from this morning, listened in on your radios. I will *end* the ones who take strangeling kids."

"Personal?" Siren asked.

"*Moy brat.* Older brother. He... slowed them down."

What? She never said a thing...

"And him?" Aisling asked, looking at me.

"Connor will be in the embarrassment of this half of the galaxy if I release my footage," Sveta said, grinning. "And I think he's used up his quota for screwing off this month. He's the Freeport Guard's department fuckup, but I needed a bodyguard and no one will miss him."

Well, thanks a lot, Sveta.

I played along, though, giving a little shrug.

The girls on the shore glanced at each other. Siren shrugged, and Aisling turned for the injured kid. Sveta and I swung our bikes inland and parked them above the waterline, then followed them over to him.

One look at his leg and my gorge rose. Pulsing black lines snaked up from the bite, and I could see exposed femur. The boy whimpered with every breath, trying to keep from screaming. A girl with copper curls and inhumanly large eyes was applying pressure, and faint healing magic glowed around her hands.

"Do you have a medic?" I asked the group. The strangelings stared at me, wide-eyed.

"Their Healer got bit herself when the fish-men attacked last night," Jainek answered. "She's poisoned bad. Real bad. You all can trust Connor. He saved the whole Sunscratcher tribe. One of the best of them."

I tried to wave that aside. Our world had still died. Nothing else really mattered.

"I've got a basic med kit, but nothing that can handle this," I said. "But... my partner in the guard is on a date with a doctor right now. I could call, ask for advice at least."

Aisling looked at the boy and back at me, hesitated, then nodded sharply.

"Do it, Elsecomer."

"Not on your duty vambrace," Sveta said, tossing me a modified comm unit. "Use this."

I shrugged and stepped away, setting it to voice only. Rellen picked up a second later.

"No, Connor, I am not delivering booze to you," he answered, and I saw a smile flit across Aisling's face. Guess she did know a bit of our language. "We all heard you were so hungover on duty that the old man pulled you off the street and left you cat sitting. Suck it up and suffer."

"Um... That isn't exactly what happened. Any chance you're with the pediatrician? I need a medic."

"Connor, Horrid's just a house cat. He can't do *that* much damage," Rellen said, sighing loudly. "Disinfect the scratches and put spray bandages on your 'wounds'. You'll be fine."

"A *cat* injured Connor?" I heard the pediatrician ask. Oh good, Sulima was with him. I snapped a couple pictures of the wounded kid. "This is *not* his week."

"Connor's on punishment detail again and wants me to bring him hangover cures," Rellen answered her. "Cat scratches are just an excuse."

"Ask Sulima if these look like some dumb spray would treat them!" I snapped, and sent the pictures.

I heard her gasp.

"Rellen, get me to that child *now*," she said.

"The black stuff is fish-man poison," I said. "A settlement in the Edgelands got hit after we drove those bastards out of the city. It's almost all kids here and their Healer is poisoned too."

"Connor, what the fuck are you doing out in the Edgelands?" Rellen said, his voice low.

"Running errands," I said. "Horrid doesn't need my company nearly as often as the old man says he does."

There was silence from the other end of the comm unit.

"Well?" I asked.

"Well, what the fuck do you want me to do?" he demanded.

"Grab Sulima's medical gear and teleport her out here," I said. "Then keep your mouth shut about who I'm with."

"Teleport?" he hissed.

"Rellen, I know perfectly well my father would have stuck a babysitter for me in the city guard," I said back, snapping back in High Kzephian for the sake of privacy. "And you got to the fish that swallowed me *well* ahead of everyone else. You train alone with Maddoc multiple times a week. Even the department fuckup can put those things together. So yes, teleport your ass over here!"

Rellen swore. The connection went dead. I tossed the comm back to Sveta. A minute later, Rellen and Sulima appeared on the beach next to me. Rellen saw Aisling and went completely still.

"I'm a doctor. What's going on?" Sulima demanded, then saw the wounded boy and practically threw herself at him. Her eyes widened in horror at the pulsing black veins.

"We've got blood loss, Squid ink, and the wound itself," Siren said, dropping to her knees next to the pediatrician. "I'm Coral. Bonnie's staunching the blood loss. I can take the ink, the tainted magic, but it'll mess me up. Mel! You go get the Healer and bring her down here. I'll take Alina's poison after I've got Jeffy's. Can you deal with the wound itself?"

"Yes. You can take the poison?" Sulima asked, confused. "What are you?"

"Right now? A sin eater," Coral said. "Slayer, I'm gonna need whatever you're sparkly with to pull me back after this. Ready, Bonnie?"

The copper-haired teenage girl started humming, and light flickered around her hands. Siren started quietly singing along with her, her voice soft but hinting at operatic power, and the black streaks climbing up the wounded leg seemed to... pause. Sulima looked down, and when she looked back up, fire flickered in her eyes. Aisling touched her hand to Coral's shoulder, and sidhe light started slipping out of her again.

Sveta, you're recording? I asked her.

In the mind link, she nodded grimly.

Rellen's breath caught as Aisling's land-bound power reached out to everyone around her, gathering strength. He knew exactly what he was seeing. He drew back and saw clearly how I didn't. I was already caught.

Connor, you are a fucking imbecile, he said into my mind.

I spread my hands out and shrugged. I was perfectly fine with this, and also couldn't *exactly* disagree.

A pair of hefty villagers carrying a wounded woman on a stretcher came down and laid her on the ground near the boy. Fever sweat drenched her, and her arm and lips had turned black. The rest of her skin was whiter than a corpse's, with dark veins running through it. Every gasping breath she took whistled.

Aisling's hand went to her mouth, and Coral looked up for a second and crossed herself.

"Pull me back, Slayer," Coral said, determination in her eyes. Her hands shook. "Or kill me if you can't. But I'm taking the ink. All of it. Dad did this, and I'm fixing what he broke."

Aisling nodded, and her fingers tightened on her friend's shoulder. Something shifted in the singer's energy, something old and dangerous and unpredictable waking up. My hand went to my weapon before I could stop it, but I kept myself from drawing.

Coral put her mouth to the wound and started sucking. The snaking black poison seemed to pause, writhing, and then turned and flowed obediently into her.

"She said they *ate* her father," Sveta whispered to Aisling.

"The bastard's body is probably what mutated them," Aisling answered, her voice low. "We dumped it in the river after I smashed his head in. Catfish scavenge corpses."

I heard Rellen's indrawn breath.

"What the fuck?" Sveta asked for all of us.

"He shot her mom and drowned her sisters. He was holding Coral underwater while she begged for mercy and grew gills. I heard her mindvoice screaming and killed him before she fully Changed. She pulled his body into the deep water and pinned it with rocks, then I shaped her Cascade to keep her human looking. We made her a new I.D. and life to keep her out of the Squids' clutches, because we suspect her dad was one of them."

"Why?" Sveta asked. "Why do they want her?"

"Monsters don't like it when children flee their nests."

Her eyes darted to Rellen and me, and her jaw tightened.

Rellen grabbed my arm and pulled me down to the waterline. Some of the fish bits were still twitching. He took out his blaster and fried them till that stopped, smiling with grim satisfaction. Then he turned to me and spoke in Kzephian again.

"Connor, *who* is that sidhe girl and what the hell is going on?"

"The big dead snake had holes from one of our weapons in it," I said. "As well as bullets and a small human rocket from the strangeling Edgeland patrol. I called Maddoc because that seemed like it might indicate a security breach. He brought in Sveta because when the border got crossed this morning, there was another kid with tech magic there. She tracked him, and found evidence Derdriu had a daughter in the outlands. The old man sent me to look for her. As you can see, that didn't take very long. Sveta wants to connect with the technomancer, and here we are."

He blinked at me.

"The old man sends you on outland missions. And tells everyone you're cat sitting for him."

"Now and then. Six times out of ten, it's a real punishment."

"How *the hell* am I supposed to guard you if you're traipsing all over the outlands?!"

"You're *not*. I'm the department fuckup, not anybody important, *remember?*"

"I remember your father is going to flay me alive if anything happens to you!"

"Well, fuck that, and that's a *gross* exaggeration anyway, he would never. And I abdicated, not that it matters since we don't have our own world anymore and my magic is broken! None of that bullshit from back then matters now! What sort of idiot would want me for a leader, anyway? Forgive me for trying to find something I *can* still do."

"You're Manannan's only surviving blood heir, Connor," Rellen growled, "Whether or not you want to be. And *I* followed you into battle two nights ago, and would again. *'That bullshit back then'* measured the depth of our honor. Maybe we failed to save Briargard, but *our honor* was to save every life we could before the world's destruction! In that, at least, the sidhe were not found lacking. Nor were *you!*"

I gritted my teeth and tried to keep from shaking.

"So? My dad wants a fever dream! There's nothing to be heir *to* anymore. And even if there was, look at me! I'm entirely unsuitable, in virtually every damned way possible! I signed abdication papers as soon as I could after waking from the coma. It's done! What you see is what you get: Guardsman McMann, Freeport pole dancing champion and Queen of Pride, useless, hard-drinking *fuckup*."

Rellen stared at me. His jaw muscles worked like he was barely keeping from screaming at me.

"You are not *just* that."

I made myself take a deep breath.

"Whatever. Look, Sveta's sworn me to secrecy already, she's got her own thing going, but can you keep the old man updated for me? He and Daire know about Aisling, no one else, and Maddoc would like to keep it that way. Tell him his granddaughter's going to need training as soon as possible. Maybe feed Horrid once or twice too. He gets out and hunts pigeons and draclets, and there's an automated feeding system, but he likes to have someone stop by so he can oppress them."

Rellen closed his eyes and took a couple deep breaths himself.

"What kind of training?"

"From what I've seen in the last few minutes, everything you'd expect Maddoc's granddaughter to need," I said. "Because she's a chip off his block, with more than a bit of the White Raven in there as well."

"*Lady Macha?*"

"You know Maddoc was her Briargard port-of-call. She left Derdriu with him when it became obvious their daughter had nothing in common with her and would follow a Black Raven path. The same cannot be said of her granddaughter."

Rellen nodded unhappily, looking back at Aisling. She glanced away from her friend and glared at us, looking both determined and afraid.

"She's landbound. And pulling you in."

"The redhead was fighting the fish-men practically alone when we arrived. Aisling got here seconds before we did, flaring bright, and pulled Sveta and I in before we had any idea what was happening. Gods, Rellen, I can *hear* the land again, feel the magic out here. I don't *care* if that compromises me."

He frowned, then tilted his head and seemed to consider that. Some of the tension eased from his shoulders.

"What?" I demanded.

"Maybe the old man's right, and this *is* what you need."

I blinked at him.

Coral suddenly reared up from the wounded boy, throwing herself away from him. The sultry redhead was gone. Her eyes had gone flat black, like some sort of deep sea monster, and her fingers clawlike. She lurched away, hunched over oddly, and then threw her head back and screamed in agony. Glassy deepwater fangs filled up her mouth as we watched, protruding out beyond her lips. Hands went to the ears of every person on the beach, trying to keep that tortuous *sound* out.

"You've got this, Coral," Aisling said to her now-monstrous friend, her armor shaping ear protection as she put her hand back on Coral's shoulder. "Hold on to yourself. Keep your center. I'm here with you."

Coral grabbed her own arms, hugging herself, and her screams died to whimpers. For a moment, she just stood there sobbing. Her skin had gone grayish-blue and almost scaly, her hair the blackish twisting green of kelp strands. Her shoulders shook. Then she straightened up and nodded. She didn't look human at all now, but she went over to the Healer and dropped to her knees next to the arm that had been bitten. It was blackened almost to the shoulder. Behind her, Sulima was working steadily, cleaning out the boy's wound and fixing what damage she could manually. Sparks rose from her, djinn magic manifesting, and determination and fear mixed in her body language. Rellen looked unhappily from me to her, then went up and put himself between Coral and his date. I followed him and stopped next to Aisling.

Coral picked up the Healer's blackened arm and drove those deepwater teeth into the bite mark. The woman thrashed and the villagers who'd carried her over pinned her down. Aisling put her free hand on the wounded woman, and sidhe light flared through her and into both Coral and the Healer. The inky poison retreated before the light, and Coral choked and gasped as she slurped it into her mouth, looking more like a deep sea terror with every swallow.

But it was working. The Healer's breath evened out first, and then that frightening pallor and odd wet texture retreated down the poisoned arm. Coral was looking... worse. When she drew back again, she looked like an oddly elegant Creature from the Black Lagoon. Her eyes were double the size they had been. Her hair writhed in the air around her head like tentacles.

The Healer drew in a breath, and it was clean. Light played over her as Sulima's magic started working to save her.

"*More,*" Coral hissed through a forest of jagged teeth at Aisling.

"The fish-men on the beach," Aisling said. "Take it from them."

The monstrous woman rose, no longer lurching but sliding with mercurial grace. Her eyes had gone pitch black. She glanced at Rellen and me, and an atavistic shiver ran through me. To such as she was, sidhe were *prey.*

But something in me knows *this magic,* I thought, old terror welling through me. Rellen had his gun in his hand, but not pointed at her. Yet. His fingers twitched with the effort of keeping the weapon down. *I have known this magic since I was a child. It has shaped me all my life...*

I put that thought away, not knowing where it came from.

"*He has it,*" Coral whispered, looking right at me. "*Purified. Not like my family.*"

And abruptly, I knew *exactly* what she was.

No. No. Oh no.

This will destroy our elders.

They thought their war was won.

Rellen's hand flickered, and his weapon pointed directly at her head.

"You can't have him," he said.

Coral hissed, and Aisling's eyes went wide and dismayed.

"That is my *blood sister,*" she said to him haltingly in our language, as if she hadn't spoken sidhe words in years. "Please don't hurt her."

Horror filled Rellen's eyes. He stepped back, closer to Sulima, and lowered the blaster slightly.

"What do you need?" I asked Coral, speaking softly, like you do with injured animals.

"*Show me. One drop only.*"

I nodded, and carefully held out my hand. Aisling glanced from Coral, swaying like kelp in the deep sea, to me. She took my hand, her fingers gentle on mine, and the touch felt like coming *home.*

The armor on her hand shifted into a catlike claw, and she pierced my little finger as if with a medical lancet. A single red drop welled out.

Coral's tongue flickered out, tasting its scent like reptiles do. She licked the air and smiled. Her tongue darted out again and left my finger clean. Then she threw back her head, as if in ecstasy, and sudden song poured out from her lips. There were no words, yet it was hurricanes and whitewater and whirlpools, water in all its ecstasy and deadliness, and oh gods of my ancestors, but part of me *recognized* it. Her magic billowed out, and it was everything I feel on stage and so much *more*.

Siren magic, I thought, stunned. *I have that too. I didn't even realize.*

Her arms reached wide, and she spun suddenly towards the river. On the shore, the fish-men carcasses shivered, and something viscous and black oozed out of them. What was left dried impossibly quickly, and fell to dust and floated away into the twilight. The inky stuff billowed and wafted through the air. Vast coils seemed to surround Coral for a moment, as if some primeval goddess of the deep rose to embrace her daughter. Her song rose and reached into the river, into the heartblood waters of the land, and I felt Aisling consciously activating her landbond as she followed Coral into the water until they were both knee deep. She put her hand on her friend's shoulder again.

Upriver of us, something seemed to chime, as if a bass gong struck through the magic of the land.

Black globs breached the surface of the river, and I *knew* there were more fish-men out there. Coral's magic reached out, *feeding*, and they rose, convulsing, from the water. More ink spilled into the air, and simple - if very large - catfish flopped back into the current and swam away.

For a minute, the monstrous woman paused on the shore. Her song died to silence. She stood motionless for a long moment, then slipped into the water and disappeared. The last light of the sun went with her.

Something stirred in the woods, woken by what Aisling and Coral had done. An old wild magic of the forest stalked through the trees, seeming to flash from root to root. Rellen spun to face whatever new threat Earth was throwing at us, and then confusion flowed across his face at the sheer shining strength of landbound sidhe magic approaching us. The world seemed to shiver, and the shadows of an old riverside cottonwood condensed into an antlered figure. His eyes glinted like emeralds and faint gold dust seemed to float from the antlers on his forehead.

Everything of old landbound, Earthly magic seemed to rise through the dusk, the sort of mantle of power all but the oldest of us have lost.

Arthur Hart looked up at us.

It was like looking straight into the wild heart of the forest.

Then he shook his head, and stared at us, completely taken aback.

"Aisling!" he called to her. "What is going *on*?"

Rellen and Sulima froze, fighting the urge to go to a knee in the old way, before the lord of the land. I had to fight that urge too, even though Aisling's land magic had already claimed me.

Then I got a better look at Hart. He'd been handsome in the footage. It had nothing on what he was like in person. Like, *omigod,* the *hotness.*

Actually, I thought, cheering up immensely, *I'd be just* fine *spending an indefinite amount of time on my knees for him.*

54

DANGEROUS MERMAIDS

AISLING

A rthur's power billowed across the forests towards us, and I felt him step out of the roots of the woodland through an ancient cottonwood on the Mississippi shore. I didn't turn around, but I couldn't keep my shoulders from hunching up. Coral was walking a knife edge between letting her twisted heritage claim its own and staying at least nominally in control. She needed me more than anyone else here.

On the shore, the Elsecomer called Connor walked over and started talking quietly to Arthur. I had a feeling Sveta underestimated him, but Connor seemed an okay sort, even if he *was* flirting with my boyfriend.

Oh hell. Is Arthur my... anything... now?

I sat down on the sand and stared at the swirling water. Coral still hadn't resurfaced, and the sun had sunk below the horizon. She could stay under a long time, though. I suspected that what she was turning into could stay underwater indefinitely.

Arthur was shaking hands with the second city guard. Connor somehow convinced his partner to call in to their headquarters that he'd been dropping off a comm unit for Maddoc and the Strangelingtown locals set off some defenses, which shook the land energies. Everything was okay now, he told them, and they didn't need to send out a patrol. Arthur offered to help the Arabic-looking woman medic. I wasn't sure what she was. Not a strangeling, not quite sidhe, with magic like ours but touched by fire. She nodded acceptance, and after a second of sort of fumbling with it, the land's power gathered around him. It flowed to her and into the injured boy, and when he was patched up, to the poisoned Healer.

"You know what your friend is?" Connor asked, coming over and sitting down next to me. He nodded his head towards the water. Unlike virtually everyone else here, there was a silence around him; no emotional projections scraped against me like fingernails on a chalkboard. Maybe he was shielding it? Could people shield like that?

He has that kindness people get after surviving being utterly broken, I thought, looking at him. *The gentleness of those who have lost everything. I wonder what happened.*

"I can make an educated guess, but I don't want it to be true," I said. "And my basis for it is just human folklore and legends. But the world's mythic heritage is waking up. We think she's born of the sidhe people's... old opposition."

Connor nodded.

"My father was born of a peace marriage with *them*," he said. "One of the neutral ones. They called him the 'son of the sea' for it. A fair number of us have some of their heritage. Helps with healing faster, among other things. I've lived through things I shouldn't have, because of their blood."

Aha. Survivor's guilt. He's drowning in it.

I nodded, staring out at the water. Coral still hadn't resurfaced.

"You have family in the Freeport," he said. "You could return with me. Your friend can come too, get... whatever help we can give her."

"You think that'd be wise?" I asked him, looking askance at him. Damn, his eyes were incredible. Almost just like the little cub in the otherworld. What did *that* mean?

"No," he said after a long moment. "Not if you and Sveta are right. She found three bugs in the 'secure' conference room where

I met her today. Your *Squids* are likely everywhere. Gods help us if they're like Coral."

"More likely they just have a lot of people beglamoured," I said, sighing. "Coral can tell people to do something, then forget it, and they do. She has an awful time in confession, trying to unburden herself to the Catholic priest she talks to without actually giving anything away. It's probably your own janitors placing the bugs, completely unaware they're doing so. Or they think they're working *for* your cause against secret infiltrators, depending on who they think recruited them."

He looked sick, as if something was chewing on the edge of his own mind.

"One's gotten to you, hasn't it?" I said. "Not recently, but..."

He shivered.

"Maybe back on Briargard," he said. "Someone close to me. Before... the end."

I waited, but he didn't say anything more.

The inhabitants of Strangelingtown were filtering down to the beach. They have a fortified place, inland and a bit upriver, stocked like a bomb shelter for when things come through that they can't fight. Most of them would have gone into hiding before Coral went "fishing", a precaution in case the town was overrun. Now the leaders were coming over to Arthur, and I gritted my teeth as I felt the binding roots of his magic spreading even here.

People look at him and see steadiness, competence, someone who can handle things: a leader, I thought. *They look at me and see someone who can kill shit fast.*

The strangeling boy who'd shared a canoe with Zahra came out and stared at her, and when she dismounted, Grayjay ran over and flung his arms around her. They started talking a mile a minute and a bunch of other kids joined them, along with the old librarian who originally got my team involved with the Underhill Railroad. They pointed at me and babbled and petted Uni-Tanky.

...And it looks like my Rue persona is totally burned, dammit. Oh, and Arthur is apologizing to Zahra. And she's accepting that it

was a miscommunication. And I bet he has some kind of mutual aid deal worked out with Strangelingtown in, oh, the next five minutes or so.

I was *slightly* landbound there, not like up by Duluth, but a bit. Strangelingtown had been under *my* protection for years. It *grated. I don't live down here, though.*

I wanted to go punch out Arthur. Or bang him brainless again. Maybe both.

"What happened between you two?" Connor asked.

"He's an idiot," I said. "And I'm an idiot. Our idiocies are somewhat mutually compatible but also extremely aggravating. He said a stupid thing he probably didn't really mean, and I knocked him out and ran away. Now I don't know if we're... anything."

Arthur overheard me, and looked over for a minute, his heart in his eyes. It hit me like a punch in the gut. I hugged my legs and rocked with the blow.

"What?" Connor asked.

"I'm an empath," I said. "And everything that made that curse manageable for the last few years just got blown out of my head. Thought I'd worked through the worst, but I was alone then. Everyone freaking out about the monsters, and Coral, and prisons... it's hitting me like sledgehammers. I'm not sure which feelings are mine and what aren't, and I'm finding ten years of backlogged emotional messes vomiting out on every second thought. I just want to run away and dive into some extremely dry textbooks and not come up for air until someone brings me *gallons* of moonshine."

He smiled and put his fingers on mine. Stillness washed over me, blessed silence, and some odd, delicate feeling I couldn't name.

Safe, I thought eventually. *I think maybe that's what "safe" feels like.*

"The Freeport has some *fantastic* clubs if you decide to come in," he said. "Some of the best bartenders this arm of the galaxy. I should know; I spent like thirty hours partying before coming into work today."

"Celebrating something?"

"Being alive," he said ruefully. "Two nights ago, one of these fish-men swallowed me whole. Shooting them just now was *extremely* satisfying. They've been attacking the Freeport every full moon for the last few years. The older trainers made some ridiculous rule that we should fight them with just basic melee weapons. I had to cut myself out of one's belly. It's ridiculous, but everyone's so bored we go along with it."

"Yeah. Gotta *live* after a close call. Been there."

"What happened?" he asked.

I put my hand up, feeling Coral returning. A vee of ripples approached the shore. She rose from the water as if its Stygian depths had condensed into the curves of a woman, ink-black, her movements inhumanly liquid, exquisitely terrifying. All sound ceased behind us, and a wave of fear washed over me from the townsfolk. The other sidhe all went cold and focused, ready to fight and kill.

Coral's eyes closed, savoring some exquisite flavor in that fear.

"Hey bestie," I said, trying to keep my voice even. "Pull yourself together. The Lumber Punks have a reunion gig in two hours, remember? And my bass skills are *not* going to hold an audience."

"Shining One," she crooned. *"I need..."*

"And I give freely," I answered, shaping a claw and piercing a vein in my elbow. Then I blinked. Light shone out of my arm, white-gold, Radiant. Connor's eyes went huge. So did Coral's. "Um, I might have eaten too many apples in the otherworld. Shot of liquid Schwartz? Let's make space tracks!"

The inky woman went still, then started shaking. It took me a second to be sure she was laughing. She flickered forwards, almost as fast as I move at speed, and I felt her lips on my arm for a second. Gold light washed over and through her. Then she fell backwards to the sand, shining from the inside. Human color washed back into her complexion, and the liquid blackness faded out of her hair until it was bright, brilliant red again. The light glimmered and faded. A soft giggle rose from her, then got louder until it was a full belly laugh.

Above the beach, people eased up.

Coral lay in the sand, just shaking and laughing.

After battle reaction. The last twenty-four hours are all hitting right now.

"Dusty! I'm having an evilgasm, and all you can do is make *Spaceballs* jokes?!?" she chortled.

I grabbed Coral and hugged her tight for a minute. Connor got up and walked up the shore, giving us space. Whatever he'd done to shield my empathy went with him, but the breathing space he'd given me had let me re-center.

"Yeah, well, my real superpower has always been excessive nerdiness, remember?"

She wrapped her arms around my back and just held me for a minute.

"Thank you," she said, quietly. When she pulled back, there were tear streaks on her cheeks.

"Of course," I said. "You're my sister. We've got each other's backs."

She looked up at the group standing at the flood line and waved. A collective sigh of relief wafted down to us.

"We're okay!" I called, but didn't get up. Arthur looked like he was trying to decide if he should keep talking to people up there or come down to us. Connor went over to him and said something I couldn't make out.

"That hotness is the guy who's been chasing us?" Coral said, disbelieving. "And *you* made your willpower check to escape his clutches?"

"They were seriously sexy clutches," I admitted. "But I had a Runner to get through. Rigs kept you updated?"

"Oh, I have been getting an *earful,*" she said. "He is not *halfway* acidic today."

"Have a feeling he's got his own trouble incoming," I said, looking at Sveta. She seemed to be coordinating something with communication technology between the Elsecomer doctor and the old librarian who originally got us into the Underhill railroad. When she saw us looking at her, though, Sveta told them she'd be back in a minute and came over to us.

"Your technomancer," she said. "Iz stupid about girls, or no?"

Coral and I looked at each other.

"Mostly no," I said. "I mean, our team is girl combatants and guys on support."

"Yeah, but *this* one's another techie," Coral said. "I doubt he'd even be able to open his mouth and make sounds come out of it if she tried talking to him. He thinks we're violent numbskulls and the absolute opposite of his 'type'. Remember what he did after he let dating distract him in his freshman year?"

Oh. That.

"What?" Sveta asked.

"Swore off relationships for the rest of university, because he got a B- on a test after going out with a girl," Coral said, giving Sveta a rather incomplete answer.

"Okay," she said. "You tell him the Russian technomancer iz 'Big Ivan'. I want to see if the Outland technomancers have found things like this."

She held out a small clear baggie with a couple of tiny electronics in it. I took it.

"What's in there?"

"Snooping technology, I think from your 'Squids'. These, I disabled the transceivers, but they are otherwise intact. Is not from the sidhe or aliens, so I break no laws giving them to you."

"How should he contact you?"

"I will contact him. Already got into his systems once. Will do it again."

"You're going to make him crazy," I said. She grinned like a shark, then left to keep talking to the Elsecomer medic and guard who'd teleported her in.

"You're sure you're okay?" I asked Coral.

"Think so," she said. "Feel pretty weird right now. Got my gills, though."

She arched her neck sideways, and gills flared under her jaw. When she straightened again, they completely disappeared.

"Huh. That a shapeshift?"

She nodded.

"Going to get myself a fish tail next time we do this," she said, smiling wryly. A *next time* was unfortunately inevitable. "I've already got the hair and know all the songs, after all."

She'd been aiming her cascade towards becoming a mermaid since the day we met. It was a better option than what we'd just seen.

"Let's get out of here," I said. "We do need to keep our band cover intact. Bad to be late for a gig, and we desperately need a meal first."

"Not going to try sorting things out with Captain Hottie, or maybe that blond? He seemed interested."

I looked at the two of them. The city guard who'd brought the doctor was arguing with both of them and gesticulating towards us, but speaking low enough that I couldn't make out his words.

Arthur and Connor looked back at me. I hadn't even imagined that much masculine beauty could exist in this world. Both of them looked like they had things they wanted to say.

Dammit. What I wouldn't give to be in the middle of that sandwich, if we could just skip all awkwardness and complications.

"Nope," I said, getting to my feet and giving her a hand up. "I'm a mess and in nowhere near the right headspace to start a relationship with *anyone*. And love triangles? *Hard* nope. I have *read* that shitty book and watched its crappy knock-off movie. Let's go."

Also, I don't like the way the other guard is looking at you, I added silently.

Coral shrugged. Arthur and Connor looked like they'd overheard what I said aloud and were both ready to object. They started walking towards us.

"Okay," Coral said. "I already took care of everything to settle in the Runners. Looks like Mrs. Rowan has Zahra now. They're good."

"Sorry guys, gotta run to make our cover gig! Toodles, all!" I yelled up at everyone, and reached inside myself for the mist. A half dozen people started waving like we should stay. Coral grabbed my hand. Fog swallowed us. As reality faded behind us, I saw Connor turn to Arthur, who was staring in stunned dismay at our sudden retreat.

"Sooo....," I heard Connor say, speculatively flirtatious. "Guess you're single?"

55

BECOMING ONESELF

ARTHUR

"**S**he ran from me," I said, staring in shock at a swirl of fading mist. "She ran from me *again*. She didn't even give me a chance to talk to her!"

The blond city guard - Connor, who I think must be the guy the Dohoulani had tried setting me up with - turned sympathetic eyes to me. He looked like a fallen angel, beautiful and dangerous and tempting. I felt this frisson every time I looked at him, like the magic in me wanted something I couldn't even define.

Not the way his uniform defined every sculpted inch of his legs and butt, anyway.

No, I told myself sternly. *We have problems enough already.*

Damn, yeah, I could get into that, the fae side of me thought. *Haven't had a boyfriend since I was fifteen, and this thing with Aisling isn't going so well...*

I tried to ignore that voice.

"She's an empath and her mental defenses are *shredded*," Connor said. "I haven't seen an overload case like that in years. If I were in any state half that bad, I'd hide in a hole until being around people wasn't actively painful."

"What would... oh fuck," I said, covering my face with one hand. "They *warned* me, and then I pulled her into a mental net with two dozen soldiers she barely knows."

"Who warned you?" Rellen asked. He had long dark hair pulled back into a sleek ponytail and the look of someone who deeply did not want any of this to be his problem. But he also seemed like the sort of competent, steady guy you want on your side, even if he *was* an invader. All three of the Elsecomers were treating me like I was one of them. And they were just two city cops and a medic, reasonable people, not exactly the conquering terrors we fear our "alien overlords" to be.

"The ladies in the ghostland... never mind."

"That child..." Mrs. Rowan said, nodding to where Aisling had just vanished. She was the steely-haired human woman who seemed to lead Strangelingtown. Not what I'd expected to find here. She had the air of an elementary school teacher, not a post-apocalyptic survivor. "That girl's waded more grief and damage than any young person should endure. Let her go. She'll come back when she's ready."

"You know her too?" I asked, surprised.

"Since she was old enough to toddle to story hour at my library. I suspected she was both Rue and the Green Lady, but didn't have confirmation until today. When she was little, she'd hide among the books when she needed space. I introduced her and her friends to the Underhill Railroad when Coral had trouble with her Change. I thought she'd need to run, but they stabilized her somehow. Hoped we'd get some eyes and ears in the local school then instead; two years later they were pretty much running the local Railroad, and have ever since."

"Wouldn't they have been teenagers?"

"Yes. And Aisling had compartmentalization of information, guerilla tactics, and what I'd consider black-ops training from when she could walk. I heard her cheerfully telling her friends what to do if they were ever questioned, and that her mom had put her through anti-interrogation training when she was eleven."

Dear god.

Rellen's mouth dropped in horror. Well, I guess at least that meant Deirdre wasn't typical of Elsecomer parents.

Good to know.

"Her mother trained her to be a weapon, and seemed to barely know what to do with an actual little girl. At least the rest of her family took care of her. But Aisling had her best friend Change and get executed in front of her in fourth grade. Then her baby brother got eaten by a redcap, and she blamed herself for not being fast enough to rescue him, even though she was across town. A few months later she showed up at the library looking like a cipher of herself, blank as a zombie, and asked for hard science books. Didn't begin really recovering herself until Coral appeared, homeless and orphaned and just as traumatized. Those two have been saving each other ever since."

"That redhead's a Fomorian. I'd bet my life on it," Rellen said.

"Maybe," Connor said. "But not a bad one."

Rellen stared at him.

"*I'm* a quarter Fomorian!" Connor exclaimed. "My father was born of a peace marriage, remember? My flipping adopted brother Lugh is too, you know! His grandmother Cethlean was a siren who could convince parents to feed her their *children*, and no one brings that up even when they're all thinking he's the *best* at flipping *everything*. And some of them used to defect to us. We're all part human. Sometimes that wins out."

"Connor, we can't ignore this!"

"We're not going to," the little lavender-haired technomancer said. Sveta looked a bit like an Elsecomer, but had a heavy Russian accent and multiple facial piercings. "I'm taking ze idiot and going hunting. I'll start by tracing Coral's family, see what I can find."

Rellen blinked at her.

"She's blackmailing me," Connor said, irony heavy in his voice. "Forcing me to obey her every demented whim."

"With what?" Rellen demanded.

"Dunno," he said, shrugging. "It's Sveta. She's sure to have options."

Rellen looked like he wanted to tear his hair out.

"Ze 'affair with the eel', among other idiotic shenanigans. I have footage of whole escapade," Sveta said, giving Connor a deeply unimpressed glance. "Two days ago, captain of city guard told him to stop being an embarrassment to entire sidhe civilization and culture. Fifteen minutes later ze dumbass let a mutant fish eat him on live camera. Think ze eel thing being released now would not go down so well."

"Oh, that's probably true," Connor said, looking amused and completely unrepentant. "Bhairton would *hate* that."

"...eel thing?" I asked, dubious.

"My favorite drag bar had a serial groper problem, so I armored up down below and stuck a biting eel in a jock strap. Guy lost a finger and I ended up sprinting down Hennepin Avenue in a Vegas showgirl outfit at two a.m. Running in nine inch platform heels is *crazy*. Best fun I've had all year. Unfortunately, I'm told that all 'lacked dignity'. Probably be cat sitting for months if footage got released."

No wonder the Dohoulani say the tabloids adore them!

I might be in love again, my fae side whispered.

Absolutely no, I whispered back. *Are you insane?*

We could collect crazy blonds. Like a hobby. Something to share.

You are out of your mind. *One is plenty.*

They were cute sitting together! And he knows what's wrong with her and how to help. And damn, that uniform makes his butt look fantastic.

Must you think about sex constantly?

I've been locked up for ten years. And you only think you're straight because an evil witch cursed you!

Stop. Please.

No.

Please.

I'm just getting started.

"You'll want to look at a triple murder in Grand Rapids, eight years ago," Mrs. Rowan said to the technomancer. "A mother shot, two daughters drowned, and another daughter and the father gone missing."

Lightning flickered in the technomancer's eyes, and her hair twitched in invisible currents.

"Got it," she said. "Connor, let's go."

"Would you like to stay for the welcome party?" Mrs. Rowan asked. "We have one every time we get new arrivals, to celebrate their new lives."

I blinked. No one ever treated Changing as anything but a curse and inevitable death sentence.

"May I?" I asked. "I've never seen free strangelings. Aisling said you do better, here, than my people."

The old librarian gave me a confused look. Oh. I still had Aisling's sweater on. They didn't realize I led the unit that had been chasing escaping strangelings. I took a deep breath.

"I Changed almost five years ago," I said. "Been in command of Strangeling Brigade since then. I'm human-born, not an Elsecomer. And we need to talk about getting people through more safely. Division 51 won't be chasing Runners any more."

"Aisling spent the day subverting him," Connor said, amused. "Guess it worked."

"Yes," Mrs. Rowan said, a smile forming on her face. "Come see."

Strangelingtown wasn't like anything I could have imagined. Some of it was built on the foundations of the pre-invasion town of Elk River, and they had reused a lot of debris from there, but the settlement was neither a ruin nor a shanty-town. The homes were half grown from living trees, and the materials re-purposed from Before had been shaped with magic into seamlessly organic shapes.

Underground greenhouses, only their glass roofs visible, fed the town, producing even through the harshest winters.

They had food, and it was delicious. They had real beer, and it was even better. There were kids everywhere, and Aisling was right, they adapted to Changing better than adults did. Some of them were obviously traumatized, but as many were happy to be what they were, and were helping those having trouble every way they could.

Rellen took off to "run cover", and the doctor he'd come with stayed to do exams and consult with the local Healer and make sure her recovery was genuine. The wan mother from the canoe this morning got some kind of IV drip and started actually gaining color. She shyly handed me back my jacket and told me her family was doing okay. I wished them all well and started making a mental list of who among my people would be most helpful here.

Two hours later, I could somehow feel my troops getting worried, then deciding to head home without me. After all, this was hardly the first time I'd disappeared chasing the Green Lady. I could almost hear Jones' voice say the words aloud.

"I need to get back to my people," I said regretfully. "They've got the truck out of the ditch and running, and they're heading back to St. Cloud."

"Going back the way you came, or do you need a ride?" Connor asked. He'd made Sveta stick around when I asked to stay. The guy made friends as easily as breathing, and had flirted incorrigibly with practically everyone here. I was pretty sure I'd gotten more of it than anyone else, though.

Ride, my fae side said, gazing at Connor and admiring the view again. *Definitely ride.*

We can just step back through the roots!

Oh, and you know how to do that all on your own, do you now?

I hate you.

A collection of crazy blonds would help you get over that!

Sharing a skull with you is torture.

Uh huh. Same.

"Honestly, not sure how I did that magic," I admitted. "I'm running on instinct and guesswork with these things."

"You want to meet your people in the woods or back in St. Cloud? I think we're going straight up the river."

Sudden pain stabbed my heart, and Connor's and my heads both snapped to the Northwest. Something was wrong; Aisling was in trouble. He felt it too.

I looked at him.

"She pulled me into something like a battle net when we arrived," he said. "It... has an effect, when a landbinder does that. Don't tell her, please, she's stressed enough."

I nodded, a weird pang of something that *surely* wasn't jealousy running through me.

"St. Cloud," I said. "Let's check on her, then you guys can head on your way."

Aisling? I called, reaching for her. I felt her wince at the contact and shield me away.

"She's not in danger," I said. "It's the empathy overload thing."

"Can we finally get moving?" Sveta asked. "I need to go bug ze crap out of *everything.*"

Connor rolled his eyes. We said our farewells, and he led us down to the speeder bike things they'd parked on the beach. I climbed up carefully behind him, trying to ignore the scent of his hair and the brush of his skin against mine.

"Apologies in advance," he said, leaning back to speak to me, something hot and wicked in his eyes. "Sveta drives like a maniac, and I have to keep up with her. So hold on tight, absolutely *anywhere* you want to."

Wait, what?

"Connor, don't be pig!" Sveta yelled at him, and kicked her bike into gear. There was a sudden feel of power underneath us and we slammed forward after her, accelerating far faster than any vehicle made by humans. I did grab him and hold on tight, squeezing my eyes shut against the expected wind.

And then I realized it was barely there. And for all that we were traveling at insane speeds, it was a smoother ride than I'd ever experienced, and Connor's hands were strong and competent on the controls. And oh god, but the body under his uniform spoke of a lot more time spent in a gym than my high school boyfriends had ever bothered with.

No. Bad. No.

I felt Connor smiling.

"What?" I yelled, the speed we were traveling at almost tearing the words away.

Just glad you aren't straight, he said into my mind as we swooped around a bend in the river. I saw the moon rising behind us as we took the corner. It was still almost full, and glittered on the water. The sudden surreal beauty of the night...and everything... took my breath away. *And very, very happy to not be the only sidhe under a century old around here anymore!*

Um... what? I repeated, going completely mentally tongue-tied.

I'm an empath too, he said. *Contact based, not wide spectrum. Don't worry, I won't start seducing you until you've sorted yourself out.*

For a second I just blinked, even my fae side having no idea what to say to that.

I felt him grin wider.

...and then? I couldn't help but ask.

Then all bets are off, he answered, anticipation shimmering through his mindvoice. *But for now, here's your stop. Okay on foot from here?*

He slid the speeder under a spreading weeping willow and I slipped off the back. It was just me and him. The silence hummed.

"Nice meeting you, Arthur," he said, his smile flashing in the dappled moonlight.

"Same. You weren't what I expected. Good hunting."

He grinned, tipped his bike into a tight turn, and vanished silently into the night.

I found Aisling behind a grimy bar on the edge of St. Cloud. THE LUMBER PUNKS: *LIVE TONIGHT!* exclaimed a sign out front. I could hear the siren's song rising over a packed crowd from inside. Damn, she had a *voice*. I briefly, intensely, wished I could go in and have a beer and listen, maybe dance with Aisling...

But then again, my actual evening has left no room for complaints.

The parking lot was full, but I recognized the shape if not the paint job of the old van at the back of it. Aisling was just beyond, ten yards back in the woods, sitting on a fallen tree. A half-empty bottle of something that stung my nose from the edge of the clearing dangled from her hands. She looked up at me and I saw the adult version of her human illusion. Her otherworldly beauty was hidden behind a plain, intelligent face and a nose that had been broken at least once, but I knew her.

Blurry, owlish eyes blinked at me, and her shoulders shivered. She looked wounded, vulnerable, so much *less* than she really was.

"Come to arrest me?" she asked quietly, twirling the bottle neck in her fingers.

I took a step closer to her. She didn't flee.

"Do you want me to?"

A fragile smile flitted across her face.

There's my girl.

"Maybe a little."

"I'm sorry," I said. "I just wanted to get you to run into the woods with me."

She took a drink from her bottle.

"Yeah," she said, looking at her feet. "I figured that out. Eventually."

I dropped to my knees in front of her, carefully leaning my forehead against hers, trying to keep my antlers from poking her. She reached a hand up behind my neck and steadied herself against me. The fumes from her breath stung my eyes.

"What are you drinking?" I asked after a minute of just holding each other. "Is that industrial alcohol?"

"Dunno," she said, her voice cracking. "It was cheaper than painkillers."

"What's going on?"

She sighed and leaned her head into my shoulder. I held her there and stroked her hair.

Let's just stay like this forever.

"I forgot how bad it was," she said eventually. "How much people used to overwhelm me. Was a minor empath when I was a kid. Then my best friend Changed in fourth grade, one day at recess, and a major projective empathic talent bloomed along with the wings that sprouted out of her back. It happened suddenly, and couldn't be hidden. I held Samantha and tried to talk her through it, tried to keep her calm... and then soldiers dragged her out of my arms and pushed her against the gym wall. Shot her so many times they had to clean up the parts with a shovel. One held my head in place and made me watch, so I'd know what happened to the Changed and their sympathizers. She screamed out her death in my mind. Ripped that minor talent open, and it never healed. I couldn't handle crowds or gatherings at all for years, not till my mom bound me up over... well, *you.* Now everything hurts and I could barely even manage being inside to play three songs before I collapsed. Don't know how I'm going to survive life without bars."

At least you aren't living behind bars. And you won't, as long as I can protect you.

"What are you going to do?"

She was silent for a bit.

"Go home, finish my Master's, try to cope. Didn't have any social life planned this spring anyway. I'll be back down here in June, after my degree work is done. Did you work something out with Strangelingtown and those Elsecomers?"

"I think so. Not till June?"

"You ever written a thesis on cryptid biochemistry? I'm going to be *living* in the lab till then."

I blinked at her.

"That sounds... intense."

"Well, it makes fighting stone giants almost alone seem a good way to unwind," she said, a wry smile twisting her mouth. "Much more exciting than dissecting mutant roadkill."

What the hell is she studying?

"You aren't at all what I expected," I said. "And you have no idea how obsessed with catching you I've been."

"Got an inkling. You can project at me *any* time you're showering."

I couldn't help but smile. Neither could she. Then her lips met mine, and we kissed in the moonlight...

...for rather a while...

...and lost a layer or two...

...and were heading towards losing a few more...

Then the music in the bar switched to something canned. I heard the bar's back door open, and a pair carrying a keyboards and amps heaved their gear over to the rusty van.

"Hey Stockholm Syndrome! Quit sucking face with Captain Compromised!" her technomancer friend yelled from the parking lot. "Concert's done and I don't wanna sleep in the van again!"

She pulled back and made a face in his direction, then laughed. Her lips brushed mine again, and when she straightened up there was a real smile on her face. Her fingers caressed me from my ear tip to collarbone.

"Well, till June then," she promised.

"Unless we come up North for a hunt," I said, holding on to her.

"Okay. Maybe I'll leave you something to kill," she said, grinning wickedly and pulling her shirt back into place.

"You do that. Want your sweater back?"

"Nope. I like keeping you warm."

"Mmm. I like that too. Well. Take care of yourself. See you soon."

She kissed me again, slowly, then got to her feet and walked back to the parking lot, giving me a little wave before she climbed into the van.

I sighed, smiled, and pulled my clothes back into place. Magic flowed through me, and I stepped through the forest's roots to the road just outside the Box.

Jones and Birch were waiting in a Jeep there, Jones snoring behind the wheel and Birch whispering something about nudist Klingons into a handheld voice recorder. I did *not* want to know what that was about. Both of them were completely oblivious to the little bronze draclet contentedly eating a windshield wiper on the Jeep's hood.

I glared at it. It froze and tried making innocent eyes at me, even though its mouth was still full of wiper. It gave a little experimental chew, eyes still fixed on me.

"No," I told it. "Bad mini dragon. No eating cars."

Its eyes went big and sad and regretful. Birch looked up and Jones startled awake and swore at the pocket dragon. I held my arm out, some sort of connection flowing through the fae side of me, and it hopped over and bent its neck for scratches.

"And what did we just tell the green kid?" I asked Jones, petting the draclet.

He raised his eyebrows at my appearance. His expression said he knew *exactly* why I was late.

"Take a shower before wrassling the hot elf girl?"

I laughed, put the windshield wiper back in place, and climbed into the Jeep.

"Best advice *ever*," I grinned. Then I held out my arm and the little draclet leaped away into the night. "Everything okay?"

"Yep," Jones said. "Troop carrier will need some frame repairs. No one was surprised to hear Captain was off in the woods chasing the Green Lady. Again. Everyone knows you'll drag in sooner or later, covered in mud, bruises, bug bites..."

"...hickies, lipstick, the reek of extremely cheap booze..." Birch muttered, putting his recorder away.

"God, I need to get that girl to drink something better, just so I don't have to taste it in her mouth," I agreed. "I think she was drinking disinfectant!"

"That's Hildie," Birch said, grinning. "Don't say I didn't warn you about her!"

"Totally fair," I said. Then I sighed contentedly and leaned back in my seat. The stars blazed bright above us. "But we didn't kill each other within five minutes of meeting, so there might be hope."

Jones laughed and turned the key, and we pulled onto the road and drove home.

EPILOGUE

It was well after midnight when Rellen caught up with Daire and Maddoc.

"Sirs," he said, walking into the entryway of the San Francisco suite they were sharing, "Are you aware of what Connor and little Sveta are up to right now?"

"I can only imagine," Maddoc said, barely looking up from the display he and Daire were examining. "But they're working under my orders, and Morganna has Sveta's server mirrored. Everything she records goes straight to the backup systems. We've been busy, but I'll be checking it later to see how they're doing."

"She followed Connor out of the city! And promptly threw away all standard espionage protocols and made direct contact with your feral granddaughter. Who is *landbound* and already accidentally tied my idiot partner to her and doesn't even realize it! He's ready to fall head over heels in love with her, and also possibly with the *second* lost kid out there. Hart's bloody five times as landbound, and to the zone *directly* on our border! And he lives incarcerated in a human prison! *And won't leave!* What were you thinking, sending *Connor* out to find lost kids who, *incidentally*, are completely inappropriate and also the only other young, un-attached sidhe in the area?"

Daire leaned back and laughed.

"You *did* remind him of the rules of engagement?" he asked his old friend.

"Of course," Maddoc replied. "Regardless. Less than a single sun's wheeling. Pay up."

Daire chuckled, walked over to his room on the far side of the suite, and came back and handed a bottle of aged whiskey to Maddoc. His friend smiled and opened it, and the scents of oak and peat and fine craftsmanship filled the air. Daire grabbed three tumblers off the hotel's bar and gestured for Rellen to sit with them.

"So. Feral?" he asked, voice mild.

Rellen blew out a frustrated breath and took a seat.

"That's the estimation of the Dohoulani I talked to," he said. "And I concur. She's wild, violent, barely speaks our language, and is up to her neck in things no child should deal with. Also, she's already starting to Navigate, and used her nascent skills to run away from all of us. Sveta knows where she lives, so that's not a problem. But thank the gods at least the antlered boy has some sense. Even he looked like wanted to scream at her when she fled Strangelingtown. And sirs, what happened there tonight... I don't even have words for how bad the news is. I've already been to tell the *Ard Rí* but he didn't believe me. *Worse.* It was like he didn't hear me. *Couldn't,* maybe. Just said he was glad his son had met a girl!"

"What did you see?" Maddoc asked, frowning.

"A Fomorian princess coming into her power," he said, and Daire choked on his good whiskey. The weapons master went completely still.

"Impossible," he said. "Utterly... bloody hells. No. It's impossible."

"Who?" Daire demanded.

"The redhead working with Maddoc's granddaughter," Rellen said. "Her *blood sister.* Goes by Coral or Siren. The only bright side is that she's in hiding from *her* people, and seems a decent person despite her heritage. *Both* girls think they come from families of monsters. Aisling fled us the second the other girl had stabilized."

Maddoc put his head in his hands and stared at the ground for a minute.

"Why would you think she's a Fomorian?" Daire asked. "We *eradicated* that old evil. We salted the ground where we buried their bones."

"You went back with a starship and vaporized it down to bedrock, too," Maddoc commented dryly, straightening up again. "So blasted on Kzephian brandy, Brennos couldn't even look at the stuff for a century afterwards."

"Good times," Daire said, waving his drink. "Should have done that earlier."

"Coral's father tried initiating her their old way, by drowning," Rellen said. "If you've got Sveta's footage, watch what happened after the fish-man attack, when they were dealing with the wounded. Coral went fully Fomor, then came back to human-passing; make your own judgments. Sulima fully concurred with my assessment of the girl, as did Connor."

"The djinn doctor you've been trying to ask out?" Maddoc asked, surprised, scrolling through his screen and accessing Sveta's footage.

"Kid out there got chewed up and poisoned by the fish-men," Rellen said. "Connor called me to ask her for help. And flat out said he knew I could teleport and was working for his father! Sulima is still in Strangclingtown, and I'm not sure how I'm going to get her to leave, given the depth of need there."

"Connor's very good at making people underestimate him, you know," Maddoc said. "Probably because he so thoroughly underestimates himself. Well. Hopefully this excursion will help things."

"Help things?" Rellen asked. "Is that why you send him to the Outlands?"

"Young Connor desperately needs to be needed, and to have something to protect," Maddoc said. "He bases his worth on things lost to him, and left to his own devices, would either drown in a bottle or waste himself away creating tempests in increasingly fragile teapots."

Rellen sighed, unable to disagree, and finally took a sip of his whiskey.

"You were *counting on* him falling for one of these youngsters?" he asked a moment later.

"His face when we were watching the footage Sveta found of them was pretty transparent," Daire answered dryly.

"He called me to look at wounds made by a sidhe weapon in a dead monster snake," Maddoc replied. "And I scanned possible futures to see the best way to handle things. I saw him flying again, and whole... *if* I sent him to take care of this."

"But... his magic's broken. He hasn't been able to fly or shield since Briargard fell."

"Shielding like he could do is only possible with the strength of a landbond behind it," Daire said. "Our people cannot afford to lose such gifts. We have too many enemies."

"Sidhe become land-bound two ways," Maddoc said, finding the place in Sveta's footage where she and Connor arrived in Strangelingtown. "Somehow chosen by Land and its people for service, and in tying themselves to someone who is already landbound. Connor lost his magic when his land was destroyed. The only likely way he could regain it would be by joining with someone who has their own landbond... and in the sidhe cities, no one does."

"Oh," Rellen said, taking a thoughtful sip. "So what about your granddaughter?"

"My daughter wished her hidden," Maddoc said, his voice soft. "I will not contradict her last wish until necessity demands."

"And if Connor falls for her?"

"Perhaps he'll convince her we aren't monsters. And that boy can hardly make worse choices in lovers than he's been making recently," the old man said, shaking his head. "To use the term 'lovers' *very* loosely."

"Well, there's a truth," Rellen said, and took a sip of his whiskey. "But what if there *are* Fomorians still out there?"

"Then they're already among us," Daire said softly. "It would explain some things. And the best we can do, for the moment, is start looking for facts that fit or disprove the theory. Perhaps youngsters they haven't already compromised may find them... but this must stay *quiet*, especially if our own *Ard Rí* is beglamoured. At the Convocation, we'll speak in person to those who need to know and were historically resistant to our old enemies. Most of them won't be on-planet until then, anyway. For now, we gather evidence... and let this play out."

Maddoc's hands shook, and he took another drink. Then he leaned back and nodded resigned agreement.

"I think Earth's about to get a lot more interesting," Rellen said. "Well. I'll take care of your cat and help cover for Connor. Anything else I can do?"

The elders glanced at each other.

Daire leaned forward.

"The boy with antlers," he said. "Did you notice if he had feline pupils instead of round ones?"

MORE

The "Children of the Broken Dawn" series will be at least seven books long and come out over the next few years. If you'd like to get updates about upcoming releases, series artwork, geekdom, and background on the book's weird science and mythology, please join the **mailing list** on my website, KiraHagen.com . Want to collab? Tag fanart and such with #childrenofthebrokendawn or write me!

Liked the story? Please leave a review on the booklover's site of your choice. Indie authors are often judged by the quantity of reviews left on their books, so even a couple words help. Hated the book? "Redcap Reviews" will get collected and used to more accurately target an audience that appreciates pansexual pole-dancing elves. ;) Found a typo? Drop me a note and I'll fix it.

ABOUT THE AUTHOR

Kira Hagen is a long term traveler, EFL teacher, photographer, and digital artist. Born in Minnesota but growing up internationally in conservation circles, she went through her first African coup d'état at age five. At the invitation of a schoolfriend from the American School of Antananarivo, she moved to Moscow, Russia for to teach English and spent about a dozen years in various countries doing that. She and now lives in Germany with an apartment full of feral parrotlets and an oblivious son and husband. She works mainly as a photographer and digital artist.

"Strangeling" is her first novel, and as you may have guessed, began as a covid lockdown project ("My main character's super power is going to be teleporting away from here!"). This story attempts to color within the lines of real Celtic and Norse mythology while re-interpreting it from the perspective of the alfar and aos sidhe. There are too many mopey vampire stories out there; what would immortals who like to *live* be like?

Made in the USA
Monee, IL
01 July 2022

98914805R00263